CONOCIMIENTOS
PRESS

ANTONIO

A MEXICAN BOY & HIS STORIES

JESSE NATAL SÁNCHEZ

CONOCIMIENTOS

PRESS

Published by Conocimientos Press, LLC
San Antonio, Texas

ISBN: 978-1-7351210-7-9

CONOCIMIENTOSPRESSLLC.COM

To my wife Norberta,
and our son Victor,
with love.

PREFACE

Jesse Natal Sánchez wrote to document his upbringing in the Texas community where he was raised. This book focuses on his experiences growing up Mexican American during the war years of 1941–45, detailing abuse and violence dispensed to keep him and his people in "their place."

Despite the trauma he experienced through exclusionary barriers and boundaries he confronted daily, Jesse demonstrates that he was much stronger than the whole lot of them. For more than twenty-five years, Jesse suffered with Multiple Sclerosis, Parkinson's disease, and other medical complications, and he moved about in a power wheelchair.

The last years of his life, his left arm was highly restricted. His right arm, which he named the "good arm," facilitated the completion of his manuscript. After he retired at age sixty-five, and using only three fingers on his laptop, he dedicated himself full-time to finishing the book. Tremors caused his arms to shake continuously, day and night. This did not stop him from achieving his dream. By July 21, 2020, he was done.

As his wife, I never imagined being involved in the publication of his book. However, since this was what Jesse most desired, my aim was to keep the promise I made at his deathbed and sought out ways of making his dream a reality.

I realize much work may be involved. I'm inspired by Jesse's desire to expose the inhumanity he survived and still pervades in our society. Jesse makes a case for an equality that must be accessed by all who reside in the U.S., even when differences continue to rule the ways in which we see and treat one another.

Now more than ever, I want everyone to learn about my husband's life. I want readers to gain an understanding about how a young Mexican American boy was marked by peers and adults as not belonging. Jesse strongly identified with his ethnic background and culture. May he rest in paradise.

—Norberta Loredo Sánchez

ANTONIO

THREAT OF THE
WHITE SCHOOL

"I don't want Antonio to go to the Mexican school," Juan Tomás said to his wife Belén.

"*¿Por qué no?*" she said.

"Because I went by the school today and talked to Mrs. Vogel, the teacher—the only teacher at the Mexican school."

Belén finished preparing supper.

"One teacher for the whole school?"

"That's right. Mrs. Vogel teaches the eighth-grade girls—there are no boys in eighth grade this year. The eighth-grade girls help her teach the other seven grades."

Belén set the table for three. "It sounds like too much work for one teacher."

"That's what I'm telling you, *mujer.* The eighth-grade girls teach, grade papers, and help keep order in the classrooms. Imagine what kind of education Antonio will receive there."

Before sitting down, Belén served Juan Tomás and Antonio.

"The school has three classrooms," Juan Tomás said.

"It sounds like they need more teachers and a bigger school," Belén retorted.

Juan Tomás nodded. "That's nothing. Let me tell you about the Negro school." He paused briefly to eat before he continued. "The Negro school is one big classroom, and the teacher teaches all grades, first through eighth, at the same time."

Belén looked up from her plate. "*¿De veras?* Poor thing. How can one teacher do all that?"

"I don't know, but I want you to know that the Negro children don't even have desks. They sit on wooden benches with their books and things piled on their laps or on the floor."

"How do you know all this, Juan Tomás?" Belén asked.

"That's what Mrs. Vogel told me when I complained about the Mexican school."

"I guess she was trying to tell you things could be worse," Belén said.

"Pero mira. José Porras, the janitor at the Anglo school, tells me the Anglo school has a classroom and a teacher for each grade. Not only that, but they also have a cafeteria, a gymnasium, and indoor toilets."

"That's the way it ought to be. It would be nice if Antonio could go there or a school like that," Belén said.

Juan Tomás lifted his index finger in the air. "That's what I'm getting at."

"You mean Antonio's going to the Anglo school?"

"Why not? That's what they do in the big cities. There they don't have Mexican schools and Anglo schools. They just have schools. Only Negros go to separate schools. Meyers has a population of only three-hundred people, and it has three separate schools. That's stupid."

"Most of the school children live on farms near Meyers, not in town," Belén said.

"It's still stupid."

Belén raised an eyebrow. "I don't know. I don't think they will allow Antonio at the Anglo school. Mexican children have never gone there, that I know of."

"Nobody has tried. It's time we did something about it. If we fail, we fail, but at least we'll give it a shot."

"This scares me. You're going to make the Anglos mad, and they'll probably take their business somewhere else," Belén said.

"Somewhere else. Where? The J T Store is the only gas station in town, and I'm the only mechanic within eight miles. They're not going anywhere. There's no one else around here who will go to the farms and fix their tractors in the middle of a muddy field."

"Well, Antonio turned six in July, and he's ready for school. Are you going to take him to the Anglo school without checking with somebody first?"

"Ay, mujer. Of course not. These things must be done correctly," Juan Tomás said. "Tom Williams is president of the school board. He's a very decent man. I'll ask for his advice."

The Second World War was raging in Europe, North Africa, and the Pacific Ocean. At the peak of the war, new cars were no longer built, and factories were retrofitted to manufacture war machinery. Studebaker began turning out trucks for the military, and Ford produced jeeps and other war materiel. Silk, previously used in women's underclothing and stockings, the government reserved to produce parachutes. Gasoline, oil, rubber articles, sugar, butter, milk, cheese, meat, eggs, tea, chocolate, butter, sliced bread, leather shoes, metal buttons, metal zippers, type-writers, cooking oil, bananas, photographic film, and good quality paper were either available only through rationing coupons, scarce to find, or even none-existent at times. Those commodities rationed across the nation nobody considered a sacrifice. They were the contribution of those who stayed home, so that the armed forces could have enough for their needs. All metals were in high demand by the military, and service stations served as gathering sites for those drives. The J T Store became the official drop-off point in the Meyers, Texas, area.

Juan Tomás saw Tom Williams pull around the back of the store with another pickup-truck full of scrap metal and went outside to help him unload.

"I don't know where you find all this metal, Tom. Nobody else brings in half of what you do. You should get an award or something," Juan Tomás said.

Tom laughed. "I'm just trying to pay for my past sins, Juan Tomás."

"In that case, you should become a Catholic. We go to confession and say a few prayers, and the *padre* forgives our sins. We don't have to beat ourselves or collect scrap metal or do whatever else you Protestants do."

Tom threw another mangled truck bumper into the heap.

"Do you remember how we used to sell metal to Japan before the war started?" Tom said.

"Sure do. The Japanese said they were making toys, and all the time they were making guns and bombs and airplanes to fight us with."

"That's my sin, Juan Tomás, a big sin. I sold a lot of metal to them, made a lot of money, too. Now, every time I hear about another American soldier killed in the Pacific, I can't help but wonder if the metal I sold them killed that American boy."

"You can't blame yourself, Tom. We all did it. They fooled all of us."

"I'll let you in on a secret," Tom said. "Some of the metal I bring here, I buy at junkyards and give it to Uncle Sam. That's why you see me bring-ing a lot of scrap iron and metal junk. I'm trying to make up for what I did. But I never will because our dead soldiers stay dead, don't they?"

"They sure do," Juan Tomás said.

When they finished stacking the scrap metal on the pile, they went in-side. Tom pulled out a Coca Cola from the icebox and popped it opened. He took two long swallows and wiped his brow with his shirt sleeve.

"The wife tells me you came by the house looking for me this morning."

"Right. I've got a problem. Thought maybe you could help," Juan Tomás said.

"Shoot. Tell me what's on your mind, and I'll do my darndest to try and help you out." Tom finished his drink and set the bottle down.

"How about another Coke?" Juan Tomás said.

"No. No. One will do it." He took some change from his pocket, and Juan Tomás immediately signaled with a wave of his hand to put the money back.

Juan Tomás came to the point. "My son Antonio just turned six, and I want him to go to the Anglo school. How do I go about that?"

"Whoa," Tom said. "That's a loaded question." He drummed his index and ring fingers on the icebox lid. "Hmm, good question. Does your son speak English pretty good?"

"I think so. Belén even showed him how to read a little already."

"Technically, that's all he needs. The reason we have separate schools for Mexican kids is because most of them don't speak English."

"So, Antonio can sign up at the Anglo school, that's what you're telling me?"

"Ah...well, it's not quite as simple as that."

"But you're president of the school board, Tom."

Tom scratched his right eyebrow. "Maybe I'll have that second soda water after all," Tom said.

"Coke?"

"Yeah."

Juan Tomás pulled out a Coca Cola, dried the dripping bottle with a towel, opened it, and wrapped it with a short piece of absorbent paper before handing it to Tom.

"Okay, *amigo*. Where do I start?"

"Juan Tomás, the truth is I don't have the authority to enroll your son in the White school. But I tell you what, you come down to the next school board meeting and present your case. Tell 'em your boy speaks English, tell 'em you want real teachers teaching him, not teenage girls. Prepare a little talk. Let them hear you out, and then they'll put it to a vote on whether to accept him or not."

"Can I speak at a board meeting?" Juan Tomás said.

"Oh, sure. We call it a board meeting, but everyone's welcome to come out and put in his two cents worth."

"What are his chances, Tom?"

"Honestly, I don't know. You're well-liked by most White folks, I can tell you that. You're considered a war hero, but I don't know, Juan Tomás. We have a few diehards that nothing will change their minds about how they feel toward Mexicans."

"I'll be there," Juan Tomás said.

With the schoolboard meeting three weeks away, Juan Tomás knew he had ample time to prepare his talk, and he knew he could not do it alone. It was going to be the most important speech of his life. His son's education depended on it.

He would consult with Belén, his wife, and Ponciano, his *compadre* and closest friend. They would know the correct words to use at such an occasion. Belén had a knack for knowing exactly what to say at the appropriate time.

Likewise, Ponciano, the manager of the Spanish-speaking radio station in San Marcos, was never at a loss for words. He was a talking machine. When KSAM, first went on the air, Ponciano was its first full-time broadcaster. He did twelve-hour stints as disc jockey, newsman, weatherman, and sports announcer six days a week in Spanish. Ponciano was nineteen years old when he took to the air waves. He was the only one in his family to break away from the stoop labor of the land for a generation.

Ponciano dropped by the J T Store after supper every evening. As usual, Pedro, Esquique, and Joaquin also showed up, and together with Juan Tomás, the store owner, they exchanged ideas on events from around the world. The progress of the war was discussed nightly. Discrimination of Mexicans was second on their list of most discussed topics, with the Mexican Revolution coming in a close third, although that war had ended over twenty years earlier.

On that night, Juan Tomás was less talkative than usual, but nobody seemed to notice. There was enough chatting going on to fill out the evening. His brief talk with Tom Williams burned in Juan Tomás's mind, but he had already decided not to bring up the subject that evening. Belén should be the first to know about important matters concerning their son.

But when he got home that night, he said nothing about his conversation with Tom Williams, nor did he tell Belén the following night or the one after that. The entire month slipped by before he mentioned the meeting to anyone. On the night before the school-board meeting, when he and Belén were already in bed, Juan Tomás finally found the courage to tell her, and blurted it all out in one breath.

"And what did Ponciano, and your other *compadres* say?" Belén asked.

He had not told them, Juan Tomás admitted.

"Why not?"

"Tengo miedo," Juan Tomás said. "I am afraid of failure. I am afraid of what people might say about us. If I go before the school board and try to get Antonio admitted to the Anglo school, our friends might think we're acting like we're better than they are, *qué nos creemos mucho.* I don't know what the Anglos will say, but they will probably be mad at me too."

Belén sat up and turned on her table lamp. *"Mira, hombre.* You were in the middle of the war with bombs falling all around you and bullets flying in every direction, no? And you came face to face with death itself, with the bodies of your friends and enemies lying dead on the ground, *¿Verdad?"*

"That's true," Juan Tomás said.

"And did you not lose some vision in your left eye and parts of your body in battle?"

"I most certainly did."

"Well, then, what are you afraid of? Don't tell me you're afraid of what a handful of ignorant, *gringo* farmers or what your *compadres* might think. Go look at your medals hanging in the parlor, especially the Purple Heart. You fought for this country, *mi amor.* We are citizens of the United States. We belong here. This country belongs to us Mexican Americans as much as it does to those blue-eyed farmers. This country owes our son the best education it can give him. You already paid for it. Afraid? *Válgame,* Juan Tomás. Get serious."

Juan Tomás lay quietly for a long time, letting her words sift into his brain. She had said what his friends, the Chicago city slickers, told him in England.

"Be bold! Be assertive!"

After a long pause, he broke the silence. *"Gracias,"* he said.

Juan Tomás's presence at the school-board meeting did not appear to surprise anyone when he entered the yellow-brick gymnasium. School-board meetings had always been open to the public, but only Anglos attended. The prevailing logic among the minority sectors was that Anglos called all the shots anyway, so why bother.

Juan Tomás pled with Belén to accompany him, but true to her Mexican beliefs, she refused to be directly involved in his affairs. It was not proper, she contended, for a wife to appear alongside her husband whenever he was called upon to fight or defend himself, physically or verbally. That was a Mexican tenet dating back to Hispanic chivalric days, when men destroyed each other in duels or in jousting matches on horseback. Of course, those were the deadly games of the elite. The poor accomplished the same results in the streets with knives, clubs, and rocks.

"Mexican women should never follow their men into battle," she said. It was unbecoming of the fair sex to witness such gory demonstrations, much less participate in them.

"What about the ladies who followed Pancho Villa's army?" Juan Tomás asked.

"Those weren't ladies. They were barflies and prostitutes—*una bola de arrimadas,*" Belén said.

FIRST SCHOOL BOARD
MEETING EVER

"We are glad to have with us this evening Mr. Juan Tomás Vásquez, proprietor of the J T Store," Tom Williams began, by way of introduction, while everyone settled in. A light applause rippled through the crowd. No introduction of Juan Tomás was necessary. He was the only Mexican in town who owned a business, and everyone, including Anglo women and children, patronized his store regularly. He was well known and accepted as a member of the community.

Juan Tomás managed a wry smile and gave a slight wave with his hand. He found a place to sit on the edge of the crowd and glanced over his shoulder at the White faces looking in his direction. He was acutely aware that he was the only Mexican at the assembly, and soon his courage began to falter.

Maybe it was a mistake going there alone, he thought. He should have taken a couple of his *compadres* for moral support. But to the end, it was he who kept secret his intentions of attending the meeting. Only Belén knew.

He listened to a reading of the minutes from the previous meeting and to the discussion of items on the agenda. Tom Williams had told him to make his presentation when new business was announced. To Juan Tomás, it seemed as though an hour elapsed, though it was only twenty minutes, until the school-board president, Tom Williams, called out, "New business? Any new business to come before the board?"

No one spoke. Juan Tomás heard his cue but did not respond.

Tom Williams looked around briefly. Nobody had a new order of business to be considered.

"Juan Tomás," Tom asked, "is there anything you want to share or discuss with this assembly?"

All eyes fell on Juan Tomás. No malicious looks, just a mild surprise to find him in their midst.

The moment of truth had arrived, and Juan Tomás arose slowly.

"Yes, Tom. I have something I want to ask. You see, my son Antonio just turned six years of age in July, and soon he will be starting school, with God's favor." He stood mute, staring blankly at Tom Williams.

Except for the sound of his own voice, the room was silent. After three weeks of rehearsing his speech, he had nothing more to say. He stood dumbfounded. His face cringed, and for a few moments, he wasn't sure where he was or what he was doing there. He stood mute, staring blankly at Tom Williams.

His stage fright was obvious to Tom Williams, who deftly came to his rescue.

"That's wonderful, Juan Tomás. I know your son will do well like you have, by starting school at the prescribed age," he said. "I wish more parents of Mexican descent would take the same initiative. But you said you wanted to ask something? What is your question?"

"Yes, I have a question," Juan Tomás said.

Blood had started flowing through his face again as he regained his composure.

"Antonio, my son, speaks English. My wife and I, we teach him, you see. He also uses English at the store with the customers. He speaks English good. Very good... I think."

The assembly laughed softly.

"I think that's wonderful," Tom Williams said, knowing Juan Tomás was not there to tell them his son spoke the primary language of the land. "Just exactly what is it you are trying to say? What's the point you're trying to make?"

Juan Tomás proceeded. "Well, the Mexican school…it is not a very good school, I don't think. I mean it is good, but not as good as your school."

"Your school? You mean the White school?" Tom said.

"Yes. The White school... the Anglo school. I don't know what you people call yourselves," Juan Tomás said.

A surge of hearty laughter broke out.

"Either White or Anglo is fine, Juan Tomás. We know what you mean. Please, continue."

"Gringos! That's what we are," someone cried out.

Again, a wave of laughter swept the bleachers.

Juan Tomás drew several small nervous breaths before he continued.

"The White school," he said, "it has more teachers than the Mexican school. It has eight teachers; the Mexican school has only one. I believe the teachers at the Anglo school are better educated, too. They have college degrees. I would like for my son, Antonio, to receive the best education he can get, an education like your sons and daughters are receiving. I don't want my son to pick cotton or to be a mechanic, like me, when he grows up. I want something better for him. That is why I am here tonight. I am asking your permission for my son to attend the Anglo school. Someday, I hope to send him away to a university to study for a career."

There. It was out, and for all of ten seconds, the big room remained stone silent. The die was cast, and it had taken everyone by surprise.

After a brief pause, the audience simultaneously came alive in a noisy drone, and Juan Tomás was astounded as the objections grew louder and more distasteful. This was not the response he had expected. He came begging like a peon before an all-Anglo assembly, the way the Chicago city slickers had told him never to do. They would have told him to demand his son's rightful education, not beg.

The Anglos attended the meeting in their work clothes. Only Tom Williams wore a neatly pressed, white shirt and khaki trousers. The navy-blue suit Juan Tomás wore to give him confidence had failed him.

"Stand tall and don't be afraid of anyone, *mi amor*." Belén's words echoed in his brain. He tried to straighten out his back to appear brave, but how could he fear no one with a gymnasium full of angry men and women snapping scornful remarks at him? Belén should have been there, he thought. She would know how to respond to their criticism.

The war, Juan Tomás thought. He should have talked about the war, as his wife had suggested. He should have told them what it was like fighting day and night so that not a single Nazi soldier would ever set foot on American soil and so that the men and women sitting comfortably in the bleachers making nasty remarks might have the peace in the homeland they currently enjoyed. A plethora of wonderful ideas rushed through his mind, things he wished he had said, but it was too late.

"Mexicans have their own school. That's where your son belongs," Jim Kearns said to the immediate assent of the assembly.

"Yeah, that's right," resounded loudly inside the yellow-brick gymnasium.

"His son don't need no other school," someone behind Juan Tomás shouted out. "Who does this guy think he is?"

"Now, now," Tom Williams said, signaling for order with a downward motion of both hands. "Juan Tomás came here tonight with a valid request, and I believe we owe him a civil reply. Let me remind you folks that the main reason the government allows us to maintain separate schools is that Mexican children can't speak enough English to attend the White school. Mexican children need things explained to them in ways they understand. Sometimes the teacher must ask questions in Spanish before they comprehend, before they get it. That's why we have Mrs. Vogel over at the Mexican school. She speaks their lingo."

"That's right, Juan Tomás. Send your son over there, where he belongs," Bob Hanson said.

Tom continued. "Another reason for separate schools is that Mexican children tend to learn at a slower pace. The problem there is that they miss so much school, while working in the fields, that they can't keep up with the regular school curriculum. Sometimes they migrate to Lubbock and other places during the harvest season and are out of school for weeks, even months at a time. In the White school, not only will those Mexican students fail, but they will also hold back the White children."

"You've got that right," Margaret Brandt, the first-grade teacher, said.

Tom Williams looked around at the nodding heads, approving his observations up to that point. But he could sense the hostility in the room.

"Now, having said all that," he continued, "along comes a Mexican boy—Antonio, Juan Tomás's son, who is six years old and speaks English. His father would like to give him a better education than he can get at the Mexican school. The question is should we allow him in the White school?"

By that time, Juan Tomás had recovered sufficiently to defend his son's cause, and he was ready to be assertive. He understood what Tom was driving at and tried to ignore the antipathy swelling up around him.

"My son is not too young or too old to be in the first grade," he said, "and I promise you he will not miss school. I will not send him to work in the fields, here or in Lubbock or San Angelo or anywhere else. I have a business here, and we live here all year round. This is our home."

"Juan Tomás," Tom Williams said, "What about your son? Do you think he will be happy at the White school?"

"Yes. I'm sure after he makes a few friends he will be happy there."

Mary Hillman stood up and pointed at Juan Tomás. "Maybe you and your son will be happy, but the rest of us here sure as hell won't."

"That's right," someone shouted.

Tom Williams wiped his brow and thought hard. He didn't want to bring the issue to a vote that night. What Juan Tomás wanted didn't have a prayer with all the ill will emanating from the crowd. Juan Tomás had stated his case succinctly, but that wasn't enough. Tom had given the usual objections against integration, and then planted the idea that perhaps those objections might not apply in Antonio's case. He knew before Juan Tomás's request came to a vote that he had to address the Anglo community alone, without Juan Tomás's presence.

"It's getting late, folks, and I must be in Austin in the morning. Why don't we table this issue until our next meeting, when we will put it to a vote. In the meantime, y'all be thinking about it." Tom Williams said.

"Thinking, hell. What for? The answer is no," Jim Kearns said.

"That's right. There's nothing complicated about this."

"Vote now, I say," came a demanding voice from the top of the bleachers.

Tom cleared his throat almost imperceptibly, and his friend Hank Smith acted on his cue without delay.

"Mr. Chairman," Hank said, "I think you're right. We all need to get on home and think about this. I make a motion that this meeting be adjourned and that we table this matter until next month's meeting."

"What is the pleasure of the membership?" Tom Williams asked. "All in favor raise your right hand...okay. Now, opposed. Hands?"

Hank Smith stood up and took a fast count. The count was twenty-nine in favor and thirty-one against. Hank reversed the numbers. "Thirty-one in favor, twenty-nine against," he announced.

"Ayes have it, and it is so ordered. We vote next month. This meeting is adjourned," President Tom Williams announced amid protests.

The recording secretary penned herself in as seconding the motion.

Belén was waiting at the door when Juan Tomás pulled into the driveway and got out of the car.

"Well, how did it go?" she asked.

Juan Tomás shook his head. "They acted like a bunch of mad wasps when they heard what I wanted, like I had knocked down their nest." Juan Tomás laughed. "You should have seen them."

"Did they turn Antonio down?"

Juan Tomás went in the house and took off his suit coat and tie. He draped them over the back of a chair.

"We didn't vote. Tom Williams asked everybody to think about it, and we'll vote on it at next month's meeting."

"Why?"

"*¿Quién sabe?* Maybe because Tom knew Antonio didn't stand a chance and didn't want to embarrass me."

Belén picked up the coat and tie and took them into their bedroom. "So that's it. They'll vote next month when you won't be there to be embarrassed?"

"Wrong. We'll vote next month, and I'll be there, only better prepared. I need your help and Ponciano's and the other *compadres* to prepare a good speech."

"*Qué guapo eres, mi amor.* No other *Mejicano* I know would have gone there tonight and stood up to all those *gringos.* I'm proud of you."

"I surprised myself, Belén. Before I went in the army, I never had the guts to stand up for my beliefs. The Chicago city slickers—that's what I called them, and the army taught me how to defend myself."

"I wish I had met your army friends from Chicago," Belén said. "What were their names?"

"Santiago Dominguez, Ismael Moreno, and Pepe Luis Olivares, three Mexican university students from Chicago, studying to be lawyers when the draft got them. You should have heard them, Belén. They were *morenitos* like us, especially Pepe Luis, he was very dark. But they all spoke perfect English. They sounded just like *gringos* talking. I couldn't believe they were Mexican until they spoke to me in Spanish."

"Smart, huh?"

"Very smart, and they talked and joked with everybody, even the commanding officers."

"Like you at the meeting tonight, *¿verdad?*" Belén said.

"When I was too quiet, they would say, 'Okay, *rancherito.* Speak up. Don't just stand there with your straw hat in your hand waiting to be noticed.'"

"And did you speak up?" Belén asked.

"I had to. They kept after me until I said something. After a while, I learned how to join a conversation in English without being afraid."

"Which one told you not to call *gringos* mister?"

Juan Tomás laughed. "That was Santiago. He said I talked to Anglos like a *peon.* He imitated me and said, 'Hello, Meester Smith; Yes, sir, Meester Smith; Thank you, Meester Smith; I really appreciate it so much, Meester Smith.' He told me over and over, 'Never call an Anglo mister, unless he's your boss or a very old man.' He also told me to quit being so polite."

"Was that good advice?" Belén asked.

"I think so. Us Mexicans overdo that kind of thing. We even thank people for thanking us."

"*¡Imagínate!*"

"Santiago believed Anglos lose respect for Mexicans and take advantage of us when we are too polite."

"Makes sense," Belén said.

"Santiago said things in a nice way. Ismael and Pepe Luis could be rude, and sometimes made me angry, but they were just trying to help me. The night before I left England, they went to see me. Pepe Luis told me, 'When you get home, don't forget what we taught you, *hermano*. Someday you'll send a postcard thanking us.'"

The following evening, when the *compadres* met for their nightly discussions, Juan Tomás broke the news about the school board meeting he had attended.

"*Compadre*," Ponciano said, "You went alone, and frankly, I'm disappointed you didn't confide in us before now. That was a very important meeting."

"All wisdom is not found in one head only," Joaquin said. "You should have allowed us to help prepare your speech."

Esquique and Pedro nodded.

"This isn't only about Antonio, *compadre*," Ponciano said. "This is about all Mexican American children. Once one of them is accepted at the Anglo school, others will follow."

"That's true," Joaquin said.

"Tom Williams invited me to speak at the school board meeting, and the truth is I didn't want to embarrass myself in front of you, my closest friends, in case they turned Antonio down."

"Well, that's water under the bridge now," Ponciano said. "The question is what to do next."

Joaquin rapped his knuckles on the Coca Cola icebox. "Now, we put together some good ideas on what Juan Tomás should say at the next meeting."

"Someone needs to go with him, so he won't get nervous again," Pedro suggested.

"Maybe we should all go," Esquique said.

Ponciano shook his head. "*No, no.* Bad idea. *Nos hacemos bola.* Only one must accompany Juan Tomás. That's enough."

Pedro nodded. "Ponciano, you're his real *compadre*, Antonio's godfather. I think you should go with Juan Tomás."

The others agreed.

ANGLOS MEET, SEPARATE AND APART

With the Anglo citizenry still abuzz after Juan Tomás's appearance at the schoolboard gathering, Tom Williams called for a special meeting the following Saturday at the First Baptist Church, directly across the street from the Anglo schoolhouse. The entire adult Anglo community of Meyers was present.

The night was warm and balmy. All the church windows were open, and the ceiling fans set for maximum ventilation. Tom took to the podium and looked over the crowd. Everyone knew why they were there, and an uneasy tension crept into the room as it filled. Tom could feel negative vibes wafting in his direction. The crowd knew he was there to convince them of something they opposed, and there were no smiles, only long taut-mouthed faces.

Tom tapped the microphone with his fingertips and waited until everyone settled down before he spoke.

"I bet Reverend Keebler would love to see this large a turnout on Sunday morning," he said.

Only one person up front managed a limp laugh. The others said nothing. They were not in a mood for humorous quips.

"All right, folks," Tom Williams said. "Let's get down to business, because I have a feeling, we're gonna be here a long while."

"We don't have to be," John Jenkins said. "Way, I see it, that young whippersnapper is trying to bust into our school, and we'll just tell him no. Our kids' school is a White school, and he ain't White. Simple as that."

"That's right," several people said.

Tom Williams scratched the side of his head.

"In plain English, I'm gonna try and tell you what we're up against." Tom said. "Every year, more and more schools are integrating Mexican students into White schools all over Texas. As you probably know, the bigger cities have been integrated for years. In some towns, like El

Paso, Mexicans have never attended separate schools. And folks, like clockwork, the government sends its agents down here every year asking questions and wondering why our schools haven't integrated yet."

"Tell 'em 'cause the Mexicans is too damn dumb to be in a White school," Reggie Skaggs said.

The assembly assented with loud howls and catcalls.

A thin woman, wearing a light green dress, stood up. "Well, Tom, I don't like it none, even if the United States government and our Texas legislators think otherwise," she said. "I know that children in the big cities are getting thrown in together, so I know it's probably been a coming here for some time, but I want to go on record saying that I don't like it. Not one bit."

"This is an informal meeting, Mrs. Hillman, but I'm asking the recording secretary to note your objection," Tom Williams said.

Mary Hillman continued. "Most of them Mexican kids are two and three school grades behind for their age, and I don't want no ten-year-old, greasy-haired Mexican sitting in the second grade next to my seven-year-old Amy. Why don't you know, folks, Mexicans has lice in their hair and boils all over their bodies, and God knows what other diseases they has that we don't know about. They're a dirty bunch. Always has been. Ooh! I don't even want to think about it."

Mary Hillman shook her head, and her entire body shuddered to demonstrate her disgust.

"I know many of you have your concerns," Tom Williams said, "but the government will not give our schools financial aid much longer unless we try to integrate our schools. And folks, we need their money. The way I see it, all the government needs is a crumb thrown their way, now and then, to keep the politicians piped down, like San Marcos and Luling did."

"Their schools is integrated, Tom," Mary Hillman said.

"I know that I know that" Tom Williams said. "The point is they held integration at bay for years, by making it appear they were trying hard to comply with the law."

"So, what are you saying, Tom, that we allow this here Mexican boy into our White school?" Reggie Skaggs asked. "Is that your solution?"

"Either that or the state is going to raise our taxes through the roof to offset the federal money we won't be getting anymore, and small districts like ours need that money bad."

Tom's remark piqued a swift uproar that lasted for over three minutes before order was restored.

"Look," Tom said. "Juan Tomás's son Antonio is six years old. He's a clean-cut boy and speaks English. He is the bread crumb the government is looking for. We've got to show the state and federal authorities we're trying, folks, that we're making every effort to comply with the law. See? We've talked about this several times in the past three years. The time has come to do something. When the federal agents come snooping around again, and they will, we can tell them Antonio is the only Mexican student who qualified to be in the White school. You people don't want the Supreme Court coming down here, throwing its weight around, maybe sending some of us off to jail for breaking the law, and getting our government money cut off to boot. Do you?"

A boisterous squabble of opinions flooded the church. This time Tom waited until the room quieted down on its own.

"Don't worry," he finally said. "If the boy doesn't keep up his grades, we'll boot his little behind right on over to the Mexican school. Then I'll challenge the Feds to come down here and find us just one Mexican student qualified to enroll in the White school."

Tom knew it was going to be a long night. "Folks," he said, "we all know Antonio from the J T Store. If we must choose one Mexican kid, he's the level best you can find, and you know it."

"I still cain't get this thing straight in my mind about why Meskins cain't go to their own school," Timothy Rawls said. "The government don't seem to pay no mind to Negroes going to a Negro school. Why should Meskins be treated any different?"

"Tim," Tom Williams said, knowing he was opening an explosive topic. "Let me tell you something, and please listen up, people. The Supreme Court of these United States of America recognizes four, and only four—mind you, categories of people. Four races." Tom held up four fingers to emphasize the point. "They are White...Negro... Oriental... and Native American Indian. Period! That's all."

"So, what happens to the Mexicans. They ain't White," Reggie Skaggs said. "Look at 'em."

"That's right," someone said.

"Now listen up. The way the Supreme Court sees it," Tom Williams continued, "Mexicans are not Negros or Native American Indians, and for sure, they aren't Orientals. There is only one category left, and that is White. Mexicans are part Spaniard and part Mexican Indian. Spaniards have always been considered White. Maybe Mexicans aren't Anglo-White, like you and me, but they are Hispanic-White. That's what the Supreme Court has to say about the Mexican race. And the Supreme Court also ruled in 1930 that Mexican American children have the right to receive a public education but may be placed in separate schools if they cannot speak English well enough to attend a White school."

"Rubbish. Mexicans ain't White," Mary Hillman shouted, looking around the room in disbelief. "Ain't that the darndest thing you ever did hear, folks?" A lot of people nodded.

Reggie Skaggs snorted. "That's bull! Pardon my French, ladies."

A lot of people agreed with his remark as well.

"It don't make a lick of sense to me, Tom," Timothy Rawls said. "Why school Meskins when all they're gonna do anyway is work in the fields? Cities is different. Cities don't have crops that needs planting or picking. But out here, that's all we got acres and acres of crops that needs tending. We don't have no fancy office jobs or factories and such. And you know it don't take no book learning to pick cotton, corn, maize, or watermelons. Or to slop hogs, for that matter. Besides, book learning will more'n likely make Meskins uppity."

"Lazier, too, if you ask me," Mary Hillman said, and cast a sidelong look at Timothy for his approval.

"Anybody else have some other thoughts on this subject?" Tom asked.

Margaret Brandt, the first-grade teacher for the last twenty-nine years, arose to speak. "I believe some of you are getting excited over nothing. If you put that boy in my classroom, I promise you he won't last six weeks. I'll have him begging to be transferred to the Mexican school in no time flat. Any time I can't outsmart a six-year-old, it's time for me to quit teaching."

The teacher's remarks drew the largest applause of the night.

Tom Williams smiled. "See. It could be a temporary thing—just long enough to show the authorities we're trying."

The heated session continued until it snuffed itself out around midnight. By that time, everything everybody wanted to say was said many times over, studied, reviewed, discussed, and commented upon. Some bitter arguments arose throughout the evening with many caustic remarks leveled at Tom Williams. He remained calm, gave his opinion on objections raised, but did not present his strongest arguments until the meeting was into its fourth hour. In the Navy, Tom had taken up boxing, and he understood the importance of letting an opponent drain his own energy first with wasted motions to the point of complete exhaustion. By the ninth round, after furiously flailing away and bouncing around for almost thirty minutes, his opponents' legs were gone, and their arms felt like fifty-pound weights. They had no fight left in them. At that point, Tom opened with a flurry of reserved energy and took over the fight.

The night of the special meeting, the assembly burned itself out as it approached the bewitching hour. When objections became repetitions already discussed and settled several times, Tom knew he had won the bout. The crowd was no longer angry and belligerent, just tired and disappointed, mostly with their government. All of them were ready to go home. They understood Tom's logic, and everyone left exhausted but satisfied he had his say on the bitter pill they had to swallow. When Tom threatened the assembly one last time with the wrath of the United States' government, they said no more. Tom had the entire gathering of Anglo men and women facing in the same direction. They agreed to the lesser of two evils. Nobody wanted jail time and higher taxes. Antonio Vásquez was in.

Three weeks later, Juan Tomás and Ponciano dressed in their Sunday best to attend the school board meeting. Juan Tomás wore his other suit, the light gray one. Ponciano had on charcoal-gray, dress trousers and a navy-blue blazer with a line of brass buttons on each sleeve. Both men wore subdued ties. Belén brushed their shoulders and sleeves free of lint.

"You look like a couple of insurance salesmen," she said.

"We will probably need the tongues of insurance salesmen before this night is over," Juan Tomás said.

"*Vayan con Dios,*" Belén said, and hurriedly made a cross in the air in their direction, as they left the house.

Juan Tomás arrived with Ponciano in tow and entered the gymnasium. The two men took their places near the bottom of the bleachers, about where Juan Tomás had sat the previous month. No one appeared surprised to see them. Some men glanced in their direction and waved on their way up the flight of bleachers. The Anglos were all smiles.

Ponciano keenly surveyed the situation and whispered in Spanish, "I think something is wrong, *compadre.*"

"*¿Qué pasa?*" Juan Tomás said.

"They look too friendly. They are smiling at us. Did you not say they were not happy with you at the last meeting?"

Juan Tomás, unaware of the special meeting held at the First Baptist Church, was perplexed as well. "Yes, that's true. Some were very unhappy. Especially that woman over there, the one with the blue dress."

Ponciano turned slowly and studied the woman's physiognomy. She looked benign enough. She was smiling.

Since the previous board meeting had ended suddenly and nothing was resolved, Juan Tomás went prepared to restate his request. He rehearsed the short speech with Ponciano, until both men knew it by heart. They took turns reciting it aloud, modulating the cadences and inflections until the delivery sounded right to their ears. It was only a sixty-word speech, carefully crafted by Juan Tomás, Belén, and the four *compadres*, but on it rode Antonio's chance at a decent education, and perhaps that of other Mexican American children.

"How I wish you could say this thing in Spanish, and that they would understand," Ponciano said. "English is not our tongue. You will probably sound as ignorant as *gringos* do when they speak Spanish. Pardon me for saying that, my *compadre*."

The school board meeting was soon underway. It was a warm night, and Juan Tomás felt uncomfortably constrained and hot in his suit. The Anglo men were in their clean strap-overalls. The four Anglo women, who were present, went nicely attired. Juan Tomás wondered if he and Ponciano appeared ridiculous in their suits. He repeated the speech mentally one last time, afraid he may have forgotten some part. It was all there, every word.

The meeting whizzed by this time, and soon Tom Williams called out, "Old business?"

"Here you go, *amigo*," Ponciano said, expecting his *compadre* to stand or raise his hand. When Juan Tomás didn't respond, Ponciano nudged him lightly with his elbow. Juan Tomás looked pale, paler than some of the Anglo faces around them. His mind was blank, the way it had been at the previous meeting. He even forgot in which pocket he had slipped the copy of the speech he carried with him in the event of a memory lapse.

Mary Hillman, the woman in the blue dress, stood up quickly. "Why, yes, Mr. Chairman," she said, in her shrill tone of voice, "I believe we were going to vote on whether Antonio Vásquez, son of our good friend, Juan Tomás Vásquez, should be allowed to enter the White school as a student at the first-grade level this September. Antonio is six years old and is said to have the required credentials. If that information is correct, I make a motion we accept him."

Reggie Skaggs raised his hand. "I second the motion."

"All right, folks, we have a motion on the floor and a second. The members of the school board have decided to accept whatever the general assembly approves. All in favor of Antonio Vásquez entering the White school, pending the favorable results of an English test, say aye."

A tumultuous uproar of ayes filled the room.

"All opposed say no." None were recorded.

"The ayes have it, and it is so ordered that Antonio Vásquez be allowed to enroll in the White school this September at the first-grade level, pending the results of an English examination."

From somewhere near the top of the bleachers, a gravelly baritone voice broke through the commotion. "What the hell's going on?" the baritone voice said.

Juan Tomás was wondering the same thing.

"Looks like you missed a couple of meetings, Russell. That's all. You can go back to sleep, now," Tom said.

The crowd responded with a round of hardy laughter.

Ponciano turned and patted his friend on the back. "You got it, *compadre*," he said. Juan Tomás did not reply. He was still coming out of a stupor and was not lucid about what had just occurred.

"Juan Tomás." Tom Williams said. "We must test Antonio's command of English before school starts. Bring him by the schoolhouse at seven tomorrow evening. Miss Margaret Brandt, the first-grade teacher, will give Antonio a short test. Won't take long. Okay? He won't need paper and pencils or nothing. Just bring the boy. That's all."

Juan Tomás would always remember that evening as one of the happiest of his life, although at the time, only Ponciano was there to share his elation. The two *compadres* shook hands, embraced one another, and tried to subdue the excitement they saw in each other's eyes. Nobody else was in the mood to celebrate. After the vote, the noisy assembly settled down. Their earlier enthusiasm and gusto waned. They were not angry, just pensively quiet, as if something valuable had been taken away from them.

When the final gavel of the evening sounded shortly thereafter, only Tom Williams went over to congratulate Juan Tomás. The crowd somberly spilled off the bleachers, ignoring Juan Tomás and Ponciano as they shuffled past them and left the gymnasium.

"Don't worry yourself none," Tom Williams said. "Your boy will do fine, just fine." He shook Juan Tomás's hand. "Don't forget tomorrow night, 7:00 p.m. at the White schoolhouse." He shook hands with Ponciano, too.

The Chicago city slickers would have been proud of him that night, Juan Tomás thought. Now was the time to send them a thank-you card, if only he had their address.

Juan Tomás got home at nine and broke the news to Belén and Antonio. They were ecstatic. Belén hugged Antonio and danced with him throughout the house. The family stayed up two hours more, listening to Juan Tomás give a moment-to-moment narrative of a meeting that had lasted thirty minutes. Juan Tomás was extremely wound up to fall asleep when they went to bed. He got up and paced through the house, opening, and closing doors and drawers, as though he were looking for something. It was a habit he employed whenever he was restless. Belén was also on edge, but she remained in bed with her eyes open in the dark. Now that the Anglo school was within Antonio's reach, serious doubts rippled through her mind, and she was not certain it was such a good idea anymore.

"I don't know, *mi amor*," she said. "Maybe Mr. Williams was right when he said Antonio might not be happy at the White school. He will be the only Mexican student there, and with no friends, either. Somebody might do something to him. Hurt him, maybe."

"Nonsense, *mujer*. Tom simply asked if I thought Antonio would be happy at the Anglo school. He didn't say anything about trouble. Anglos are like you and me, just trying to make the best of things, working, and raising their families. Besides, we live only six blocks from school. If anything happens, I'm there. *¿Me entiendes?*"

Belén was not sure this was making the best of things for her Antonio. That night she prayed she would never regret not having fought against her husband's obstinacy. One of the things she admired about Juan Tomás was his persistence in getting things done. He was a dedicated man who knew how to bring his dreams into the light of reality. But this dream could involve her son's safety, and that troubled her.

The moment of the unanimous vote echoed in Juan Tomás's brain throughout the night and would not go away. At five-thirty in the morning, when he could no longer tolerate his bed, he arose a second time, fixed himself three fried eggs with bacon, toast, and black coffee. He ate his breakfast alone and hurried off to open the store while it was still dark, hours before daybreak, earlier than he had ever opened it before. The unanimous vote followed him there, too. The incredible dream had come true.

COMPADRE JUAN AND PONCIANO ATTEND THE MEETING

Juan Tomás asked Ponciano to break the news to the Mexican community during his newscast at KSAM. It embarrassed him to crow about the good fortune that had come to his family, especially since he had not spoken a single word before the assembly. He knew the credit was due elsewhere. Somehow Tom Williams had maneuvered for Antonio's approval from behind the scenes.

By noon, the story of Antonio's acceptance to the Anglo school had reached the remotest homes and fields in the Meyers area. The Mexican community was elated and shared in Antonio's victory. This was an important step in the right direction, they said. It was an achievement for all Mexican Americans. Many men went by the J T Store after work to congratulate Juan Tomás and his son. Soon the hour came, Antonio found himself preceding his father and thirteen of his father's friends into the first-grade classroom, where they found standing room only. Some Anglo couples had already gathered inside by the door to witness the event.

Margaret Brandt, the first-grade teacher, a petite woman with long, black hair, which she tied into a matronly bun at the back of her head, took immediate charge of the gathering. She stood five feet tall and had dark penetrating eyes with a glint of anger and immediacy. Those angry eyes the town gossips blamed on her inability to catch a husband. She was fifty-one years old and single.

She picked up her pointing stick, a three-foot-long, wooden dowel, and slammed it hard against the flat surface of her desk, taking the crowd by surprise. Instantly, all talking ceased. Everybody straightened up and stood stiffly at attention.

"Antonio Vásquez," Margaret Brandt said in a roaring voice one would expect from a much larger person. She pointed to the back of the room. "Sit down in the last desk on the right side of the room at the very back."

There was no equivocation. She pointed the stick at the desk as she spoke, and Antonio went there at once and sat down. The Anglo couples recognized Antonio. He was the little boy who helped his father at the J T Store. His hair was black, and his skin was brown, like his father's.

"Antonio," Margaret Brandt said, as soon as the boy was seated. "Where is the door to the room?"

Antonio pointed to the door, the only door, and said, "There."

"Is the door open or closed?"

"The door is closed," he said

The teacher tapped the top of her desk with her pointer softly. "Good. Now, go open the door, and then go back to the desk and sit down."

The boy arose, crossed the room, opened the door as instructed, then returned to the desk and sat down.

Margaret Brandt tapped her pointer softly. "Good," she said.

She was an intense woman. Without much effort, Juan Tomás pictured the teacher as an army drill instructor. The voice, the brashness, and the sardonic look, they were all present.

His reverie did not last long. The pointer came down firmly the instant the teacher said, "Now." The teacher continued. "As you can see, we have drawings of animals pasted high on the walls all around the room, even over the blackboards. See?" She waved her pointer from side to side.

"Antonio, what is the animal directly behind you called. Also, the animal behind me."

Antonio turned around and saw a spotted tan-and-white giraffe. On the wall behind her was a white bear. "The animal behind me is a giraffe. The one behind you is a bear."

The teacher tapped her pointer lightly. "Good. What kind of bear is it?"

Antonio knew the answer. His father bought ice cream for the store from the Polar Bear Ice Cream Company, and there was a large, white, polar bear, like the one in the picture, painted on both sides of the refrigerated truck.

"It's a polar bear," he said.

Juan Tomás exhaled in relief. He wasn't sure if his son knew the answer.

"Antonio," the boy heard the teacher say, while rapping her stick on the desktop, "Where is the door to this room?"

"There," Antonio said, pointing to the door.

"Is it open or closed?" she asked.

Antonio looked at the door. "Open."

"Well, what are you waiting for, boy?" she said, rapping the pointer continuously. "Go to the door, close it, and then go back and sit down."

Antonio was out of his desk and headed for the door before she finished the sentence. He was noticing a pattern. The teacher slammed the pointer to get attention. She rapped it lighter to give instructions. She tapped it softly to indicate approval.

As soon as the boy sat down, the pointer rapped again. "Antonio, what is the big, gray animal in that corner?"

"An elephant."

"And the one with horns next to it?"

"A buffalo."

Antonio knew animals from comic books his father sold at the store. He especially enjoyed the comics featuring Tarzan, the king of the jungle, and Gene Autry, the king of the cowboys. His mother, Belén, read them to him many times over, and Antonio was familiar with the pictures and many of the words.

"And the animal to the right of the buffalo?"

Antonio did not turn around. "A horse," he said.

"And the one next to the horse?" she asked.

Again, he knew and did not turn around to look. "A camel."

"And the one to the elephant's left," she asked.

He replied instantly, without looking. "A rooster."

Margaret Brandt looked squarely into Antonio's eyes. Was this a display of some special powers or an incredible memory?

"Where is the exit?" she said, as soon as he gave his last reply.

"Do you mean the door?" Antonio said.

"Bingo," she said, followed by a rap of the wooden rod. "Well, go close the door, and then go back and sit down. *¡Ándale! ¡Ándale!* You know the routine."

Juan Tomás was not sure what the teacher was up to. Every time his son went to the door, the Anglo couples either laughed or smirked. Just how many times did Antonio have to open and close the door anyway? Was she playing Antonio for a fool or was this a valid English examination.

"Now," the teacher said, waving the stick like a wand, "I'm going to point to different parts of my anatomy and to articles of clothing I am wearing. Name the body part or the article of clothing when I point to it."

She touched her arm with the pointer.

"Arm," Antonio said.

"And this?" Pointing to her head.

"Head."

"And growing out of the head. What's this?"

"Hair," he said.

And this?"

"Shoe."

"And this part of the shoe?"

"Toe."

"And this?"

"Ankle," Antonio said.

"And this?"

"Neck."

"And this?"

"Elbow."

"And these?"

"Teeth."

"And this?"

"Nose."

The oral examination continued for another few minutes, by which time Antonio had named many more objects in the room and opened and closed the door another three times. Margaret Brandt scoped the four walls, finally aiming at the picture of a wolf she had passed over before.

"What is that animal? The one that looks like a big dog."

Antonio was not sure.

"A fox?" he said.

"No. It's a gray wolf. Foxes are smaller." She closed the folder before her on the desk and placed it under her arm. "What color did I say the wolf is?"

"Gray," Antonio said.

"Antonio," she said, with a medium rap, "where is the door?"

"There," he said, pointing to it.

"Is it open or closed?"

"Closed," he responded.

"Good. Go open it," she said.

Antonio advanced toward the door when he heard his father's voice intervene.

"Just a minute, Miss Brandt." Juan Tomás said. "How many more times does the boy have to open and close the door? He answered all your questions correctly, except one, and I think Antonio knows where the door is by now. Don't you?"

Margaret Brandt's dark, steely eyes focused intently on Juan Tomás's disdainful scowl. "Yes, I do," she said. "I asked him to open and close the door before to see if he could follow instructions. Now, I'm asking him to open the door so we can all go home. The examination is over. What do you have to say about that…sir?"

"Ah…I guess I didn't understand what you were doing," Juan Tomás said.

She gave Juan Tomás a scornful look of her own and didn't withdraw her eyes from his until he looked away in defeat.

"I'll turn in my report to the board of directors in the morning, saying that Antonio understands and speaks English well enough to attend this school. Congratulations, Antonio. I'll see you in class soon."

The group of Anglo parents closed ranks around Margaret Brandt and snickered and laughed in a muffled sort of way that irked Juan Tomás. When he and Antonio walked past them, Juan Tomás knew they were ridiculing him.

"*Malditos*," he said. But he got what he went for. The teacher said Antonio had passed the examination, and that was the important thing.

Out in the schoolyard, Juan Tomás's friends shook his hand felicitously. They had just witnessed history in the making. They patted Antonio on the head and called him a good boy. Juan Tomás beamed with pride. Antonio is a great boy, he thought—smart, too. Someday his son would be like his army friends, the Chicago city slickers who spoke perfect English. In the Anglo school, his son would learn to speak English the way Anglos did. He wished Belén had been there to witness their son's brilliant performance before a roomful of spectators.

On the way home, Margaret Brandt reflected on the events of the past hour. She could have easily structured the test for Antonio to fail dismally, but those were not the instructions given her. The Anglo school needed a token Mexican American student. Now they had him, and no one expected her to treat Antonio equal to her White students. She rolled around in her mind the end of the meeting and smiled. She had made a stammering fool out of Juan Tomás. What a perfect conclusion to the evening. She had never addressed a Mexican as "sir" before. She meant it to sound sarcastic and hoped everyone understood it that way.

Margaret's first and only job, to date, was that of first-grade teacher at the Meyers elementary Anglo school, the position she currently held. She lived alone and prided herself of the fact that she had single-handedly purchased her home, in an era when few women could obtain loans of any kind, much less a home mortgage, without the inevitable signature of a man as cosignatory. Margaret had spent a generous part of her life at the little school. She got her elementary education there, after which she went off to high school and college in San Marcos, only to return as a novice teacher three months after obtaining her teaching diploma from Southwest Texas State Teachers College.

Now she was going on twenty-nine years of teaching—twenty-nine years in the same classroom, the same walls and windows, the same desk. But in all that time, her love for teaching had not burned itself out. Teaching was still as fresh and exciting as it was the day she faced her first roomful of students. In the classroom, she wielded all the authority she craved, albeit if only over five and six-year-olds, and she found great joy in imparting knowledge to the supple, young minds in her charge. And since she was single and had no children of her own, her profession became the most cherished pursuit of her life.

The following morning, Margaret drove out to her aunt Kathe's house. After her uncle Karl's death, her aunt leased out the farm, except for the main house, where she lived. She had recently reached her seventy-second birthday and had some difficulty in getting around without a walking cane. Her aunt was Margaret's only surviving relative in America. Aunt Kathe was a liberal and her views often provoked Margaret's anger. Margaret made her visits as short as possible, just long enough to quiet her feelings of guilt that she had abandoned her lone relative.

As usual, she found her aunt sitting in her dark living room, sipping tea, and worrying about the future. Margaret poured herself half a glass of tea from a pitcher in the icebox and sat down with her aunt.

"I can only stay a couple of minutes, but I'll join you for tea."

"Marge, have you heard they are building a concentration camp for Germans in Ethan, Texas, about forty miles south of here?"

"Oh, aunt. Those are just rumors."

"No, really. Anita Wilson's son told her. He's one of the carpenters building the camp. It's a real hush-hush project."

"What makes you think it's for Germans anyway? It could be just another training camp. They're always building training camps around here."

"Marge, it's a prison, it will hold thousands. They already have some captives there. Germans, all Germans."

"I don't believe it."

"Well, that's what Anita tells me."

"Don't believe everything everybody tells you, aunt."

"Do you think they'll come take me away, too?"

"Oh, aunt. Just because you were born in Germany doesn't mean they're coming for you."

"Do you remember I told you that the Friesenhahn brothers were arrested last month for waving German flags? Well, they are still missing. I'll just bet they're in Ethan. And they were born here," her aunt said.

"They were doing more than just waving German flags," Margaret said. "They were organizing a Nazi sympathizers brotherhood."

"They are good boys, but I haven't seen them since they were little. Sometimes they came with their father before dawn, helping him on his milk route."

"That was ages ago. They're in their thirties by now."

"Be careful, Marge. The government suspects all Germans of something."

"Aunt Kathe, most White people around here are German. They're not going to lock up everybody."

Aunt Kathe cleared her throat and sipped on her tea. "How did the boy do?"

"Um...Oh, you mean the Mexican boy? He passed."

"So, he's going to be in your classroom this fall?"

"It appears so. I don't have much choice in the matter. The school board let him in."

"Wolf would turn over in his grave if he knew you are going to teach Mexicans. He considered them a lower class of people, you know," her aunt said.

"It's just one Mexican, not Mexicans, but he won't last long. I agree with father, but there's nothing I can do, if I want to keep my job. There's a lot of politics behind this."

"Mexicans aren't a bad lot, really. They're just different, Marge."

"I don't know about that. You should see the boy's father. You could see him seething with hatred toward Whites."

"Your father believed in Aryan supremacy—the great White race, Wolf called us. He was fanatical about racial differences. He believed the

White man's God-given burden was to keep non-Whites in their place. He took his beliefs with him to the grave. A lot of good they did him in life. Just made himself miserable every time he met up with a Mexican or a Negro on the street."

"Father was right, though, Aunt Kathe. You should see how insolent and disrespectful Mexicans are getting these days."

"Really? I wonder why?"

"It's the war. They're coming back from the war demanding all kinds of things. Look at Juan Tomás Vásquez, the boy's father. They say he's receiving a nice monthly pension from the government for injuries sustained in battle, but he's not disabled. He runs the J T Store and works as a mechanic in the back of the store. He doesn't limp or anything. Somebody should check it out. Now, he's got his son enrolled in the White school, and let me tell you, that boy isn't White, not by a long shot."

"As I said, they are different, but they're human beings," Aunt Kathe said.

"You don't know those people. The first time I heard Juan Tomás speak before the school board, I despised him immediately. He's exactly the kind of troublemaker father warned me about."

"The poor man is probably just after what he thinks is best for his son," her aunt said.

"Hah! Next thing you know, they'll be demanding to eat at the same restaurants and use the same public bathrooms as Whites."

"Well, maybe they should."

Margaret grimaced and stood up. "Aunt Kathe, you don't know what you're saying. I must run to pick up some papers at school before noon."

"Thanks for coming by Marge. Come again soon."

Margaret rushed out the door before her aunt could get her completely riled up with talk about minorities and their rights. It was ground they had covered before, and each time Margaret went off displeased with her aunt's liberal views.

ENGLISH LITERACY
AND COMPREHENSION

Even though the Vasquez family lived only a short distance from the schoolhouse, Juan Tomás and Belén drove Antonio there on his first day of school.

"Imagine." Juan Tomás said. "Our little Antonio, the first Mexican at the Anglo school. Can you believe that?"

Belén sat quietly pondering that very question, but her husband was too distracted to notice her uneasiness.

Juan Tomás proudly drove his burnished, black '38 Ford sedan into the large, half-moon driveway, and parked behind a string of cars. He had the flashiest car in town. After spraying the vehicle with five, thin coats of jet-black lacquer, Juan Tomás buffed the car until he could comb his hair on the doors and fenders. The chrome on it glittered like polished silver. He would show those *gringos* that Mexicans had class too, he told Belén.

A small group of Anglo men had gathered in front of the school. The men knew Juan Tomás's car, and all eyes turned to look in his direction as he pulled in and parked.

"*Mira*, Juan Tomás. Everybody is looking at us," Belén said. "*¿Sabes qué?* Maybe Antonio is still too young to go to school. He's just a little boy."

"*¿Otra vez?* What are you talking about?" Juan Tomás said. "He speaks English, he is six-years-old. We've been through this a dozen times. Don't worry yourself silly, *mujer.* Those men are just talking and looking around."

Belén studied the faces of the men standing by the front door of the building. "Juan Tomás," she said, "they are not just looking around. They are facing this way, staring at us, and moving their mouths. They look angry. *Mira*, they even have the doorway blocked."

"Bah. You always imagine things, Belén. I know those men. Come on, Antonio. *Muévete.* Time to go. You remember where your room is, no?" Juan Tomás turned to see if Antonio was listening.

Antonio nodded.

"*Bueno.* Grab your school bag and lunch box. *Vámonos.*"

Juan Tomás went around the car and helped Antonio with his leather bag. It was light, now, with only the required school supplies. Soon it would be heavy with the books Antonio needed to begin his education, the books that would transmute the small-town boy into a city slicker who would speak perfect English. In his mind, Juan Tomás pictured Antonio as a young man already attending college. All things were possible in this country. He held Antonio's hand as they headed up the walkway toward the front door. The first steps of a long journey, he thought to himself

Belén was right. He could see the austere faces of the men by the entrance. They looked anything but friendly.

"Good morning," Juan Tomás said.

The cluster of men inched ever so slightly to the right, just enough to allow Juan Tomás and his son passage. A solitary voice replied, "Mornin'." The others were silent. Juan Tomás would forever wonder who had responded.

Two women were at the door: Jane Schneider, the principal, and Margaret Brandt, the first-grade teacher. Without greetings from either woman, Margaret stepped forward and said, "This is fine. I'll take him from here." She clenched Antonio by the upper arm and led him through the first doorway down the hall.

Antonio was the first student in the classroom that morning, and the teacher directed him to a desk at the rear of the room. It occupied the same space as the desk he sat on the night of the English examination, but it appeared different. It was larger, much larger.

"This is your desk," the teacher said. "Take out your school supplies and arrange them neatly inside. If you brought lunch, it goes on the table by the front window."

Antonio sat down at the desk and was almost lost in it. He was unable to place his elbows or forearms on the desktop. Without uttering a word, Margaret Brandt brought him an old Sears catalogue and dropped it on the seat. She motioned for him to sit on it. Now, he could reach the desktop, although not comfortably, and his back was two inches from the back of the desk.

"There you go," she said, and went outside to welcome more students.

Weeks later, Antonio would learn from José Porras, the janitor, that his desk had been discarded from the seventh-grade classroom. Margaret

Brandt ordered José to bring it out of the basement and exchange it for the smaller one already in place, one the size of the other desks in the room. This was the beginning of the ordeals Antonio encountered throughout his first year of school.

Juan Tomás started the Ford's engine and threw it in gear. "I forgot to remind him to make friends," he said. But the advice was not necessary. He had lectured Antonio on the necessity of having friends every day since his son was accepted to the Anglo school.

Before driving off, he and Belén looked back at the school. The group of men, who just minutes before stood at the entrance, had dispersed, and more students were hurriedly entering the schoolhouse. If there was a message to the men's presence at the doorway, it was lost on Juan Tomás. He was too elated to notice.

When the second bell rang, his classroom was full. Antonio knew almost every boy and girl in his grade. He saw them frequently with their parents at the J T Store. Sometimes they bought candy and ice cream or a toy. Only older boys went to the store by themselves. They bought caps for their guns and BBs for their Daisy air rifles, but they did not linger. They purchased whatever they went for, then looked around a little and left.

During the first recreation period, leadership and natural abilities in sports quickly surfaced and were permanently established. Ross Wentworth threw the football to his cousin, John Riley, and appointed himself captain of one team and John captain of the other. Ross and John were the tallest boys in the first grade. The two boys drew players for their teams, and they remained captains for whatever sport was played thereafter. Besides being the tallest boys, Ross and John turned out to be the roughest and best players in every sport, so no one questioned their leadership abilities. Girls did not participate in organized sports. They were happy to waste away their recesses talking and screaming on the monkey bars, the seesaws, the slides, and the merry-go-round.

At the first recess bell that morning, the first graders enthusiastically started pouring out of the classroom, headed for the playgrounds, when a sharp rap from their teacher's pointing stick on her desktop froze their progress.

"Antonio Vásquez, remain seated. I need a word with you," Margaret Brandt said.

When the room had cleared out, the teacher closed the door and approached Antonio's desk with the wooden pointer clenched in her right hand. Antonio and his teacher were alone, as they would often be throughout his first year at school.

He viewed the round, unpainted stick in her hand from up close. It was splintered, and he was wondering how often she replaced it when the pointer unexpectedly rose and came crashing down on the edge of his desktop. The loud sound made Antonio jump. The stick broke, and a third of its length bounced off the wall and landed on the floor. She was clutching the remaining two feet firmly in her hand.

Antonio bent down to his left to retrieve the broken piece.

"Let it be," she shouted. Her face was only inches away from his, and he could feel her breath on his cheek. "Let's get one thing straight right now. The only reason you are in my classroom is because certain individuals think you belong here. I don't. I may have to teach you, but I don't have to like you, so don't expect any favors from me. The law doesn't say I have to be nice to you, and, by golly, I don't intend to be nice. Is that clear?"

She slammed down the pointer a second time with enough force to cause Antonio to jump to his feet. She towered over him, and Antonio stood trembling with his arms hanging at his sides. He didn't dare place his hands on the desk where she might strike them.

"I asked, is that clear?"

"Yes, ma'am."

"Sit down!" she said, and Antonio dropped on the Sears catalogue at once.

"How often do you take a bath?" the teacher said.

"Every night, before I go to bed," Antonio said. His eyes studied the scratched surface of the old desk. Rage in adults was nothing new to him. It was the kind of behavior his father resorted to when Antonio did something unacceptable. Not necessarily bad or wrong, just unacceptable.

"Look at me, not at the desk. I'm the one asking the questions," she said.

Her voice was loud, and yet it wasn't loud at all. During the reprimand, the teacher's face was never more than six inches from Antonio's, and every word was amplified in his ears. She spoke in shrill, harsh tones, without one sound penetrating the walls of the classroom.

"And how often do you shampoo your hair?"

"Every night, when I take a bath." His eyes welled up, and he ran the back of his right hand over them.

"Crying doesn't spell cat in my classroom," she said. Reaching into her pocket, she produced a black comb with several of the large teeth missing. "Sit still. I'm going to run this comb through your hair a few times, and if I find any lice—just one louse, dead or alive, I'm sending you home. Do you understand?"

Antonio nodded. "Yes."

"Yes, who? I have a name."

"Yes, Miss Brandt," he said.

She ran the comb back-to-front, front-to-back, and side-to-side. After every few strokes, she stopped and studied the spaces between the smaller teeth for specimen, but there were none. No little critters. She went to the window and viewed the comb carefully, then returned to Antonio and continued her search. No lice, parasites, or nits of any kind were visible. Her last strokes went in all directions, and when the inspection was over, she left his hair in complete disarray. She started to slip the comb into her pocket, but on second thought, she walked back to her desk and dropped it in the waste basket.

"Tell me. How did you remember the position of the animals on the wall without looking, the other night?"

"I don't know. I saw them when I came in the room," Antonio said. "I guess I just remembered them after that. My mother says it's a gift."

"What do you mean a gift? A gift from whom?"

"I don't know. My mother says we all have gifts. She says some people can run real fast, some can jump high, some even know about the future."

"The future?"

"Yeah. They can tell people's fortune."

"And what is your gift called?" she said.

Antonio turned toward the window. It was too high for him to see the activity outside, but he could hear the children at play. He wished he could be out there with them.

"I don't know. I just remember things."

Miss Brandt stared at him with disdain.

"Can you tell somebody's future?" she said.

"No. I don't think so."

"You Mexicans believe in things like that, don't you? In witches and ghosts, and what do you call them—*curanderas*? Why you even worship statues in your church, don't you?"

Antonio shrugged his shoulders.

"Have you ever known anything about somebody's future?" she said.

Antonio thought the question through.

"This one time I dreamed my mother had a new hat with little flowers on it, and that same week she bought one like the one I dreamed," he said.

"You also like to tell stories—little white lies, don't you, Antonio?" the teacher whispered in his ear.

"No… Miss Brandt."

"Antonio Vásquez, in this room, we speak only the truth. No lies. Do you understand?"

"Yes, Miss Brandt."

"I don't for one second believe that story about your mother's hat, and as punishment for lying to me, you are grounded for the rest of the day. Do you understand?" the teacher asked.

Antonio did not respond.

His silence infuriated her. "Do you know what grounded means? You should understand something as simple as that," she said. "Your father claims you understand English. Remember? Grounded means you cannot go out to play.' Tomorrow, I'll ask you again. If you lie again, you will be grounded all week. *¿Comprende?*"

"Yes, Miss Brandt," Antonio said. He wondered if she would strike him. His father usually did when he went into a fit of anger like hers.

But she didn't strike him. Instead, she slammed the stick on his desk with all her might. It struck the edge of the desktop at an angle, and another large piece of the stick went flying across the room.

"Dammit," the teacher said, and walked back to her desk, where she dropped whatever remained of the broken pointer into the waste basket.

When the children returned from recess, Margaret Brandt announced, "Antonio is not going out to play, today. He told me a lie, and I'm punishing him for it."

The children turned and looked at Antonio. He must have told a whopper, they thought. Antonio sat embarrassed over his alleged misconduct.

"In my classroom, we don't put up with lies. We speak only the truth. Is that clear?"

"Yes, Miss Brandt," the class said in unison.

"Shame on him," Liz Blevins said.

"That's right," the teacher said.

Antonio was almost home when he saw his father standing in front of the store waiting for him. He panicked. His teacher must have called to report on his behavior. That meant a sure spanking.

"How was school, *m'hijo*?" Juan Tomás called out.

Antonio was relieved to hear his father's calm tone of voice.

"It was good," Antonio said.

"Did they give you your books?"

"Yes, but I didn't bring them home. We don't have anything to study."

"Tell me what you did all day," Juan Tomás asked.

"First, we went to the gym, and a lady talked to the whole school. Then Miss Brandt, my teacher, took us around the school. She showed us where the restrooms are and the place where we eat. Then she took us outside to show us the swings, and the slides, and the merry-go-round. Oh, yeah, and the monkey bars. They're a lot of fun. Later, we ate lunch, and after lunch we went back to our room, and teacher gave us our books. She showed us how to cover them, but I didn't need any help, *papá*. I covered my books all by myself, and I even helped Harold with his."

"Good. Did you make any friends?"

"Just Harold, the boy I helped," Antonio said.

"So, what do you think of school? Do you like it?"

"Yeah. I think so."

"Was Miss Brandt nice to you?"

Antonio felt his whole body stiffen. If his father knew what occurred between him and his teacher, it was sure to anger him.

"She's nice," Antonio said.

"Good. Go on home. I think your mother is fixing one of those egg *ponches* you like. I heard her cranking the eggbeater a while ago."

"Yes, *papá*," Antonio said, and obediently went home.

If he had learned anything in his young life, so far, it was that a child's word was nothing against an adult's. Antonio decided he would never divulge any rebuke or harsh treatment he received at school from his teacher. There were some things his father could not understand.

ANTONIO PLAYS HORSESHOES

"Today, we start learning the alphabet," Margaret Brandt announced on Tuesday morning, the second day of school. "The alphabet consists of the twenty-six letters we use to write down the words we speak. Does anyone here know the alphabet?"

Three hands went up: Liz Blevins's, Antonio Vásquez's, and Ross Wentworth's.

"Liz, come up here and recite the alphabet for the class," the teacher said.

Liz stood before the class and recited the alphabet in the singsong version her mother taught her.

When she finished, the teacher applauded. "Very good. Let's give her a big hand."

The students clapped their hands.

"I can write my first name, too," Liz said.

"I think that's wonderful," her teacher said.

The students applauded again.

"Ross, you're next."

Ross went to the front of the class and delivered the twenty-six letters of the alphabet in a single breath.

"Excellent. Very good," Margaret said, and everyone applauded Ross.

"Now, can anybody here write all the letters of the alphabet."

Antonio raised his hand. "I can, in capital letters."

"That's not good enough," the teacher said. "We are going to learn both the capital and the small letters. After that I'll teach you how to write your first and last names."

Antonio raised his right hand. "I know how to write my first and last names and my mother's name, too."

"Antonio don't interrupt me when I'm talking," the teacher said. "Speak only when I ask you a question, and don't waste the class's time with extraneous remarks. Do I make myself clear?"

"Yes, ma'am," Antonio said.

"What does extraneous mean?" Harold asked.

The teacher ignored Harold and proceeded with the lesson of the day.

During the afternoon recess, Jane Schneider, the principal, met Margaret in the hallway.

"How's it going so far, Margaret?" she asked.

"Well, I already had to ground Antonio for lying."

"Yes, I heard, but be careful. You're under the microscope. Everybody in town is waiting to see how Antonio pans out."

"I'm not going to do him any favors, Jane. If he wants to hang himself, I'll give him plenty of rope."

"What do you mean?" the principal said.

"He's a smart aleck, thinks he knows everything."

"Is he intelligent?" the principal asked.

"I don't know. I guess."

"Margaret, remember we're here to instruct, not to obstruct."

"I know, but I'm not going to let him disrupt my classroom."

"If it's a matter of discipline, there's always my office, but go easy, the school year has just begun."

"And already I have two prospects for your office," Margaret said.

Nothing terrified students more than to be called into the principal's office by their teacher. It was the designated room for whipping boys who could not be otherwise controlled. Girls were never whipped, not by any teacher, not at the Anglo school anyway. The only girl ever subjected to the rod at the school was a thirteen-year-old who attacked and injured smaller children on two occasions. That student had her calves properly thrashed by the school principal in the presence of her parents. She was an unfortunate young lady given to periodic fits. Later, in her freshman year of high school, she almost killed another student with her bare hands. In the end, it is said, she was quietly withdrawn from school and institutionalized in an asylum for deranged children in Austin, Texas. But all that happened decades ago. Her family had long since moved away, and no one was even certain of the girl's name anymore. Jacqueline. Madeline. Something like that, French.

Antonio's second friend at school was Ross Wentworth, the tallest boy in the first grade. They walked together most of the way home after school. The two boys had a lot to talk about.

"Why didn't you say the alphabet like me and Liz?" Ross asked.

"Teacher didn't ask me to," Antonio said.

"You really know how to write all the letters of the alphabet?"

"Yeah, but only in capital letters."

"I can write my name, but that's all," Ross said.

"I can write my name and my mother's. Her name is Belén. B-E-L-E-N."

"Does your daddy really own the J T Store?" Ross asked.

"Yeah. How did you know?"

"Pop told me. So, if you want a candy bar or something, you just take it. You don't have to pay for it?" Ross said.

"No. I must ask for it. Most of the time Papá says yes, unless it's close to supper time."

"So, you can eat ice cream and stuff anytime, if it's not close to your supper time?"

"Yeah. Most of the time," Antonio said.

"Wow. If I was you, I would eat ice cream, and fig cookies, and candy all day. Then I'd wash everything down with a strawberry Nehi soda water."

"You'd be sick. Most of the time, I just have me a soda water or a chocolate ice cream after school. Momma says my teeth will rot and fall out if I eat too many sweets."

"I wish we could trade places," Ross said.

The boys came to the corral where Ross's father kept three horses and Ross's Shetland pony, Mighty. It was the boy's fifth-birthday present. Ross picked up tufts of hay from an enclosure the horses could not reach and fed the pony through the fence.

Antonio picked up some hay and gave it to Ross. He was afraid of the pony's big teeth. "Me and my *papá* see Mighty all the time when we go to the post office. Sometimes we stop and watch him run with the big horses. I wish I had a pony."

"Ask your daddy," Ross said.

"I already asked so many times he got mad at me."

Ross smiled. "Yeah, I know what you mean. Pop gets mad when I ask for cowboy boots."

"Don't you ever ride Mighty? I've never seen you on him," Antonio said.

"Daddy only lets me ride Mighty when he's around. He says ponies are more dangerous than a big horse. When a pony is full grown, he is still small, but he is stubborn like a mule. He likes to kick and bite. He has big, sharp teeth like a horse. Mighty can kick so hard he can bust your arm or crack your skull. That's what daddy says. He's like a jackass. Never stand close behind or in front of Mighty. There's no telling what he might do to you."

Antonio moved away from the fence when the pony came near, but when the pony started prancing around in the corral, Antonio was enthralled.

"I wish we could trade places, too," Antonio said.

One Friday, Ross invited Antonio to his house to play horseshoes. As soon as school let out, Antonio ran the six blocks to the store. With luck, there would be only a few tools or car parts to wash in kerosene. That was his new after-school chore, and his father allowed nothing to interfere with it until the obligation was fulfilled. But that afternoon, Antonio didn't have to worry about cleaning anything. When Juan Tomás heard who had invited his son to play, he couldn't get Antonio on his bicycle and off to Ross's house fast enough. The next few customers who stopped at the J T Store received an earful on Antonio's whereabouts. Ross was the grandson of the largest landowner in the county, namely: W.W. Wentworth, III.

Juan Tomás felt his son had arrived.

In the backyard at Ross's house, two, short, steel pipes were permanently set in beds of sand to prevent the horseshoes from rolling away, and scant grass existed between them. Small craters had formed at the foot of the pipes, where the horseshoes had landed again and again. Their first game had just begun when Ross's mother came out of the back door with two glasses of lemonade and a small dish of cookies on a tray.

"Ross," his mother called out, "this is for you and your little friend." She turned to see who her son had brought home. One swift glance and her pleasant attitude spun on its heel.

"Ross," she said in an ominous voice, as though she were warning Ross of some impending danger he had not noticed. Ross ran across the yard to show Antonio his ringer.

"Ross Lee Wentworth," she shouted. "Get in this house… now! And I do mean right this instant."

It was seldom that Ross's mother addressed him by his full given name, but when she did, she always said it with the same scathing fury, and every time it meant he had done something exceptionally bad that demanded the immediate discipline of his father's belt.

Ross's cheeks turned red, and he started sobbing as he ran toward the house.

"What, Momma? What did I do?" he asked, leaping on the back porch.

Ross's mother reached out and grabbed his left arm and hurled him inside the house. She slammed the wooden door behind them, taking the lemonade and cookies with her.

Six-year-old Antonio stood transfixed, facing the door, not knowing what to make of what had just occurred. Five minutes went by, and when Ross did not appear, Antonio gave a fleeting thought to the notion of knocking at the rear door. Not a good idea, he decided. Ross's mother was very angry. Antonio stood locked-kneed waiting for the door to open. He studied the windows at the back of the house. No sign of Ross or his mother anywhere. Twenty minutes passed. When it was evident that Ross would not return, Antonio straddled his bicycle and pedaled away slowly, looking back at the house from time to time. There was no telling what Ross had done.

"Back so soon?" his father said, without looking out from under the hood of the car he was repairing.

"Yeah," Antonio said, and ingenuously related what had happened. Juan Tomás showed his face from under the hood. It was as red as Ross's when he ran to his mother's side.

"Did that woman tell you anything? Did she say anything mean to you?" Juan Tomás asked.

"*No, Papá*. She didn't say one word to me, just to Ross."

"Good. Then don't worry about it, *m'hijo*. Ross probably had something important to do. You have a lot of other friends anyway. Don't you?"

"*Sí, papá*" Antonio said, and he wondered why the question needed to be asked.

Ross's desk was close to the front of the classroom, so it wasn't possible for him and Antonio to talk at school, except during recess. When it finally arrived, and the students poured into the recreational grounds, Antonio ran after Ross, who was kicking around a deflated volleyball.

"Ross, what happened? I waited and waited for you. Were you in a lot of trouble?" Antonio asked.

"No, I just can't play or walk home with you anymore," Ross said.

"Why?"

Ross shrugged his shoulders. "'Cause Momma says you're a Mexican. She told the teacher not to let us talk anymore." And with that, Ross kicked the deflated ball and went chasing after it.

"Don't worry, you have a lot of other friends."

His father told him when he learned his friendship with Ross was over. From that day forward, Ross never walked home with Antonio or spoke to him again. When Ross went to the J T Store with his father, he remained in the truck. He smiled from a distance, and Antonio smiled back. The boys understood they were friends caught up in an adult world.

RACISM OR WHAT?

Antonio's short-lived friendship with Ross had shielded him from the school bullies. Even older boys respected Ross, because of his height and strength. But once Ross was no longer there to protect him, it wasn't long before Antonio became subjected to jeers and rock throwing. The distance between the schoolhouse and the J T Store became a six-block-long nightmare he sprinted through every afternoon. The moment he was out of sight from the teacher patrolling the schoolyard, a fuselage of rocks, large and small, began with angry calls of "Dance, Mexican." Monday through Friday, Antonio ran the course. There was no one to protect him anymore.

Ross walked home by another route. He went down Main Street through the small business sector, past his grandfather's offices, the post office, and Anderson's blacksmith shop, before he turned left and headed home. It was a round-about way that added seven minutes to Ross's walk home. He no longer saw or fed Mighty. Those were his mother's orders.

Antonio protected the back of his head with his schoolbag, but the rest of his body was exposed to the onslaught of stone projectiles. When cars went by, the ordeal ceased momentarily, only to resume and continue until the J T Store came into view, or his tormentors ran out of rocks. Some of the boys participating were in the third and fourth grades and brought rocks to school in their pockets and schoolbags for that purpose.

After a week of the harrowing experience, Antonio disclosed the truth to his mother. She examined the welts and bruises on his back, arms, and legs. They must tell Juan Tomás, she said, even though he probably would not understand. That night, Belén had Antonio strip down to his shorts. There were nine distinct purple and black bruises on his body. Some with welts.

"*¿Qué pasó?*" Juan Tomás asked.

"Some schoolboys are throwing rocks at Antonio on his way home every day."

"Why?" he asked. "Let Antonio answer."

"Because they don't like me, *Papá*."

"That's true, they don't like you," Juan Tomás said. "Otherwise, why would they throw rocks at you? But why don't they like you, Antonio? Do you make faces at them in school, or maybe you don't talk to them? People treat me nice when I'm nice to them. You're doing something to make them dislike you."

"*Papá*, they don't like me because I'm Mexican."

"That's not true. Children your age don't know what discrimination is," Juan Tomás said. "It's you, Antonio. Be friendly, and those boys won't bother you. Or else, learn to defend yourself."

It's Miss Brandt, Antonio wanted to cry out. She's teaching the whole school to hate me, but he knew how futile those words would set with his father.

"Listen to yourself, Juan Tomás," Belén said, "your words have no wisdom. We're talking about a serious problem, and you're talking about making friends or defending himself against several boys. They're killing him, Juan Tomás. What are we going to do about it, now?"

"The boy must learn to be a man, and you're raising him like a girl. Don't interfere, or I'll straighten you out, too. That's all I have to say," he said, and left the room.

Belén's helplessness settled deep in her throat and threatened to choke her. Her husband would not come to their son's rescue when he desperately needed his father's help, and all because of his *macho* nonsense. It was an old Mexican belief that boys should be tough as wild animals and ready to withstand any adversity.

When Juan Tomás forbade Belén to interfere, she did not take it as an idle threat. On more than one occasion, she had seen her husband smash the faces of men who provoked his anger. Belén prayed for a miracle. There was nothing else she could do to help her son.

Two days later, Antonio received a flying, red brick to his upper back that left him windless and almost unconscious on the ground. Donato Juárez, the sacristan, witnessed the incident, as he left the church grounds. He saw the boy go down and the bullies scatter when they saw him approaching. Donato helped a sobbing Antonio to his feet and walked him to the store, where he gave Juan Tomás a full account of all he had seen. Donato said he knew the boys by sight only, none by name.

"There were six White boys," he said. "They were older than Antonio—ten, maybe eleven years old. It is hard to say because sometimes White children are tall for their age."

Belén removed a hot pan from the stove and hurried to the store as soon as she saw Donato assisting Antonio by the arm. She had had enough.

"I told you last week, but you refused to listen. They're killing him. *¿Vez?*"

Juan Tomás ignored his wife and thanked Donato, offering him a Hires root beer. Donato wiped the neck of the bottle with his handkerchief and savored the cold refreshment, while Juan Tomás reprimanded Belén and Antonio.

"You got what you deserve," Juan Tomás said, and backhanded Antonio across the face, sending him sprawling on the loose gravel. "They chase you like a dog, and then you crawl home crying like one."

Belén helped Antonio get up and away from Juan Tomás.

"This is all your fault, Belén. You are raising a sissy. He cries about everything. *Es un llorón.*"

Belén stood between Antonio and her husband. "And you think getting him killed is raising him like a man? *Estás bien loco,*" she said. "Isn't that true, *Señor* Juárez?"

Donato Juárez took a quick swallow from the bottle and shrugged his shoulders. He set his sights on a passing truck carrying a load of watermelons and did not reply.

"From now on, every time you come home crying because someone hit you, I'm going to whip you," Juan Tomás said. "You are a boy, not some sissy girl. *¿Entiendes?*"

"*Sí, Papá.*"

Belén went to church twice the next day, once to hear the celebration of the Mass, at eight in the morning, and a second time in the afternoon to pray the rosary to Our Lady of Guadalupe for a miracle. She remained on her knees on the wooden kneeler, praying for over two hours, until Donato approached her and whispered that he was locking the church doors in five minutes.

"If you want to continue with your prayers," Donato said, "I open the church at seven-thirty every morning and close it at three."

"At three?" she repeated.

"Yes. Is there something I can do for you, *señora*?" he asked.

"*Señor* Juárez, my son gets out of school at three. I would like to hire your services for fifteen minutes every day."

"I am aware of his problem, *Señora* Vásquez, but don't worry. Those boys will not bother Antonio again."

"Of course, I will pay you," Belén said.

"Don't insult me, *señora*. It's a sad world if we cannot help each other in a time of need."

"Well, then, I promise to remember you and your family in my daily prayers," Belén said.

"Ah, prayers we can all use. *Gracias*."

"I came here today looking for a miracle, and I found it. The miracle is you," she said.

The nightmare had finally ended for Antonio and his mother. Donato finished his chores at church ten minutes ahead of schedule every day and appeared across the street from the schoolhouse in time to walk Antonio home. There were no more shouts of "Dance, Mexican" or rocks thrown.

Juan Tomás went about his work oblivious of the world outside his store. Belén, who missed little from her kitchen window, prayed for the Lord to hold Donato and his family in the palm of His hand forever.

Donato Juárez was a small man of some five feet and four inches in height. He was docile as a dove in the company of adults and a bully with children. Boys dreaded his acrid tongue, which he felt at liberty to use whenever no other adult was present. In his shirt pocket, he used to carry a Scripto fountain pen filled with indelible, royal-blue ink with which he kept score when he and his cronies gathered under Isidoro Chávez's shed to play dominos every afternoon. He drew diagonal lines for fives and x's for tens. No names were necessary, a simple 1, 2, 3, 4 identified every player. They always sat in the same place.

When more than four players showed up, they switched to penny-poker, and no written record was kept. The tips of the pen's nib had become separated, rendering the pen almost useless, and when Donato failed to screw the cap on tightly, ink seeped out, leaving dark blotches on his shirts. It happened with such frequency that no one bothered to question the old man about his mottled shirts anymore. Donato's fingers were perpetually stained with blue fluid, but even so his wife tolerated the pen until he had ruined most of his shirts.

One night, she filched the pen and hid it in a jar of cinnamon sticks in the pantry. The loss of the pen was of no great consequence to anyone except Donato, and then only prestige-wise, because, as things turned out, Donato could neither read nor write, other than diagonal lines, x's, and a few numbers. The charade was for appearances only. Displaying writing instruments on his shirt pocket gave him a sense of importance because surely any man who could write was a man of profound ideas and serious thoughts. Donato searched desperately, but the pen never surfaced. His friends, on the other hand, who used endless excuses to keep away from the leaky instrument, were grateful that the fountain pen was gone at last.

But good fortune was on Donato's side. Soon after the fountain pen disappeared, Pedro Garcia died. He had been the church sacristan for the past thirty-two years, and Padre Luna promptly selected Donato Juárez as the new sacristan of Santa Monica's Catholic Church. Even though it was a small church, the sacristan held a position of true importance, as only the *padre* and his sacristan had the Church's sanction to lock and unlock the church's doors. That kind of authority over the house of God imparted more prestige on Donato than all the fountain pens he could carry in his pockets.

The following Sunday, in a little ceremony before Mass, Padre Luna presented two shiny, new, brass, keys into Donato Juárez's care. The new sacristan displayed them proudly at the end of a short, gold chain that hung from the fob pocket of his khaki trousers. The other end of the chain was attached to a gold watch, an heirloom he inherited from his father. The keys and the watch were his most treasured worldly possessions.

Donato had a lot of time to dedicate to his new ecclesiastic duties, as men his age were no longer expected to work. At age seventy, the dark, sinewy man kept himself in good physical condition by walking or riding on his bicycle wherever he went. Every morning, he walked three miles to church, and once a week, he rode his bicycle to San Marcos, eight miles up the road, where he joined his friends. It was the habit of men his age to gather on Saturday afternoons outside the county courthouse.

Anchor stores surrounded the Hays County Courthouse: Piggly Wiggly, 5 & 10 Cent Store, J.C. Penney, Kress, First National Bank, Woolworths, Western Auto, Cordero Grocery Store, Carlisle Drug Store, and Karotkin's Furniture. Interlarded between them, plying their wares and services, were two movie theaters, three dress shops, a hardware store, a sporting-goods store, a Mexican restaurant, a shoe store, a bridal shop, two beauty salons, a barbershop, an ice cream parlor, two law firms, two jewelry stores, a curio shop, a cloth store, a leather shop, an optometrist's office, a dentist's office, and a shoeshine stand. This was the place men went to buy a car battery—or mother and daughter, a wedding gown. The county courthouse stood at the center of town and was at the hub of most business activities.

Saturday was the shopping day for laborers, and most of the people shopping were Mexican. The women were constantly on the move, going into this store, then that one. Young girls in their teens were a joy to behold. They went dressed in their flashiest outfits and walked around the plaza decorated like Christmas presents with their colorful ribbons and bows. They walked in coveys of five or six girls, constantly laughing and giggling, especially when they walked past a group of boys their own age. The young men stationed themselves alongside the store fronts, leaning against the walls. Whenever a group of young ladies walked past them, the young men let out sibilant and hissing noises, attempting to get the girls' attention. If a girl was particularly beautiful or well endowed, the boys threw in a groan in her direction or bit their lower lips, as if in pain. Their antics caused the girls to giggle and blush, as they quickened their pace to leave the wolves behind.

The girls were not without their own flirtations, although more subtle. They played an innocent game of boys and girls getting to know each other. As the young ladies walked past their admirers, they pretended to be too preoccupied talking to each other to notice the young men vying for their attention. It fell on the kid-sisters, who trailed their older siblings, to notice whom the boys were ogling. They were the eyes and ears of their older sisters. They reported which boy was calling for the attention of the girl in the blue dress. The girl in blue then wanted to know everything about her admirer. Was he tall or short, light, or dark, skinny, or fat? Good looking? If the feedback was to her liking, the next time around the plaza, which was every few minutes, she would look intently at him and treat him to her best Mona Lisa smile. Then the covey of girls laughed together and hurried away.

This ritual, along with the shopping done by their mothers, took place every Saturday afternoon. The mothers and the young singles were there, come rain or shine.

The parade of young ladies in their colorful clothes was not lost on the husbands who took their wives shopping. The men stood in small groups at a distance, watching their sons make fools of themselves, trying to get some girl's attention. The men smoked and discussed the events of the week. The topic of women's shopping habits was often discussed. It was a mystery to them.

"Makes no sense at all," Ponciano said, "You would think that if a woman goes into a store and finds the kind and color of yarn she is looking for, she'd buy it and leave."

"No woman shops that way," Joaquin said.

"That's what I'm saying," Ponciano said. "They have to check out every store that sells yarn, and along the way, they look at everything else in the store, even though they have no intention of buying anything other than yarn. They take inventory of every item in all the stores, so that if anybody should ask about a specific product, they can tell her which stores carry it and at what price."

The promenade of girls encircling the courthouse had deeper implications for many men than just the festive atmosphere of the moment. Chances were that in the maelstrom of humanity before them walked their future daughter-in-law. The men smoked and talked as coveys of young ladies walked past them, but all the while they made mental notes of who was out there, available for their sons. In theory, this was the purpose of their girl-watching, although there were those who looked for their own gratification and who would have liked to make hissing and groaning sounds, if the rules of propriety had allowed it.

When an attractive woman their own age came along, the men's conversation suddenly stopped, as they all turned to observe her graceful arrival. Some doffed their hats and uttered afternoon greetings. If there was someone in the group the woman recognized, she would smile and return their pleasantries. Otherwise, she gave them all a go-to-hell look and proceeded ahead while the men watched her sway away.

Across the street from the stores, on the sidewalk that surrounded the courthouse in front of the parked cars, stood the patriarchs of the families, the *dons*. These men had reached the age where they no longer worked and were provided for in every way by their sons and daughters. They had passed from being addressed as *señor* to *don*. It was a title of utmost respect. Donato Juárez—rather *Don* Donato Juárez, took his place among them. Since the *dons'* interest did not lie in girl-watching, young or old, they stood away from the crowds, where they could talk and not be disturbed. These men rolled their own cigarettes from Bull Durham pouches. Some of them smoked pipes with tobacco that smelled as sweet as honeysuckle in the evening. They all wore either black or brown felt hats and spoke with all the gravity expected of them. They talked of illnesses and of times gone by. They remembered well the drought of 1936, the great influenza pandemic of 1918, and the Mexican Revolution. Misty-eyed, they recalled sons who went off to war and never returned. They no longer discussed buying land, cars, or houses. Their pride was in their families: their sons and daughters, their grand and great-grandchildren, whom they eagerly introduced to their friends with pictures from their wallets.

"I love all my children and grandchildren," *Don* Donato said, "even though some of them are not always as respectful as they should be."

"They are all like that these days," *Don* Florentino said. "In Mexico, when we saw our grandfathers, we ran to kiss their right hand, and we bowed to them. Then our grandfathers would place their hands on our heads and gave us their blessing. In those days, a grandfather's birthday was a day of great celebration, something like a holiday. In this country, our children and grandchildren have lost those customs. By the next generation, they will be calling their elders *tú*, instead of the respectful *usted*."

"Let me tell you," *Don* Silvestre said. "My grandchildren from Chicago do that now. They used to call me *abuelito*, then *uelito*. Now they call me Willie, like I was their age. They hardly speak Spanish, but what can I say? I'm lucky to see them at all. My son drives down from Chicago with his family once a year for a week. Last year, he brought two of my great-grandchildren. You should hear them talk. Only seven and eight years old and they sound like *Americanos*, but they can't speak a word of Spanish."

"That's not a bad thing," *Don* Donato said. "They are losing some of their Mexican customs, but they're learning to be real Americans. If they're going to live in the United States, I believe it's better for them to speak English correctly."

"Do you mean they should forget about learning Spanish?" *Don* Silvestre asked.

"Yes, if Spanish is going to keep them from learning English the way it should be spoken," *Don* Donato said.

Not all the *dons* agreed.

ANTONIO KEPT IN HIS PLACE—
A YEAR IN THE SAME DESK

One day, a strange drawing appeared on Antonio's desk. It was the image of a swarthy-faced boy with a long, slender knife piercing his chest. The vividly colored drawing jolted Antonio. Red was everywhere. Blood gushed from the wound, and the lifeless body lay face up in a large pool of blood. The artwork was too sophisticated to be the creation of a first grader. With tears in his eyes, Antonio approached the teacher's desk and handed her the paper.

She unfolded it and shrugged her shoulders.

"Oh, Antonio, you're such a crybaby. You can't come up here crying about every little thing that bothers you. Who drew this?" Margaret Brandt asked.

"I don't know." Antonio said.

"It is a pretty good drawing. Lots of detail. Humorous, too."

"What is it?" Liz Blevins asked.

"Oh, just a picture somebody drew. Here, it's kind of funny."

The teacher handed it to her.

"This is funny," Liz said, and passed it to the student behind her.

As the picture wove its way from one desk to the next, the students laughed and agreed with their teacher. It was a funny picture of Antonio.

By then, he had become the classroom scapegoat.

"Antonio is a crybaby," Liz said.

"And where do crybabies belong?" Margaret Brandt asked.

"At home with their mommas," the class replied.

The classroom exploded with laughter, and Antonio regretted taking the picture up front. He was sorry he did not follow his first impulse to tear it into small pieces and throw them away on the way home.

Jane Schneider, the principal, waited until the next afternoon before she called Margaret to her office.

"Tell me, how is Antonio coming along?"

"Not good. I don't think the boy's going to last long," Margaret said.

"What do you mean?"

"Well, he just isn't. The other children don't like him. They call him names and don't want to play with him."

"Do you treat him fairly?"

"Of course, I do. He just doesn't fit in, that's all," Margaret said.

"What's this I hear about a drawing found in your classroom of a Mexican boy distastefully portrayed?" the principal said.

The question caught the first-grade teacher by surprise. "Where did you…?"

"Never mind that, Margaret. Just tell me about it."

"I don't know anything, really. It was just a drawing that showed up on Antonio's desk after lunch yesterday. I think some kids were trying to spoof him, show him he's not welcome here."

"Where is the drawing?"

"I threw it away. It was just a crude sketch, Jane."

"I heard it was very graphic. Showed a dead Mexican boy with a knife in his chest, lying in a pool of blood. That's serious stuff, Margaret. You should have reported it to me immediately."

"It was kid stuff, Jane, meant to scare Antonio."

"Did the drawing frighten him?"

"Not that I could tell," Margaret said.

"I heard he was so upset he took it crying to your desk."

Margaret remained silent.

"You don't like Antonio very much, do you, Margaret?" the principal asked.

"No, I don't. He's a smart aleck and keeps holding back my class with dumb questions."

"He is part of your class, you know."

"Well, you can't tell by looking at him. Sits there like a smudge at the back of the room, always talking at the wrong time."

"I noticed in the log he has been in my office for disciplinary action twice in two weeks. Also, Harold Stern. What did they do?"

"Antonio kicked the football into the street where somebody could get seriously injured or killed, chasing after it. I think the other time was for running in the hallway. He bumped into a second-grade girl. Made her cry. Harold kept bothering the girls during study period. The second time was for fighting."

"With whom?"

"Billy Smith."

"Did you punish Billy?"

"No. Harold started it."

"You don't like Harold, either. Do you?"

"He's a pest."

"That's four whippings in the first two weeks of school. Four more than all the other teachers combined."

Margaret shrugged her shoulders. "They deserved it," she said.

"Do you know what your obligation is as a teacher?" the principal asked.

"I should know it. I've been teaching almost thirty years."

"In case you have forgotten, it is to teach. We don't harass or mistreat children here, regardless of their race or background."

"And that's exactly what I do, Jane, so I wish you wouldn't listen to gossip about what goes on in my classroom," Margaret said.

The principal opened her top drawer and pulled out a sheet of paper. She dropped it on the desk blotter. It was the drawing of the brown-faced boy with a knife in his chest.

"Don't ask," Jane Schneider said. "Just be careful. You're skating on thin ice."

Margaret's face blanched when she recognized the picture. "Yes, ma'am," she said.

As was her custom once a month the first-grade teacher moved her students around the room to another desk so they wouldn't become bored from sitting at the same desk every day. Margaret prepared thirty slips of paper with a number and placed corresponding numbers on the desks. When the students returned from lunch, she sprang her little surprise on them.

She clapped her hands over her head to get their attention. "Okay, class. You are moving today. You don't have to sit in the same old desk anymore. Would you like that?"

"Yes, Miss Brandt," the class said.

The prospect of moving anyplace always excited the children.

"See the number on the paper on top of your desks?" she asked. "Well, in this shoebox, there are thirty pieces of paper with numbers matching the ones on your desks. Stand to the left of your desk and come up here one at a time, starting with the row next to the door. Take a number and find the desk with the same number on it. That is your new desk for one month. Isn't this fun?"

"Yes, Miss Brandt," they answered, and shuffled their feet noisily toward the shoebox.

Antonio was at the rear of the row by the windows, which meant he would go last. When everyone had picked a number and found his new desk, the teacher rapped her stick for attention. "Okay. Now, as quietly and orderly as possible, go to your old desk and move your books and supplies to your new desk."

There was no heeding her command with thirty students jostling across the wooden floor, struggling with two arms-full of books, supplies, and personal belongings. Antonio drew number three. He would be moving to the opposite side of the room, close to the door.

Margaret allowed them ten minutes, then said, "Okay class. Sit down at your new desk."

A fragile-looking girl with strawberry-blond hair started crying. It was Liz Blevins. Her books and supplies were on top of Antonio's over-sized desk. Nothing had been put away.

"What's the matter, honey?" the teacher asked.

"My mother told me not to touch anything Mexicans have touched, and I don't want to sit where he sat," Liz said, and pointed at Antonio. "I'm going to tell my mother." The young girl cried with her face buried in her hands.

Margaret glared at Antonio. "See what you did? You upset Liz. You're nothing but a troublemaker, but your father got you in here anyway, didn't he?"

She embraced Liz.

"No, sweetie, you're not going to sit where Antonio sat," the teacher said.

With a swift rap on the desk, she got the class's attention and modulated from her compassionate tone of the moment before to her authoritative voice.

"All right, class. Let's start over. Put the pieces of paper with the numbers back in the shoebox. We're going to pick numbers, again. Isn't this fun?"

"Yes, Miss Brandt," the children said.

A second time, the students lined up and drew numbers. Antonio followed closely behind Billy and saw him pick the last number out of the shoebox.

Antonio looked up at the teacher.

"Take it," she said.

Antonio looked in the box, again. Where there had been an empty box a moment earlier, it now contained a folded piece of paper. Antonio picked it up and unfolded it. He wanted the desk next to Ross's. Maybe this time, he would get lucky. It was number thirty. He had picked his own desk, which meant he would not be moving.

The teacher was not through with him and said, "Antonio, look at the trouble you've caused. You made Liz cry, and we had to draw numbers all over again, wasting everybody's time. Go stand in that corner facing the wall for an hour. I'm so disgusted with you."

Antonio went up front and followed her orders.

A hand went up. "Miss Brandt, isn't Antonio supposed to wear the dunce cap?" Jimmy Spears asked.

"Not until I get Antonio his own dunce cap," the teacher said. "Mexicans have these little bugs in their hair called lice, you know. They bite and suck blood out of your head. You wouldn't want to get his lice on your head if you must wear the dunce cap tomorrow. Would you?"

"No-o-o!" Jimmy said.

"That's sick," Carol said.

Liz Blevins stopped grieving. She felt vindicated.

The story of the "Mexican's Desk," as the classroom incident was dubbed, circulated fast throughout the Anglo community. It was the news of the town. A few parents congratulated Margaret for the tact she displayed in handling the situation. She had simply outwitted a six-year-old child, the teacher explained. That was all. Some quieter souls saw injustice but said nothing. Only Reverend Keebler confronted the first-grade teacher. He met Margaret at the foot of the church steps one Sunday after services.

"You've become a celebrity, Margaret," he said.

"Some things I do because they're expected of me, Reverend. They're part of my job."

"Even if it's a miscarriage of justice?" he asked.

"These days I am under the microscope. My job is on the line, you might say. If I don't perform according to the wishes of the people that matter, I may soon be seeking other employment, Reverend Keebler. That's all I can say."

"Just following orders, right? Remember, we are all God's creations. God has a special place for children in His heart. As a teacher, you should always bear this in mind. 'Woe unto him that scandalizes one of these little ones,' says the Lord. He tells us it would be better for that individual if he had never been born. Someone will have to answer to God Himself for every mistreated child."

Margaret found herself receiving a tongue lashing from the pastor, while her friends and neighbors looked on. He was no threat to her job security, and she became livid. "Okay, Reverend. Do you really believe Mexicans are equal to Whites? And Negroes, too?"

"The Lord says that it is so, Margaret. In the eyes of the Lord, we are all created equal."

"Well, Reverend, I didn't see any Mexicans or any Negroes in church this morning. How many did you invite? How many?"

Reverend Keebler was suddenly at a dearth for words. "Well... no. I don't think you understand."

"That's what I thought," Margaret said, pointing a finger at him. "You're a bigger racist than I am, and a hypocrite, too. If you really believe what you preach, you will invite all races. Think about that before you come preaching to me, again." Then she turned on her heel and walked away.

A crowd had gathered to listen to the heated discussion and stood gazing at their dumbfounded pastor after Margaret's hasty departure. Reverend Keebler remained speechless, wrapped in his thoughts about what had just occurred. He could not find the proper words to tell Margaret that he personally believed in the equality of mankind, but with his congregation looking on, his cowardice had prevailed, and he did not say what was in his heart. He wanted to explain that the time was not right to admit other races into his church. Not yet.

The pastor remained in front of the church with his head lowered in shame. He had excelled in debate classes at the seminary, putting together irrefutable arguments and exposing fallacious lines of thought. But that Sunday morning, confronted with the reality of the moment, he was left speechless. Margaret was right, he thought. He was a hypocrite without the fortitude to speak the truth. Peter the apostle had separated himself from Jesus by denying Him three times. Now he had denied the teachings of Jesus Christ, hiding the light of His truth under a bush.

Long after his parishioners departed, and all the cars left the parking lot, Reverend Keebler entered the church. Eight months later, he resigned his position as pastor of the Meyers First Baptist Church.

At the end of October, it was moving time again for the children. The white shoebox reappeared from the closet, and once more, the class picked numbers and moved to a new desk. Everybody, that is, except Antonio, who, through the same mathematical unlikelihood as before, drew the number thirty again. November and December were repeat performances of the previous months, as was all the second semester, and Antonio remained at the scratched, oversized desk at the far right-hand corner at the rear of the room until the end of May.

ANTI-MEXICAN CULTURE

One evening, the *compadres* turned their attention to the topic of discrimination, a subject which was never far from the minds of Mexican Americans in those days. The discussion was well under way, with everyone citing incidents of discrimination committed against them or their relatives and friends.

"My brother-in-law says his son Homer was not allowed to eat in a New Rhine restaurant last week," Ponciano said.

"*Compadre,*" Juan Tomás said. "Everybody knows about New Rhine. Tell him to stay out of that town. They're a bunch of prejudiced square heads or Germans. They discriminate against Mexicans in restaurants, theaters, barbershops, even at the public swimming pool in Verde Park. A long time ago, I stopped there at a Sinclair station on the way home, and they refused to sell me gasoline. They would rather lose money than sell to a Mexican."

"My nephew Homer went there with the basketball team from his school to play the New Rhine team," Ponciano said. "After the game, the coach decided to celebrate their victory with hamburgers and cokes, so they stopped at this little place on the way out of town. While they waited for their order, the manager came over and told the coach that everybody could eat inside except Homer, my nephew, the only Mexican on the team. He said Homer was welcome to eat at the tables outside."

"*Qué desgraciado,*" Esquique said.

"Did your nephew eat outside?" Joaquin asked.

"I haven't told you the best part," Ponciano said, "the coach told the boys about Homer's situation. When the food came, the boys took a big bite out of their hamburgers and complained to the manager that the meat tasted bad, like it was spoiled."

"What did the manager say?" Pedro asked.

Ponciano chuckled. "I don't know. The coach told everybody to get back in the bus and leave the hamburgers on the table. They left without paying."

"Serves that *méndigo* right," Esquique said.

"Talk about discrimination," Joaquin said. "I once saw a bar in Laredo, Texas, with a sign over the front door that read, "Mexicans and dogs are not welcome here."

"In other words," Ponciano said, "they were putting us in the same category as dogs."

Esquique made a fist. "How do you fight ignorance like that? I never saw anything like that in Indiana."

"That's because people up north are more civilized," Pedro said. "I never heard of anything like that either when I lived in Michigan. Children go to school together in Michigan, and you never see a restroom, or a drinking fountain marked 'Whites Only,' like you see in Texas."

Juan Tomás shook his head. "I fought the Germans in North Africa, and now I'm fighting them here at home."

"Up north workers have unions," Esquique said, "and the unions negotiate the wages you make. It's not like here where they pay *gringos* more than Mexicans to do the same work. When I was loading trailers, everybody got paid the same hourly wages. Didn't matter who you were. We had *gringos*, Mexicans, Negroes, Puerto Ricans, and Chinese. And my boss couldn't fire me just because he wanted to give his brother-in-law my job. He had to prove to a committee of union and company officials that I broke the rules of the union contract before he could fire me, or anyone else."

With the *compadres* riled with indignation at the way Mexicans were treated in Texas, Ponciano asked a pointed question.

"Would anyone of you prefer to be a *gringo*?" he asked.

Most immigrants, who had known a life as adults in Mexico, dreamed of returning there someday and exhibited a fierce patriotism for their homeland. Those who came to the United States as children were more like second generation immigrants, with no real ties to the mother country and felt no compunction to return there. Their roots were here in the United States. Even so, discrimination against Mexican Americans forced them to think of themselves as Mexicans first and Americans second.

Their reply to Ponciano's question was an emphatic, "No way."

"Hell no," Esquique said.

Ponciano laughed. "Let me put it another way. If you had a choice between being born into a well-to-do Anglo family or a poor Mexican family, which would you choose?"

Juan Tomás shook his head. "That's different. We are proud of who we are by birth, but what you are asking is ridiculous. If we were born Anglo, of course, we would be proud to be Anglo, but we're not Anglo."

"So, what is your answer?" Ponciano asked.

They considered the question, and although no one wanted to betray his Mexican heritage, they concurred it would not be a bad thing being born into a life of affluence, even if it were that of the despised Anglo.

"I'm an American citizen, but I'll tell you one thing," Esquique said. "If I was a *gringo*, I wouldn't be one of those big chicken shits who mistreats Mexicans because he doesn't like how we look."

"In Texas," Pedro said, "all *gringos* are like that."

Juan Tomás disagreed. "They have good people, too."

"Name one."

"Tom Williams," Juan Tomás said.

"Is he your friend?" Pedro asked.

"I consider him a friend."

"Has he ever invited you and your wife to his house for dinner?"

"No, but that doesn't mean he's not a friend. I talk to him here, and I can see he's a decent man. We enjoy our conversations. Like us, Pedro. I consider you my friend, and you have never invited me to your house either, have you? And you live right across the street from me."

The *compadres* laughed.

"I think you made your point, Juan Tomás," Ponciano said.

"I find it strange that Anglos treat Mexicans so badly," Joaquin said. "Without our labor, their lands would be worthless. They need us as much as we need them."

"If God had reversed our positions, and we were the landowners, I don't think we would treat Anglos like they treat us," Juan Tomás said.

Ponciano disagreed. "You have some Spanish blood in your veins, don't you? Well, think back at how the Spaniards treated the Aztec Indians, and there's your answer."

Joaquin agreed with Ponciano. "The Spaniards slaughtered Aztecs by the thousands. It is said that streams of blood flowed down the streets of Tenochtitlan, the capital of Mexico, and all in the name of Christianity. That is why, to this day, there isn't a single statue in Mexico honoring the conquering Spanish captain, Hernan Cortez. He's considered a tyrant, another Hitler."

"Spaniards may be like that, but not Mexicans," Esquique said, "We Mexicans are a warm-hearted race. Anglos are the opposite. They are cold natured."

"Anglos are colder than you can imagine," Pedro asked "Have you ever gone to an Anglo's funeral? I have, and I'll tell you it makes one sad."

"Why?" Ponciano asked.

"Because nobody cries. Everybody just stands around the grave site, and after a couple of prayers, everybody goes home, and that's the end of that. If their dog died, they'd show about the same emotion. It's sad. When you go to a Mexican funeral, you see women and children crying. But not *gringos*. With them it's *el muerto al pozo, el vivo al negocio*—the dead to the grave, the living back to business."

"That's true," Esquique said. "When I worked in a factory, a *gringo* named Gilbert took a long lunch break. Just kidding, I asked him if he had gone home for a nooner, and you know what he said? He told me he skipped lunch because he went to his father's funeral. Can you believe that? He went to his *papasito's* funeral during his lunch break, and then went back to work. That's cold, man."

"That is cold," Ponciano said.

They all shook their heads in disbelief.

Juan Tomás removed his glasses and wiped them clean with his handkerchief. "I believe that in a few years discrimination will no longer exist. We will be Americans like all the other nationalities who have come to America."

Pedro said, "It's happening now. In Michigan, I saw Mexican girls married to Anglo men and a few Mexicans with Anglo wives."

"Someday soon, we will be true Americans, in spite of our brown skin," Juan Tomás said.

"The first Spanish missionaries who came to Christianize the Mexican Indians called us the bronze children of God," Joaquin said.

"Education is the weapon that will end discrimination," Juan Tomás said. "It's too late for us, but we should see that our children get a proper education. When the Mexican people become an educated race, our status will rise."

"What will we become?" Esquique asked.

"Americans, of course, the real kind, not second-class citizens like us," Juan Tomás said. "When our time comes, we will become a strong political force, who will pass laws to benefit our people. We will no longer depend on handouts from the *gringo* ruling class. We will be part of that ruling class."

"The Mexican race is like a beautiful song which Americanos dislike because it is so distant from their song," Joaquin offered. "Juan Tomás is right. Education is the key, but it will take time before we are accepted as equals. Someday Anglos will understand and love the song of the brown people who came here from Mexico."

"When that happens, we will no longer be despised," Esquique said.

"*Dios te oiga,*" Pedro added.

CHRISTMAS FOR ALL,
EXCEPT ANTONIO

Aunt Kathe unlatched the screen door when she saw her niece coming up the walkway. "I'm glad to see you back so soon. Pour yourself some iced tea and sit a while. Helps to calm the nerves."

Margaret went into the kitchen and filled a glass with ice cubes and tea.

"Is everything all right, Marge?" Aunt Kathe asked.

Margaret threw up her arms. "The school's going to hell in a hand-basket. Would you believe that dog, Jane, threatened to fire me?"

"Oh, my. She said that?"

"She told me I was skating on thin ice for giving the Mexican boy a couple of well-deserved whippings."

"Whippings? Maybe you're too severe with the boy,"

"There you go again, aunt. Don't you understand? Antonio doesn't belong in the White school.

"I thought the school board accepted him," Aunt Kathe said.

"Yes, they did, after Tom Williams scared them half to death with talk about higher taxes and what-not. The way I understood it, after a couple of weeks we were going to expel him and send him to the Mexican school."

"Maybe you misunderstood?"

"No. In fact, Agnes Blevins and Mary Hillman dropped by the house last night, wondering when I'm going to expel him. They said they've been talking to other parents, and everybody wants him out of there."

"Can you expel him?"

"No. Only Jane Schneider, the principal, has the authority, but she acts like she's protecting him."

"Well, don't go getting yourself fired."

"If it happens, it won't be the end of the world. After Jane threatened me, I started looking around. Just in case."

"Are you serious? What are you going to do for a living?"

"Aunt, right now there are two government job centers in San Marcos looking for women. The jobs they have are connected to the war effort. Do you know the starting pay is more than what I earn after twenty-nine years of teaching?"

"But gasoline is rationed, and they probably won't give you enough gasoline coupons to travel out of town every day?"

"There's a way to get around that. I talked to three women who work at one of the plants. The say they take turns driving their cars. That way they don't have a shortage of gasoline coupons. It's a new concept brought on by the war's restrictions. They call it car-pooling. If I ride with three other women, I'll drive my car only every fourth week. I think I'll enjoy being Rosie the Riveter for a while."

"You mean you'll be working on heavy machines?"

"No, I'll probably sew and fold parachutes. Any woman working at a defense plant is called Rosie the Riveter."

Aunt Kathe cleared her throat and sipped her tea. "You'll be throwing away your teaching career, and may wind up with nothing, Marge."

"What do you mean?

"Well, the war could end tomorrow, and there go the jobs at the defense plants you're talking about. Won't be any need for them. The soldiers will be coming home. Then what?"

"I've given that some thought," Margaret replied.

"Don't stick out your neck where you can get your head chopped off like a turkey. By this time next year, that boy will be in second grade, and he'll be somebody else's problem."

"What am I supposed to do in the meantime?" Margaret asked.

"Tell those busybodies, like Agnes Blevins, that only the principal can expel him—which is the truth."

"I did, Aunt. You wouldn't believe how fed up I am with that Mexican boy."

"Tolerance, Marge."

"Oh, by the way, this year my first graders are putting on a square dance for the annual school pageant. Talk of ignoring someone, guess who isn't in it?"

"The little Mexican boy?" Aunt Kathe responded.

"Right. We've been rehearsing for only a week, and the children have the steps down pat. The first day, I paired them off by height into boy-girl couples, until only two girls and Antonio remained. I put the girls together and ignored Antonio."

"Poor boy."

"Are you serious? How would you like for a Mexican to hold you by the waist. I'd be run out of town if I paired him with a White girl."

"He's just a little boy."

"Thanks for the tea, aunt. Gotta go."

As Christmas drew near, John Schneider, the principal's husband, took the eighth-grade boys on an outing north of Wimberley, where they selected and hewed down eight evergreens. The following day, with help from José Porras, the janitor, John Schneider, and the boys set up a Christmas tree in each classroom. The trees were a beautiful dark green and exuded a fresh, sweet aroma. With the evergreens in place, the spirit and scent of Christmas permeated the schoolhouse. The star on the tree in the first-grade room touched the nine-foot ceiling.

Margaret Brandt's students pasted multi-colored links made from construction paper and formed colorful chains to decorate their tree and to festoon over the doorway and the blackboards. The first-grade teacher hectographed images related to winter and the yuletide season from coloring books and distributed them to the class.

"All right, everyone, take out your crayons and color the picture I placed on your desk," the teacher instructed. "Color carefully and stay inside the line. Do the best you can because we're going to tape them on the wall for the whole school to see."

Harold Stern's hand shot up immediately. "Teacher, I gots a snowman. He's already White. How do I color him?"

Two girls turned and glared at Harold. They disliked him because he questioned everything.

"Harold, you mean 'I have', not 'I gots,'" Margaret replied. "Leave your snowman the way he is. Just color his scarf, his hat, his eyes… anything you think needs coloring."

She glanced at her watch. "I'm allowing you fifteen minutes to finish… starting now. Take your time and don't look at anybody else's picture. When you finish, print your first name at the bottom of the page…repeat, at the bottom of the page, and lay it face down…like this…on my desk"

"How many minutes?" Harold asked.

"Fifteen," came the impatient echoes from around the room. Only girls bothered to answer Harold's question.

One girl said, "Duh?"

The students worked diligently, trying to finish within the allotted time, although at their age none of them had yet grasped the concept of time. There was a large clock with Roman numerals behind their teacher's desk that only she could decipher. The first graders judged time at school by bells and their teacher's commands to start and to stop. Likewise, at home, time was a matter of alarm clocks and oral instructions that it was time to do this, that, or the other thing.

Harold finished first. He dashed to the teacher's desk and slapped his snowman facedown. Antonio finished second. He worked fast, using only two colors. Drawing and coloring did not interest him yet, and his artwork was seldom neat. He went up front and placed his picture on top of Harold's snowman and returned to his desk.

Everybody else took much longer to finish, and Antonio began to wonder if he and Harold had failed to follow instructions. Gradually, one by one, the other students went up to the teacher's desk and turned in their pictures.

"Okay," Margaret Brandt said. "Since Ross and John are the tallest students, I want them to come up here and tape the pictures on the wall behind me. Start as high as you can, boys, because you will need to form two rows of pictures."

As the pictures went up, the first graders looked enthusiastically for their creations.

"That's mine," someone cried out, every time a picture was pasted.

On the bottom row, the second picture from the left was of a dark brown animal with black eyes and black hoofs. It stood out in contrast to the others, which were colored in festive hues.

"What's that?" Carol Williams said.

The teacher answered the question. "It's a burro, a little Mexican donkey. Most of them are grey, but Antonio colored it a dark brown, like himself. Are you a burro, Antonio?"

The class turned to look at Antonio and giggled.

"Why did you choose that color, Antonio?" the teacher asked.

"Because that's the color of the burro on your desk.

"You mean my paperweight? That color is bronze, a dark tan color like your skin." A spiteful glint appeared in her eyes. "Burros are slow, dumb animals" she said. "Do you feel like a burro, Antonio? Sometimes... maybe?"

The students snickered and laughed.

"No, Miss Brandt," Antonio replied.

From that day on, burro became the singsong name the children whispered whenever Antonio was in the playground. He became the object of their derision, the donkey anyone could pin ill words on. Children do not forget easily, and on the last day of school of the second semester, the word burro could still be heard.

Whatever indignities came his way, Antonio kept to himself. Juan Tomás expected him to blend in with the other children, and the boy dared not disappoint his father. At the store, Antonio sometimes heard men discuss Mrs. Vogel and the Mexican school. He wondered why he couldn't go there.

A week before Christmas, the teacher sent her students home with a note. Antonio waited until after supper to give it to his father. It was a simple message: "Please have your child bring to school a gift-wrapped present of not more than fifty cents, and suitable for a boy or a girl. We will be exchanging gifts at our Christmas party on Dec 23."

"*¿No qué no.* What did I tell you?" Juan Tomás cried out.

"What are you so excited about?" Belén asked.

"Antonio is taking a gift to school. They're having a Christmas party."

"I don't understand," Belén said.

"This means he will be receiving a gift, too."

"So?"

"What do you mean 'so'? How many other Mexican children do you know who get Christmas gifts from their Anglo friends?"

"*Ay, por Dios.* It's no big deal."

"Of course, it is. It means they accept him."

Belén got up and began to clear the table.

"Forget what the note says, Antonio," Juan Tomás said. "Take as many toys from the store as you want. Take three or four presents for some of your other friends."

"*No, Papá.* One gift is all I'm supposed to take. Something a boy or girl can play with."

"Who's your gift for, Antonio?" Belén asked.

"I don't know. We are going to put our gifts under the tree, and teacher said she will pass them out at the Christmas party."

"So, you really don't know whose gift you will get or who will be getting yours," his mother said.

"No."

"Well, anyway it shows he's included like everybody else in his class," Juan Tomás declared.

At the store, Antonio scanned the assortment of games and toys behind one of the glass cases. Cap guns, police whistles, checker sets, dominoes, jump ropes, ball and jacks sets, flat kites, box kites, playing cards, American bingo, Mexican bingo, and a cup-and-ball magic trick that everyone in town knew how it worked, but kept buying it anyway.

A box kite, Antonio decided. There were six furled kites in various colors, and Antonio selected the blue one, along with a skein of kite string. He took them home for his mother to help wrap them. It was a toy suitable for a boy or a girl. All the recipient needed was a light wind, which in small towns is almost always present. Not even a tail was necessary to steady the box kite.

It wasn't long before all the space beneath the nine-foot evergreen was filled with colorful packages of various shapes and sizes. It was a magical time, and the excitement of Christmas was everywhere. The boys wanted the largest package under the tree; the girls hoped for something pretty and cute. Size didn't matter to them.

From the shape of the packages, it was obvious several gifts were balls of some kind or other. Some were apparently checkers, by their rattle. Some, most guessed, must be coloring or comic books. Nobody could guess Antonio's gift. It was light, cylindrical, and long, with a bulge on one end. Belén hid the box kite inside one of the hard, pasteboard tubes in which Juan Tomás gave away Gulf Oil calendars and secured the ball of string to one end. She wrapped the gift in festive Christmas paper with teams of reindeer flying over snow-capped houses.

Almost nothing scholastic was accomplished on the last day of school before the Christmas holidays began. It was time to celebrate. The teachers went noisily in and out of each other's classrooms, exchanging gifts and proudly displaying the ingenious decorations their pupils had created. Margaret served the adult guest's eggnog in paper cups and thin slices of fruitcake. She wore tiny jingle bells on her shoelaces that rang with every step she took.

At 2 p.m., with a rap from her magic wand, the long-awaited Christmas party with red punch and green cookies, shaped like Christmas trees, began. Margaret turned on her radio to an FM station playing Christmas carols. For once, she allowed her students to enjoy themselves and become as rowdy as children will be. She served them punch and cookies and chatted with her pupils until the food and drink were gone. It was the first time Antonio heard his teacher laugh.

After twenty minutes, Margaret Brandt announced, "All right, class. It's time to exchange Christmas presents."

"Hooray," the class shouted together. The children looked at one another, giggled, and moved their arms and legs anxiously with anticipation.

"Come up to the tree, one at a time, as I pass out the gifts. As usual, we will start with the row by the door, and the row by the windows will be last."

Margaret passed out presents until only one gift remained and one student to receive it. Antonio went up and retrieved his gift. It was the present he brought from home, the one his mother wrapped for him. He took it back to his desk and did not open it.

Meanwhile pieces of wrapping paper flew in all directions, until the aisles were a collage of colors and designs.

"Aren't you gonna open up your present?" Harold said, waving a new, green top in Antonio's face.

"What for? I know what it is. It's a box kite. It's the gift I brought to school," Antonio said.

"A box kite? Hey, I'll swap with you. I already gots three tops at home."

Antonio's face lit up.

"Deal," he said.

Antonio also owned three tops, but he was glad to go home with someone else's present—anyone's. His mother would be heartbroken and sad if he took home his own gift. Juan Tomás would be furious.

Antonio had already decided to dump the kite in the ditch on the way home and claim he had forgotten his present at school. Hopefully, by the time the holidays were over, Juan Tomás would forget about the Christmas gift from an Anglo, which seemed so important to him. But that was before Harold came to his rescue.

Margaret admired the presents from the front of the room but didn't go down the aisles. There was too much wrapping material littering the floor. Three girls brought their teacher gifts, and she opened and showed them to the class. Eventually, she sidled back to her desk.

A swift rap of the pointing stick on the teacher's desk brought the class to attention. "Listen, everybody. As soon as you put all this wrapping paper and ribbons in the waste baskets—all of it—you are free to go home until next year, until the eighth day of January. Oh, and don't forget your coats and schoolbags…and your lunch boxes."

Within five minutes, all the wrapping litter was off the floor, and the students were hurrying out of the door.

Margaret stood by the exit, smiling.

"Merry Christmas…Tell your folks Merry Christmas for me…Happy Holidays, everybody," she stated, and touched her students on the shoulder as they filed out of the classroom.

As usual, Antonio was the last to leave. His desk was the farthest from the door.

"Antonio?" she called out. "What did you get?"

"A green top."

"A top? In that long package?"

Antonio waved the top for her to see.

"See you next year," she said. The teacher followed Antonio outside and waited until all her pupils had left the school grounds before she re-entered the building.

Margaret spent Christmas with her aunt. They cooked a sumptuous meal that lasted them for three days. Margaret enjoyed listening to stories about her family and the old country. She was fascinated with the story of how her parents and her aunt came to America.

"So just like that you and my father decided to pull up stakes and leave Germany, Aunt Kathe?"

"It was Wolf's idea. He wanted to come to America. He was my youngest brother. We were so close I decided to come with him."

"What did Grandfather and Grandmother say?"

"Our father was furious. Our family had lived in the same house for a hundred years, and he couldn't conceive of anyone leaving all that behind. Mother preferred that we stay home, of course, but she didn't try to stop us."

"It must have been exciting not knowing what to expect," Margaret exclaimed.

"Scary, too. But it didn't bother Wolf. He said if we didn't like America, we could always go home or to Argentina."

"How old were you?"

"Eighteen. Your father was twenty. We got jobs in a factory in Philadelphia, and three months later, Beth, your mother, joined us. She was nineteen and skinny as a corn stalk. They got married two weeks later. They had a small wedding, and I was Wolf's only relative present. Beth had no one, but they were so happy."

"Love conquers all things," Margaret replied.

"A line from a famous poet?"

"Yes, but don't ask me who... a Roman poet, I believe. Probably Ovid or Virgil."

Aunt Kathe stared sadly out of the window. "Those were exciting times. We thought we were so bold and brave. We were probably just foolish."

"You were bold and brave. You were trailblazers."

Aunt Kathe shook her head. "I don't know. Wolf and Beth are gone now, and only you and I are left here in America. I worry that when I die you will be left all alone."

"Well, don't worry on my account. I belong here. This is where I have my career and my house and my friends."

Margaret studied her aunt's pensive face.

"Would you like to go home, aunt?"

"To Germany, you mean? Heavens no. This is home, where my husband's buried. This is where my friends live, and of course, you."

"Don't you miss your relatives?" Margaret said.

"No. I went to Germany for three months after my husband passed away. It was like visiting strangers. I'm not like your father. I became Americanized. I have loved this country from the moment we got off the ship in New York."

"Why didn't my father become Americanized?"

"Because he never let go of the absurd belief that Germans are superior to all other nationalities. America is a melting pot of foreigners, but Wolf never melted."

"Is that so wrong?" Margaret asked.

"Truthfully, yes. You grew up learning your father's values and his outlook on life. Consequently, you are still single and unhappy with half of the population because they are not White."

"That's an insulting accusation, Aunt Kathe."

"Sorry, but you asked."

"But there's some truth in what you say. Right now, I've just about had it with Antonio. I'm going to flunk him."

"That's not right. Besides, how can you do that? I thought he was a bright boy."

"I'll figure something out. Any time a teacher can't outsmart a six-year-old student, it's time for her to take down her teaching certificate."

LUIS OROZCO AKA LUIS LOCO

That year's Christmas season was especially memorable in Meyers, Texas, because it was about that time that a four-month-old mystery was finally solved. The whimsical story of Luis Orozco, whom the children dubbed Luis Loco, will linger in the minds of people for many years. The story has been told and retold so many times, and there are so many versions of what happened that only one fact seems to remain constant, which is that in the end poor Luis Orozco was ingloriously apprehended and sent away.

It started with a subject too indecorous to mention in mixed company in those days. To be bluntly exact, and come to the point, women's panties were mysteriously disappearing from clotheslines on laundry day. Since there were no clothes dryers or privacy fences, every family's clothes were exposed for the world to view on Mondays, fluttering in the wind, suspended on clotheslines with wooden clothespins.

Every housewife knew that sheets, pillowcases, trousers, dresses, towels, and men's shirts were hung on the outer lines. The inner lines were reserved for clothing considered too personal to flaunt. In this way, all clothing was properly dried and sufficiently aired, while maintaining a minimal exposure to the public. After all, no woman wanted her neighbors to know she wore a corset or mended underwear. And no woman wanted her husband to see their neighbor's disembodied, black bra and panties, lest his imagination might run amok. After all, if chance permitted, it was not beyond even the most respectable of husbands to sneak a peek at the neighbor woman's underclothing, even though she wasn't in them. A vivid imagination readily filled in the complete picture. Nothing exasperated wives more than to live next door to a loose woman who disregarded the accepted practices of hanging wet clothes by parading her unmentionables on washday.

Early that autumn, women noticed they were losing panties from their clotheslines. Young dogs sometimes played games with the frolicking laundry, as it gamboled in the wind over their heads, and it was not uncommon to find an occasional sheet or towel on the ground, since these hung low where the playful pups could reach them. But panties? Not really. Those articles of clothing were hung too high to be tampered with. This was the work of careless clothes' hangers or of a pervert.

Carl Hanson couldn't help noticing the pronounced increase in panty sales at his store. The Hanson General Store had long ago made an agreement with farmers in the vicinity that their farmhands could charge whatever they needed throughout the year, with the understanding that when the crops were harvested and the stock and pigs were sold, the farmers would come in and settle the debts incurred by the families they employed. Nobody knew how long this custom had existed, but that's the way things were when Carl inherited the store from his father, John Hanson, thirty-four years earlier. This method of doing business worked well for the farmers, since they needed to pay their employees only part of their salary every weekend, and it worked well for the farmhands, because they had access to the necessities of life year-round, regardless of whether they were working. Much to everybody's credit, the storekeeper's, the farmers', and the laborers', the system was never abused by anyone.

Two years earlier, Carl Hanson attended a liquidation sale in Dallas, where he purchased, for a song, eight hundred pairs of pre-war, crimson-red, silk panties, made before the government started reserving silk for the war effort. "Genuine Silk" a sign above the counter read. Carl rationalized that since pink panties were his best sellers, red should sell almost as well. He dedicated a large glass case to display his special purchase, and there the red panties lay for a long time. Teenage girls pointed at the display and giggled, while their mothers hurried them past it, as though there were something sinful lurking there. Only loose women wore such scandalous underclothing, they told their daughters. How they arrived at that conclusion is hard to say.

With the panty thief at large for months, it wasn't long before the regular supply of panties was exhausted at the Hanson General Store, and shortly thereafter, crimson-red silk panties made their first appearance on many clotheslines. In ordinary times, no respectable woman would have bought, much less worn, crimson-red panties, but given the urgency of the moment and the availability of credit at the Hanson General Store during the fallow season, more red underclothing began appearing, until crimson red was just about the only color of female underwear fluttering in the wind on Mondays in the inner clothes lines between the sheets, pillow-cases, towels, shirts, and men's trousers.

Poor *Doña* Chole, Trinidad Ochoa's widow, seriously considered confessing to Padre Luna that she was guilty of wearing red, silk panties, but her embarrassment was so great, she decided instead to light a seven-day, votive candle to Our Lady of Guadalupe in atonement for her shameless-ness. But in her heart, she knew she was a fallen woman.

Men, on the other hand, must have been pleased with the new underclothing, because during those months, there was considerably more excitement in the bedrooms. After the panty thief was apprehended, and the crimson underwear became gradually replaced with godly hues, the bedroom activity returned to normal. Months later, there was a noticeable upsurge of babies born in Meyers, Texas, but no one bothered to change the statistics on the signs on the outskirts of town. Those numbers never changed, even after an official, nation-wide, government census, which took place every ten years. The signs continued to read: "Meyers, Texas, 301 pop."

About eight o'clock one Saturday night, when the Cortez Bar & Grill was jumping to the blaring sounds of a jukebox and the clamor of men drinking beer and having a good time, Luis Orozco made his appearance.

Pedro Cortez, the proprietor, met him at the door.

"Luis, you know the rules," he said. "If you behave yourself, you can stay until closing time. If you make trouble or get drunk, I'll have to throw you out, the way I do almost every Saturday. *¿Me entiendes?*"

"No problem, *Señor* Cortez," Luis said. "I'll just drink a couple of Lone Star beers and mind my own business."

"And don't scare the ladies by screaming like a wild animal or any of that crazy stuff," Pedro warned.

As was the custom, every Saturday afternoon, men took their families to do their weekly shopping. With that duty accomplished, they headed for a bar with their entire family in tow. Many men chose the Cortez Bar & Grill because it was the first bar across the county line from Thimble County, which was dry. Also, they were allowed to carry a tab until payday. There was no grill as the name of the establishment indicated. If the idea of a grill ever existed, it never materialized. Certainly, no one ever ordered a hamburger or a BLT sandwich there. Properly named, the big blue neon sign should have read Cortez's Bar & Dancehall, but the dancehall part was a well-kept secret from the wives outside. The jukebox blared Mexican polkas and *rancheras* at deafening decibels. Meanwhile the wives sat outside in their cars fanning themselves with a piece of cardboard they carried in the glove compartment for that purpose. They talked to whoever's wife happened to park next to them and got out of their vehicle now and then to mollify rock-throwing skirmishes between their children and other wild factions.

The Cortez Bar & Grill provided women. They were not call girls, but women, nonetheless, who danced with customers for a dime. The dancing area was dimly lit, and the ladies would dance cheek-to-cheek and allow the men to get *free-feels*, which were not exactly free either, but another dime would usually allay whatever inhibitions the girls might have about being manhandled. Although female companionship was available from the day the bar opened, the wives outside were not aware of the dancing ladies. They assumed all the women inside were waitresses. Pedro Cortez, the proprietor, was astute enough to put the entrance on the side of the building with two sets of double doors, so that whatever went on within could not be seen from the parking area.

By eleven-thirty that night, Luis Orozco was unequivocally soused. He sat with his head and arms sprawled on the bar, leaving his last Lone Star bottle of beer untouched. The bartender helped Luis walk outside through the double doors and laid him on the porch. Luis remained there until he awoke to the taunting shouts of children.

"We don't have no more Lone Star beer, Mr. Luis Loco. How about a Pearl beer?" they shouted.

"Yeah, yeah. Pearl is okay, too, but I like a Lone Star more better," Luis said.

He sat up, teetering on the edge of the porch, blithering while he waited for the bottle of beer that never arrived. The children ran past him in every direction, and Luis knew they were scurrying off to bring him a beer. Luis reached out for his bottle of beer each time someone dashed by. Somehow, he kept his balance and didn't fall off the porch. The game went on until the children got tired of running and decided to stop and rest.

Rosalinda Perez was sitting on the hood of the family's Chevy sedan, watching her children play. She had spent two hours inside the humid car until the wind arrived from the Northeast, and she decided to get out and enjoy the breeze. Like the other wives, she didn't complain. She preferred waiting outside the bar to sitting at home, worried about her husband's whereabouts. This had become part of her social life.

The gusty breeze was like those preceding a rainstorm, and some of the other women were coming out of their cars too.

"Qué linda brisa," Rosalinda said to the woman in the next car. Suddenly a strong gust of wind engulfed her, sending Rosalinda's wide skirt flying up over her face, exposing her legs and her crimson-red underwear.

Luis was sitting on the porch directly in front of Rosalinda. He caught a glimpse of her underclothing and sprang into action like a police dog trained to attack on command. He pounced on Rosalinda and struggled to remove her panties, while she fought back just as hard to keep the garment on. Amid her cries for help, all the other women rushed to her aid, beating, and scratching her assailant. Luis finally got his trophy, as he successfully came away with her panties at the price of scratches, high-heel lumps on the head, and all the punishment to his body that thirteen women could inflict in two minutes.

And that was just for openers.

When the men inside heard the women screaming, they galumphed drunkenly out of the bar and caught Luis before he could drive away. Dozens of women's panties fell to the ground when they dragged Luis Orozco out of his truck. Instantly everyone understood. They had nabbed the panty thief.

"Get a rope," someone shouted, and no sooner were the words spoken than a rope appeared with a hangman's noose already in place. The angry mob of drunks threw the rope over a thick branch of the pecan tree in front of the bar and pushed the noose over Luis's head. They lifted him onto the bed of a pickup truck, and only a command for the truck to proceed forward kept Luis from reaching immortality then and there.

Pedro Cortez pushed his way through the crowd.

"Now, just wait a minute, boys. Let's not be too hasty about this. Let's think this over. You have all been drinking and drinking sometimes makes you do things you normally wouldn't do. If you hang Luis, you are all a party to his murder. Not only will Tacho Longoria get the electric chair for driving his pickup forward to hang Luis, but so will the guy who put the noose around Luis's neck, and the one who tied the other end of the rope to the tree. Maybe all of you, too, for cheering them on while a man is murdered. It's called aiding and abetting."

The mob mumbled in disgust and confusion. Their enthusiasm suddenly dwindled.

"Oh, I guess some of you won't get the electric chair," Pedro clarified, "but you sure as hell will go to prison. And who's going to care for your family while you're gone? Think about that."

By then, Pedro was standing next to Tacho Longoria, who was sitting in his truck with the engine idling. "Okay, son," Pedro said. "Turn off the engine and hand over the keys before you do something you'll regret for the rest of your life." He stuck his hand in the truck, and Tacho dropped the keys in his palm.

Someone untied the rope from the tree, and Luis removed the noose from his own neck just as Sheriff Krause pulled into the parking lot. He got out in the middle of the crowd.

"Something going on here, Mr. Cortez?" he asked.

"I think Mrs. Rosalinda Perez can explain it better than any of us, Sheriff," Pedro told him. He held a meek and repentant Luis Orozco by the arm, adding, "I think we found the underwear bandit."

Luis stood with eyes downcast, mumbling strange sounds, while Rosalinda recounted the events of her attack at the top of her lungs. She reached into her purse, pulled out her panties, and shoved them in the sheriff's face.

Sheriff Krause quickly stepped back, and advised her, "Put those away, lady."

The children had aptly named him Luis Loco. After a short hearing, the judge sent Luis Orozco for rehabilitation at a state institution for the insane in Austin, and he was heard of no more in Meyers.

EVE OF FINAL EXAMS: ANTONIO SENT HOME

On the eve of the first-semester's final exams, Margaret Brandt was reviewing her pupils, when she noticed Antonio reach up and scratch the side of his head. Moments later, he did it again.

"Is something wrong, Antonio?" she asked.

"No, Miss Brandt," he said.

"I noticed you scratched your head a couple of times, and I believe you have a problem. Does your head feel itchy?"

"A little."

"That means you probably have lice. Go home, and don't return until the lice are gone."

Antonio was not certain he understood. "Do you mean now?"

"Yes. Right now. Go home and don't come back until your hair is completely clean. It takes about a week to get rid of lice."

She pointed toward the door with her stick.

"*Pronto, pronto,*" she said. "You're holding up the class review for tomorrow's exams," she said.

Antonio grabbed his empty book bag from under the desk and hurried out of the room.

It was the first period after lunch, and school would not be over for another two hours. Explaining the situation to his father was impossible. Juan Tomás would immediately conclude he had done something wrong if he was sent home early.

Antonio approached the J T Store stealthily and darted past it once he saw Juan Tomás was not in sight. He dashed into the house through the side door and excitedly blurted out the whole story to his mother.

Belén listened, and when he was finished, she asked Antonio to stand still while she combed his hair with a barber's fine-toothed comb. There were no lice. She knew there wouldn't be.

"You know, *Mamá*, Bobby Ray, the boy who sits in front of me, has a big ringworm on the back of his head. It's like the one Billy had last month, and teacher didn't send them home.

Belén asked, "Did Miss Brandt see the ringworms?"

"I think so. She sends us to the blackboard to write, and she can see the back of our heads," Antonio said.

"I see. I have a feeling your *papá* will listen to us this time."

After supper, Juan Tomás hurried back to open the store and was reading the newspaper with a toothpick in his mouth when Belén came in with Antonio trailing behind. She wanted to catch him relaxed. She knew Ponciano and the other *compadres* would be along soon for their nightly discussions, so Juan Tomás was not likely to create an ugly scene.

"*¿Qué pasa, mujer?*" her husband asked.

Belén never set foot in the store unless it was an important matter. Their tacit agreement was that she took care of her house, and he managed his business.

"I've tried telling you before that *la vieja* Miss Brandt, his teacher, discriminates against Antonio and does things to him, but you always choose to deny it, *mi amor*," she said. "*Pues, bien,* look at Antonio's head and comb it with this comb. Here."

It was not a flighty request. Juan Tomás understood that from her somber face and the determination in her voice. He took the comb and ran it through Antonio's hair.

"Look at his hair, and look at the comb, Juan Tomás. No lice on his head. No lice on the comb. *¿Verdad?*"

"That's true," came out from Juan Tomás. "*¿Qué pasa?*"

"Today, Miss Brandt humiliated Antonio in front of his class. She accused him of having lice and sent him home. She told him not to return until the lice were all gone. She said it takes a week," Belén said. "You know why? Tell him, Antonio."

"Because I scratched my head like this two times."

"You found no *piojos* when he came home?" Juan Tomás asked.

"Of course not. *Nada.* The teacher is just picking on him. She didn't even look at his hair. Antonio has final exams tomorrow, and he will get "F's" on every subject on his report card if he doesn't take those tests. He may have to repeat first grade."

Juan Tomás drummed his fingers on the chair's armrest. "All right, I'll take him to school in the morning. Have him ready at seven."

He could forgive a teacher many things but keeping his child out of school was not one of them. Juan Tomás had the school board's unanimous approval to send Antonio to the Anglo school, and he wasn't going to let a first-grade teacher interfere with his son's education.

At a quarter past seven the following morning, Juan Tomás stood with Antonio outside the principal's office. Jane Schneider was the principal of the three elementary schools in Meyers. Like José Porras, the janitor, she arrived at school an hour before the first bell rang.

"What can I do for you, Mr. Vásquez?" she asked. The principal manipulated some keys from her purse and opened her office. "Come on in and have a seat."

Juan Tomás and Antonio followed her into the office. Nothing about the small room exuded warmth. It was a practical place with several large, dark, wooden file cabinets taking up half of the office's space. There was an executive desk in the middle of the room with an L.C. Smith typewriter on top and two wooden chairs positioned so that their occupants would face her.

Antonio's mind immediately went to the times he had been in the room with his pants and shorts down to his knees, bending over with his forehead on the same chair he now occupied, getting whipped by his teacher. The principal had not been present. She was away, teaching her eighth-grade class.

Juan Tomás came to the point. "Miss Brandt sent Antonio home yesterday. She said he has lice, but that is not true." He signaled for Antonio to stand up. "Go over to Mrs. Schneider so she can see your head."

Antonio did as he was ordered.

Juan Tomás followed his son and slipped his left hand under the boy's chin. He drew Antonio's head within inches of the principal's face. "Now look at his hair, ma'am. See? No lice. Comb it back and forth with the comb like this. No lice. His teacher said he should stay home for a week, until all the lice are gone. He has important tests today. He must be in class. If not, he gets F on the report card, maybe flunk first grade."

Mrs. Schneider smiled. "No, no. Antonio is doing very well in school."

She knew about the previous day's incident, and after questioning Margaret, she was inclined to believe that the first-grade teacher had acted in haste and sent the boy home not only without sufficient cause, but also without consulting with her. Principal Schneider was glad Juan

Tomás had gone to see her. This allowed her the opportunity to unravel an unseemly situation with the proper decorum.

"I can see Antonio's head is clean, Mr. Vásquez. I don't know all the details about what happened yesterday, but I agree with you. This young man belongs in the classroom, not at home. Yes, I think your son can go back to school this morning," she said.

"Thank you, ma'am. I knew you would understand. To miss a week of classes—*ay, no.* That's too much. I do not allow him to miss even one day, and he knows it. Headache. Stomachache. Those are not excuses to miss school. Believe me I must see blood before Antonio skips school," Juan Tomás stated. "His blood, of course."

The principal looked at Juan Tomás's resolute face. The man really means it, she thought. She jotted a short note on a memo pad and handed it to Antonio.

"Don't lose this. Give it to Miss Brandt when you go to your room at the usual time this morning. She will gladly allow you to stay and take your exams."

Antonio and his father left the principal's office, just as a busload of students arrived.

"Thank you for coming," she said.

She thanks me for coming to her with a problem. This woman has class, a lot of class, Juan Tomás said to himself.

"*M'hijo,* don't forget your book bag and your lunch. They are in the backseat of the car," Juan Tomás told him, before Antonio could dart off toward the playground.

"You brought his lunch?" Mrs. Schneider said.

"Oh, yes. I knew this was going to be a good day."

LA LLORONA:
LOSSES AND PAINS

On any given evening, one could count on the same habitués at the J T Store: Juan Tomás, Ponciano, Esquique, Pedro, and Joaquin. What had started as a friendly exchange of knowledge and opinions months earlier between Juan Tomás and his *compadre*, Ponciano, Antonio's baptismal godfather, soon attracted the other three men, and it became a nightly ritual that lasted over twenty years. Antonio was there from the beginning, until he finished high school and went off to college. He listened to their nightly debates, discussions, stories, and songs through the window between the small office and the store, while he worked his school assignments. He wondered if someday he would have numerous friends like his father. So far, he had only one close friend, Harold Stern. Antonio was not interested in their debates and discussions, but when they told stories, he put his pencil down and listened. He liked to hear stories about buried treasures, stories about war in faraway places, and stories about Mexican folklore.

His favorite tale was the legend of *La Llorona*, the crying woman. The telling of that story was reserved for stormy nights when lightning bolts lit up the firmament without warning every few seconds, and the rolling thunder that followed in their wake shook the earth frightfully. It was told only on the rainy nights when José Porras, the school janitor, was present, which was almost always, as it was his habit to stop in for a Butterfinger candy bar around closing time. José Porras was one of those timid souls who is easily frightened, even by his own shadow. Ponciano told the story best. He waited until José Porras decided it was raining too heavily to leave and joined the *compadres*.

"The legend of *La Llorona*," Ponciano began, "is a word-of-mouth lore known in every Hispanic community from the United States to the southern tip of South America. She goes by other names in some countries, but whatever she is called, it is always the same sorrowful story of a young mother who, overwhelmed by the demands of life, in a moment of madness hurls her two infant sons into the raging waters of a swollen river. She regretted her great sin almost immediately and returned frantically looking for them at the site of her crime, but the swift currents had already swept the children downstream, and she could not find them. From that day on, it is said that on rainy nights *La Llorona*, remorseful and heartbroken, skims over bodies of water, large and small, looking for her infant children. Even after her death, she continues to search. Her bloodcurdling wails are familiar to countless adults and children, and almost everyone who hasn't seen her knows someone who has. It is said that her soul, instead of being cast into the depths of Hell, when she died, was condemned to search hopelessly for her children forever.

"Those who have seen *La Llorona* say she is very old and transparent as a thin puff of smoke, something like a sheer, white veil suspended in midair. This is correct because that is what a ghost looks like. According to some, she has a long, gaunt face with piercing orange eyes. Others say her eyes are a glowing green. Who knows? Some say she has long, jagged teeth, while others don't remember seeing her teeth. But all who have seen her agree she resembles a mist with the outline of a woman, white and luminous.

Her shrieking screams have turned men's hair completely white overnight, as though they had aged many years. Fortunately, for those individuals, they soon regain their natural color of hair, but mentally, they are never quite the same. Coming face-to-face with a condemned spirit is too much for human beings to endure, too much for us mortals who are still on this side of the curtain of eternity.

Most of the time, *La Llorona* appears where there is water. She is also known to appear on rooftops, outside of houses looking in through windows, and in bedrooms, standing at the foot of the bed. One instant she is there, then poof, she's gone.

"Just last week, *Don* Donato's wife saw *La Llorona* flying back and forth under the bridge at the *Rio de Cleofor*—the little creek that runs under the road going toward Wiley, José Porras reminded them. José Porras didn't want to hear that. It was the creek he crossed going home. Fear overtook him, and he munched faster on his Butterfinger. He would have to buy another candy bar before the night was over. He wasn't enjoying his first one at all.

"Sometimes when *La Llorona* is around, people mysteriously disappear," Ponciano continued. "It happened some time back when my *tío* Cleto was playing poker and drinking beer with some friends in the shed behind his house. Fermin Patlán, his good *amigo*, skipped a hand and went outside to relieve himself behind a tree. Said he'd be right back. He was gone a long time, so my *tío* went looking for him. *Tío* Cleto worried a little because there was only one tree on his property, and it was only fifty feet away, not far at all. Fermin couldn't get lost very easily.

As soon as my *tío* left the shed, he said he heard an explosion and saw a blast of light flying up out of the tree. He said it looked like a lightning bolt shooting up toward the sky. *Muy grande.* Then he heard the frightful screeching of *La Llorona* and screams from Fermin that sounded like somebody was hurting him."

"Was Fermin hurt?" José Porras asked.

"Well, that's the funny thing. Not funny, really...strange. *Tío* Cleto looked everywhere and found nothing. Fermin had disappeared."

"So, what happened to him?" Esquique asked.

That was the question José Porras had in mind, too.

"Nobody knew for months," Ponciano said. "Three months went by before they found Fermin Patlán wandering in the downtown streets of San Antonio, sixty miles away. He was living under a bridge with hobos. His family took him home, but to this day, he's not the same. That was six years ago. He doesn't play cards anymore, and he doesn't remember a lot of things. He hardly ever leaves the house."

Slowly José Porras squirmed his way to the center of the little circle of friends. He wouldn't be the one grabbed and taken away. Juan Tomás shot a telling sidelong glance toward José Porras, and everyone laughed, including José, although he had no idea what the sudden outburst was about.

"Nobody knows what happened to him," Ponciano said. "Maybe a tree branch fell and hit Fermin on the head, and he walked away dazed."

"Amnesia," Joaquin chimed in.

"Yeah, something like that."

Ponciano got up and stood in the doorway. "Looks like the storm is over."

"And just in time. It's ten o'clock, *señores.* Time to shut her down for the night," Juan Tomás said.

José Porras knew nobody was going his way, so there was no point in asking for a ride. He helped Juan Tomás and Antonio lock up while the others left, and he waited until they were outside in the dark before he asked.

"Antonio, I'll give you a dime if you follow me home," José said.

"It's drizzling," and "I'll get mud all over my bike."

José Porras knew he held a losing hand. He upped the ante to "*una peseta*, a quarter."

Antonio called out to Juan Tomás, who was checking the side doors. "*Papá*, can I walk José home? He forgot his flashlight. I'll help him home with mine."

"It's drizzling, *m'hijo*. Let's give him a ride home."

José Porras lived a mile from the J T Store.

"I wish nobody had mentioned the scary lady." *La Llorona* was so real to José Porras, he would have paid a dollar for Antonio to walk him home that night.

José Porras was twenty-three years old, and he thought Antonio was the bravest boy on earth. Antonio had walked him home several times at night. José was a simple man, who preferred the company of children— people he understood. He liked to play games children played. He taught his little friends how to fly kites, showed them how to play *concos* with their tops, and introduced them to the art of shooting marbles out of a circle drawn on the ground with the finesse of a billiards' grand master. Sometimes on weekends, he sat with Antonio on the bench in front of the J T Store and played "My Car, Your Car." If he chose left, all the cars approaching from the left side were his, and all the cars coming from the right were Antonio's. It was a game of make-believe that children in small towns enjoyed playing, and so did José Porras. He would roar with laughter when Antonio's vehicle was a broken-down, vintage rattletrap, and he would whistle loudly, bracing his bottom lip with two fingers and beamed with genuine pride of ownership when his car was a shiny, latest-model vehicle, the likes of which nobody in Meyers owned. The women of the town said José Porras was born simple because his mother was badly frightened by a rabid dog in the third month of her pregnancy, when she was carrying him. The poor woman had a recurring nightmare for months thereafter of raving dogs snapping at her with their contaminated, foaming jaws. Most people were inclined to believe that explanation, because José had other brothers and sisters, older and younger, and they were all normal.

When stories ran short at the J T Store, Ponciano and Esquique brought out their musical instruments and played for the *compadres*. They were talented musicians.

Ponciano owned an old violin. It was a relic passed down to him by his father, who had inherited it from his father, and so on back up the family tree for several generations, from progenitor to progeny. It was not an expensive instrument, even when new, but to Ponciano it was an heirloom almost as priceless as the fingers of his hands. He carried it in a worn violin case, which he believed to be the original, and he treated the violin with reverence. When he played, it humbled and fascinated him to know that several generations of his predecessors had lovingly placed their chins on that same instrument to render their melodious interpretations, and now it was his turn. He wondered "who were those men, and what were they like?" But other than his father, he had not known them, so these were questions that could never be answered. At times, Ponciano envisioned those defunct musicians guiding his right arm as the bow crossed majestically over the strings. He preferred playing the old, traditional waltzes, which he knew his ancestors must have known and played.

His friends did not know with any degree of certainty how accomplished a violinist their friend Ponciano was because their knowledge of the violin was limited to listening to local musical groups, which seldom included an accomplished violinist. But when they saw him with his eyes closed, enraptured in his music, so that Ponciano and his instrument became one entity, they knew he must be very good.

When Esquique brought out his guitar, it was time to sing and reminisce. They sang authentic songs from the Mexican Revolution to the accompaniment of his guitar. Songs the revolutionaries sang while riding aboard military trains, when General Francisco Villa's army was on the move, and songs soldiers sang at camp to keep their melancholia away. They sang songs about trains, ships, horses, mules, and lost loves. Nonsensical songs about an ugly woman they once knew, a dark-skin woman they would gladly die for, and even about the woman they wanted most for a mother-in-law. They sang songs celebrating victories won in battle and about getting gloriously drunk. There were songs recalling the good life that once was, although real life before the Revolution was never idyllic. *Adelita* and *La Cucaracha* had been Pancho Villa's favorites. They belted out those songs and many others.

The great irony of it all was that these men patriotically sang out their hearts to a revolution that had driven them out of home and country, which sent them fleeing to the nearest border with only those possessions they could carry on their backs. As time passed, the Revolution and most of its colorful characters became enshrined in a mystic aura. Rancor about the inconveniences the war caused abated and settled solely on those men who had blatantly abused their political power, like Porfirio Diaz and Victoriano Huerta. Pancho Villa became a national hero, the defender of the poor and underprivileged. Even the Mexican government, which for many years considered Pancho Villa nothing more than a bandit, eventually declared him a patriot of the nation. They exhumed his remains from his humble grave in the *Panteon de los Dolores*, in *Hidalgo del Parral, Chihuahua*, and laid him to rest in Mexico City in a place of honor among the other great heroes of the Revolution.

LEGENDS OF REVOLUTION AND MIGRATION

Of the five *compadres*, only Joaquin migrated to the United States as an adult, and he never became an American citizen. The other four were under ten years of age when they crossed the Rio Bravo into a haven called Texas. Their recollections of the Revolution were hazy: a lot of gunfire, women and children crying, soldiers barking orders, traveling north by night, and hiding in tall grasses by day.

Joaquin, who first migrated to California before settling in Texas, described the brutal summers he spent in the fields, gathering fruits and vegetables at the frenzied pace demanded by the American *mayordomos*. Laborers, he said, lived in shallow, dugout caves on the sides of hills, where there was neither running water nor electricity. To add further insult, the bosses charged the laborers twenty-five cents a week for the crude living quarters.

In the evenings, when they convened at the J T Store, the *compadres* related their personal experiences, along with interesting stories they picked up along the way. One topic they all knew well and discussed repeatedly was the Revolution. Spelled with a capital R, it meant the Mexican Revolution of 1910–20. Sitting in the tranquility of Texas, their fathers filled in the gaps about the country they had left behind and gave their own spin on how and why the Revolution happened. Joaquin knew that phase of Mexican history firsthand but kept it to himself. He never admitted favoring any political faction, and there were many: the *Diazistas*, the *Maderistas*, the *Villistas*, the *Carranzistas*, the *Obregonistas*, the *Zapatistas*, the *Huertistas*, and other lesser-known ones.

"When an army marched unexpectedly into town," Joaquin argued, "it was a healthy idea to side with the faction that had just arrived."

Ponciano opened the discussion at one of their first meetings with a question.

"Did you know that Pancho Villa was not Pancho Villa's real name?"

Before Ponciano could elaborate, four voices were clamoring that his true name was Doroteo Arango. With everybody talking at the same time, each one gave his version of why Doroteo Arango was renamed Pancho Villa, and no two versions coincided.

"That was easy," Esquique said.

"Yes, but which is the true story? Even in books, the story is not told the same way all the time," Pedro said.

"Have I told you about the time I saw Pancho Villa?" Ponciano asked.

Now that was a bit of exciting news. After several discussions, when one was prone to believe all that they knew about Pancho Villa and the Revolution had already been said, a new revelation surfaced, as happened every time the topic arose.

Ponciano continued. "*Sí, señores*. One day Pancho Villa rode into Arroyo Seco with *Los Dorados* at his side, his most trusted bodyguards. We lived in a small village, smaller than Meyers, maybe two-hundred souls, something like that. Villa called the men of Arroyo Seco together and told them they were joining his army the following morning.

"'And don't worry about your wives and families,' Pancho Villa told them. 'My men will look after their safety, and they will have plenty of food on the table.'"

"But my father and the other men did not like the idea of leaving their wives and children with strangers. They were for the Revolution, yes, but Villa was demanding too much.

"My father owned a small *hacienda*, which he inherited from his father. We had horses, pigs, and chickens. It was the kind of *hacienda* the revolutionaries loved to raid whenever they came through.

"The citizens of the town respected my father and looked up to him. In times of need or trouble, they went to him for help or to seek advice. So, my father was speaking for the town when he looked at General Villa in the eye, and told him, 'We are all on your side, *mi general*. But we would like to choose four men from our town to stay behind and protect our families. Just four.'

"Pancho Villa threw back his *sombrero* and wiped his brow with the kerchief tied around his neck. He was very angry. '*Mi amigo*,' he said to my father. 'I did not ask what you think I should do. I am ordering all men, sixteen and over, to join me here tomorrow morning. And don't worry about your *patrones*, I will take care of them. *¿Me entienden?*'

Then Villa gave a wicked laugh.

"'*Sí, mi general*,'" my father said.

"'Be ready to join my troops when we come through here at dawn. Bring your pistols and rifles, whatever you have—*machetes*, knives,' Pancho Villa commanded from his horse."

"That night, my father and the men of Arroyo Seco met at our house and decided what they should do. At midnight, our family fled, as did all the town. I was five-years old at the time," Ponciano said. "When people asked for the escape route, the instructions were simple. 'Take any road going north and follow it until you get to the Rio Bravo. Cross the river, and don't stop until you see *Americanos*—lots of *Americanos*. Only then will you be safe from Pancho Villa and the revolutionaries."

"That is how we got here, too," Pedro said. "But we didn't wait until Pancho Villa was knocking at our door. We lived in Noriega, and one night some revolutionaries came and shot up the town. Bullets were flying in every direction. We slept outside on our *petates* in the corn field behind our house. If someone came into the house to shoot us, they would think we had left town. The Montemayores, next door, slept inside, and that's where they died—assassinated in their own beds."

Juan Tomás said, "I was six years old when we left Mexico. We settled on a farm not far from here, between Meyers and Redden. We were a hundred and fifty miles on this side of the border. My father said this was a safe distance from the Revolution.

"One day soon after we arrived, I went to Redden with my father and mother to buy groceries. We took Chona, our mule, and our wagon, the same mule and wagon that brought us all the way from San Luis, Potosi. We were at the grocery store buying our *mandado* when a tall, dark man with guns on both sides of his gun belt entered. He was a stranger. He wore black pants and a black shirt and black boots with noisy, silver spurs. His *sombrero*, like his clothes and boots, was covered with dust. You could tell he had traveled a long distance, and from the way he stared at people, you knew the man was not there to buy groceries. He was looking for someone."

"Who was he? Don't tell me you thought it was Pancho Villa," Ponciano said. "Villa never came to Texas. He went to New Mexico."

Esquique jumped in. "He did come to Texas. He came to El Paso."

"No, he didn't," Ponciano retorted.

"Let Juan Tomás finish his story." Pedro said. "Maybe it was Pancho Villa."

"No way," Ponciano insisted.

Juan Tomás resumed his story. "You could feel the tension build up in the store as the man in black walked around. Everybody was aware of his presence, and you could hear a low humming sound of people whispering to each other about the stranger. But nobody dared to look the man in the eye, and everybody stayed out of his way.

The stranger paced up and down the aisles with a hard look on his face. He was looking for someone, but who, he did not say, and no one dared to ask.

"*Doña* Juana, an old woman who worked at the grocery store, watched him at a distance from the moment he entered the store. It was her job to make sure nobody stole anything. She was trying hard to recognize the man, but no, she didn't know him. As he edged closer to where she stood, *Doña* Juana sensed big trouble, and when finally, he turned into her aisle and headed straight in her direction, at that very instant, she knew. There was no doubt in her mind.

"'*Dios mío*,' she cried out, as though the Devil himself had appeared to her. At the top of her lungs, she screamed, '*Aquí está Pancho Villa*.'"

"*¡Híjole! ¿De veras?*" Esquique cried out in disbelief.

The *compadres* were astonished by this incredible disclosure.

"The customers panicked, and in less time than it takes to tell you, everybody went running out of the store to safety. They flew out the front doors and ran straight ahead toward the low hill to the north, where they would have protection from the bullets that were sure to follow. But nothing happened. No guns were fired. The funniest part, my friends, is that the stranger dressed in black, with two guns hanging at his sides...well, he was the first one out of the store, and he went running up the hill to safety ahead of everybody else."

The *compadres* exploded in a burst of laughter, knowing they had been had.

"Juan Tomás, you're mishandling the truth again," Esquique told him.

"It's a true story," Juan Tomás insisted, but the *compadres* were too busy laughing.

Joaquin asked, "Did they find out who the man in black was?"

"Yes, it was *Don* Donato's nephew Arnulfo. He had just arrived on horseback from Mexico and was looking for his uncle. Someone told him *Don* Donato went to the Redden grocery store on Saturday. You see, Arnulfo deserted Pancho Villa's army and escaped to Texas, knowing he would be executed before a firing squad if he was caught. That's why he outran all the others. He thought Pancho Villa was in the store looking for him"

They laughed a while longer, chortled, and wiped their eyes one last time, before moving on to the next story.

WHIPPINGS A-PLENTY

At the Meyers elementary Anglo school, students who misbehaved were whipped only in the principal's office, since it afforded the privacy no other room in the school provided. During the discipline, the principal was never present, unless she was the teacher meting out the physical punishment. In his first semester, Antonio went five times through the humiliation of lowering his pants and shorts in front of his teacher, after which she administered three swift raps to his buttocks with her wooden dowel, while he bent over with his forehead touching the seat of a chair. His first whipping was the outcome of kicking a football into the street. The second was for running in the hallway and knocking down a girl. The third was for talking after the bell rang. He completed a sentence just as the second bell sounded. The next time was for getting a tennis ball stuck in the rafters of the gymnasium ceiling. Margaret Brandt never gave an exact reason for Antonio's fifth whipping, but the indignity lingered in Antonio's mind long after the pain of the stick was forgotten. No notices regarding his bad conduct were sent home, and his report card was glazed over with a B+ in deportment. His teacher, Margaret Brandt, chose not to confront Juan Tomás and offer explanations.

Harold Stern was forever amid trouble, too. Harold came from poor, Anglo parents, who were raising their young family of seven rowdy children on a small farm east of town. Harold was their youngest child, and there was a Stern student in almost every classroom. Because they were poor, the Stern children had no clout with Margaret Brandt. She had no reservations about taking the rod to Harold for minor infractions, which she might have overlooked for certain other boys.

Margaret whipped Harold Stern five times in his first semester. He visited the principal's office as frequently as Antonio. On one occasion, both boys found themselves in the principal's office at the same time. Harold went first. He lowered his pants and shorts and remained stone silent while the teacher struck his buttocks. When the whipping ended,

Harold pulled up his clothes, and said, "Thank you, Miss Brandt," as instructed to say, and returned to the classroom with a grin on his face. Antonio didn't cry either, but he couldn't help himself and uttered short grunts every time the rod struck him. From that day forward, he had an admiring special respect for his friend Harold.

During their first school year, Margaret Brandt went through six pointing sticks, as she called them. Antonio and Harold smiled at each other whenever one of the menacing ferules—what they also knew as boards of education—cracked in half, only to be disappointed the following morning when their teacher appeared with a new pointer in hand, rapping it on desktops much to her heart's delight.

THE ALAMO,
THEIR STORY NOT OURS

Juan Tomás had misgivings about Mrs. Louise Lazlo, the music teacher. He found the choice of songs she taught Antonio's class unrealistic and absurd.

"In her music class," he complained to Belén, "she's teaching the children songs about white Christmases, snowmen, and a Santa Claus who dashes through the snow on a sleigh. I don't see what meaning or usefulness those songs have in Antonio's life, or for the rest of his class. It has never snowed enough in Meyers to make a snowman, and I don't know anyone who owns a sleigh. Most certainly, there has never been a white Christmas in this part of the country. She's probably a Yankee. They have a different climate up there."

"*Ay, qué* Juan Tomás. You find fault with everything." Belén said, "Those are children's songs, songs intended to stir up a child's imagination. What do you want them to sing for Christmas? *El Rancho Grande?*"

"I don't know. Something true to life."

The following week, Antonio went home from school singing a song that stirred up a lot more than Juan Tomás's imagination. He became enraged and forbade his son to sing the ballad even at school.

"That song is an insult to all Mexicans," he said.

That evening during their nightly discussions, Juan Tomás asked Antonio to sing the new song he learned at school.

"You mean the song you told me not to sing?"

"That's the one. I want my friends to hear the trash they teach at school."

Antonio left the office, where he was working on his school homework, and went into the large room of the store where the *compadres* were seated.

"Sing that part that mentions the Alamo," Juan Tomás said.

Antonio cleared his throat and sang the first four lines of the ballad.

"Oh, beautiful, beautiful Texas,
Where the beautiful bluebonnets grow.
We're proud of our forefathers,

Who fought at the Alamo."

"That's enough. See. What did I tell you, they're teaching children to dislike Mexicans even in grade school through songs like this one about the Alamo. What do you think?" Juan Tomás asked.

"You're right. Any song about the Alamo is an insult to us Mexicans, and you should complain about it at the next school-board meeting," Pedro said.

"This is very serious," Esquique said. "I would complain to the principal tomorrow morning."

Joaquin chuckled. "I don't know. It sounds more like a patriotic song to me. They're just remembering their fallen Texas heroes. The Mexican army won the battle, you know, and all the soldiers inside the Alamo were killed."

"That's right," Ponciano said, "Besides, Antonio should be proud of his ancestors who fought at the Alamo. They were the Mexican soldiers who stood outside the Alamo shooting in.

"If that's true," Juan Tomás conceded, "maybe that little song isn't an insult after all."

"So, can I still sing it at school?" Antonio asked.

Juan Tomás nodded. "But remember your ancestors won that battle. Let's sing the song right now. You lead, *m'hijo*, and we'll follow."

That night, Juan Tomás and his *compadres* sang the Texas ballad several times, always ending it with the resounding refrain; *"Viva Mexico."*

The Alamo wasn't a bad place after all.

For over a century, since the cessation of Mexican lands to the Republic of Texas and to the United States of America, Mexican children learned at home that Anglo Americans were essentially bad people. *Gringos* was the erstwhile pejorative name given them by the Mexicans, but the word's etymology is so foggy that no one can say with any degree of certainty when it first came into use or what its origin may have been. Some say it originated with songs American soldiers sang by campfires, such as *Green Grow the Rushes, Oh! Green Grows the Laurel,* and *Green Grow the Lilacs.* Or perhaps it originated with the American Irish soldiers whose uniforms were green, and the Mexicans chanted to them, *"Green, go home."* Some Europeans claim the term *gringo* was used much earlier in Europe and designated someone or something not understood. It was a derivative of *griego,* which meant Greek or foreign.

Who knows? What is known is that in the beginning, *gringo* was just a way of designating an Anglo American, with no malice intended. It became a derogatory term during the fight for Texas' independence and the subsequent Mexican American War, where many lives were lost on both sides. Finally, after over a century of constant usage, *gringo* became just another slang term designating an Anglo American, although some might argue it still carries a tinge of disparagement.

Most Mexican parents taught their offspring that Anglos stole from Mexico the lands that now comprise the border states from Texas to California. There was a pact, they said, called the Treaty of Hidalgo, wherein were spelled out, among many other things, the rights that protected Mexicans who owned and lived on lands that Mexico ceded. But in the end, the United States government conveniently looked the other way while those specific rights were violated, and Mexicans living on those lands lost the right to own their lands. Their lands were, in fact, stolen from them.

During that era, it was not uncommon for Americans to arrive from the east, armed with a deed in one hand and a rifle in the other, and announce that the American government had awarded them lands which Mexican families had cultivated and lived on for generations. Some Mexicans were given only days to pack up and vacate their homesteads. Others were driven off their lands immediately at gunpoint. Even less fortunate were the Mexican families shot on the spot and buried on what had been their *haciendas*. Those were the Anglos that Mexicans knew back then, the *gringos* whose corrupt legacy came down by word of mouth and little in the way of written historical note in American history books.

Juan Tomás and his friends sometimes discussed the events of those turbulent years, and it inflamed their minds with indignation. The *gringos* had stolen the very land on which Meyers, Texas, was located, they said. Not from their fathers or grandfathers. It happened to the unfortunate Mexicans who lived in *Tejas* in the middle of the past century, the Mexicans who were killed or driven south of the *Rio Bravo,* as Mexicans called the Rio Grande. The lands were not stolen by Carl Hanson, the man at the grocery store or by W.W. Wentworth, III, the rich landholder, or even their fathers, but by men who came before them—maybe their great-great-grandfathers.

In discussions by the *compadres,* Antonio heard of General Antonio Santa Anna, the Mexican commanding general, who was captured by the Texans and who relinquished the lands now called Texas in exchange for his life. Juan Tomás and his *friends* held the general in low esteem.

"He should have accepted an honorable death by execution, rather than surrender lands which were not his to give," Esquique opined.

"But Santa Anna must have had his redeeming graces," Joaquin argued. "After all, why was he called on to lead Mexico as president and commander of the Mexican armies eleven times?"

Up until the time of the battle of the Alamo, Mexicans and Anglos coexisted well, to the extent that there were intermarriages between the two races. The fight for Texas independence and the subsequent Mexican American War changed all that. Now the two races had a reason to dislike and distrust each other. The struggle to pry Texas loose from Mexico brought on intense bitterness, even toward those Mexicans who had fought with the Texans against Mexico, like the celebrated Colonel Juan Nepomuceno Seguin, a soldier of Mexican descent who fought with distinction on the side of Texas. He had been mayor of San Antonio. But despite his personal recognition as a hero, the wealth of his family, and his education, ultimately, he fled to Mexico for his own safety, as did many other affluent Mexican families who were stripped of their lands.

Anglo children learned in Texas history books of a battle in which Mexican soldiers slaughtered mercilessly almost two-hundred Anglo soldiers, perhaps some of their own distant ancestors. This was not a fable enshrouded in a mist of hazy recollections. The old mission of the Alamo still stood as a reminder of the massacre that took place there in 1836, and "Remember the Alamo" remained the battle cry within every Anglo-Texan's heart over a century later.

CRUELTY AND PUNISHMENT—
DISCIPLINE AT SCHOOL

The second semester began badly for Margaret Brandt. At the school-board meeting, her unfulfilled prediction came back to haunt her. Timothy Rawls was among those ready to remind her of her boast.

"When we met over at the Baptist church last August, you promised the Meskin boy would be gone in six weeks, so we went along with Tom Williams and let the boy in. I don't know what kind of calendar you have, but this is already February, and he is still at the White school."

"Maybe she's using the almanac to make her predictions," Mary Hillman spoke.

A baritone voice from the back broke through. "I said y'all was nuts to let him in. Now he's dug in like a bedbug, and you cain't get rid of him."

"Margaret, I thought you said it was no big deal outsmarting a six-year-old kid," Agnes Blevins declared.

Timothy Rawls demanded some answers. "Like the Meskins say, *¿Qué pasó?*'"

Margaret got up to defend herself. "Give me a little more time. He'll be gone for good soon enough."

"You've been feeding us that claptrap for months, Margaret," Mary Hillman reminder her. "Like my late husband used to say, 'That hound dog don't hunt no more.' We need action."

"Yeah. action," someone repeated.

"Just what have you done to get rid of him?" Reggie Skaggs questioned her.

Nobody asked about Antonio's grades. His excellent school marks were known to everyone and lamented by some Anglos.

The first-grade teacher felt her knees tremble. "I've discouraged him every way I know how. I whipped him five times last semester. The boy has no friends, and nobody plays with him. I discipline him for every-thing he does wrong. I don't cut him any slack. I keep telling him things would be a lot easier for him at the Mexican school. I even had Gladys

Vogel, the teacher at the Mexican school, come over and talk to him. You tell me. What else can I do?"

Margaret sat down. Her face was flushed with anger.

The room was silent. Nobody had any suggestions.

"All I can say is remind you to stay within the law," Tom Williams warned.

Margaret raised an eyebrow. What was he saying? Their ridicule stung her hard. Every criticism leveled at her was true, but she wasn't thinking about shooting anybody. Why had Tom Williams made such a remark? Suddenly the jobs at the defense plants were very appealing.

On Saturday, Margaret arrived early at her aunt's house. Her aunt was already up with a cup of coffee in her hand. She was having a good day, walking around without the aid of her cane.

"Aunt Kathe, excuse me if I look a fright, but I didn't get a wink of sleep last night."

"That boy, huh?"

"Yes, that boy, again. Everybody thinks it's my duty to get rid of him, but I don't know how."

"I thought you were going to flunk him."

"I can't do that. Grades are sacred to me. They reflect a student's God-given intelligence and how much he applies himself. In my classroom, if a student makes an A or an F on an assignment, that's what he gets. I don't care if it's Governor Coke Stevenson's daughter or Antonio Vásquez."

Aunt Kathe's eyes glistened. "Noble ideals well spoken, but you didn't learn that from your father. Wolf believed only Germans have brains."

"Maybe I'm becoming Americanized."

"And you should, my dear. You were born here. But don't worry, it's already February. Three more months and the boy won't be your problem anymore."

"You make it sound so easy, but I've got most of the town blaming me for this mess," Margaret said.

"Tom Williams is the one who created the mess, as you call it," said her aunt.

"That's true, but I opened my big mouth last year and promised I'd get rid of Antonio in six weeks. You should have heard them at the meeting last night. They wanted blood. Tom Williams even told me not to do anything illegal."

"Stay away from those meetings, Marge. People get vicious when they're in a crowd."

"Just tell me about it. Believe me, I'm not going back there again, but that boy is going to be the death of me yet. God, I hate him."

"Well, as they told you, don't go doing anything foolish."

"Illegal."

Margaret had a miserable weekend and spent hours planning her next move. Since she couldn't expel him, she had to convince Antonio of the advantages in attending the Mexican school. She had to get the Anglo community off her back.

On Monday morning, she waited until the first recreation period to confront him.

"Antonio," she called out as the classroom emptied out for recess. "Please remain at your desk. I have something important to discuss with you."

Harold looked in Antonio's direction and mouthed, "Watch out."

Antonio remained seated. He had no idea what awaited him, but he knew it wouldn't be good.

When the last student left the room and they were alone, the teacher closed the door and walked casually toward him. The pointing stick lay back on her desk. She sat down on top of the desk next to Antonio's and smiled at him.

"How are you today, Antonio? Are you okay?"

"Yes, Miss Brandt."

"Good."

The teacher continued to smile.

"You know, Antonio, sometimes I think about how much happier you would be at the Mexican school. You would have lots of friends over there. Mrs. Vogel is a very nice lady, and do you know the boys and girls are allowed to speak Spanish during recess?"

"No."

"Yes, they are. Isn't that great?"

Antonio did not reply.

"I bet you would have a wonderful time over there."

"My father doesn't like that school," Antonio said. "That's why I'm here."

"Forget about what your father likes. Wouldn't you rather be there?"

"My father doesn't want me to go there," he told her.

"Maybe you should try it, though. Think of all the fun you will have. I can arrange it for you."

"He won't let me," Antonio said.

"For the moment, let's forget about what your father wants. Let's talk about what Antonio would like."

Antonio shook his head. "I have to do what he tells me."

"But wouldn't you at least like to try it?"

"No," he declared.

The teacher pulled back her arm and struck the boy with all her strength with her open hand on his left cheek. The blow caught Antonio by surprise and knocked him off the Sears catalogue onto the wooden floor. He jumped up immediately and sat down again and began crying softly. Margaret stood frozen in disbelief of what she had done. She knew she had crossed the line, that she had become a tyrant, but she did not apologize. Somehow it felt right. Antonio was not White. He didn't belong in her classroom.

"Damn you," she murmured almost inaudibly and staggered back to her desk, crying with frustration. She felt a sharp pain in the center of her chest and sat still until the pain subsided.

After a while, she reached in her purse and pulled out a handkerchief. She tamped her eyes and cleared her throat.

"Antonio, if you say one word about any of this, I swear I'll do more than just slap your face the next time. Don't you go telling anybody. If they ask at home why your cheek is puffed up, tell them you fell off the merry-go-round or the monkey bars. Understand?"

"Yes, Miss Brandt."

"Okay. So, what happened to your cheek?" she asked.

"I fell off the merry-go-round or the monkey bars."

"Stupid, not both! Choose one. Stick with the merry-go-round. Forget the monkey bars.

"Yes, Miss Brandt."

She turned and looked at the clock behind her.

"There's twelve minutes of recess left. Get out of here," she exclaimed.

Antonio wiped his eyes with the back of his hand and slipped quietly out of the classroom. Margaret slumped farther down into the chair, face buried in her hands. She was drained.

PONY RIDE:
NOT FOR MEXICANS

When Margaret Brandt announced to her class that on Friday Ross Wentworth's father was bringing a pony to school for the first and second-grade students to ride, Antonio's fondest dream was about to come true. Every day, since the beginning of school, he had envisioned himself riding the mottled pony whenever he passed by the corral. He knew it was going to be the happiest day of his life.

At home, he blurted out the news and talked excitedly about the pony ride to his parents. He couldn't believe it was going to happen. He drew pictures of Mighty, complete with its tan splotches in the right places. Antonio knew the pony well. He drew the diminutive horse gamboling freely across an open meadow, where there were no fences. Ross showed him the pony's tan saddle before their walks home together abruptly ended, and Antonio drew pictures of Mighty with the saddle and harness in place, poised as for a portrait or awaiting a rider. The loose-leaf paper images of Mighty formed a little mound on the left side of the boy's desk-top, which his teacher could not help but notice. His anxious anticipation of the event was contagious, and soon that was all the boys talked about. Friday. Friday. Friday.

The girls eyed the pony ride with some apprehension. They weren't sure if riding a horse was something they would enjoy.

It was the second year the Wentworths took the pony to school. Maurice Wentworth, Ross's father, lifted the children one at a time onto the spotted horse and gave them a slow ride around the baseball field, while holding the reins. Irene Wentworth, Ross's mother, took pictures of each rider, which she later gave the children for their family albums.

On Thursday, after her pupils had gone home, Margaret sat down at Antonio's desk and went through his files. There, in the cubbyhole for tablets and loose papers, she found the sheaf of drawings of the pony. Mighty running. Mighty standing, Mighty jumping over a fence, Mighty with a blonde-headed boy rider. One drawing caught her eye. It was meticulously delineated and carefully colored in. The rider was a boy with a batch of black hair, and his face and arms were brown. The sketch was hidden in the middle of the other twenty drawings. It was the best artwork he had produced all year.

"Not bad," Margaret whispered to herself.

Antonio didn't sleep well the night before the long-awaited event. He had a hard time falling asleep, and once he did, he kept awakening throughout the night, wondering how soon dawn would come. He was awake when Belén entered his room to rouse him. He hardly touched his breakfast, jabbering the whole time about the pony ride. When he arrived at school, he looked around the schoolyard. Mighty would be there that day, but it was not there yet. He went to his room without stopping to play on the monkey bars and pulled out a new loose-leaf sheet of paper. On it, he drew his last image of Mighty.

Finally, the second bell rang, and school began. Classes, recess, and more classes came and went. After lunch, the students returned to the classroom for study-hall period and waited. The anticipation of the pony ride filled the room, but nowhere more than with Antonio. Ross's father would arrive with the pony at any moment.

Halfway through the study-hall period, Ross's mother entered the classroom smiling. A camera hung by a strap from her shoulder. She spoke briefly to the teacher. This was the first sign that Mighty had arrived, but nothing boded what was about to happen.

"Okay, class," their teacher said. "The pony is here."

The classroom erupted with cheers and howls of enthusiasm

"Mrs. Irene Wentworth is going to take a picture of each of you on the little horse. Anybody who wants a ride, follow her outside. The pony is behind the gym, where the baseball diamond is. The rides are very safe. Mr. Wentworth will help you get on and off the pony."

Irene Wentworth cupped her hand and whispered to Margaret, while looking in Antonio's direction.

"That's the insolent Mexican boy who came to play with Ross. I'm not about to take his picture," she said.

Up until then, Margaret had not given the matter any consideration. Now she had no choice. She was not about to place her job in jeopardy. Irene Wentworth was a very influential woman. She had married into the richest family in the county.

"You're right, Mrs. Wentworth. It won't happen," Margaret said to the younger woman, and her chest pain flared up as it often did during stressful times.

Some of the girls were still not sure they cared for the adventure. Nevertheless, the entire class headed for the door en masse with Ross's mother leading the way.

The three words that followed would remain imbedded in Antonio's memory for life. The teacher's pointing stick suddenly came down with one sharp rap on the desktop. By now, everyone knew their attention was demanded, and the children stopped instantly. Margaret pointed to the boy at the rear of the room.

"Not you, Antonio," the teacher ordered. "Remain seated. Everyone else can go on outside now."

After the room emptied out, and only teacher and student remained, Margaret busied herself with the papers on her desk. Antonio sat staring straight ahead, waiting for an explanation. The silence in the room was broken by the gleeful screaming and laughter of Antonio's classmates, clearly audible, as they rounded the building and headed to the back of the gymnasium.

Antonio sat stunned. It was incomprehensible that this should happen. When no explanation came, his eyes welled up, and in a papery voice, he said, "Why, Miss Brandt?"

He asked so softly he wasn't sure she had heard him. Margaret did not look up. He attempted it a second time, but no sound came out, and he began to sob. He wiped his eyes with the palms of his hands.

"What did I do wrong?" he asked.

Margaret was pondering the same question. *Somebody will have to pay for injustices committed against children. Will God really send me to Hell for not allowing a boy to ride a stupid horse?* In recent months her chest began to hurt with more frequency, and she worried about having a heart attack. Her chest was hurting now. This was an injustice, she knew, but she was not the culprit.

"I can't help you, Antonio," she said. "Mrs. Wentworth is taking pictures, and she doesn't like you. It's their horse."

Antonio didn't understand. "I don't hate anybody," he said, "unless they are bad, like the evil."

"You mean the Devil," his teacher said. *Am I the Devil?* she wondered.

"I want to ride the pony. I don't need a picture," Antonio said.

Margaret stopped shuffling her papers and placed both hands firmly on her desktop. "Look, Antonio, the Wentworths don't want you on their horse, and that's all I know. I don't want to hear anything else about it," she said, and found anger and sadness in the answer she was coerced to give. For once, she felt compassion for the boy.

Antonio's eyes remained fixed on his teacher for a long time, but she didn't look up again.

Soon the room was a stir with laughter as the children returned in small groups. Most had never been on a pony and entered the room excited and noisy. Antonio sat morose at his desk, wiping his eyes, trying to regain his composure. He knew his father would be very angry if he found out he had cried at school.

After the last student returned, Maurice Wentworth entered the room and stood by the door. He was a tall, rancher-looking sort of man. "Did you boys and girls enjoy the ride, eh? Was that fun?"

There was an uproar of excitement as they answered in resounding yeses and yeahs.

Irene Wentworth entered the room and stood smiling by her husband.

"Did we miss anyone?" Ross's father said. "Did everyone who wanted a ride get one?"

Antonio stood up. "I didn't."

Margaret saw the thwarted look on Irene's face and instantly called out, "No! Antonio can't ride the pony. He knows why...I'm punishing him for something he did."

Antonio remained standing.

"Are you sure?" Maurice asked.

"Positive," the teacher replied.

Ross's father shrugged his shoulders and gave Antonio a helpless look. "Sorry, son. Maybe next year, okay?"

Margaret could not face Antonio. She knew the boy was overwhelmed, that his spirit had been crushed. There was tightness and pain in her chest, but she could not risk losing her job.

Irene smiled broadly, clinging to her husband's arm.

"Let's go, hon," she said.

At that moment, Margaret Brandt hated Irene Wentworth more intensely than she loathed Antonio. She felt manipulated. How dare another woman come in her classroom and dictate what her pupils could or could not do.

TEACHER RESIGNS

Something new was blowing in the wind as the school year neared the end. The Texas legislature voted to desegregate schools across the state and to integrate Mexican American children with Anglo schools by the beginning of the new school year in September.

Simply expressed, as Tom Williams put it, "What with the war going on and a shortage of cash all around, they say it's too darn costly maintaining separate schools in every little, dinky town. In the minds of federal and state legislators, if the big cities can consolidate their schools, so can we. Those of you who don't see eye to eye with our legislators can send your children to private school if you so desire. That's it, folks. It's been coming for a long time, like I told y'all before, and here it is. Come September, there will be no more separate White and Mexican schools in Meyers."

Parents and students learned of the merger at the end of April, one month before school let out for summer vacation. The news exploded like the walls of a weak dam suddenly filled beyond capacity, and at the Anglo school, the uproar of "The Mexicans are coming" intensified progressively louder with each passing day.

The drastic shift in school policy captivated the town. It became the most debated topic of conversation, and it burned like a red-hot branding iron on the sanity of those who opposed it. Many Anglos considered the merger the most ill-advised measure that could befall their children's education. For days, the news upstaged even the ongoing world war, and whenever three or more people gathered to talk, it was a safe assumption they were discussing the merger.

The Anglo community vented its frustrations with a litany of objections that was repeated in every small community throughout the state. It was as though there had been a state-wide convention, where a list was passed out on what to say. They were the same concerns Jim Kearns, Mary Hillman, John Jenkins, Reggie Skaggs, Timothy Rawls, and others had expressed almost a year earlier at the school board meeting and at the special gathering at the First Baptist Church. They were the same complaints Margaret Brandt snapped angrily in Antonio's face. Anglos could not understand how the federal government, 1600 miles away in Washington D.C., could claim to know the educational needs of their children, and their own Texas legislators, up in Austin, didn't appear to know them either.

The Mexican community, which in rural areas was never enthusiastic about their offspring's education, suddenly became very interested. Every family with a child attending the Mexican school received a letter from Tom Williams, advising them of the upcoming merger. It was unbelievable to Mexican parents that the federal and state governments, which had suppressed and ignored them for so long, were now actively promoting something positive for their children.

The black parents, whose children's education was a disaster, looked at the new developments with interest. They knew their turn was next. "Not yet" the Reverend Fortune Walker told his flock. "But I see that our children's time is in the offing, and hopefully not that far into the future."

Aunt Kathe heard a car door slam. Only her niece closed her door with such determination. Margaret took after her father, she was an intense person.

"It's open," she said, when she heard Margaret's footsteps on the porch.

"The end of the world is here, Aunt Kathe."

"Oh, my. Is there an invasion?"

"Only at school," Margaret responded. "Today Jane Schneider called a teachers' meeting after school. Gladys Vogel was there, too. They're closing the Mexican school at the end of May, and they're merging it with my school.

"Will that affect your position?"

Margaret glared at her aunt in disbelief. "Will that affect my position? Are you serious? Of course, it does. My class will be half Mexican come September, and I'm not about to teach a bunch of grease-heads."

"That's ugly talk, Margaret. They're innocent children. You sound like your father."

"There you go, again. You never stand up for your beliefs. You just roll over and accept whatever comes your way."

"Marge, what's the harm in educating Mexican children."

"Now that, my dearest aunt, I can tell you from first-hand experience. They're nothing but trouble, and a little education will spoil them for sure. They'll start thinking they're somebody important."

"They are," Aunt Kathe said. "They're human beings."

"You and your liberal ideas. They're a lower class of people, aunt."

"I don't believe that for one instant. That's your father talking."

"Of course, you don't believe me. Your head is always stuck up there somewhere in the clouds thinking everything around you is agreeable," Margaret said.

Aunt Kathe set her tea glass down on the doily.

"A good rule in life is to live and let live, Marge."

Margaret stood up suddenly and headed for the kitchen, where she dumped her iced tea in the sink.

"Wake up, Aunt Kathe. Don't you know Hitler is at war trying to keep the world a pure and decent place for the White race to live in?"

"Be careful who you say that to. It could get you in a lot of trouble."

"This conversation is going nowhere. I came here for a little encouragement and reassurance from my only aunt, and I end up getting a lecture."

"I'm sorry, Marge. Of course, I'm concerned about you. It's just that at times you're too caught up with beliefs from the past."

"I'm not modern enough to suit you?"

Aunt Kathe shook her head. "So, what do you intend to do, my dear?"

"I don't know. But this much I know, I won't be teaching."

"Maybe you can get one of those defense jobs you were talking about."

"I don't think so. I've given that a lot of thought, and Father would say I'd be contributing to Germany's demise. At this very moment, I must have cousins fighting under the swastika banner."

"Forget Germany. You don't owe that country anything. Think about yourself first."

"I have to go, aunt."

Margaret went home to wrestle with the twin horns of her dilemma. She saw two options. Either she would accept Mexican students in her classroom, or she must resign. She had acquiesced to teach Antonio, and a year later, her classroom was on the verge of a Mexican invasion. Her anxiety intensified, and she did not sleep well. Her chest pains increased. A dark cloud loomed over her future.

Without employment, her lifetime's savings would dry up in a couple of years, and she was still years away from retirement age. She looked at the bronze-faced boy at the rear of her classroom and winced with disgust. It was Antonio and his kind who would cause her downfall. She did not have a husband to support her like the other teachers. During the war, gasoline was rationed, which meant she could not seek a job in another town without a major upheaval, such as selling her house and starting over elsewhere. The war-effort jobs she had considered were now out of the question. She was a trapped animal.

Margaret's distress ultimately led her to examine darker solutions to her problem. Suicide had always been such a foreign and unthinkable act that her own thoughts frightened her when she found herself considering the concept in earnest. She could not recall when the ludicrous, little idea first entered her consciousness, but by the end of May, she was seriously contemplating suicide.

For days, she filtered through various ways of carrying out self-murder. For the moment, there was no urgency in taking her own life, but it comforted her to know that if her world collapsed in the worst way imaginable, she still had a viable exit.

Once Margaret Brandt made up her mind, she knew there was no turning back. On the last day of school, she tramped into the principal's office with her letter of resignation in hand.

"This is it, Jane," she elaborated "Just thought I'd drop by and tell you in person I don't intend to teach school after today."

The principal looked up astonished. "You mean you're resigning, Margaret?"

"Right. I have no desire to teach that wild bunch from the Mexican school."

"I had no idea you felt so strongly about it, but don't be hasty," Jane said. "You have all summer to think about it."

"I want out. I'm not about to disgrace myself any further. Teaching Antonio was bad enough. No more."

"You're throwing away your life-long career, you know," the principal reminded her. "You possess a lot of wonderful knowledge and experience that will be invaluable, now with all these changes. Give it some more thought."

"I've done all the thinking I'm going to do, and I want out. When Gladys Vogel became headmistress of the Mexican school, my father said he no longer considered her a German. She had sold her soul like a street harlot. Imagine what he would think of me?"

"So, this is it. I should find your replacement?" Jane asked.

"It's the end of the line for me. Start looking." Margaret handed the principal her letter of resignation and left the office in tears.

The news of her resignation traveled with the speed of vicious gossip, and for a few days Margaret found comfort in the approval of her sympathizers, who assured her she had done the right thing. Still, she didn't have the palest idea about her future.

Margaret prayed to awaken from the nightmare and discover it was just that, a bad dream. Only after the principal dropped by her house with the news that Gladys Vogel had signed up as the new first-grade teacher did reality smite her. She had taught first grade going on three decades and fancied herself as irreplaceable. Now that someone else held that position, she was devastated.

She locked herself in her house and didn't answer the telephone. For two weeks she was a recluse. During that time, demons raced about in her mind faster and faster, whispering evil thoughts in her ears, and suicidal images darted across her vision at all hours of the day. She was getting little rest and even less sleep.

To stop the interminable train of suicidal thoughts, Margaret settled on one option: hanging. There were seven cross beams in her car garage, and a demon selected the middle one. He told her the ten-foot beam was sturdy enough to support a hundred and ten-pound woman. Another demon told her to purchase a rope and to learn how to tie a noose. But even after selecting the method and the venue of her demise, the train of madness roared on at full tilt in her head.

One evening in the middle of June, Jane Schneider called to offer her the position of second-grade teacher. Sara Evans had decided to retire. It was the only teaching stint available for the coming autumn-spring semesters. Margaret had to decide soon before some outsider snapped up the one-year contract.

"Stop calling me," Margaret screamed.

"It's just that I'm worried about you. Give it some thought. Please."

Margaret hung up.

Later she wondered if she should have considered the offer. *I know, Father. I will be no better than Gladys Vogel, if I accept that position, but what am I to do? You and mother are gone, and I am here. I must survive.* She wondered if her parents could see the unfolding debacle from the great beyond and asked for their advice before she sullied her reputation. She asked for their approval to commit suicide, if it came to that, and explained how simple it was to snuff out her own life. She could execute the act swiftly and easily. Yes, that was the precise word, she mused: *execute*. Hopefully, painlessly, too.

Margaret was in a terrycloth gown with a towel wrapped around her damp hair when she heard a knock at the door. She had just stepped out of the shower, and there was no one she cared to see. She shuffled quietly to a front window and opened a slit in the curtains, just enough to see the street. There was a car in front of her house she didn't recognize. She was about to close the curtains and ignore the caller when she caught him staring at her.

"Hello," was his salutation. "I'm here to see Miss Margaret Brandt."

"What do you want?" she said.

"I'm Bob Kellum, the minister of the First Baptist Church. I came by to meet you and chat a while, if possible."

"I'm very busy. I can't talk to you right now."

"Will tomorrow be a better day...better than today?"

"I guess, I don't know."

"Fine. I'll be here at one tomorrow. My card is on your screen door."

After he drove away, she retrieved his card. It read Bob Kellum, Pastor of Meyers First Baptist Church. Margaret had not attended church services since her confrontation with Reverend Keebler, but the name on the business card was familiar. Her aunt Kathe spoke highly of him.

Although she had no desire of meeting the minister, she decided to dress for the occasion, in the event he talked himself into her house. Ministers were a persistent breed.

At exactly one, there was a knock at the door.

"Bob Kellum," the tall man in the light gray suit announced.

"Hello. I'm Margaret Brandt. Sorry I couldn't see you yesterday."

"That's quite all right. I shouldn't drop in on people without calling."

"Please come in and sit down. Would you care for some iced tea?" she asked.

"That sounds like a good idea at this time of day. I see it's the beverage of preference in your family."

"Dear Aunt Kathe. Yes, I'm afraid she got me hooked on iced tea during the hot summer months. She's the only relative I have...in the United States, I mean."

Margaret went to the kitchen and returned with a pitcher of tea and two ice-filled glasses on a tray. She poured tea in both glasses and set them down on the coffee table between her chair and the sofa where Reverend Kellum was sitting.

"Nice house. Very nice," he said.

"Thank you."

"I won't stay long. I dropped by to meet you and to invite you to our Sunday worship services. Your aunt tells me you're Baptist."

"Well, I considered myself one, until I had a run-in with Reverend Keebler, and I suppose you've heard all about that."

"Actually, yes, I have," he admitted.

"Where is he now? We've heard several different stories," she announced.

"I don't know. I've never met the man. When I came here, he had already left."

Margaret put her tea down and cleared her throat.

"Reverend, I'd like some straightforward answers, if you don't mind."

"Not at all. I have no secrets."

"Very well. To begin with, can you tell me in one sentence why I should accept your invitation?"

"Make that two sentences. Because your soul is immortal, and because we want to be sure it goes to the right place when your body dies."

Margaret repeated his answer in her mind. "That's the whole purpose of religion, isn't it?"

"Well, not quite. That and learning to love the Lord. My ministry is preparing souls to reach heaven. Praying, charitable deeds, obeying the ten commandments, tithing, and many other things are all a part of that preparation."

"Let me ask you the same questions I asked Reverend Keebler, the ones that have kept me away from church. Are all men and women created equal?"

"Obviously not, if we're talking about natural abilities. But if you mean equal as human beings, in terms of a body and a soul...then yes. Even a mentally impaired child has an immortal soul like ours. And that child may be fortunate to suffer his misfortune because he will leave this world innocent of any wrongdoing."

"Do you allow all races in your church?" Margaret asked.

"In the first sermon I delivered here, I made it clear I would welcome all races and nationalities to hear the word of the Lord in our church. Some members objected, but I think they've come around. The issue hasn't arisen again. Mexicans here consider themselves Catholics, even those who only attend church once a year, on Ash Wednesday to have ash crosses scrawled on their foreheads. The Negros, and there are only nine families in the community, attend their own Negro Baptist Church. Makes me wonder what the good Lord thinks of that. In Heaven, there is no such nonsense as White souls and Negro souls. Just souls."

Margaret sipped her tea and set the cup on the table. "We've just met, Reverend, and already I dislike you."

"Well, at least I know where I stand, but as I said, I'd like to invite you to this Sunday's services. I'll be glad to pick you up around eight-thirty."

"I don't think you're listening, Reverend. Besides, you should consider your family first."

"I would like to, but I don't have a family."

"No wife?"

He shook his head. "We buried her in St. Louis three years, four months ago. Cancer. We didn't have children."

"I'm sorry," Margaret offered him comfort.

"That's the way the Lord wanted it. We were married twenty-eight years."

"I didn't mean to pry into your personal life"

Reverend Kellum finished his tea. "Well, I'm off," he said. "Pick you up at eight-thirty Sunday morning?"

"Yes."

This was the beginning of Margaret Brandt's first friendship with a man, other than her father. In a way, he reminded her of her father. He was sure of his convictions.

Thanks to the minister, Margaret found a fulfilling religious experience that summer, which transformed her life.

As Reverend Kellum put it, "Religion sands down the rough edges on people's otherwise beautiful personalities." That summer, many of her lifelong beliefs crumbled with her thrust into the spiritual world.

One afternoon, Reverend Kellum invited her to go to San Marcos. They sat on a bench under a large pecan tree in front of the courthouse. It was Saturday, and the stores surrounding the courthouse were teeming with shoppers. Reverend Kellum was wearing khaki trousers, a short-sleeve, light blue *guayabera*, and penny-loafers.

"No one would believe you're a minister," Margaret stated.

"Oh, I'm your normal, average sort of guy. I wash and hang up my clothes to dry on Mondays. I cook, mow the yard, go to picture shows... everything the average guy does."

Margaret laughed. "What are we doing here, Reverend?"

"Looking," he said. "And please, call me Bob."

"What do you look for, Bob?"

"People."

"I sense there is a lesson to be learned here."

"A simple lesson. Tell me, Margaret. If this were a marketplace, let's say, in the time of Jesus Christ, and all these people milling around us were Greeks, Romans, Jews, Babylonians, and so forth, would you automatically dislike any of them?"

"The Jews," Margaret said without hesitation.

"That's my point. You are prejudiced against Jews. The word prejudice means a pre-judgment. You were raised believing that certain people are a menace to society, so before a Jew even appears, you dislike him."

"Can't help it. Same goes for Mexicans, Negros, and Orientals."

"Yes, you can help it, but you can't do it overnight."

'You sound like my Aunt Kathe. But for the sake of conversation, where would I start?"

"With tolerance. I can teach you how to look at people you dislike and focus on their good qualities. In time, you will learn to accept and even like them. You will do it for the glory of God and the salvation of your soul, which won't make it into Heaven scarred with hatred."

"Brimstone and hellfire, the old scare tactics, Bob?"

"Call it what you like, but can you take the chance that I may be right, and you may be wrong?"

Margaret reflected on his statement. Then she asked something that had troubled her for months. "Would God send someone to Hell for not letting a boy ride a horse?" she asked.

He knew the question must have relevance for her to ask. "Off hand, I would say no, but I imagine there's a story behind that question."

There, beneath a pecan tree in front of the courthouse, Margaret suddenly decided to bare her soul to a man she had known for only a few days.

"Do you believe in demons, Bob? I mean real demons who whisper evil thoughts in your ear and urge you to do bad things, even to yourself."

"You mean like suicide?"

Margaret's hands were trembling. "Yes, but please, don't ever mention this conversation to my aunt. How do I get rid of them?"

"By cleansing your soul of whatever is troubling you. Do you want to be cleansed?"

"Yes, but I need help."

"All right. Let's begin by praying for divine guidance."

Pastor Kellum took a special interest in Margaret and spent countless hours, in the months that followed, helping Margaret resolve the problems troubling her soul. Together they prayed and read the scriptures. They discussed the resurrection of Christ and the meaning of life. She admitted her innate aversion toward all non-Anglos and told him about the demons that haunted her. He was the only person she could confide in. No one else was aware of the turmoil afflicting her soul. In the minister, she found depth and sincerity. He was not a hypocrite.

He patiently explained the mysteries of life and death in phrases she understood. "Life on earth is short, the twinkle of an eye. Life after death is forever. That is why we must make sure we get to heaven."

Yes. That made sense.

By the end of summer, Margaret was a transformed woman. The demons had abandoned her, and the rage in her heart evanesced. The anger in her eyes was gone, and she decided life was worth living. Following Reverend Kellum's advice, she signed on as the new second-grade teacher at the Meyers' grade school.

INTEGRATING SCHOOLS

That September, the Mexican American students enrolled at the Anglo school much to the dismay of the Anglo community, and the Mexican school was no more. Across town, the little, unpainted, one-room schoolhouse, where Mary Shivers had taught Black children, closed its doors, and her students reported for school at the four-room house, which had served as the Mexican school for fourteen years.

Never could Margaret Brandt have envisioned Anglo and Mexican students sitting together under one roof in her school. Had her parents been alive, they would have been appalled at the prospect of their daughter even considering educating a non-Anglo race. Her father would have accused her of being no better than Gladys Vogel, whom many in the Anglo community held in low esteem from the moment she became the director of the Mexican school.

Margaret's classroom would now include Antonio, about a dozen other Mexican children, and all the Anglo second-graders who had not fled to other schools.

As the beginning of the new school year drew near, Antonio heard rumors that Margaret Brandt was going to be his teacher, again. Surely it was a joke, he thought. She had always taught first grade. Antonio's great anticipation in passing to the next grade was that she would be out of his life. But the unthinkable happened. When he entered his new classroom, there she stood—smiling and wielding a new wooden pointing stick firmly in her hand. Mrs. Evans, whom he expected to see, had retired.

"Oh, man," Antonio said, and sank into the remotest desk at the back of the room.

Harold Stern was sitting in the next row. "Told ya," he said.

"Oh, shut up," Antonio retorted.

Margaret Brandt was also distraught. Five of her Mexican second graders were eight, nine, and ten years old. Her nightmare had come true. Her White classroom with only one token Mexican had drastically changed. Even after decades as a teacher, on the first school day, she faced her class with some trepidation.

Before leaving the house that morning, she drank two cups of black coffee to settle her nerves. The taller dark-skin boys intimidated her. She was used to teaching five and six-year-olds. Margaret stood as erect as possible, so the class could appreciate her superior height, which was exactly five feet.

The moment the second bell rang, she slammed the wooden pointer on her desktop, and the room became instantly quiet, with all her pupils sitting stiffly at attention facing her. Margaret smiled. Up until that moment she had not known how her new pupils would respond to her commands. She had feared the tall Mexican boys would be rowdy and intractable. Reverend Kellum was right. This was going to be a good year for her after all. If she had control of her classroom, she knew she would be all right. Margaret looked at all the bronze faces staring back at her.

"My Mexicans have multiplied," she whispered to herself.

Age difference was a school-wide problem. At every grade level, there were Mexican students one to four years older than their Anglo counterparts. Teaching pupils with different levels of emotional maturity at the same time proved to be an additional problem, but nothing compared to the language barrier the teachers and the new students encountered.

The cry of "the Mexicans are coming" started in the spring by Anglo students, frightened enough parents to send about half of the Anglo students scrambling to public and private elementary schools in San Marcos and elsewhere. Some Anglo parents had serious concerns that the quality of education would flounder. Their grievance was not so much with the merging of schools, but the fear that their children might be held back while the Mexican students could catch up. Other parents did not want their children associating so closely with Mexican children. Whatever their reasons, the school year opened with an enrollment about equally divided into Anglos and Mexicans.

Antonio looked around the classroom. There were many dark faces like his, and he knew almost everyone in the room by name. Some of the boys were his buddies, the boys he swam and fished with all summer. Despite Mrs. Brandt, he knew it was going to be a better year. He felt comfortable being among his friends.

Liz Blevins enrolled in a private school in Kyle, and Antonio was glad to hear the news. It was because of her whims that he sat in the ugly, oversized desk, number thirty, throughout first grade. Gone, too, were Gloria Wentworth, Ross Wentworth, John Riley, Reggie Skaggs, Jr., Carol Sparrow, and Arthur and Jerry Mudd. They had enrolled in a public school in San Marcos, but their transfer seemed pointless because their new school had integrated four years earlier.

When Juan Tomás heard of the exodus of Anglo students from the Meyers Elementary School, he observed that only affluent parents withdrew their children. "Let them leave. Let them all go," Juan Tomás said. "We got what we wanted for our children, *¿qué no?* Don't our children have a better school now with better facilities and the best teachers in town?"

His *compadres* nodded. Juan Tomás had not brought about the change singlehandedly, but they knew he had fought a personal battle for the change one year before the merger became law.

Sports changed at the newly integrated school with the influx of the Mexican students. All competitive sports became dominated by the Mexicans, who were on average older, taller, and stronger at every grade level. Antonio found himself in a curious situation. He was the extra wheel, the odd man out in his class. There were seven Anglo and eight Mexican boys in second grade, and when the team captains chose sides to play baseball at the first noon recess, the selection went down along ethnic lines. It was Anglos versus Mexicans.

Billy Evans, the Anglo captain, chose first, so he also chose the thirteenth and last player, who was Antonio, the smallest boy in his class. Immediately, dissension flared up. The Mexicans contended that Antonio belonged on their team.

"No. He belongs on our side," Billy Evans insisted. "He didn't come from the Mexican school. He was already here. He's one of ours. Besides, I chose him first."

"But he is *Mejicano*. He don't belong with you *gabachos*," Arturo Lopez the Mexican captain argued.

Antonio could hardly believe his ears. In the first grade, he was summarily excluded from organized sports. Now everybody laid claim to him. The dispute escalated until Mrs. Schneider, who was observing the boys from the cafeteria, came out to see what the disagreement was about.

Both sides stated their case.

"Well, since each team already has six players without Antonio, and neither side needs another player," the principal offered, "let's appoint him the umpire. You need an umpire."

Antonio reluctantly umpired the game, but it was not the same as playing. He found it ironic that the Anglos who rejected him in first grade should now consider him as "ours." Now he was wanted, but not needed.

After that game, he found his way back to the monkey bars, whenever the boys played baseball or football.

Jane Schneider, the principal, tried to structure the teaching curriculum to meet the new demands of her school, but there were serious language barriers, as had been anticipated. Learning at all levels became stymied and delayed. In desperation, the principal issued Spanish-English dictionaries to all eight teachers, with no effect. Some Mexican students were lagging dismally in their education, and the principal soon realized tutoring was the only solution. Otherwise, some would continue to fail school grades they had already taken once, even twice in some instances.

The principal sent a carefully crafted letter to the parents of Mexican students. It read:

Dear Parents,

Your child's education is very important to us. I am sure you are very proud of your rich Mexican heritage, as you should be. You probably speak Spanish to your children at home, and I think that is wonderful. Here, at school, however, we teach all classes in English, so it is imperative that your child knows English. If you hear that we do not allow Spanish at school, it is only because we want our students to practice speaking English as much as possible. Students learn by repetition.

Next week, we are starting one-hour tutoring classes on conversational English immediately after school, Monday through Friday. It is a voluntary program, but we urge you to help your child speak better English by enrolling him or her in this program.

Sincerely,
Jane Schneider
Principal

Tutoring, which was paid by the state, was a welcomed windfall in the pocketbooks of the very teachers who initially balked at educating Mexican children. They conferred nice bonuses on themselves. Even Sarah Evans, the recently retired second-grade teacher, benefited from the program. The one-hour tutoring sessions consisted of one instructor for seven to eight students. It was a time-consuming program that kept all teachers and many students an extra hour at school, but it worked. By Christmas, the lagging students were steadily catching up.

Margaret Brandt was the second-grade teacher for only three days, not long enough for Antonio to notice the radical change in her attitude toward him and Harold Stern. During the first week of school, Margaret dropped by her old classroom daily, offering suggestions on how to teach first-graders.

"There is a correct way and a wrong way to teach beginners," she told Gladys Vogel. "First-graders are very impressionable and must be handled carefully." If she needed assistance, Margaret assured Gladys, she was available.

By Wednesday afternoon, Gladys knew it was high time for a frank talk.

"You know, Margaret. I would be just as satisfied teaching second grade as I am teaching first grade. If you would like to swap classrooms, I have no objection."

"Am I that obvious?" Margaret asked.

"I've watched you," Gladys said. "Every time you come in this classroom, your face lights up."

"I always thought I wanted to teach other grades, and now that I am, the truth is I miss my little ones."

"Take a good look at my class, Margaret. This class is different from what you are used to teaching."

"I know, but children are children. All first graders are like thirsty, little sponges, eager to absorb knowledge. These are the kids I want to teach. I taught Antonio last year, and he was no different from the other children. In fact, he was one of my top students."

On Thursday morning, Gladys Vogel became Antonio's teacher, and twenty years would pass before Margaret Brandt had her next real conversation with Antonio.

It was a credit to Reverend Kellum that Margaret's dowel became a pointer only. She never again found sufficient cause to beat another child. In the past, she had at times employed the stick for punishment, and the practice escalated until it peaked with Antonio and Harold, whom she marched into the principal's office nine times each in their first year at school. That summer Reverend Kellum taught her patience, and with her newfound forbearance came a sense of fairness that wasn't there before. She felt sadness now, whenever she saw the two boys at school. As a teacher, she had failed them. She had abused and scandalized them just as

Reverend Keebler said, especially Antonio, whom she slapped and otherwise mistreated.

After the merger, it took only a couple of months for the Anglo and Mexican students to become friends. By November, team captains were choosing up sides based on athletic prowess. Compared to the ordeal of the previous year, second grade was a joy for Antonio. After school, he and three friends walked home together, and nobody bothered them. They stopped and talked to Mighty, and Antonio told them about Ross, the boy who owned the pony, but he didn't mention the day Ross's father took Mighty to school. The memory was too painful to talk about.

As the school year progressed, events fell into their customary cycle. In December, Mr. Schneider once more took the eighth-grade boys on a trip north of Wimberley to find and cut down evergreen trees for the classrooms. The children rotated seating arrangements, and Antonio moved to a different desk at the end of every month. Never again did he sit in the same desk for more than a month. The second graders celebrated Christmas with a punch-and-cookies party and exchanged gifts by drawing names. Enrique Gutierrez drew Antonio's name and gave him a red top, and Antonio drew Monica Knight's name and gave her a ball-and-jacks game.

Antonio enjoyed second grade with his friends. He and Harold remained close friends, and often recalled the whippings they received in the principal's office at the hands of Margaret Brandt. They spoke of the punishment with pride, as though they were describing a badge of honor earned through manly valor. This was not something the fainthearted could endure. Their second year in school brought no physical punishment regardless of how much they boasted about being whipped, they were glad it was all in the past. Antonio guessed that he alone had been slapped and was ashamed to tell even his closest friend. When he asked Harold if Miss Brandt had ever slapped him, Harold gave Antonio an astonished look.

"No way. Why? Did she slap you?" Harold asked.

Antonio felt the muscles in his face cringe. "No. I think she wanted to, but she didn't," he replied.

When the second semester was well underway, rumors began to circulate that Mr. Wentworth was taking Ross's pony to school, but when it didn't happen Antonio wasn't surprised because Ross was no longer a student at the school. After the big letdown of the year before, Antonio wouldn't allow himself to get excited over a pony ride, only to have his hopes dashed at the last moment. He no longer drew pictures of Mighty and tried to bury the entire episode in the forgettable past.

A year after the school merger, some of the Anglo students, who were whisked off to other schools, started trickling back, so that by his fourth grade most of Antonio's first-grade classmates had returned, including Ross, John, Carol, Gloria, Doris, and Reggie. Liz did not return. Jerry and Arthur Mudd returned for one year, and then were gone again. The Mudd family moved to Colorado.

Even after Ross reappeared, Antonio led his class with the best grade average.

"His writing looks like chicken scratching," Juan Tomás complained to Antonio's new teacher.

"He does excellent work in everything else," Gladys Vogel said. "Maybe he's going to be a doctor or a scientist someday. That's how most of them write."

A doctor?

The ring of Doctor Antonio Vásquez had the same breathtaking effect on Juan Tomás as it did on Belén. After that, Juan Tomás never felt compelled to question Antonio's handwriting.

"Did you hear that Miss Brandt doesn't whip her students anymore?" Harold asked.

"Yeah, but I don't believe it," Antonio said.

"No, really. The first graders like her."

Antonio rolled up his eyes. "Sick," he said.

But it was true. Margaret Brandt, the teacher who had inspired terror in the hearts of students she disliked, had softened her manner. Her reign of terror ended the summer Reverend Kellum came to town.

Margaret stood in the hallway every morning, until all her pupils were in the classroom. Whenever Antonio and Harold went by on the way to their room, she made it a point to give them a cheerful, "Good morning. How are you today?"

But try as she might, the only acknowledgement she received from either boy was a forced "morning. Ma'am."

She knew she had failed them as a teacher.

Antonio's second and eighth grades were his most cherished years at the elementary school. Gladys Vogel taught him both grades. She was the school's favorite teacher. She was a big German woman with an understanding and kind heart. She was the first Anglo adult with whom Antonio felt comfortable. She was the antithesis of Margaret Brandt, before her conversion. All her students loved Gladys, and amicably mimicked her thick German accent, which was as evident in her English as in her Spanish.

BUS DRIVER SABOTAGES ATTENDANCE

As expected, integration did not land softly on the shoulders of many Anglos. The new regulations did not deter dissenters, like Albert McLeod, from retaliating in their own way. Driving the yellow school bus was Albert's proud domain. On Fridays, after dropping off the last student, he drove the bus home to prepare it for the coming week. He changed the motor oil every three thousand miles, lubed the vehicle as needed, and kept the engine tuned up for maximum performance. On Saturday afternoons, he parked the bus in the shade of his house and washed it with a mop. He treated the bus as though it were his own vehicle, and after twenty-eight years behind the wheel, everybody associated one with the other.

Before the merger, Mexican students never rode Albert's bus. They got to school by whatever means they could find, so it came as a great surprise to Albert when the principal ordered him to pick up all students attending the newly integrated school, except those living in town or less than a mile from school. This change increased the number of students picked up and created additional routes for the bus to travel. Albert loathed Mexicans and dreaded the mess they were sure to make in his bus.

As Albert predicted, the first day got off to a bad start, and he delivered the last busload of students long after the second bell had rung. All students were accounted for, and the classrooms were full.

The following day, Albert completed his routes on time, but many of the desks were empty. All the teachers reported heavy absenteeism. Many of their Mexican students were not in class. On Wednesday, the Mexican students were back, only to miss school again on Thursday.

The principal turned to Gladys Vogel, who confirmed that at the Mexican school erratic attendance was not uncommon, but never in such large numbers. Jane Schneider wondered if this was some type of protest, although she couldn't imagine the motive. When the principal approached the children, she quickly discovered the culprit. Some Mexican students said the bus had not gone for them on Tuesday and Thursday. Others claimed the bus went by but didn't stop.

It was time to bring in Albert McLeod.

Mrs. Schneider, the principal asked, "What do you know about all this, Albert?"

"Mrs. Schneider, all I know is that this has been the worst week of my life."

"If there's a problem, I need to know about it."

"Well, Monday got off to such a terrible start that I had to make some minor adjustments in my routes," Albert said.

"What kind of adjustments."

"For one, I fixed the stops so as I pick up several students at a time, not just one or two, here and there."

"How did you do that?" the principal asked.

"Simple. I told the kids where the bus would be stopping—every mile or so."

"You're making them walk farther to catch the bus?" the principal queried.

"Yeah, some of them. Otherwise, I can't get them to school on time."

"Something's not working right, Albert. We have a lot of students missing school."

"Well, yeah. I had to skip a couple of stops to get the White children to school on time."

"You what? You mean you left some students behind because they aren't White?"

"It don't hurt them none to miss a day, now and then. Besides, they're lucky to ride on my bus. Never did before."

The principal shook her head. "Albert, I don't even know where to begin. Let me just say that from now on you're going to pick up all the students every day, not just some days, and you're going to get them to school on time."

"Cain't be done," Albert took exception.

"Why not?"

"There ain't enough time. I'd have to start picking up students half an hour earlier."

"Then start half an hour earlier. The school is open. I'm here by seven every morning. You think that will solve the problem?"

Albert sat crunching his baseball cap between his massive hands. "Should."

Jane stood up. "Good. I'll get word out to the whole school to expect the bus thirty minutes earlier from now on. No more busing problems, right?"

"Yeah," Albert McLeod responded.

Albert left the principal's office angry she disapproved of the way he was handling his job. He did not mention other creative ideas he had considered. In his initial plan, Albert tried to gerrymander the routes so that Anglo students were picked up first, and it pained him that his logistics did not work out. He had not foreseen that at most bus stops Anglo and Mexican children waited for the bus together.

That evening Albert discussed the latest changes with his wife.

"On top of everything else," he told her, "That skinny-assed principal ordered me to start my routes half an hour earlier."

"My Lord. You're already getting up at six. You'll have to be up by five-thirty now," his wife commented.

"Well, she couldn't care less about that. Ain't no skin off her nose. She's siding with the Mexicans like everybody else."

"Did you tell her about the mess the Mexicans are making in your bus?"

"I didn't get a chance. She was all fired up about getting everybody to school on time."

"Well, I think you should ask for a raise. That's what I think. The Mexicans are creating extra work for you."

"Don't worry about that. She'll pay for it. You just wait and see."

A week later, Albert was back in the principal's office.

"Albert, Albert," Jane Schneider said. "I thought we had solved the busing problems."

"We did."

"I had seven students in my office this morning who claim that yesterday you went by their pickup area without slowing down. They say they screamed and waved at you to stop."

"Sometimes them Mexican kids act like jackasses, Mrs. Schneider" Albert said. "They stand just outside the area where I told them to wait for the bus, and they stand there facing in the opposite direction, like they ain't going to school that day. They're just trying to aggravate me, you know that. Would you pick them up when they behave like that?"

"Albert McLeod, I expect you to honk your horn, get out and call them, and bring them to the bus by the hand, if you must. Whatever it takes, but no rough stuff. I'm putting you on notice. One more incident of leaving students behind, and I may be looking for a new bus driver, my friend. *¿Comprende?*"

Albert sat incredulous of what she had said. There was so much he wanted to tell the principal, but he knew it was futile. She had sold out to the Austin politicians.

"Yeah, I understand," he said.

Judging from the noises coming from outside the house, Albert's wife knew he had a bad day. His pickup truck's door slammed shut hard, followed by Albert's shouting, "Get out of here," when their dog ran out to meet him. Loud sounds came from the storage shed of heavy equipment getting thrown around before she finally heard his footsteps on the porch. Three long strides and he was inside the house.

"That bitch threatened to fire me," Albert said.

"What? Whatever for?" his wife asked.

"Because I didn't pick up some smart-ass Mexican kids yesterday."

"Did you forget about them?"

"Nah, they were trying to aggravate me, so I skipped 'em"

"Don't do that, Albert. They'll get you fired."

"That's probably what Jane Schneider and her bunch would like. Then they can hire some Mexican to drive my bus. That's what they did whenever old man Schmidt, the school janitor, retired. Remember? They hired José Porras, a mentally retarded punk, to replace him. It's all a part of an evil conspiracy hatched up at the capitol in Austin. Everybody knows they're a bunch of communists up there. They claim everybody's equal to everybody else."

"Where on earth did they get that silly notion?" his wife asked.

"From the Russians, their friends. In Russia everybody's equal to everybody else, but that's because they don't have no Mexicans or Negroes over there. Just Russians."

"No Japanese or Chinese, either?" his wife said.

"Nope, just White folks like me and you live there."

"Can you believe that?" she commented.

After the principal's second warning, Albert never missed picking up a student, but that did not prevent him from cursing the Mexicans with bated breath, as they dragged themselves yawning into the bus. Albert had one trick left. He began driving slower, and the last busload turned into the schoolyard fifteen minutes late almost every morning. He wanted to demonstrate the difficulty in busing so many students. But when Jane Schneider suggested that moving his starting time another half hour earlier might solve the problem, Albert quickly relented, and the last busload arrived on time after that.

HAROLD'S CIGARETTE PROBLEMS

At age eight, Harold Stern, Antonio's best friend, smoked his first cigarette, and he was a nicotine addict before he reached his teens. His habit started innocently enough, as do most vices. He observed two of his older brothers and their friends stuff some strips of cedar-post bark into their pockets, so he stuffed his, too. Later that day, down in the dry bed of the *Rio de Cleofor*, which was a big misnomer because it never was a river but only a creek, at best, the boys took out their cedar bark and began rolling cigarettes wrapped with newspaper. They helped Harold roll his first cigarette, and when everybody was ready, they lit up and sat with their backs against the creek bank to enjoy their creations.

"Man, this is good," his oldest brother said.

"You bet," another boy replied.

Harold wasn't so sure. By the time he puffed away less than half of the ten-inch cigarette, his lips were scorched, his eyes watery, his lungs full of smoke, and his mouth tasted of burnt newspapers. If there was some pleasure to be found in smoking, it completely eluded Harold.

That weekend, he visited his cousin Charlie Johnson. Charlie was older by two years and knew about things.

"Newspapers!" Charlie howled. "That's the funniest thing I ever did hear. How big was your cigarette?" he asked.

"'Bout a foot long."

"A foot?" Charlie dropped to the ground and rolled around gasping for air. Tears ran down his cheek. "I ain't never heard such an outlandish thing."

Harold ignored his cousin's melodramatics. He lamented confiding in Charlie.

"That's funny, man, a real hoot," Charlie sat up, wiping his eyes. "Tell you what, 'cuz, I'm going to learn you how to make a real cigarette."

They walked to the shed where Charlie's father stored corn for the hogs. Once a day, his father went there to feed the pigs. He ripped the husks from a few ears of corn and dropped the ears into a hand-cranked grinding machine that separated the kernels from the cob. Nothing was wasted. The corn went to the pigs, the cobs went into the left bin in the shed, and the husks went into the right bin. Later the corn husks were washed in boiling lye water and cut to serve as wrappers for tamales. His father sold the husks to a Mexican restaurant in town. The cobs went to the outhouse.

Charlie took a dry corn husk from the bin and put it under his nose. "Umm. Now here's a cigarette wrapper. Smell this."

Harold took the corn leaf and put it to his nose. "Don't smell like nothing," he said.

"That's right. You want to taste the cedar bark, not the corn husk," Charlie said. He took small strips of cedar bark and prepared a thin cigarette which he handed to Harold and fixed one for himself. "Now these are cigarettes, not those newspaper monsters you been smoking."

It was February, and the weather was still cold, so they stayed inside the shed. Charlie pulled out a house match and lit his cigarette and then Harold's. There was no breeze in the shed, so he didn't have to cup his hand over the flame to keep it alive. Once the cigarettes were lit, Charlie blew out the match, and when it stopped smoking, he threw it into the husk bin.

"Good, huh?" his cousin said.

"It's a lot better than the one I smoked yesterday," Harold said. "Tastes kinda sweet."

The boys smoked until only short stubs remained. Then they went outside and stomped the stubs with the heels of their shoes until no one could recognize them as cigarettes.

It was almost dark, and the lights of a truck were coming up the long driveway.

"Pa's home," Charlie said. "Let's go wash up. We always eat supper when he gets home."

Pete Johnson, Charlie's father, was a quiet, predictable man. Each morning he arose, ate breakfast, and went to work. In the evening, he came home, ate his supper, fed the pigs, took a bath, and went to bed. There were few joys in his existence and few disturbances. He preferred it that way. If there was news about anything, his wife Clara would initiate a conversation, otherwise they ate in near silence.

That evening they had a guest.

"Harold came over to spend the weekend with Charlie," Charlie's mother said, while she put supper on the table.

Pete served himself a hefty plateful. Without looking at Harold, he said, "How's your 'pa?"

"Good. Real good. Mr. Vásquez added another car-repair area to the back of the J T Store, and Pa's helping him fix cars."

"How 'bout the farm?"

"Pa's helping Mr. Vásquez only two days a week, Tuesdays and Thursdays."

There the conversation for the evening might have ended had it not been for Mrs. Johnson's sudden discovery.

"Fire," she cried out. "The corn shed is on fire."

Pete and the boys ran to the back porch. The shed was in full blaze. The pigs in the pen next to the shed were squealing and desperately trying to escape.

"Quick, grab some pails of water and throw them on the pigs while I let them out," Pete said.

It was a dark night, but the flames leaping from the shed illuminated everything. Pete broke down a section of the pigpen with his work boots and chased the frightened pigs into the open field. None were injured. They were just heated up and frightened.

"Well, thank God the fire didn't spread to the barn like it would have if the wind was blowing. Wonder what caused it?" Pete said.

The shed was a total loss, but the boys kept hauling and pouring water on the embers until the last glow was gone. Pete walked through the ashes, where the shed once stood, and salvaged his cast iron corn grinder. Another hour passed before he was satisfied there would be no more flare-ups. It was 9:30 p.m. when they returned to the house. Even at that late hour, they sat down again to finish their supper. The boys complained about how sore their arms were from carrying endless pails of water.

Pete was quiet, too quiet, but it wasn't until everyone had finished eating and his wife started picking up the dishes that he spoke up.

"Funny thing that a fire got started in the shed, you know. There's no 'lectricity out there to cause a spark; no hot engine, like from the tractor. Real strange," Pete said. "You boys have any ideas?"

Harold looked at Charlie. His cousin was staring straight ahead at the wall.

"Maybe a mouse chewed on a match and set the place on fire," Harold said. Harold shifted his weight on the bench where they sat, causing Charlie to lose concentration on whatever he was staring at.

"Clara," Pete said. "What do you think of that?"

"It's possible. But maybe just a little bit possible," his wife said.

"Harold, you really believe that's possible?"

"Yes, sir. Very possible. I remember this here time my mother lost some rolls of yarn she had just bought, and mice had taken them to make a nest. Mice sometimes do a lotta weird things."

Pete sat pensively for a short time before turning to his son.

"Charlie, you never lie to me, son. Tell me what really happened out there," his father said.

Charlie looked down at the table. "We was smoking, Pa'," he said. "I was showing Harold how to make cigarettes out of corn shucks and cedar bark. Guess we started the fire, somehow."

Charlie's admission of guilt spilled out as casually as talking about the weather. Harold knew that in Charlie's shoes he would have lied all the way to Hell and back. His credo was "Never admit to nothing."

Pete smirked when Charlie mentioned the cedar-bark cigarettes. Maybe the words took him back to his own boyhood. Maybe he happened to be in an extremely generous mood that night.

"Well, the shed and the pigpen was no big loss," Pete said. "We have plenty of lumber around here so as you boys can help me build another one tomorrow. But first we must round up the hogs and put them in the barn. They won't go far. Understand?"

"Yes, sir," the boys said, and they could hardly believe his generosity. "No whuppin." Imagine that.

It wasn't until Harold turned eleven that he got his first taste of a real cigarette. He went to the J T Store intending to buy an ice cream cone. Instead, he found himself studying the ready-rolled cigarette packs in a glass display case. There were several brands: Lucky Strike, Chesterfield, Camel, Kool, and Phillip Morris. They were factory made. Nothing to roll. Just put them in your mouth and light up. Twenty cents for a pack of twenty cigarettes.

"MUST BE OF AGE TO BUY," the sign on top of the case read.

"How old is that?" Harold asked.

Antonio looked toward the second bay, where his father was working. He was lying on a creeper under a truck's transmission.

"If you have twenty cents, you're old enough. Which ones do you want?"

"Camel," Harold said, without knowing the difference.

The pack of cigarettes was in his pocket faster than Antonio could ring up the four nickels on the cash register.

On the way home, Harold found some shade under a cluster of trees, and sat down with his back against a chinaberry tree, facing the road. He peeled off the red cellophane strip that encircled the top of the pack and pulled back just enough foil to expose two cigarettes. He put the pack to his nose. They smelled even better than he had imagined. He fired up his first Camel and leaned back to enjoy it. Fine smoking. This was smoking, real smoking. Not like the cedar-post varieties his brothers and his cousin Charlie introduced him to.

From that day forward, Harold was hooked, a five-cigarettes-a-day addict. Progressively his habit intensified, until he reached ten a day. At that stage, twenty cents every other day became a problem. His parents noticed the change. Harold was asking for twenty cents at every turn, offering to run errands, large or small, always at the same price—twenty cents. Rick Stern, his father, was a heavy smoker, and it didn't take him long to figure it out.

"He's smoking," Rick told his wife. "Twenty cents is the price of a pack of smokes. That's why he's always asking for that amount."

When Harold got home that afternoon, his mother had already gone through his room and found no trace of tobacco in any form.

"They're not in his room," she told her husband.

"That means he's got them on him, in his pockets," he said.

Harold sat down to eat, completely unaware of the conspiracy brewing. He ate well, and just as he got up to leave, his father said, "You know, son. We noticed you've been asking for twenty cents a lot lately. Now, twenty cents is the price of a pack of cigarettes. I've also been missing a few cigarettes now and then. Are you smoking?"

"Who, me?" Harold said. "No way. I spend my money on Tootsie Rolls and ice cream and soda waters. Oh, and I also buy war-bond stamps at school. They cost a dime a piece. When my book is full, I get to bring it home."

"Stand up and empty your pockets," his father said. "Put everything on the table."

Nothing thrilled Harold more than to prove his father wrong. He stood next to the table and unloaded his pockets. A broken watch, a partially eaten Tootsie Roll, a rusty pocketknife with one blade out of the original three still intact, a dirty kerchief, a wad of kite string, four house matches, a tube half full of air-gun pellets, a chunk of road tar, a page from a magazine advertising some new bicycles, four soft-shell pecans, and two rocks. No cigarettes.

Harold's parents looked at each other. Then, their attention went back to the boy.

"By God, I know you're smoking," his father said. "I don't know where you stashed the cigarettes, but I know you've got some."

Silence ruled for the next few seconds. Then his father exploded, jumped up and grabbed the wooden board on the kitchen wall, kept there for such occasions, and paddled Harold's bottom until his mother intervened and pulled Harold away. By then, Harold's buttocks were on fire, and it would be days before the boy could sit down in comfort

"I tell you what," his father shouted. "If I ever catch you smoking or even with a cigarette on you, your mother will be scraping your ass off the kitchen walls. You hear?"

"I hear," Harold said.

"Do I make myself amply clear?" his father asked.

"Yes, sir."

But bad habits die hard, and Harold wasn't about to quit smoking. Not altogether, anyway. He went back to five cigarettes a day, then two. A pack of cigarettes lasted him ten days. If he mooched here and there from his father and his friends, he could stretch his private stock twice as long.

But all that nonsense came to an end one muggy spring day in the middle of a corn field his father was seeding. Harold went along, riding on the back of the tractor. When they encountered rocks the size of an orange or larger, Harold got off and gathered them in a gunny sack. It was his father's hope to rid the field of all large rocks someday.

They entered the field at dawn to take advantage of the coolness of the morning before the sun rose high in the sky. By mid-morning, Rick Stern was out of cigarettes. He was a heavy smoker and consumed four packs daily. With each row he planted, Rick became more restless, and he was suffering intense withdrawal pangs after two hours. There was no point in going back to the house. He had taken the last pack of cigarettes from the two cartons he brought home the previous week. His hands started trembling, and he became irritable. When noon arrived, he didn't eat lunch. Instead, he chugalugged his entire jug of water, which usually lasted the entire day.

At about two in the afternoon, Rick jumped off the tractor and went off to catch a breather under a tree. On the way, he picked up rocks and threw them as far as he could. He looked like a man ready to explode. From the tractor, Harold watched his father writhe in agony. Rick picked up his son's burlap-wrapped water jug and tipped it for a long swallow. He sloshed water on his chest and shoulders and watched the dark rain clouds moving in from the West.

On the horizon, he could see lightning bolts riveting the ground every few seconds. They were far away, but the wind had already picked up, so he estimated it was a matter of an hour, or so, before the rain moved in. Perspiration beads formed on his face, but he was tired of wiping his face with his sleeve, and he let them be. Rick set the jug down against a tree and started back toward the tractor, wondering if he could spare the time to drive into town on the tractor for cigarettes. Five miles there, five back. About a third of the sky was covered with dark clouds. The rain was moving in faster than he had anticipated only minutes earlier. He knew he could not get away. The fields would be muddy and unworkable for days if it rained hard. The corn seed had to be in the ground before it rained.

Meanwhile Harold faced a critical decision, and he had to make it quickly. A month had passed since his severe paddling, and the last of the purple bruises, now yellowish, were still visible on his rear end. With every step, Harold's heart was beating faster, and his father guided his direction. He had never seen his father so emotionally distraught, and there was no time to consider all the consequences. Rick was only fifty feet away when Harold made his move. He pulled out an unopened pack of Camels from his pants' pocket and laid it on the tractor seat. Quickly, he jumped off the tractor and met his father coming.

"Guess I'll get me some water, too," he said, and walked past his father.

"Hurry it up, it'll be raining soon. We've gotta finish today."

Rick climbed up the side of the tractor and was preparing to sit down when he saw it. His eyes walleyed at the sight of the fresh pack of cigarettes lying in the middle of the tractor seat. It was a moment Harold wished he had witnessed from up close. Without questioning their source, Rick tore into the top of the pack and fired up a cigarette. He finished it in a couple minutes and lit the next one with the first one. Then he sat down and slid the pack in his shirt pocket.

From under the shade tree, Harold could see his father light up. When he lit the second cigarette, Harold knew it was safe to return to the tractor. He walked back slowly, until Rick revved up the engine and called out, "Come on, son. Let's go. We're running late."

Rick finished planting the field, peacefully smoking. His rage was gone, and he said nothing about the pack of Camels. Not that day nor any day during the next eight years that Harold lived at home. Nor was Harold ever admonished or accused of smoking again. The incident in the field became a hallowed matter. The boy had exposed himself to severe punishment so his father would not suffer any longer. Rick wished there was some way to tell his son how much he admired him for that, but he was ashamed to talk about it. From that day forward, there was a special bond between Harold and his father that wasn't there before.

But on other occasions, it doesn't pay for a boy to tamper with the emotions of adults. Antonio learned this bit of wisdom the hard way one Sunday afternoon. After church, Juan Tomás drove the family out to Belén's father's farm to see the feral cattle his in-laws had brought up from the valley. The animals were wild and mean, Antonio's grandfather assured everyone. To keep the cattle from escaping, his uncles added extra strands of barbed wire to the corral.

The unruly animals snorted menacingly at the small crowd that had gathered to observe them, and paced the length of the enclosure, looking for a way out. The restless animals were not used to fences and corrals. They came from a ranch with an open range so vast they could graze for days without encountering a barrier.

Antonio was wearing his most despised suit, which at age ten he considered inappropriate for any boy to wear. It was his white First Holy Communion suit. He couldn't play ball, or climb a tree, or chase after the goats in it. All he could do was stand around like a girl and try to stay clean.

Antonio trailed behind his parents and relatives, bored with the cattle, when he saw an old baseball about sixty feet on the wrong side of the fence. It lay there calling only to him.

"Finders keepers, losers weepers" it whispered.

Antonio dropped back and waited until the group of adults had walked farther away before making his move. He looked at the two cows nearest him. They were busy grazing, facing in another direction. His grandfather, his parents, his aunts, and his uncles were distracted for the moment, looking at two newborn calves in another pen.

Quietly, Antonio separated two strands of the fence. He pushed the bottom wire until it almost touched the ground and the one above it as high as his knees. Then he bent over and slipped to the other side, careful not to snag his suit on the sharp barbs. No one saw him cross the fence. Slowly he made his way toward the ball without taking a wary eye off the cows nearest him. The baseball continued calling him as he moved cautiously toward it. He tiptoed the last few feet and picked up the ball.

Then, all hell broke loose.

It started with his Aunt Frances' shrill scream. "*Toñito*. Look out! There's a bull behind you!"

Antonio twirled around, and indeed, there was a bull behind him, and it was approaching him rapidly. Its lethal horns were low on the ground and ready to attack. Antonio's parents stood pressed against the fence, waving him on and shouting for him to run faster, but Antonio was no match for the bull. Seconds before the bull was twice the distance to the fence as Antonio, but they were in a dead heat the final moments before reaching it. The entire family stood petrified and blanched. They could no longer scream and stood helpless with their hearts in their mouths.

A split second before the impact of the bull's horns on the boy's fragile body, and with no time to crawl between the strands of wire, Antonio dropped to the ground and rolled swiftly under the fence to safety. The bull managed an abrupt stop before ramming the fence. It huffed and snorted viciously but was no longer a threat. The boy was out of its range.

Antonio got up and dusted himself off with his hands. He looked up at the pale onlookers, who remained in a trance.

"That was nothing," he said and showed them his baseball.

Thinking back about that incident many years later, Antonio said he would have been better off if the bull had caught up with him that day. His father gave him the worst spanking of his entire life, while his relatives and the bull looked on.

DEATH AND MURDER AMONG US

The first time Padre Juan de Dios Erasti stopped at the J T Store after his transfer to Santa Monica's Catholic parish, he took one look at ten-year-old Antonio and knew he had found an altar boy.

"There should always be two altar boys assisting me at Sunday Mass, and I have only one, José Torres," he said. "José will teach you all you need to know, including the responses in Latin. Every other Sunday you get to ring the bells during the consecration."

He was a resolute man. He didn't ask Antonio whether he was interested in the position. He drafted him.

Belén was elated. Every *padre* she had known began his religious career as an altar boy, and nothing would please her more than to have a religious man in her family someday.

"The best part about being an altar boy," José Torres explained, "is that we get to drink the wine in the cruet left over from Mass. It's a special wine that only priests can buy. It's delicious."

"What's a cruet?" Antonio asked.

"It's the little glass jars the *padre* uses during Mass. We use two cruets: one for wine and one for water. But don't worry. You'll catch on fast," José said.

Antonio wasn't comfortable with the prospect of wearing a red cassock with a laced, white surplice over it. The vestments looked too much like women's clothing. What would his friends think?

"Don't worry about that. They're like the vestments Padre Erasti wears. If anybody laughs at you, let me know. I'll straighten them out."

José was one of the toughest boys at school, and Antonio knew no one would ridicule him if José was backing him.

For a week, Antonio spent an hour a day sitting on the riverbank learning the Latin Ordinary of the Mass from José. Latin sounded so much like Spanish that learning the responses came easy, especially since he was permitted to read them from a printed card.

The following Sunday found Belén sitting in the front pew on the women's side of the church, swelling with pride as Antonio assisted in the celebration of the Mass.

"In nomine Patri, et Filii, et Spiritus Sancti. Amen. Introibo ad altare Dei," Padre Erasti intoned.

"Ad deum qui laetificat juventutem meam," Antonio and José responded. Antonio kept an eye on José to know when to kneel, when to genuflect, and when to go up and assist the *padre.*

After Mass, they returned to the sacristy, the room behind the main altar, where José and Antonio helped Padre Erasti remove his vestments. He wore shirt and trousers underneath the vestments. Until that morning, Antonio had assumed the celebrant wore only shorts under the heavy ceremonial clothing. Padre Erasti kissed each article of clothing as he removed it, starting with the large green chasuble. He hung each item carefully in the great armoire that housed other vestments, each color representing a season of the church. They came in an array of colors: green, red, white, purple, and even black. The black ones were reserved for funeral masses, not for a religious season. In another corner of the room was a closet where the altar boys hung their cassocks and surplices.

After the *padre* left, José Torres picked up the wine cruet.

"We're supposed to pour the unused wine back in the bottle," he said, "but we drink it instead. We always have. It's not consecrated or anything. It's like the wine in the bottle."

He lifted the glass container up to the light and estimated where the line for half of the remaining wine should be. Then he took a swig and looked again to see if he was at the imaginary line. He handed Antonio the cruet.

"Here you go. That's yours. Drink it fast before *Don* Donato comes snooping around."

Antonio downed the wine. It tasted like grape juice, only better. It was sacramental wine.

Minutes later, Donato, the sacristan, entered the room. One of his duties was to make everything ready for the next Mass, which was cele-brated the following morning. Donato assisted the *padre* at Mass during the week when the altar boys were at school. He eyed the cruets. The one containing water was partially full. The wine cruet was empty.

José pointed at the water cruet. "Antonio, now empty out the water cruet in the sink and rinse out both cruets. Leave them upside down in the sink to dry."

"Don't forget to put out the altar candles, boys" Donato said, and went out the back door toward the parish hall.

José made a face at Donato the instant the door closed behind the sacristan. "One of these days, when he's not around, we'll use the big cruets," he explained. "They're real fancy. They're made of thin glass with brass handles that look like real gold when we polish them. They hold twice as much wine. Last time we used them I was woozy for a couple of hours."

"Why don't we just pour ourselves some wine out of the bottle? I mean when *Don* Donato isn't around," Antonio said.

"Nah, can't do that," José said. "We can only drink what's left over. If we take wine from the bottle, that's stealing. It's a sin. Next time we go to confession, we'll have to tell Padre Erasti we're stealing his wine, and he'll most likely get rid of us and start locking up the bottles."

"Yeah, I see what you mean," Antonio said. "No way around that."

For reasons known only to Norma Gonzales and Padre Erasti, Norma went away one Sunday morning without receiving absolution in the confessional. A year earlier her only child, Adriana, had married Eliseo Morales, after he completed his tour of duty in the United States Marines Corps. Norma was impressed with the young man when he went to her home to ask for her daughter's hand in marriage. By custom, it was the intended groom's father or a close uncle who handled such matters. But not Eliseo. He spoke for himself, after making his appearance in full-dress marine uniform with his chrome-plated sword at his side. He spoke politely, but assertively to Adriana's parents, explaining his plans for their beautiful daughter's future.

Norma was awed by the young man's uniform and the grand lifestyle her daughter would live after her marriage.

The girl's father was not impressed. He knew Eliseo's family well. They were poor like everybody else, except the Anglos who owned the farms where the Mexican families worked. He listened to the young man's plans to exchange currency in various foreign markets netting him exorbitant returns in a matter of months. He heard Eliseo talk about buying rental apartment houses and of paying for them with the monthly rents. The young ex-Marine even talked about buying precious stones in Mexico. He claimed he would make a killing selling them to American jewelers, who would pay up to four times the price he paid for the rocks. It all sounded well-conceived to Norma, but to Adriana's father, with no more business expertise than tilling the soil and gathering crops, it was all youthful dreams.

"And where will the money come from to finance all these businesses?" he asked.

Eliseo looked smugly at him. "Most people don't know this, Mr. Gonzales," he said, "but banks get rich by loaning out money people deposit with them. Otherwise, banks would go broke. That's where I come in. Banks are looking for people to loan money to, people with good, solid ideas like mine. In three years, five at the most, neither you nor your wife will ever have to work again. That's the way the *gringos* do it, and that's what I intend to do."

Adriana's father sighed deeply. "Well, I wish you well, and I give you and Adriana my blessing."

With that, Mr. Gonzales stood up and left the room.

Later in the privacy of their bedroom, he asked his wife how she perceived their intended son-in-law.

"He's wonderful," Norma said. "He looks so tall and handsome in his uniform. He's very intelligent. You heard him. Adriana says he can do anything. They look so good together. Don't they?"

She was completely taken in.

"That boy can do nothing," Mr. Gonzales said, raising his voice. "He went off to the Marines and heard all that nonsense from others, and now he believes he can do them. Maybe he can, but it's going to take hard work and a lot of money. I didn't hear him say one word about working hard, just borrowing. If he shows up at a bank with those insane ideas, they'll throw him out. Bankers aren't stupid. They lend money to people who own something of value they can take in case the borrower fails to pay his loan. Things like a house or a tractor. Not just promises to pay."

Norma sighed. "I don't know anything about those things. I just know they belong together. They were meant for each other."

"Nobody is meant for anybody," Mr. Gonzales said. "We choose a partner to marry, and hope things turn out for the best. That's life."

Eliseo and Adriana were married two months later and set up residence in his parents' small home, which they shared with his parents and two younger brothers. For a week, Eliseo made his rounds looking for capital with which to finance his ventures, but as he soon discovered, the rule of bankers is to loan money to people who don't need it. And the more a person doesn't need it, the more likely bankers are to help. Bankers are very fond of something called collateral, he learned, and without it, he could forget about a getting a loan.

When the planting season came, Eliseo was out in the fields with his father and brothers. If he was disillusioned, he didn't show it. Adriana accepted the fact that her husband's dreams had not materialized. It was Eliseo she had been after anyway. Only Norma, Adriana's mother, resented the fact that he turned out to be such a common coin, after he sat in her parlor and promised the family the moon in three to five years.

Then disaster struck. One night on the way home from a dance, Eliseo crashed his father's truck into a telephone pole. Adriana died at the scene. Eliseo was drunk, but the wreck was ruled an accident, and no charges were filed against him.

Norma was devastated over the death of her only child. Adriana was gone forever. After the funeral, Norma locked herself in her bedroom, brooding over her loss. Mr. Gonzales blocked out his daughter and her short existence from his memory for the rest of his life. He refused to speak of her again.

"If Eliseo comes to the house, tell him I'm not here," Mr. Gonzales told his wife.

Norma decided not to see Eliseo, either. She wasn't sure she could face him, much less forgive him. But Eliseo never went by to apologize for their daughter's death, and his lack of concern for them further infuriated Norma and her husband.

Several weeks later, two friends approached Norma at church after Mass.

"Why isn't Eliseo observing the usual year of mourning?" one of them asked.

In defense of her son-in-law, Norma offered, "Just because he isn't wearing a black arm band doesn't mean he's not in mourning. Today's young people don't observe some of the old customs we grew up with."

"Oh, we're not talking about black arm bands," the woman said adding, "I wouldn't want to be quoted on this, but I hear Eliseo goes to the Saturday-night dances in San Marcos every weekend now."

"That's what my daughter tells me, too," the second woman said. "He dances with all the girls, like poor little Adriana never existed."

The first woman patted Norma on the shoulder. "Don't be mad at us. We're your friends. We just thought you should know."

"That's right," the second woman said. "If we were in your shoes, we certainly would want to know."

The thought of Adriana lying in her cold grave while Eliseo danced and flirted with other girls festered in Norma's heart like a tumor. Her two friends reported on Eliseo after Mass every Sunday, and Norma's anguish grew with each new rumor about her son-in-law's social affairs, until the night Eliseo was found dead between two cars in the parking lot of a dance center. He was having sex in the front seat of a car with a sixteen-year-old girl when he was assaulted. The slender blade of a knife had penetrated his heart from the back.

No one saw the killer. By the time the girl pushed Eliseo's limp body away from her and got out of the car, the security guards arrived and were examining the body on the ground. At first, the girl's only concern was explaining her blood-drenched blouse to her mother, but at the police interrogation, the teenager admitted to willingly having sex with Eliseo. She did not know anything about the assailant, she said. She had not seen or heard the attacker. It happened fast, while she was on her back. The girl's two brothers were immediate suspects. They were at the dance when the murder occurred. They were taken in and questioned, but the police concluded they were not involved in the murder and released them.

At Mass the following morning, Norma's confidants sat next to her, bursting with anxiety to be the first to tell her.

One of the women, unable to contain herself any longer, leaned over and whispered in Norma's ear, "He's dead."

The woman had not said how or when or even who. Just that he was dead, which was all Norma needed to know. Her fingers released the tense grip on her rosary beads. She could relax now.

As soon as Mass ended, the three women huddled closely outside the church. Eliseo had been murdered in the parking lot of a dance center in San Marcos, they said. Some unknown girl's brothers were suspects, as were the girl's ex-boyfriends. Eliseo was murdered with a knife, and the knife was missing. The three women conjectured about the murder long after everyone else had left the premises.

That afternoon Norma visited Adriana's grave. She took her daughter a small bouquet of yellow flowers from her garden and the news about Eliseo. She knew Adriana and Eliseo were together in Heaven, where they could resume their marriage.

Whether they were reunited in Heaven or not, no one knows, but Norma saw to it they remained together forever here on earth. Two days later, Eliseo was buried next to Adriana in full-dress United States Marine Corps uniform, including his chrome-plated sword.

If anyone suspected Norma Gonzales of complicity in the murder of her son-in-law, those thoughts were as soon dispelled. The God-fearing woman attended Mass every Sunday, received the body of Christ, and observed all the holy days of obligation.

Norma kept the dark secret tucked away in her mind for almost a year. No one else would understand, but in her heart, she knew that killing Eliseo was not a sin. Everybody dies sooner or later—everybody. She had simply moved up Eliseo's demise by a few years for his own good. Eliseo needed to be with Adriana. As simple as that. No malice was intended. It was an accident she made happen, and everybody knows accidents are guilt free. In her eyes, her hands were not stained. Otherwise, she would feel remorse, which she did not.

Norma confessed her sins once a year. She went for the last time at Santa Monica's Catholic Church one Sunday morning.

The church was filling for Mass, and a small queue of penitents had formed outside the confessional. Padre Erasti heard confessions from 8:30 until 9:45 am. This allowed him fifteen minutes to get into his vestments to celebrate the 10 o'clock Mass.

At 9:43, Norma entered the confessional, and after reciting the introductory imploration to be blessed, she delivered in rapid sequence a litany of her transgressions for the past twelve months. She did not stop until she had recounted the entire list. Then she clutched her rosary with both hands and waited for the *padre* to absolve her.

Somewhere in the torrent of sins and peccadilloes, Padre Erasti thought he heard, "...and I accuse myself of stabbing my son-in-law to death."

"The taking of another person's life is one of the most serious sins the woman can commit," her confessor said. "It is strictly forbidden by the sixth of God's commandments. Did you do it?"

Norma did not expect to be questioned. "Yes," she said, "but he deserved it."

"Are you sorry for your actions?" he asked.

"He deserved it."

"If you are not sorry, I cannot give you absolution."

The *padre* was talking louder now, and people in the pews close to the confessional listened nervously. They could hear his voice clearly.

"An unforgivable sin is one for which the penitent is not sorry," he said.

"I am not sorry I killed him, *padre*" Norma whispered.

"Then we have nothing further to discuss, and I have a Mass to celebrate in ten minutes." With that, Padre Erasti bolted from the confessional, leaving Norma dumfounded.

Ten minutes elapsed before she stepped out of the confessional box with her face hidden behind a black veil. She left the church quickly and did not return for many years, long after Padre Erasti had left the parish. For the rest of her life, she stayed away from the Sacrament of Penance, until she was on her deathbed. The old *padre* who heard her final confession did not give her sins a second thought. He was used to hearing final confessions. That is the time when sinners thoroughly cleanse their consciences, when they turn their trunk-full of indiscretions upside down, divulging everything—sins that were hidden away and forgotten for decades.

For a while, Norma feared Padre Erasti might report her to the authorities, but nothing came of it. The *padre* was oath-bound to observe the secrecy of the confessional. Moreover, most people, including the clergy, preferred not to get involved with the police.

The authorities saw the murder as one that was probably deserved. No point in wasting more time and money on the investigation. Eliseo probably had it coming, anyway. He was fooling around with a sixteen-year-old girl. After a month, the murder of Eliseo Morales went into a cold-case file and was never reopened or investigated, again.

STORIES AND THE TITANIC

When Antonio turned twelve, he landed his first real job and became the town's delivery boy for two of San Antonio's rival newspaper publications: the San Antonio Express and the San Antonio Light. As soon as he got home from school, he went straight to the bundles of newspapers that awaited him and began rolling them individually, securing them with twine. On good days, he pitched the papers on front lawns. On rainy days, deliveries took much longer. He walked up to each house and placed the newspapers on the driest part of the porch, sometimes between the screen door and the wooden door. By then, Antonio rode a Western Auto Doodlebug, a small gasoline-engine-powered scooter.

At the end of the month, he made his rounds and collected from his subscribers. On those days, he removed the Doodlebug's muffler, and the small scooter took on the airs of his father's Indian motorcycle. Its roar let subscribers know he was coming to collect, and just as important, the loud noise scared dogs away. A sudden twist of the wrist on the throttle sent most dogs scrambling under the house.

Collecting was the best part of having a paper route. It was payday. Now came the time to meet his customers face to face, one at a time, and present his bill for the past month's deliveries. It took two afternoons.

Except for Juan Tomás and Ponciano, only Anglos subscribed to the dailies. Mexicans for the most part could not read English, and those who could found it foolish to buy a newspaper when they could listen to the news on the radio in Spanish at the top of every hour free of charge.

In the three years Antonio worked his route, the area manager didn't receive a single complaint from his customers. Nevertheless, Antonio wondered why Claude Anderson didn't cancel his Sunday subscriptions. Monday through Saturday, Antonio delivered both publications to Anderson's Blacksmith Shop, where he usually found the outsized gentleman sitting on a steel rocking chair, while his four dogs slept comfortably in the shade cast by their owner's enormous girth. Besides being the town's blacksmith, Anderson was also the locksmith and the horseshoe maker and fitter. His turtle eyelids never opened completely when Antonio handed him the two newspapers. He rolled the dailies onto his huge belly and secured them by crossing his thick arms over them before going back to sleep. Antonio then rode off as quietly as possible.

Antonio found it hard to believe those were the same four dogs he encountered on Sunday mornings. Anderson's dogs were small but horrible in disposition, whenever their master wasn't around.

Early every Sunday morning, Antonio hurled the large edition of the San Antonio Light over the chain-link fence onto the old man's wooden porch. Immediately, the four dogs appeared from the back of the house and shredded the newspaper to smithereens. They resembled starved wolves that have just been fed a lamb. Antonio waited until the newspaper had disintegrated and the dogs came to the front of the porch in unison, facing him with their ears up on alert, awaiting the second paper. Antonio hurled the San Antonio Express dead center in line with the front door. As always, old man Anderson didn't open the door to retrieve the publication, which was suffering the same fate as the San Antonio Light. Sunday after Sunday, month after month, for three years, the same scenario played out on the blacksmith's front porch. Yet, when Antonio presented his monthly bill, the chubby Claude Anderson reached into his old-fashioned pouch wallet, peeled out some dollar bills and change, and paid his bill in full. He always thanked Antonio and never complained about the Sunday deliveries.

Antonio finished his paper route one Tuesday afternoon and returned to the store. There weren't any cars in the mechanics' bays, and his father was resting in the office. Antonio parked the scooter in one of the bays and went in to talk to his father. He was anxious to tell his father a story.

"*Papá*, teacher told us a real interesting story at school today." He continued, "It was about the biggest ship in the world. She said it was on its first trip to the United States from England when wham, it hit a huge iceberg that made a big hole on the side of the ship, and the ship sank. She said most of the people on the ship drowned. Teacher said this really happened."

"She was talking about the Titanic," Juan Tomás said.

"That's what she called it, the Titanic. You've heard about it, *papá*?"

"A long time ago."

"Say more about it. What do you remember?" Antonio asked.

"I know very little about it. I was only two years old when the Titanic sank. But when I was about your age, I used to hear people talk about it."

"How big was the Titanic?"

"Teacher said it was the biggest ship ever built."

"I don't know. In the army, I was on several warships, and some of them were very big. Most passenger ships are even larger."

"About how big was the Titanic, do you think?"

"I really can't say," Juan Tomás responded.

"A hundred times bigger than the school bus, you think?"

"Bigger, I'm sure."

"Really? That's big?" Antonio opined.

"Take our church, for instance, it holds about two hundred people. The Titanic carried over two thousand passengers, so it had to be at least ten times larger than the church."

"Wow!" Antonio exclaimed.

"But I'm sure it was even larger because it had engine rooms, kitchens, dining rooms, playrooms, laundry rooms, bedrooms, bathrooms, and a lot of other rooms," Juan Tomás explained, "It even had a swimming pool."

"Twenty times bigger than the church, you think?"

"More than likely."

"Golly," Antonio marveled.

"Some ships are as big as tall buildings, *m'hijo*."

"Teacher said the sides of the Titanic were made of iron. How could it float if it was so heavy?"

"Like an empty tin can. Throw an empty tin can in the water, and it floats. If you fill it with water, it sinks. "

"Harold asked teacher that question, but we didn't understand her answer."

"Someday I'll take you to Corpus Christi so you can see the ships. You'll be amazed at their size," Juan Tomás promised.

"Teacher said the reason so many people drowned was because they didn't have enough little boats to save everybody."

"They're called lifeboats. They had them on the ships I was on during the war."

"Teacher said everybody hurried to get on the small boats, and when they saw there weren't enough boats for everybody, the men got off and gave their seats to the women and children. The men stayed on the Titanic and drowned.

"That's what people used to say," Juan Tomás responded.

"*Papá*," Antonio asked, "would you give up your seat on one of those small boats to a woman, knowing you would die?"

"Of course," his father answered.

"What if you didn't know her?" Antonio asked.

"It makes no difference. If that person is a woman, I owe her that respect. It doesn't matter if the woman is Anglo, Negro, Mexican, Indian, German, or Japanese." Juan Tomás explained.

"Why?" the boy inquired.

"Because women are special human beings, and God put us men on earth to protect them."

Antonio swelled with admiration for his father.

"What if she was the woman, you hated most in the whole world, *papá*?" Antonio queried and looked into his father's brown eyes.

"*M'hijo*, she could be the Devil's wife, and I would still get off the lifeboat, and give her my seat."

With that, Juan Tomás had said everything that could be said on the matter.

It would be hard for me to do that, Antonio thought. It was like caring for somebody else more than you cared for yourself. Antonio sighed deeply. His father was a hero like the men of the Titanic.

"I'm sure you would do the same thing, wouldn't you?" Juan Tomás asked.

Antonio shrugged his shoulders. "I guess. I would do it for *Mamá* and for Mrs. Vogel. She's nice like mother."

"How about the Devil's wife?"

Antonio laughed. "I don't know about her."

"You mean you would let poor Mrs. Devil drown?"

"Probably. Serves the Devil right for being so bad."

Juan Tomás smiled. His son was probably right.

Antonio had doubts about his own courage. I hope I don't grow up to be a coward, he thought. I don't think I could give up my seat for Miss Brandt or Liz Blevins.

"Your teacher sure tells some interesting stories," Juan Tomás said. "I told my *compadres* the story she told you last week, the one about the soldier who was fighting the war in the Tennessee mountains twenty years after the war ended."

Antonio laughed. "Yeah, poor man. Teacher said nobody told him the war was over until twenty years later."

MANUEL DE JESUS MIGRATES, ASKS FOR BELÉN'S HAND

Meyers, Texas lies south and west of the beautiful, hill-country landscapes for which Texas is known. There are no mountains in that part of south Texas or rolling hills with majestic trees and lush undergrowth, which usually accompany lands graced with sudden changes in elevation and an abundance of rainfall. The land there is flat. It was cleared for planting over a century ago. When crops are at their peak, the fields explode for miles upon miles with white cotton fields and seven-foot, green cornstalk rows that run ad infinitum. During the fallow season, the land is almost featureless and bare, sparsely speckled with gnarled shrubs and a few low trees, like the hardy live oaks, hackberries, and mesquites. Only along riverbanks do plentiful trees and tall grasses abound. A farmer can stand in the middle of the crossroads' junction on the edge of town and see as far as good vision will allow. Some say five miles, others ten. There is nothing to obstruct the view because no hills assert themselves until the beginning of the hill country, about eighty miles to the northwest.

To Manuel de Jesus Vásquez, Juan Tomás's father, and to many of the 900,000 of his compatriots, who fled across the Mexican American border into the United States during the Mexican Revolution, these lands became their harbor. The struggle for power in Mexico was into its eighth year in 1918, without signs of abating. Ten different men had occupied the presidential throne in Mexico City since the inception of the Revolution. Families crossed the border in droves and settled primarily along the four border states, far enough inland to stay beyond the grasp of the revolu-tionaries. Their intentions were to weather the war in the safety of the United States and return to their homeland once peace was restored.

But when the Revolution ended in 1920, few immigrants returned. They did not trust the unrest that lingered back home. Civil discord continued as Mexico struggled to get back on its feet, and riots erupted in every major city. Worse yet, massive epidemics broke out across the war-torn nation, which ultimately accounted for more deaths than did all the bullets fired in combat.

Manuel de Jesus Vásquez had been a professor at the Universidad de San Luis Potosi before the Revolution. As chair of that university's prestigious mathematics department, the professor was a highly respected man. He was not wealthy, by any means, but he and his family enjoyed a comfortable existence among the literati of the city and lived in their modest home with a maid, a cook, and even a gardener, not of flowers, but of their fruit-and-vegetable gardens.

On the contrary, in the United States, the professor's formal education meant nothing without a command of the English language, which he did not have. The instant he crossed the Rio Grande, his employment opportunities sank to the level of a labor farm hand.

The cotton fields were in full bloom when Manuel de Jesus arrived with his wife, Pola, and their two sons, Juan Tomás and Ramon, at the Ellison farm near the town of Meyers, Texas. His cousin, Irineo Cordero, who had arrived a year earlier, was expecting them. Irineo had been chief editor of *El Nacional,* San Luis Potosi's most widely read daily. He fled from Mexico after receiving death threats from two opposing political factions because of his editorial *exposes.* Apparently, nobody was pleased with his points of view.

"Manuelito, mi primo," Irineo greeted his cousin. "I've worried about you these past few days. Monica and I almost wore out the road, looking so hard for you. Thanks to God, you and your family have arrived safely."

The cousins embraced and then stood back, taking measure of each other. Irineo had the tanned look of a field hand. Manuel de Jesus, who only recently became exposed to the sun for hours, had a shiny, ruddy glow.

"The road kept getting longer every day," Manuel de Jesus said adding "I thought we would never get here."

Irineo welcomed Manuel de Jesus's family apologetically to his stark home. It was a farmhand's house, like the other nine that surrounded the owner's stately farmhouse. The two families exchanged greetings and talked about the long trip before entering the little house. Irineo and Manuel de Jesus remained outside.

"This is home, *primo*. This is where we live and work," Irineo said. "Monica and I work the fields with eight other families. As I told you in my letters, without a command of the English language or a viable trade, this is the only employment people of our professions can find in this country."

Manuel de Jesus could see the shame on his cousin's face and placed a caring hand on Irineo's shoulder. "Don't worry, *primo*. This is only temporary. We too come prepared to labor on this side of the border, doing whatever it takes to survive until the Revolution ends."

"I'm pleased to hear you say that" Irineo said. "After dinner, I'll introduce you to Chato, the foreman. See that little house over there, the one with the number five painted on the side? It will be yours, but don't expect too much. Only the *patrón*, Mr. Ellison, has a decent house."

"*Primo*, we were both poor at one time, when we were young. Remember? This is nothing new to us. Don't worry about us."

"It's not only a matter of poverty. The *Americanos* do not treat Mexicans as equals. They own the lands, they are our *patrones*, and they let us know it. The best thing for us to do is to work and mind our own business—until it's time to return to San Luis, I considered these things before we left home," Manuel de Jesus said, "and I decided manual labor and discrimination by the *Americanos* are preferable to having my family killed in the Revolution. *¿No?*"

Sunrise the following morning found Manuel de Jesus in a cotton field crouched down in a row next to his cousin with his long, canvas bag trailing behind him. He learned quickly from Irineo and was holding his own against the most productive cotton pickers by the end of the week. He did not complain. After all, it was his decision to leave San Luis Potosi. He had a family to support and was determined to do whatever was required of him.

When Pola, his wife, saw other women in the fields, she asked to do likewise.

"*Nunca*," Manuel de Jesus said. "That's what our sons and I are here for, to provide for you."

"Don't be such a hard head, Manuel de Jesus. Look at Irineo and Monica, and the other families. All the wives pick cotton, and they earn more *pesos* than us."

"*¡Basta!*" he said. "I have other ideas. Take care of our needs at home and don't worry."

Manuel de Jesus's true reason for not allowing his wife to pick cotton was that he didn't want her associating with the men in the fields, most of whom were not only illiterate but ill-mannered as well. When they spoke, it made no difference to them if they were in the presence of refined ladies or drunkards at a *cantina*. Their gross, offensive speech and manners dismayed Manuel de Jesus. They blew their noses on the ground, spewed dark chewing tobacco juice out of the sides of their mouths, and released gastric gases through whichever orifice their bodies found most expedient. He found it appalling that some men thought nothing of scratching their testicles through their pants while talking to the ladies at the cotton weighing scales.

The insolence began the moment they moved into the small house at the Ellison farm. Gone were the respectful titles of *Profesor* and *Doña Vásquez*. Everybody now addressed them simply as *tu*, the casual form of you, customarily reserved for close friends, servants, and children. But they were not alone. Immigrants who crossed the Rio Grande, between 1910-1920, were for the most part thrown into the same melting pot, like it or not. Manuel de Jesus's only solace was that his relatives and friends back home could not see the depths to which he and his family had fallen.

A year went by, and the latest arrivals from Mexico held little hope that the Revolution would end soon. Nine years had passed since the Revolution started. By that time, immigrant families who had lived in the United States for several years began to take root. Some of them bought land and built houses. Others married and had children born in the United States, natural American citizens. Even Irineo began losing hope of ever returning to his homeland.

Manuel de Jesus hated Americans and believed they were heavy-handed opportunists, who usurped everything of value: land, oil, gold, minerals, even dark-skin human beings from Africa. He knew from history books that Americans had stolen the very lands he had migrated to, and he often quoted one of President Porfirio Diaz's favorite lines: "My poor Mexico. So far from Heaven, and yet so close to the United States." He refused to learn English and were it not for the protracted war in his homeland, Manuel de Jesus would have never left his beloved Mexico.

Es mi bandera querida,	My beloved flag
Verde, blanca, y colorada.	Is green, white, and red,
Verde, la esperanza amada,	Green is for cherished hope,
Blanca, la inocente vida,	White is for the innocence of life,
Colorada enrojecida,	Resplendent red,
Es la llama del amor,	Is the flame of love,
Es el patriótico ardor,	It is for the patriotic ardor,
Con que el niño mejicano,	With which every Mexican child,
Debe de empuñar en su mano,	Should grasp in his hand,
El pabellón tricolor.	The tricolored pavilion.

Manuel de Jesus taught Juan Tomás and Ramon Mexican history and patriotic songs and poetry, so they would know and be proud of their Mexican heritage. By ages six and seven, Juan Tomás and Ramon could recite poetry like professional declaimers. The two brothers stood erect like toy soldiers, using their arms and hands for expression, while reciting *Mi Bandera Querida*, their father's favorite poem.

In San Luis Potosi, Manuel de Jesus's avocation was photography, and on weekends, he could be found out and about photographing the miracles of nature. In his youth, he studied art, and that knowledge gave him a well-developed sense for a balanced composition in his pictures. The night of their flight out of San Luis Potosi, he intended to travel light and limit his load to bare necessities. He was already sitting in the wagon, anxious to depart, awaiting the rest of the family to climb aboard, when he threw down the reins and rushed into the house to retrieve the large, flat trunk from under the bed. He could not leave without it. Without realizing it, this impulsive action would help mitigate an otherwise dire existence in Texas. The trunk contained his photographer's camera, two lenses, a wooden tripod, and some picture-developing equipment and supplies.

When he arrived in Texas, he mistakenly believed a good living could be found in photographing weddings, first communions, anniversaries, *quinceañeras*, and birthday parties, but as he soon discovered, those events did not pay sufficiently in small, poor communities to sustain a family. Nevertheless, his photography provided additional income to his meager earnings as a farm worker.

Quite by accident, he also became an *escribano*, a professional letter writer. When people heard that Manuel de Jesus could read and write, they flocked to his door on weekends to have him compose letters for their loved ones in Mexico. It became a thriving sideline. For fifteen cents, including paper and envelope, he wrote letters up to three pages long. On Saturdays, he usually had a parlor full of customers awaiting his services.

It was not long before this sideline expanded to include love letters. Young men approached him to compose romantic letters for the young ladies they fancied. At first, they were awkward in confiding their sentiments to him, but Manuel de Jesus' demeanor was professional, and whatever reticence the young men had at first soon disappeared. Most men are not by nature expressive in matters of the heart, especially when relayed through a third party, and neither were these young men. Two or three lines were all he could extract from them. Then Manuel de Jesus reached back to thoughts he had committed to paper for his wife, when they first met. He penned them into the letters at hand and asked what they thought. The young men were delighted. He charged ten cents for love letters because they seldom exceeded one page, and because he often wrote the replies from the young ladies, as well.

The girls were bashful and giggled, covering their faces after every word they uttered. Manuel de Jesus tried his best to put them at ease and gave them the privacy of a confessional by turning his chair so that they did not face him. His signature touch was sealing the envelope of the love missives with a drop of perfume from his client's purse, or from the vial of Blue Waltz cologne he kept on hand. Manuel de Jesus saw many of the letter romances flourish into marriages with families, and when he saw their children running about, he wondered just how much those little ones owed their existence to him.

In the 1920s, Mexican Americans couldn't enroll in public schools. Manuel de Jesus gave his two sons a well-rounded education at home, including mathematics, Spanish grammar, literature, poetry, Mexican history, and a thorough grasp of the Greek and Roman civilizations. But these subjects he taught in Spanish. Mandatory schooling of Mexican

American children did not become law until the early thirties, and several years elapsed before schools for them were erected and attendance laws enforced. Consequently, Juan Tomás and Ramon completed only four grades in a parochial school run by the Cordi-Marian nuns from Mexico, and their English was poor.

Manuel de Jesus wanted more for his sons. At first, he took them along to the cotton fields, where they worked side by side with him and the other field hands. Soon he was saving money, and within three years he bought two acres of land and built a house. Later, when Juan Tomás and Ramon came of age, Manuel de Jesus took them out of the farm and sent them to San Antonio to learn a trade. He decided his sons would not be tied to the land like serfs.

Juan Tomás spent a year at the *Escuela Automotriz y de Electricidad.* It was a boarding school with a well-rounded curriculum in theory and hands-on practice of automotive repairs under the supervision of two master mechanics. Classes were conducted in Spanish. His brother, Ramon, spent a year apprenticed to a master carpenter who built and repaired houses under the name of Joe Ramírez & Sons: Contractors.

Manuel de Jesus had chosen wisely. One year of learning and practice was exactly what his two sons needed to acquire lifelong trades. Upon completing their apprenticeships, his sons lost no time in seeking employment. Juan Tomás went home and was hired out as a mechanic to Polanco's Garage in San Marcos. Ramon remained in San Antonio, where there was year-round work for carpenters. Thanks to their father's determination, by age twenty Juan Tomás and Ramon possessed trades which earned them an income superior to that of a farm hand. Never again would Manuel de Jesus's sons be seen in the cotton fields working like unskilled migrants.

"And this is just the beginning," Manuel de Jesus told his wife, Pola. "Soon our sons will have their own businesses, and they will take orders from no one, much less from an *Americano* boss."

But for Juan Tomás, owning a business would have to wait. Now that he had a steady income, Juan Tomás's thoughts turned to his sweetheart Belén and marriage. After all, as he reminded his father, he was already twenty-years old. Manuel de Jesus attempted to discourage his son from a hasty marriage, but after weeks of trying to dissuade him, and the boy remaining resolute on the matter, father and son set out one Sunday afternoon with a basket of fruit to ask for Belén's hand in marriage.

Guadalupe Chagoya met them suspiciously at the door. He accepted the fruit and called to the kitchen for someone to take it away. After the customary greetings and the discussion of crops and weather, which always followed, Manuel de Jesus broached the topic he had gone to discuss.

"You are, in truth, a very blessed man, *Don* Guadalupe," Manuel de Jesus said.

Guadalupe sat farther back in his chair and narrowed his eyes into thin slits.

"Yes, you are blessed because God gave you such a handsome and proper family. Everyone is in awe over the way you raised your family alone, after the Lord took *Doña* Anita away from you and your children. She was a fine, decent woman. May God have her in the light of His divine grace."

Guadalupe nodded, and Manuel de Jesus continued.

"The night we arrived here from San Luis, *Doña* Anita was the first person to go where we were camped to see if we needed anything. She offered us food and blankets for my family and hay for the mule. We will always remember her kindly for her hospitality. We were weary of traveling... almost five-hundred miles by wagon. We were told to cross the border at Nuevo Laredo and to continue north until we saw more white faces than brown ones. There we would be safe, my cousin Irineo Cordero assured us, because the Revolution would not come this far north. We did not know what to expect, *Señor* Chagoya, but we knew life could not be worse than in Mexico. Still, this was a foreign country, and we feared the unknown, you might say. By the Lord's hand, night fell just as we arrived at the edge of your farm, where we decided to set up camp. We knew no one, and for a kind person like your wife, *Doña* Anita, to feed us and allow us to spend the night on your land was more than we could ask for.

"The following morning, we moved on and found work and a house on the Ellison farm, where my cousin Irineo and his family lived in those days.

"Now, fourteen years later, *m'hijo*, Juan Tomás, and I are back on your property. This time we come to ask the greatest favor one can ask of a parent. I assure you, *Don* Guadalupe, we come to you only after giving this matter a grave consideration. With your permission, my son, Juan Tomás, wishes to ask for *Señorita* Belén's hand in marriage."

When *Don* Guadalupe remained silent, Manuel de Jesus pressed on.

"I understand *Señorita* Belén is the first-born of your children, just as Juan Tomás, here, is my oldest. He is a good son. Never has been a problem. He graduated from an automotive-repair school in San Antonio after a year of study and practice. He is presently employed by Polanco's Garage in San Marcos. If I may boast about my own offspring, *Don* Guadalupe, he earns a decent salary with which to support a wife and family. Up until now, *Señor* Polanco is quite pleased with his work."

"And how long has he worked at Polanco's?" Guadalupe asked.

Manuel de Jesus turned and nodded for his son to reply.

"It will be a year next month, *señor*," Juan Tomás said.

"I see," Guadalupe said. "As you pointed out, *Señor* Vásquez, Belén is my oldest child, and in the absence of my wife Anita, my children's mother, I depend on Belén to help raise my seven younger sons and daughters. So, I must tell you now, even if she is agreeable to this union, she cannot marry for a year. It will take time for my other daughters to learn and assume Belén's responsibilities. If that is acceptable, I will discuss these matters with Belén, and you should have my reply within a week."

"But of course, *Don* Guadalupe," Juan Tomás heard his father say. "There is absolutely no hurry. A year, two years. Whatever you say. We understand. Is this not true, my son?"

"*Sí, papá,*" Juan Tomás said.

True to his word, Guadalupe sent notice inviting Manuel de Jesus and his son to dinner the following Sunday.

On their second visit, Juan Tomás took a small box with a silk handkerchief for Belén and a basket of vegetables for Guadalupe's kitchen.

Manuel de Jesus and Juan Tomás sat at the large dining table opposite Guadalupe, while Belén served the three men. There was subdued talk and laughter emanating from the kitchen, where Belén's brothers and sisters were eating. When she finished serving, Guadalupe asked her to bring her plate and join him and their guests. She sat across the table from Juan Tomás but did not look at him. This was something she could not yet do in her father's presence.

When the meal was over, Belén arose to clear the table, but her father took her by the arm, motioning for her to remain seated.

"Your sisters will tend to the table," he said. "They need to learn these things."

"*Sí, papá,*" Belén said.

Her father cleared his throat. "I have given careful consideration to your proposal," Guadalupe said, "and yes, I will bless the marriage of my daughter Belén to your son Juan Tomás. As we discussed, there will be a *plazo* of approximately one year before the wedding can take place. It is the end of February, so in a year we will be in the season of Lent, as we are now, and no one should marry during that holy, penitential period. Let us plan for a wedding in the middle of June, when the Lenten season has passed."

Belén knew that Lent lasted forty days and would be over the second or third week of April, but she said nothing.

"That is perfect, *Don* Guadalupe. I agree." Manuel de Jesus said. "I, too, am a believer in tradition. According to our customs in Mexico, once an engagement of marriage is entered upon, the intended groom must take care of his future wife's needs. With your permission, Juan Tomás will come once a week with vegetables and fruits, and sometimes fresh meat for *Señorita* Belén."

"Yes, that is acceptable. His visits will afford these two youngsters the opportunity to know each other better," Guadalupe said.

Belén and Juan Tomás silently agreed. Up until that time, their communication had been limited to infrequent meetings in town, where they exchanged a few passing words or smiling glances at a distance. They had never touched or been alone in the fourteen years they had known each other.

During the *plazo*, the waiting period, Juan Tomás bought an acre of land on the edge of town, and together, he and Belén drew up plans for a two-bedroom house. At first, they would live with his parents, but only for a short time, he promised her. He spent three hundred dollars on the land and began to buy the lumber for the house a little at a time.

On April 15th of the following year, exactly two months before the wedding date, Belén's uncle Fermin died after a four-year battle with tuberculosis. He was Guadalupe's half-brother by his father's first wife. Immediately, the wedding plans were put on hold. Belén's father told her there would be no more talk of a wedding for the time being and to inform Juan Tomás to stop his weekly visits. This unexpected development left Juan Tomás and Belén in the dark about their future.

By chance, Manuel de Jesus met Guadalupe in town one Saturday soon thereafter. He extended his condolences again on the death of his half-brother, which he had already done at the funeral. Guadalupe was still wearing a black band on the sleeve of his shirt.

"Juan Tomás tells me the wedding will not take place as planned," Manuel de Jesus said.

"Yes, that is true. My family is in mourning, and out of respect to my brother Fermin, we feel we must observe an adequate grieving period."

"Of course. It is a painful loss to you and your family. I understand. For how long you suppose we should postpone the matrimony?" Manuel de Jesus said.

"I haven't given the matter any thought, but I would say one year is sufficient. Do you agree?"

"Yes. Quite adequate," Manuel de Jesus said.

"A year, *papá*? He hated his half-brother. Belén says *Don* Guadalupe and his half-brother hadn't spoken to each other in years. We have already waited an entire year," Juan Tomás cried out. "It's not fair."

"I know, *m'hijo*," Manuel de Jesus said, "but for the moment, we can do nothing. *Don* Guadalupe is grieving his half-brother and is in no mood to discuss weddings. Give it a little time, and then I'll speak with him."

Three weeks later, Manuel de Jesus saw Guadalupe in town again. He no longer wore the band of sorrow on his arm.

"You have been on my mind these past few days," Guadalupe said.

"You are always welcome at my house, whenever you wish to discuss anything, *señor*," Manuel de Jesus said. "How can I be of service?"

"Well, I've been thinking that my half-brother, Fermin, would not mind if Belén and Juan Tomás exchanged their wedding vows soon, although he has been gone for only a short time."

"What is your opinion?" Guadalupe said.

Manuel de Jesus placed his hand under his chin and considered the question. "With all due respect to your brother—whom we have now only in memory, I do not believe an early wedding would be improper or disrespectful. After all, we, the living, must carry on."

"*Muy bien*. I'm glad we think alike. In that case, please inform Juan Tomás he is welcome to visit Belén again," Guadalupe said. "*Ay*, I will tell you, *Señor* Vásquez, Belén has done nothing but cry day and night since the wedding was postponed."

"And when are they to marry?" Manuel de Jesus asked.

"Whenever they please. The sooner the better. Maybe then there will be peace in my house."

JUAN TOMÁS WOUNDED AT WAR

It was from this rural community that Juan Tomás went off to war in January of 1942, and discovered the world beyond Meyers, Texas. The tranquil life which America had enjoyed since the end of the First World War, in 1918, was threatened again. In Europe, the Second World War started when Germany invaded Poland in September of 1939, and within days the domino effect began as country after country declared war on Germany. With the war expanding in Europe and North Africa, Americans knew it was only a matter of time before America was drawn into conflict. In the United States, draft registrations began in September of 1940, but Americans managed to stay out of battle for two years and three months. When it came, the United States found itself facing war on two fronts. On December 7, 1941, the Japanese air force attacked the American fleet of battleships lying at anchor in Pearl Harbor. Four days later, Hitler declared war on the United States.

Since his family's arrival in Texas from San Luis Potosi, Mexico, when Juan Tomás was five years old, he had not ventured farther than sixty miles from Meyers, the small community his family first called home in their adopted country. Juan Tomás had never experienced a train ride, sailed on a ship, or flown in an airplane. He had never seen the ocean or visited another state. To him, Europe and Africa were faraway places where troops from many nations were presently engaged in a world war, but, of course, he had not been there either. When it happened, it came so swiftly he did not have time to reflect or to be afraid. He accepted events as they unfurled before him, one amazing adventure after another. The day Uncle Sam inducted Juan Tomás into the army, his life changed forever.

Here was basic training, here was traveling by train, here was New York City, here was crossing the vast Atlantic Ocean on a naval cruiser, here was Europe, here was North Africa, and suddenly, there before him, he did not know exactly where the enemy was, the dreaded Nazi army with its omnipresent swastika, the reason for the upheaval of his life. It was all incredible, like phantasmagoric images darting rapidly toward him. And although it seemed to Juan Tomás that he had stepped out of his front door only yesterday, there he was, sitting in his tent, writing his sixth letter home from another continent.

In Texas, Juan Tomás had no Anglo friends, and he associated with Anglos only when it was necessary. His limited command of English made him feel ill at ease among them, and besides, most Anglos were not particularly friendly toward Mexicans.

In the army things were different. For the first time in his life, Juan Tomás was thrown in with strangers who hailed from all parts of the United States and from many walks of life, not just the narrow agrarian life he knew, where people fell primarily into two categories: landowners and laborers, Anglos and Mexicans.

The Anglos Juan Tomás met in the army were young men his age, who eagerly struck conversations with anyone and talked at length about everything from family life to their newly government-issued .30 caliber M1 rifles. They appeared genuinely interested in becoming his friends.

Even so, Juan Tomás hesitated to become closely acquainted with them and addressed them in polite terms, the way he did at home, where all adult Anglos were either sir or ma'am.

In his letters to Belén, he wrote enthusiastically about military life. Everything was new and exciting to him. Soldiers lived in tents, practically outside, largely exposed to the weather with most of their time spent on physical exercises and maneuvers, preparing to meet the inevitable enemy sometime soon. He told her about the extraordinary camaraderie and goodwill that prevailed at camp.

"At the present time," he wrote, "we are in England. It is a beautiful country, I am told, but we don't get to see much of it. All we do is drill, drill, drill and exercise, exercise, exercise until our arms and legs are ready to fall off."

But apparently some GIs did have time to socialize. The British were polite hosts to the American troops training in their countryside until the American GIs began showing too much interest in British girls. Then the native boys became less than enchanted with Americans. It seemed to them that the Americans had too much time and money on their hands with which to court the local girls.

As one resentful Brit wrote, "The trouble with American GIs is that they are oversexed, overpaid, and over here."

To which the Americans quickly responded, "The British troops resent us because they are undersexed, underpaid, and under Eisenhower."

Five months after his arrival in Europe, Juan Tomás's unit was on the move again, destination North Africa. There, American troops camped side by side with troops from other nations, and because of the superior number of troops from America and the United Kingdom, English became the language of preference.

Just hearing how poorly some of the foreign soldiers spoke English gave Juan Tomás renewed courage to speak up, and he began talking to those men whose command of English appeared inferior or about equal to his. Always careful with whom he associated, he limited himself to converse with soldiers wearing plain uniforms like his, without any fancy embellishments.

There were men in other uniforms at camp, uniforms resplendent with bars, medals, medallions, chevrons, stripes, cords, ribbons, and stars. Those men carried the entire history of their military careers proudly displayed on their chests. Juan Tomás knew they were important soldiers, maybe officers or heroes, so he saluted them politely, but did not speak to them unless they spoke to him first. It amused him that Europeans did not believe he was American. Some said he looked Greek or Mediterranean. Besides, they said, his English was different from that of the other Americans.

"That's because I'm from Texas, and Mexican Americans talk different there," Juan Tomás said.

The Europeans had all heard of Texas. It was that vast land they knew from motion pictures. A land replete with cowboys and Indians, cattle drives, great train robberies, sheriffs possess, and shoot-'em-ups between the bad guys and righteous lawmen whose trusted six-shooters never ran out of ammunition.

The Europeans were inquisitive and forever questioned him.

No, he didn't own a horse, but many of his friends did, Juan Tomás said.

Cows?

No cows, but his father owned two milk cows.

Cowboy boots?

Yes. He had a pair of cowboy boots.

He did own a pistol. Yes, like the ones in western movies, a Colt six-shooter.

No, there were no Indians where he came from, no American Indians, anyway.

Despite the war and being so far away from his loved ones, Juan Tomás enjoyed army life. When he left England the second time, headed for home, he was no longer the naive country boy Uncle Sam had drafted two and a half years earlier. The army gave him a crash course in what the world was all about. He met men with diverse views on life and witnessed first-hand the barbarities of war, humanity at its worst. He saw things that opened his mind to new concepts, and he had time to reflect about his own place in the scheme of world order.

Juan Tomás became certain of things he would do after the war, things that would mold his life, whereas before he merely wondered about them. He began thinking on a grander scale and no longer settled for the small goals that had once satisfied him. For one thing, he would no longer sell his skills to a middleman. He would follow his father's advice and become his own master, the master of his own destiny. The notion of framing a mechanic's shed behind his house, where he could pick up a few extra dollars, trans-formed itself into a full-blown service station, situated along a busy highway, with four gasoline pumps out front, a repair shop with two mechanics' bays at the rear, and an amply stocked general-merchandise store in the middle. Every detail of his business became so well etched in his mind that when the time came to initiate his plans, he later said, it was like connecting the dots in a picture that appear in one of his son's coloring books.

Soon after arriving in North Africa, three young men from his unit went looking for Juan Tomás. They were fellow Texans who hailed from small towns near Meyers: Jimmy Skaggs, Jack Jones, and Tommy Wright. The three men shook hands with Juan Tomás and chatted like old ac-quaintances in disbelief that they were united so far away from home. Juan Tomás knew Tommy Wright, the freckle-faced, dusty-haired twen-ty-three-year-old from San Marcos, although he did not remember ever talking to him before. The other two men were new faces.

Back home, these were the Anglos who chose to shun Mexicans, the Anglos that Mexicans referred to as *gringos*. Strange how war changes perspectives, Juan Tomás thought. In Meyers, Texas, socializing of Anglos with Mexicans was a divisive issue. Not one of those three Anglos would have acknowledged his presence in Texas, had they chanced to meet on the street, much less go eagerly looking for him. But in the face of war, as most soldiers discovered, many old customs were soon forgot-ten, or at least, for the moment, laid aside.

In Tunisia, in the face of the encroaching enemy, men fought side by side in synchrony. They covered and looked out for their fellow-soldier's welfare as though they were protecting a blood brother, risking their lives for one another as they crept forward, without pausing to reflect on the color or beliefs of the man whom they were shielding or who was watching over them. Feelings ran high in battle that either they would survive together, or they would perish alone. Fear was the great bonding factor. There, in a location unknown to any of them, in a foreign continent, crawling on their bellies on the cold ground, rifles in hand, with eyes scanning the horizon, the young soldiers were a formidable war machine.

During lulls, the four Texans gravitated toward each other. They swapped stories about home, laughed, and smoked cigarettes together, while hunkering down behind the crumbling walls of bombed-out buildings, as German machine guns sporadically strafed the area where their unit was spread out. The young GIs discussed food, family, girls, and their plans for after the war. Each one poured out his heart about his own dreams on a future that was, for the moment, tenuous at best. In a matter of months, separated from family, with the perils of war in their faces, and without societal influences from home to warp their minds, a century of animosities between races vanished.

When Tommy Wright bought the farm, as Jimmy Skaggs put it, somewhere south of Tunis, the three remaining Texans grieved their fallen brother as though he were their brother by birth. It hit them hard. The three cried separately at night when no one could see or hear them, because they were from an era that said men didn't cry. With Tommy's death, the others realized it could have been anyone of them, and this frightened them. When Juan Tomás went down with shrapnel wounds to his face and chest, he vaguely recalled Jack Jones holding his head and crying in his ear, "You're going home, you lucky dog. I wish I was you."

Juan Tomás did not know the extent of his wounds, as he lay writhing in pain. He could not believe anyone wanted to trade places with him. The next day, he left the front lines with only one good eye and two damaged floating ribs and was flown to England for surgery. After a three-month stay in an army hospital, Juan Tomás received his discharge papers and headed back to America, leaving the war churning in Europe and North Africa.

Jack Jones had spoken with premonition. A week after Juan Tomás was flown out, Jack took a bullet to the head and died instantly. Of the four young soldiers from south Texas, only Jimmy Skaggs made it through to the end of the war physically unscathed, after pushing back the Nazis in Tunisia, Italy, and France. Tommy Wright and Jack Jones went home in coffins draped with the American flag when WWII ended in Europe in the spring of 1945.

Juan Tomás had fought bravely against the German forces in Tunisia. Nobody knew with any degree of certainty if it was an enemy shell that disabled him, as the army command claimed. Up close to the line of fire, in no-man's land, injuries could just as easily be sustained from one's own backup artillery, the big guns, whose volleys often fell short of their intended targets. Friendly fire, the military chose to call their mistakes in later years, a euphemism, if ever one existed. A dead GI or a wounded GI was just as dead or just as wounded regardless of who pulled the trigger. This was not a new phenomenon of war. Juan Tomás remembered reading an account of the War of 1836, between Mexico and Texas, in which General Santa Anna's troops, blinded by clouds of black gunpowder smoke, shot down other Mexican soldiers as they scaled the walls of the Alamo. No excuse or euphemism was used or thought necessary at the time. History's hand simply recorded the facts.

J T OPENS THE STORE

The J T Store opened its doors for business four months after Juan Tomás returned home. It was a business unlike any that anyone had ever seen. It was not exactly a grocery store, or a hardware store, or a service station, or even an automotive repair shop. It was a combination of all those businesses under one roof. Customers could purchase Gulf ethyl and regular gasoline for their vehicles, white gasoline for small engines, motor oil, kerosene, kerosene lamps and heaters, oil lamps, lamp wicks, fan belts, tires, inner tubes, oil filters, air filters, spark plugs, inner tube repair kits, car rear-view mirrors, transparent plastic steering knobs, ground coffee in bags, soda waters, Bayer aspirin, gauze, iodine, tape, flashlights, BB's for air rifles, canned food, including chili-con-carne, sardines, Spam, salmon, and a variety of soups, corn chips, potato chips, candy bars, Fig Newtons, Dentyne, Wrigley's chewing gum in all flavors, Chiclets from Mexico, Chinese candy, raisins, fruit jams and jellies, peanut butter, pickled pigs' feet, roasted Spanish peanuts, pocket handkerchiefs, hair combs, toothbrushes, toothpaste, shaving lather soap bars, shaving cream mugs, double-edged safety razor blades, boot and shoe laces, shoe polish, licorice sticks, ice cream on cones or by the pint, Eagle brand canned milk, packages of Kool Aid, Sen-Sen, unsliced loafs of bread, saltine crackers, boxes of white oleomargarine sticks for frying with packets of yellow powder to convert the oleomargarine into faux butter, ice in 12 ½, 25, 50, and 100-pound blocks, nails of all sorts and sizes—including square horseshoe nails and roofing nails with lead collars—needles, iodine, gauze, tape, house matches, chains, rope, twine, spools of sewing thread in nine different colors, Big Chief tablets, pencils, fountain pens, writing ink in bottles, packages of two and three-hole loose-leaf note-book paper, light bulbs for home or auto, votive candles, cap pistols, caps, bolts and screws, cigars, cigarettes, loose tobacco in tin cans with paper to roll cigarettes, garden tools, fan belts, radiator hoses, sparkplugs, sparkplug cables, lug wrenches, gas tank and radiator caps, two-gallon gasoline cans, five-gallon gasoline cans, car batteries, flashlight batteries, small toys, table games, toy cars and trucks, water guns, kites, playing cards, dominos, balloons. The store carried whatever fruits and vegetables were in season. The shelves of the two front rooms of the store were replete with commodities from floor to ceiling. On the floor of the front room stood an ice-cooled soda-water box, an electric refrigerated freezer with ice-cream, and glass cases, also offering their wares. If one looked hard enough, one could find just about anything sold in hardware stores and service stations, along with many grocery items, and surprises, including black bow ties, sewing thimbles, and a clever device for threading needles which was popular with grand-mothers with faltering eyesight.

Juan Tomás could wash and dry a car, change the oil, and lube it in a lickety-split thirty minutes flat, or so the sign said. He changed the time to twenty-five minutes after he installed a hydraulic car lift. If a customer knew him well and belonged to the male gender, Juan Tomás might sell him bootleg whiskey (Meyers was in a dry county). He also honed gaffs for cockfight roosters, even though cockfighting was strictly forbidden by law.

Occasionally, Sheriff Krause dropped in and snooped around the area where the bench grinder was bolted down, but he never found any evidence of gaffs, nor did he ask. At the rear of the building were two mechanic's bays. There, Juan Tomás and his part-time helper fixed any-thing mechanical larger than a pocket watch. They tuned cars, did small and major repairs, painted vehicles with hand-painted pin stripes thrown in free of charge. Now and then, he also took in gasoline-operated clothes washing machines and water-well pumps. The only thing Juan Tomás could not do was refurbish car upholstery.

Juan Tomás called his enterprise the J T Store. It said so in ten-inch-high, black letters on the large signs that projected out on three sides over the canopy of the building. To the Mexican clientele, the store was known as *La Tiendita*, the little store, the three decades it remained open. The business was a success from the get-go. Meyers was an ideal location for the garage. It was the only automotive repair shop within eight miles. Automobile manufactur-ing came to a standstill during the war, and people looked to Juan Tomás to keep their pre-war vehicles up and running. New automobile wet-cell batter-ies were available only at a premium, and Juan Tomás collected casings from discarded batteries and produced his own line of rebuilt batteries, which he sold at a handsome profit, yet at lower prices than new ones.

An old-timer, passing through one afternoon, marveled at the array of wares and foodstuff items on display. He suggested the name be changed to the J T Emporium. He explained to Juan Tomás that, in years gone by, stores with large assortments of merchandise, such as his, were called emporiums. But to Juan Tomás, that sounded too highfalutin. The J T Store was just fine, thank you.

Rubber was in high demand by the military forces at one point during the war, and there were rubber drives across the country. But rubber proved too costly to recycle. The solution to the rubber shortage was alleviated by the development of synthetic rubber and the rationing of gasoline, whose real intent was to conserve tires, not fuel. There was an abundance of gasoline. The United States was soon mass-producing synthetic rubber, and the military did not suffer a scarcity of tires. For some unexplained reason, however, gasoline remained rationed in the United States until the end of the war.

Someone, somewhere, with more authority than knowledge of what was needed at the time, initiated a massive paper drive, and soon there were hills of wastepaper all over the country with no place to go. The paper recyclers were deluged far beyond their capacity to process the quantities of used paper available, and the paper hills remained where they were until they rotted or caught on fire. When the paper fiasco became apparent, word got around that the paper drive was intended to give citizens the patriotic feeling they were helping with the war effort, but that bit of logic most people attributed to the guy who started the senseless drive.

Many cities got carried away with their metal drives, and in their patriotic haste donated bronze park statues and plaques, which they later regretted when they replaced the memorabilia at post-war prices. Irreplaceable relics, such as cannons and cannon balls, from the First World War, and even the Civil War, were often melted down for the cause.

For months after his return from the war, Juan Tomás was something of a celebrity, and people regularly stopped by to shake his hand and wish him well on his business venture. Anglo men called him son and patted him on the back. Many of them had loved ones fighting in Europe and North Africa, and it was important for them to talk with someone who had been there, who could tell them what their sons were experiencing.

Were their sons in a lot of danger? they asked. Was it cold over there this time of year? What do soldiers do all day? How do they stay dry and warm when it rains? Do soldiers live in foxholes? Son, did you see many dead American soldiers?

Juan Tomás tried to allay their anguish as much as possible, assuring them their loved ones would return soon.

"Your sons are all dry, comfortable, and in good spirits," he said. "You should be proud of their bravery and the cause they are defending. The Nazis are now retreating on every front. American troops and their allies are advancing and liberating city after city, the way you see on newsreels at the movie theatres. When the GIs enter a town, men and women come out to greet them in large numbers, cheering and waving small American flags. Our soldiers are liberators. They are heroes in Europe and North Africa. People at home should not worry. The end of the war is near."

Juan Tomás did not mention that liberating cities was an infrequent occurrence when he left the front. When it did happen, there was only a small group of forlorn looking women and their threadbare-clad children without shoes and dirty, who stood by the roadsides and watched the latest conquering forces roll by. No smiles, no flowers, no cheers, no little American flags—just gaunt, starved faces, gazing blankly at the troops and their war machines in motion. The women looked like human beings whose souls had been stolen yet remained alive somehow. At one time, those wretched women may have been attractive, maybe even beautiful, but after years of rapacious physical and mental cruelties, they had become empty shells. One who saw into the abyss of their vacuous eyes—no anger, no anguish, no fear, no emotion. Nothing. They had no husbands and no families, other than the small children who clung to their tattered skirts. Those desolate women and their broods were aimless vagabonds without warmth or shelter. Worse yet, often without food.

The war persisted another two long years before the American troops finally came home to their families. All the American troops, that is, except the 416,800 American men and women who died defending their country.

CANTANKEROUS JUAN ANTONIO

When Antonio learned the word *irascible* in high school, he knew whoever coined the term must have had someone like Juan Tomás in mind. *Marked with a hot temper and easily provoked*, the dictionary said. Yep, that was dear old dad.

Looking back over the years, the consequences of some of his father's fits of anger now appeared comical, even ludicrous, although at the time they were serious business. Like the time Juan Tomás hurried to finish repairing Keith Ellison's '38 Nash. It was a transmission-overhaul job, which he had promised Keith would be ready to drive away the following morning. He could not foresee any reason for a delay. The transmission was rebuilt, filled with transmission fluid, tested, and in place. Only minor adjustments and tightening of a few nuts and bolts remained to be done.

Juan Tomás was under Keith's car, using his only 3/16-inch socket with a ratchet wrench when the socket suddenly slipped, smashing his knuckles against the frame of the car. Juan Tomás flew out from under the car on a wooden creeper, cursing and screaming. He hurled the wrench with all his strength against the wall, missing its mark, and the tool went sailing into the night through one of the windows opened for ventilation. Juan Tomás looked for the wrench for twenty minutes before he pulled Antonio away from his homework to join in the search. Together, they scoured through the tall weeds that covered the side of the building and came up empty handed. Around midnight, they finally gave up. Neither the '39 Nash was ready by morning, nor was Antonio's school homework.

The wrench turned up the next morning outside a window, but not the one Juan Tomás insisted it had gone through.

Few things provoked Juan Tomás's hot temper faster than drivers who would not dim their headlights at night. Juan Tomás had cataracts, and bright lights from oncoming traffic were blinding globs of bright light rushing toward him. He decided to teach those irresponsible drivers some driving manners and installed a spotlight on his car.

One night, soon thereafter, Juan Tomás took his family to the movies in San Marcos. On the way home, a light fog started rolling in, which enhanced the luminosity of headlights approaching. He switched his lights from high to low every time a car came his way on the narrow road, but nobody dimmed their lights for him.

"I'm going to show the next idiot who comes our way what bright lights are," Juan Tomás said.

Soon a car came around a curve in his direction with its bright lights on. Juan Tomás grabbed the control handle, and when the two cars were about thirty yards apart, he switched on the spotlight, aiming its intense beam in the driver's face.

"Take that. You ignorant road hog." He cried out and didn't let up on the spotlight until the car drove past his.

At the last moment, he recognized Sheriff Krause's cruiser. The police car swung around in the middle of the road with its alternating red lights flashing rapidly and went roaring after Juan Tomás. The cruiser pulled up behind Juan Tomás's Ford, as soon as it stopped, and Sheriff Krause jumped out, flashlight in hand, he shined the light in Juan Tomás's face.

"What in the hell was that all about?" the lawman said.

Juan Tomás was so shaken up to see the sheriff, it took him some time to give an explanation.

"Juan Tomás, I can understand your frustration with people who don't lower their bright lights. I get that all the time. But I can't have you running around blinding people with that danged spotlight. You're taking the law into your own hands, and you can't do that. Do you understand?"

"Yes, sir," Juan Tomás replied.

The sheriff opened his pad and began writing. "I'm giving you a ticket for endangering other drivers. It's up to the judge to decide the proper fine or punishment, but it will go a lot better for you if you can tell the judge, you no longer have the spotlight mounted on your car.'

Juan Tomás agreed. "I'll take it off as soon as I get home."

When Sheriff Krause finished writing, he shook his head. "Juan Tomás, that was one of the dumbest things I've ever seen anyone do. Now, sign here, and be careful getting home."

That little outburst in temper cost Juan Tomás two-hundred dollars in the court of the Honorable Judge Horatio Clemens.

Whenever Belén asked Juan Tomás to do something for her, he regarded it as a request. The second time she brought up the same topic, he accepted it as a reminder. He had heard her loud and clear the first time and assured her he would get around to doing whatever it was she needed done in due time. Any reminders thereafter, he considered nagging, which was the source of much of their bickering and arguing. Such was the case the summer an opossum began sneaking into Belén's chicken coop, killing some of her prized White Leghorn laying hens.

"Juan Tomás," Belén said in a tone of voice that told him, "Here it comes, again."

"I know, I know. The opossum," he said.

"It killed another hen last night. That makes three dead hens in three days," she said.

"And that makes nine times you've told me about the damn opossum."

"It is not!"

"It is so. I've heard about the opossum at every breakfast, lunch, and supper since you found the first dead chicken. Get off my back. I'll get around to it if you just give me some breathing room."

"And how soon can I expect you to find time to get rid of that dreadful animal? After all my hens are dead?" she said.

Three days of constant nagging was all Juan Tomás could withstand. Then it was time for action. After supper that evening, he, and Antonio did not return to the store. Instead, they hid in the tall weeds, armed with a shotgun, in front of the chicken coop, where the hens were visible through the mesh wire.

Belén raised only White Leghorns, and she was as proud of them as she was of her quarter-acre vegetable-and-fruit garden.

"We're dealing here with a very clever animal," Juan Tomás told Antonio. "He burrows his way into the chicken house at night and bites off their heads while they roost. He eats only the head and leaves the rest of the chicken untouched."

"Why does he do that?" Antonio asked.

"Your guess is as good as mine, son."

"How are we going to trap the opossum, *papá*?"

"Trap nothing. I'm going to blow his brains out. This varmint goes on the prowl once it gets dark, and we'll be waiting for him."

In fifteen minutes, it was almost dark.

"When the chickens start moving around like something's bothering them," Juan Tomás whispered, "be ready with the flashlight, Antonio. When I say 'Now,' aim the light where the chickens are moving. As soon as I see the opossum's eyes, I'll let him have it."

They waited quietly until there was a commotion toward the center of the coop. Some hens were clucking nervously, trying to get away from the intruder.

"Now," Juan Tomás cried out, and the instant the beam of light came on, the reflection of the varmint's eyes was clearly visible.

The shotgun blast that followed sent the coop into a state of pandemonium, as the hens abandoned their roost squawking loudly, trying desperately to escape. Seven White Leghorns fell dead to the ground, and chicken feathers and blood went flying in all directions. The opossum lay on its back, covered with blood. But before Juan Tomás could claim victory, the opossum was on its feet, again, and scampered under a cluster of hens that had bunched up in a corner of the coop.

"Over there," Antonio called out, and aimed the flashlight in their direction.

The second blast from the shotgun left another batch of dead hens.

Belén ran out of the house toward the coop.

"*¿Qué pasa?*" she called out.

"I got him," Juan Tomás cried out. He walked into the chicken coop and picked up the nemesis by the tail.

"*Papá* killed the opossum and about twenty chickens," Antonio said, and shined the light on the hens lying motionless on the ground.

"*Dios mío*, this is worse than what the opossum did," Belén said.

"This opossum won't be bothering your chickens anymore," Juan Tomás said.

Belén looked at the dead hens inside the coop and raised a trembling hand to her lips in disbelief. She wanted to cry, and she wanted to scream at Juan Tomás. But she knew it was pointless to cry or say more. What was done was done. She would always remember that Friday evening as the Night of the Massacre.

It was well past one in the morning before Belén finished preparing and packaging the slaughtered hens. First, she cut off their heads, and immersed their pellet-riddled bodies in boiling water to ease the plucking of their feathers. She then gutted and rinsed them thoroughly before wrapping each hen separately in freezer paper. Finally, she marked the packages for contents, and stored them in her freezer.

Early the following morning, Antonio went out to view the aftermath. His mother was already there, taking count of what was left of her White Leghorns.

"Where's the opossum?" he asked, looking around. "*Papá* left it over there by that tree last night."

"Good question," Belén replied. "I think it was only pretending to be dead. It was gone when I got here."

In a way, Juan Tomás's anger had won out. The opossum never returned.

As with everything else in life, there is always an ultimate story that tops all other stories in the same category. And so, there existed an ultimate story about Juan Tomás's wrath and the ludicrous consequences it spawned.

As a child, Antonio felt closer to his mother than to his father. He respected and obeyed Belén, but he did not fear her in the way he did his father. Belén played games with Antonio and touched him lovingly in tender ways Juan Tomás never could. During adverse times, when his father was excessively harsh with him, Belén sided with Antonio and defended him. Likewise, Antonio sided with his mother when his parents had serious fights.

Those fights usually occurred at suppertime, and their course was predictable. They began with a sudden flare-up of tempers, followed by a loud exchange of accusations, and ended when Juan Tomás turned violent and smashed something, usually a bowl of food, against a wall.

Antonio could confide things to his mother which he could not reveal to Juan Tomás without arousing his wrath. His father's pleasant mood could swing to one of extreme anger in an instant. Consequently, Antonio and Belén were careful about which topics they discussed with Juan Tomás, and they had their secrets and private jokes about things they knew would provoke Juan Tomás.

All Antonio had to say was, "Mamá, remember the snake?" and it brought Antonio and his mother to tears with laughter about a snake Belén had killed many years before, when Antonio was four years old. At the time, Juan Tomás swore he would deal with the perpetrator of the prank and wreak excruciating pain on the "idiot's" body. But Belén and Antonio kept their secret stowed away for life, and it remained a mystery to Juan Tomás.

The story began one morning, when Belén and Antonio entered the chicken coop to gather eggs. Antonio held a wicker basket while his mother reached under the hens, as they sat in hay-lined, wooden crates. She had gathered about a dozen eggs when Belén cried out:

"Snake. Get out of the coop fast."

Antonio hurried outside and watched his mother through the doorway as she slid her hand back into the same crate and jerked out a large garter snake. Gripping it tightly behind the head, she dragged the writhing animal to a grassy area behind the house and threw it down.

"Keep your eyes on it, and don't let it get away, while I get something to kill it with," she said, and disappeared in the direction of the tool shed. Antonio shuffled his feet nervously, terrified by the snake. He wondered what he was supposed to do if the snake started to slither away, or worse yet, if it moved in his direction.

Soon Belén returned, armed with a hoe, and on the first swing chopped the snake's head off.

"That's the longest snake I've ever seen," she said. "Look how fat it is. Probably from eating our eggs and baby chicks."

Belén picked up the dead snake and held it over her head. It was longer than she was tall.

"Wow! Let's go show it to *papá*," Antonio said.

"No, he's probably busy. Let's put it by the kitchen door, where he'll be sure to see it when he comes home for supper."

Belén dragged the animal around the side of the house and stretched it across the small wooden deck outside the kitchen.

By the time Juan Tomás walked home for supper that evening, it was dark, and Belén had not yet turned on the porch light. He felt something squeeze under the weight of his foot before he glanced down and saw the viper clearly in the moonlight. It was wider than his shoe. Juan Tomás dove off the porch before the snake could strike. He landed hard on his elbows on the concrete walkway below, and immediately got up and ran to the store. Moments later, he emerged with a long-handle axe, and chopped the snake into pieces.

Belén and Antonio were in another part of the house, and by the time they reached the kitchen door to see what the pounding was about, the snake lay in ten separate parts. The small wooden porch was destroyed.

Belén flipped on the porch light.

"*Me las van a pagar*, or you'll get yours," Juan Tomás screamed.

"*¿Qué pasó?*" Belén asked.

Before her stood her enraged husband wielding an axe. His elbows and forearms were scraped raw and bloodied.

Juan Tomás was beside himself. "Somebody left a dead snake on the porch to scare me and look at me. I almost killed myself. After I made mincemeat out of the darned snake, I noticed the head was missing."

"I'm sorry," Belén said.

"Not half as sorry as the sorry no-count who did this is going to be. And I have a good idea who it was."

"Who?" Belén asked.

"John Cross, Jr. He delivered gasoline today. He likes to play jokes on people."

"So do your *compadres*, especially Esquique and Ponciano," his wife said.

"That's true, but don't worry about it, I'll get to the bottom of this, and they're going to pay for it. I mean really suffer."

Belén had never seen her husband so angry. This was not the time to be truthful.

"Juan Tomás, you suffered quite a shock. Come on in and wash up before your supper gets cold," she said.

Antonio had been standing quietly by his mother's side, observing the family crisis, but the moment Juan Tomás went into the bathroom to wash up, Belén pulled him aside, and swore him to secrecy.

Seeing what his father had done to the snake and the porch, Antonio was readily convinced that he knew nothing about the snake.

FRANK MORRISON, THE CHECKER PLAYER

A customer drove up to the gasoline pumps, and Antonio hurried out to wait on him. The man was new in town. His name was Ennis Frank Morrison, but he preferred to be called Frank or Mr. Morrison. Nobody dared to call the big man Ennis. Only on those rare occasions when legal documents required his signature with his name exactly as shown on his birth certificate did Frank begrudgingly sign his name in full, after making it amply clear to all present that he did not answer to that hideous name. Frank was a retired fireman from Houston. After his wife died, he retired and went to live with his daughter Dorothy in Meyers, Texas. Like many retired firemen, he was something of an expert at dominoes, poker, checkers, crossword puzzles, Monopoly, and mahjong.

One day shortly after his appearance in Meyers, he went to the J T Store for gasoline.

"You've got candy and stuff like that in there?" the robust man said from behind the steering wheel.

"Sure do. Candy, ice cream, soda waters, fig cookies, Fritos. All kinds of stuff."

Ennis J. Hannegrief Frank Morrison let himself out of the car, and immediately it rose three inches on the driver's side.

On top of the candy counter lay Antonio's homemade checkerboard with its improvised checkers of Coca Cola bottle caps on one side and 7-Up caps on the other.

It had been three weeks since the retired fireman Ennis J. Hannegrief Frank Morrison came to town, and all he had done was sit on a rocker on the front porch of his daughter's house, reading the newspaper and watching an occasional car drive by. He waved at everybody. When children walked past his house, he bellowed something or other at them, and then he roared with laughter when they ran away in fear that he might chase them. After a while, the children chose to walk on the opposite side of the street, as they did with houses where unfriendly dogs lived.

Ennis J. Hannegrief Frank paid for the gasoline and bought three candy bars. He unwrapped and ate them on the spot.

"You play checkers, boy?" he said.

"Yes, sir. I always keep the board set up, in case someone wants to play," Antonio said.

"I'll play you for a Baby Ruth." Ennis J. Hannegrief Frank said.

Antonio shook his head. "My dad will give me a whipping if he catches me doing that. It's not my candy. But I'll play you for a nickel. If you win, you can buy your own Baby Ruth. They cost a nickel."

Antonio reached in his pocket and placed a coin next to the checkerboard. "You challenged, so you go first."

Ennis J. Hannegrief Frank had never heard that rule, but he made the first move anyway. After two more moves, he tried to figure out what Antonio's game strategy was, or whether the boy had a plan at all. By the fourth move, he knew he was in trouble if the boy knew what he was doing, and as it turned out, Antonio did.

"Let's go again," Ennis J. Hannegrief Frank said, when he saw the game was lost. "This time, you go first."

Antonio opened from the left side. After three moves, he started bringing out the pieces from the right.

"Hmm," Ennis J. Hannegrief Frank said, wondering if he was in trouble again. He was.

Before the game was over, Frank pushed all his remaining bottle caps toward the center of the board. "Okay, fella, let's try it again."

They reset the checkers, and a third game began with Frank starting his attack from the left. Five moves later, he was cussing. With his fat fingers he raked all the bottle caps to the center, again. "That one's yours. Just one more, and I gotta go."

Antonio came out with two checkers from the middle, then one from the right. He moved out another checker from the middle and took one of Frank's checkers but lost two of his own. He missed an opportunity to do the same to Frank on his eighth move, and now he was in trouble. Antonio played on and did not concede until he lost his last checker, which Frank devoured with gusto, leaping high over it with his king.

"Gotcha," the big man said. "I gotta go home. We'll play again some other day."

Frank got in his car, and the entire left side sank. He drove off with a big smile. "See you next time, boy."

Antonio put the newly won silver dime in his pocket and watched Frank's blue Chevy hum away. He would be back. He would be back many times, and each time, Antonio would see to it that Frank went away happy, like the other people he played regularly. Antonio was very good at checkers and adjusted his game to the skill of his opponent. If the player was of mediocre ability, Antonio slacked off and played down almost at the level of his competitor. If his opponent was skilled, Antonio showed little mercy.

Juan Tomás told him, "Son, nobody likes to play a game they can never win at. It's not fun anymore. It's like beating one's head against the wall. Pointless. Let the other player win once in a while."

It was good advice. After that Antonio never won all the games.

One afternoon, Ennis J. Hannegrief Frank stopped at the J T Store. "Fill her up," he said, and went inside for some candy.

"The checkerboard's all set up," Antonio called out.

Frank didn't reply.

When Antonio entered the store, he found Frank eating his second Baby Ruth and a third wrapped candy bar lay on top of the glass case. The checkerboard was gone. Antonio registered the sale and gave Frank the total. It was then that he saw his homemade board and bottle-cap checkers dumped in the wastebasket.

"Here you go," Frank said, and handed him a ten-dollar bill.

Antonio rang up the sale and gave him his change.

"Be right back," Frank said. He went out to his car and returned moments later with a large package under his arm. "It's all yours," he said, and slid the package across the counter toward Antonio. It was very heavy, and Antonio used both hands to pick it up.

"What's this?" Antonio asked.

"It's something for the Meyers' champion checker player. Open it."

Antonio tore open the square package. It was a black and white onyx checkerboard with a black, onyx border. The game pieces were also made of onyx. Half of the twenty-four checkers were ebony black, the other half, alabaster white.

"Anybody as good as you at checkers ought to have a decent checker set," Frank said. "I saw it in Nuevo Laredo this past weekend, and I told my daughter Dottie you ought to have one, so I bought it for you."

It was the most beautiful checker set Antonio had ever seen. The checkers and the board glistened like polished marble. Antonio could hardly believe it was his.

"I'll pay for your candy bars the next few times you come here," he said. "I don't know how else to pay you."

"Don't worry about it, boy. If you're happy with it, I'm happy."

"Yes, sir," Antonio said. "I'm very happy."

"Well, set 'em up. Let's give it a whirl. Maybe I'll have better luck with this checkerboard."

Antonio felt like he was doing something important, the way the pieces clicked when they tapped the onyx board. The stone gave the common game of checkers a certain solemnity. They played their usual five games, but on this day, Frank won three of them. Frank suspected the boy had thrown at least one game his way. Frank seldom won more than two games.

JULIO CORTEZ AND ANTONIO PLAY CHECKERS

Julio Cortez stood on his front porch, smoking his first cigarette of the day. From across the street, he watched Antonio trudge his way through the crusty, frozen grass from the house to the store. Julio was single, thirty-nine, and fancied himself a lady's man and a good checkers player. He was still miffed at himself for allowing Antonio to beat him four out of five games twice the night before. Juan Tomás and his friends had witnessed the crushing debacle. Now he wanted to sit down one on one with Antonio and play another five games with no witnesses to make him nervous. The boy had a system, and Julio decided he would discover what it was.

Antonio opened the J T Store at 7 a.m. If the mornings were cold, it was his chore to fire up the pot-bellied heater between the mechanics' bays. For the store, he lit a small open-faced, propane gas heater. Once both heaters were burning, winter was tolerable. By the time Juan Tomás made his appearance, the entire building was warm. On school days, Antonio slipped off to school the minute his father walked through the door.

"How about some checkers?" Julio said.

"Sure," Antonio said. "The checkerboard is in the back where we left it last night, but I have to light up the heater in there first."

Julio remained at the front of the store with his back to the gas heater. Through the doorway, he watched the boy prepare the pot-bellied heater. Antonio stuffed the bottom of the cast iron stove with two crumpled pages of a newspaper, and laid three, short, mesquite logs on the grate. He lit the paper and watched the flames gradually ignite the wood. The bark on the logs hissed and popped softly. Normally it took eight to ten minutes for the fire to reach its peak and another fifteen minutes for the room to warm up. Antonio was in a hurry that morning and decided to take a shortcut. He wanted to play a couple of games before going off to school.

His father kept a small wash tub on the floor with two inches of kerosene for washing car parts and tools. Antonio took the dripping brush out of the tub and opened the heater's door. With a snap from the wrist, he sprayed the inside of the pot-bellied heater. Instantly, the old heater sprang to life, and the brush in his hand became a burning torch. A few drops trickled down the handle to his hand and fingers, and they also caught on fire. Antonio panicked and threw the brush back in the tub, which roared as it immediately caught on fire. Flames shot up all way to the rafters and the sheet-metal panels that formed the roof. He beat his hand against his pants to extinguish the fire burning his hand. Antonio knew if the wooden joists and rafters caught on fire, the entire building would go up in smoke.

"Help me open the side doors," Antonio called out, but Julio didn't move. He stood frozen with fear in the other room. The accidental fire overwhelmed him.

Until that morning, Antonio had never opened the large, sliding doors through which cars entered the mechanics' bays. They were too heavy. But that was about to change. He pulled out the large, steel pin that secured the doors, and put his shoulder against the frame of the first door, throwing all his strength behind it. The door slid open four feet in one push. Antonio grabbed a tined rake from the wall, snagged the tub by an ear, and dragged it outside to the middle of the gravel parking lot. There, he flipped the tub over and let the fire burn itself out safely.

Throughout the entire episode, Julio remained in a trance. Antonio waited until the flames outside were in their waning stages before he re-entered the store. He placed his shoulder on the door again and slid it shut.

"I forgot Dad said we were out of kerosene, and he put gasoline in the tub instead. Whew, glad that's over. It was kinda scary. Are you ready to play, Mr. C.?" Antonio said.

Julio looked pale. "I don't feel too good," he said. "I don't feel like playing anymore. Maybe tomorrow."

"Okay. Anyway, it's almost time to go to school," Antonio said.

When Juan Tomás showed up minutes later, he noticed the scorched rocks outside and the black soot where the flames had licked the rafters.

"What's that all about?" he asked.

"Oh, we had a little fire in here when I lit the heater," Antonio said. "The tub caught on fire, so I threw it out in the parking area."

"You have to be careful, *m'hijo*," Juan Tomás said.

Antonio slung his schoolbag over his shoulder. "See you this afternoon, Pops," he said and went out the front door.

"That's *papá*, not Pops," Juan Tomás called out.

"Oh, by the way. I don't need your help to open the sliding doors anymore. I can do it by myself," Antonio said, and flexed his right arm to display a bicep that was well-hidden beneath his jacket and a corduroy shirt.

EL TELEFÓN AND THE FIRE
IN LUBBOCK

Juan Tomás was the only Mexican in Meyers, Texas, who had a telephone—*el telefón*, as the Mexican clientele called it—mounted on the east wall of the store's office, next to the cash register, where Juan Tomás could listen in on conversations, in case someone might try to sneak a long-distance call at his expense. It was his personal phone, but his customers were welcomed to use it. *El telefón* was the old-type instrument. You held the earpiece up to the left ear while briskly turning the crank with your right hand three or four times in rapid succession to get the operator. Then speaking loudly, you announced to the operator, and to everyone within hearing range, the telephone number of the party you wished to speak to. Small-town areas had few telephones, and Juan Tomás's was simply number seven. Large cities, like Dallas, Houston, and San Antonio had fancy prefixes: Capitol, Fannin, Garfield, General, Pershing, and the like. Not Meyers, Texas. There you cranked up the operator, and if you asked for number seven, you got Juan Tomás, who answered, "J T Store?" For reasons unknown, he always made it sound like a question. It was there that people without telephone service went to place and receive their calls.

After the cotton and corn were gathered in the Meyers' area, many families moved on to West Texas in search of late crops. Juan Tomás's telephone was especially active during that period. Emergencies, large and small, arose and were first made known through his telephone from the outside world. Cars and trucks broke down, and people called home for money to repair them. Sometimes the calls concerned wrecks by the migrant workers or serious illnesses.

A local telephone call was a somber matter in those days. A long-distance call was a serious and, at times, a grave undertaking. No one called to gossip unless the gossip was weighty enough and serious enough to warrant using *el telefón*. Certainly, no one telephoned his girlfriend to tell her how much he loved her. Such matters were best handled in person or by mail.

All calls went through the Meyers Telephone Exchange Company's switchboard, manned by Miss Juanita Ramírez, who listened in on all calls, in and out, just to pass the time of day. As luck would have it, she was also the town's main gossip, so naturally she withheld no secrets. Sometimes Ramon called his brother Juan Tomás from San Antonio. They would use the vilest language they knew, which was enough to drive the red-faced Miss Ramírez from their line. After they heard her click off, the two brothers enjoyed a good laugh before continuing with their conversation.

If you called home for money because your truck broke down, the entire community knew exactly where you were, the nature of repairs required, and the cost involved, long before Western Union could transmit the money. If your daughter eloped or your uncle was in the slammer, you could count on those tidbits of juicy information to travel fast far and wide, compliments of Miss Ramírez.

At times, appalling, terrible, and very sad news travelled through *el telefón*. Such a call came through one Saturday morning in late January.

When dawn broke, the ground was covered with packed ice. It was an unusually harsh winter, and it had sleeted through the night for the third time that week. Winter always came in January and February.

The call came in at 8:17 a.m., and Maria Evencia took the call. She was Juan Tomás's youngest sister. Whenever the store was very busy or Juan Tomás was gone for more than an hour, Maria Evencia was called in to manage the store. On that day, Juan Tomás and Belén had gone to Austin to buy a bedroom suite.

Maria Evencia wrote down the message word for word. On the other end of the line was a police chief calling from Lubbock, Texas. After Maria Evencia explained to the officer about the community telephone at the store and that all messages were relayed, the officer came to the point.

"Inform Tomás Allende that his daughter, Beatrice Esparza, died last night in an accident. Her body is at the Pennington Funeral Home in Lubbock, Texas. Tell him to contact the funeral home at Capitol 181270."

After the officer hung up, Maria Evencia could not help but wonder if the policeman was even remotely aware that he had entrusted the responsibility to a thirteen-year-old girl. On the telephone, she came across as being older, more mature. Everybody said so, and she was proud when people noticed. But not that morning. She would have preferred that Juan Tomás had been there to take the call.

It took Maria Evencia seconds to decide on what to do next. She would have the message delivered as soon as possible. Whenever Juan Tomás and Belén went to Austin or San Antonio, they made it a whole-day's trip, leaving early and returning well after dark. The message was too important to wait until they returned. Besides, Juan Tomás usually sent Antonio to deliver the news. She rewrote the message and compared it to the original. When she was satisfied, they were the same, she handed Antonio the copy to deliver.

Antonio took special pride in being the town's messenger. He had read a comic book about the Pony Express riders and fancied himself the last of a dying breed. Besides, the tips were good—sometimes. When the news was very bad, such as this, chances were that with all the grieving and consoling going on, the recipients would forget about him. He could expect only a thank-you or a handshake from some penniless relative of the bereaved family who happened to be visiting

The roads leading into farms were messy affairs during the wet season, too muddy for the small wheels of Antonio's motor scooter. He mounted his old bicycle and headed north to the farm where Tomás Allende lived. There was nothing as nostalgic as wild Indians to be encountered on his trip, only dogs. But dogs had to count for something. They were not as interesting as redskins shooting arrows at him on the run, but they posed a danger to be reckoned with, especially on farms and ranches, where every family kept a half dozen dogs more vicious than old man Anderson's wild bunch.

The trip turned out to be a tough five miles. The sleet on the ground was hard and slippery, and the wind that picked up from the north packed a wallop that penetrated his clothes and his wet tennis shoes.

Tomás Allende was feeding the cows some winter hay and breaking the thin ice that had formed at the surface of the water troughs. No dogs were in sight.

By custom, adults did not acknowledge children's presences too hastily. Tomás went on about his business, although he had caught sight of Antonio coming up the icy road long before Antonio turned into his muddy entrance way. When he saw Antonio approaching with a paper clutched in his hand, he quickened his pace and hurried toward the barbed-wire fence that separated them.

"*Buenos días, Toñito*," he said. "What can possibly bring you out in this kind of weather so early this morning? It can't be good news. Can it?"

"*Buenos días, Don* Tomás." Antonio knew this wasn't the time to chit-chat. Besides, he never knew what to say to adults, aside from answering their pointless questions. "We got a call for you from the police chief in Lubbock this morning, just a little while ago."

Tomás wiped his brow with his shirt's sleeve, more out of habit than from necessity in the crisp morning. "And what did he tell your father?" Tomás asked.

"My father is out of town in Austin, but my aunt Maria Evencia took the call and wrote everything down. I have it here," Antonio said, and held out the paper for Tomás to take.

"What does it say, *Toñito*? Read it, *por favor*," Tomás said. "I am ignorant of reading and writing."

Antonio read the note. When he was through, Tomás Allende took the note and meditated, paper in hand, for a few seconds. Then Tomás opened his hand and stared at the message. This little paper says all that, he said to himself in disbelief. It said a lot, but it left important questions unanswered. Facts he needed to know.

Antonio was not sure whether he should leave or stay. He had read the message and given Tomás the note. What more could he do?

But there was much more beyond the message on the paper to be learned, as Tomás knew.

"Tell me, *Toñito*. What else do you know about the accident?"

"That's the whole message, *Don* Tomás. Nothing else was said. I was there when my aunt Maria Evencia wrote it down."

"*No, mi hijo*," Tomás said. He reached over the fence and placed a gentle hand on the boy's shoulder. "Let's lower our heads and close our eyes and see what else the Lord will show us."

Tomás lowered his head and said a prayer. When the prayer ended, Antonio saw a man pouring liquid into a kerosene heater in the center of a small bedroom. The metal container read Kerosene, but the liquid that poured out of it was red. It had the pungent odor of gasoline, not the soft, inoffensive fumes of kerosene. He saw the match ignite and the heater explode. A young woman leaped out of bed, frantically trying to douse the flames enveloping her husband. An instant later, the fuel can explode, hurling burning fuel into every corner of the room, the walls, the ceiling, and the floor.

"My God," Antonio said, and covered his eyes.

The woman screamed. Now she too was on fire. Her night clothes first, then suddenly her hair. She screamed in pain as the skin of her fingers and forearms melted before her eyes. She had no hair left. She reached for her throat as if to help herself to get a lungful of oxygen, but there was none. She fell beside her husband, who never uttered a sound throughout the ordeal, and both lay still on the burning floor. It seemed to Antonio that the small house burned to the ground in a matter of seconds, although it must have taken minutes, but not many. It was a horrific scene.

Tomás removed his hand from Antonio's shoulder, his face contorted with pain. Antonio wondered how much the old man had seen. The experience drained both, and they remained still, breathing heavily.

"The message," Antonio finally said. "That is all we really know."

Tomás took out his wallet and extended the two one dollar bills it contained across the fence. Antonio shook his head. It was a generous tip, but it felt wrong accepting money for bearing bad news. Tomás worked his body between the fence strands to the other side without touching a single barb. On the porch lay six ten-pound sacks of potatoes. He picked up one and handed it to Antonio.

"Give this to your mother," he said. "Thank you, *Toñito*. Now I must go in and prepare for the trip."

Inside, Tomás Allende gave a simple command. "Everybody get ready. We're leaving for Lubbock as soon as possible."

Faustina, his wife, seized upon the urgency of his request. "*¿Qué pasó?*" she said.

Tomás turned and looked at her. "Beatrice and her husband had an accident. We must go to Lubbock, right away."

"What kind of accident?" his wife asked.

Tomás gave her a stern look. He had not intended to say anymore, but seeing the desperation in the woman's face, he decided otherwise. She was Beatrice's mother. She had a right to know.

"A fire," he said. "But hurry, *vámonos pronto*. It is a six-hour drive."

"*Dios mío,*" Faustina said in astonishment, but asked nothing further of her husband. She would learn the details on the road.

Antonio had heard his father say that Tomás Allende was a saint. Now, he understood.

ILLUSTRATED COMICS
AND THE RAFT

When Illustrated Classics first appeared in comic-book form in the spring of 1941, the world of adventure opened to a new generation of youngsters as never before. Great stories were suddenly made available in life-like, colored drawings with simple dialogues. They filled young boys' minds with nostalgia for a time in the past when swashbuckling adventurers fought to the death with bearded pirates for the honor of a beautiful princess or a trunk filled with Spanish gold coins. Youngsters donned capes, improvised from bath towels, and fought fearlessly with broom handles and sticks, in lieu of swords. The Corsican Brothers, The Three Musketeers, The Last of the Mohicans, Treasure Island, The Count of Monte Cristo, Robinson Crusoe, and Robin Hood became popular hits the moment they appeared on the stands. But nothing captured the imaginations of Antonio and his young friends more than the publication of The Adventures of Huckleberry Finn in comic-book form. It was more than a tale. It was a calling. There, on the edge of town, flowed the meandering San Isidro River, and what could be simpler than building a raft that would take them all the way to the sea. The boys sat on the riverbank mesmerized, reading, and absorbing the pictures, imagining Huck and Jim as they sailed downstream, until Antonio said the magic words. "We can do that. We can build a raft and sail all the way to the Gulf of Mexico."

This was something within their reach, and the very thought of seeing themselves drifting downstream on a raft excited them immensely. Everybody began talking at the same time.

"I'll be Huck," Felipe said.

"No, I wanna be Huck," Luis argued.

"I'm Huck," Harold said, "Huck was a White boy."

"Well, then, I wanna be Jim," Luis said.

"You can't be Jim. I'm Jim," Clear Walker asserted.

"You want to be a runaway slave?" Antonio queried.

"Well, I'm the only Negro in our group, so I gotta be Jim," he said.

"Who am I going to be?" Mario wanted to know.

"Wait a minute. Nobody's going to be nobody," Antonio said. "We're going to do the things Huck and Jim did, but we're going to be ourselves."

And that appeared to be the best solution to everyone.

The gods of raft construction were favorable to the boys. There was no need to chop down trees and trim off their branches. Nearby lay the town's dump in a deserted gravel and sand pit, where the principal materials required to build a raft were available. The boys scavenged the quarry for two days, selecting and hauling posts and boards to the riverbank. When they determined the stack of materials gathered was sufficient for their needs, Antonio brought out his comic book again.

"We'll build a raft like the one in these pictures," he said. "All we need now are tools and some nails."

"I can bring a hammer from home," Lupe said.

Harold said, "Me, too."

"I can bring a saw. My dad won't miss it," Mario added.

"I'll bring a bunch of nails," Antonio said.

With a half dozen borrowed hammers, an axe, a saw, and a bucketful of four-inch finishing nails from the J T Store, building the raft got under way the next day. The boys nailed boards to posts until darkness set in.

"When we finish it," Antonio said, "we're going to sail all the way to the Gulf of Mexico. That's where the San Isidro River ends."

"All rivers flow south until they reach the ocean," Julio said. "Mrs. Vogel showed us on a map."

"Liar. That's not true. The Nile River in Egypt goes north." Harold said, "It starts somewhere way down in Africa."

"Africa?" Mario said. "We ain't in Africa, we're in the United States. Look at the river. It's going that way—south."

"The main thing is that it'll take us to the ocean," Luis said. "I've never seen the ocean before."

"I saw it in Corpus Christi. It's humongous," Mario said.

Antonio shook his head. "I've never seen it either, but my dad promised to take me there someday to see the ships."

"We'll get there before he takes you," Clear said.

"How many are going on the trip?" Antonio asked.

Eight hands went up.

"Lalo's not here, but he told me he wants to go too," Felipe said.

Nobody asked how long the trip would last, what they would eat along the way, or how they would return home. Such frivolities would work themselves out, just as they had for Huck and Jim.

"That's nine of us. I hope the raft will hold nine people without sinking."

"It should." Antonio said. "If it's not, we'll make it bigger."

"We cain't make it bigger," Harold said. "It will be too heavy to carry."

"Carry? We're not going to carry it. We're going to ride on it, dummy," Felipe chided.

"Not all the time," Harold said. "We ain't going over dams on the raft. We'll get killed. We must get off and carry it around dams every time we get to one."

"There ain't no dams on the San Isidro," Manuel said.

"How do you know? Maybe there is."

"Maybe there ain't," Manuel said.

"How do you know?" Harold repeated.

"What about the dam by the Jennings' dairy?"

"That one don't count. It's upstream," Lupe said.

"All I know is I ain't going over no dam on no raft," Harold said.

It took three days to complete the raft. The hard part had been finding and dragging the materials to the building site. Their creation, however, was by no means the sleek vessel depicted in the comic book. Their raft was a conglomeration of boards and posts crudely assembled, and it was very heavy. With considerable effort, the nine boys dragged the craft the short distance from the riverbank into the water, where it barely remained afloat with no one on board. But it was so exhilarating to see it in the water, after three days of hard labor, that no one was ready to ruin the moment by admitting the raft was not truly river worthy.

Nor did they have to. Nature took care of the vessel the boys had toiled and bickered over. It was the start of a new year when nature tries to make up for the shortage of rainfall for the entire previous year. It rained continuously for three days, hard and light, but never completely stopping. By the time the rains let up, the river had left its banks and crept twenty yards toward town. The site where the raft was moored lay under water for days, and when the flood receded, the raft was gone. Nobody had thought of securing the craft properly. Branches and debris were strewn along the banks of the San Isidro River. The swift currents had swept the raft away and smashed it to pieces to become part of the debris floating downstream. The boys went to the river's edge and lamented the fate of their efforts. Inwardly, though, they sighed with relief. Building the raft had become too much like real work, and no one suggested building another one.

The boys quickly erased from their minds what might have been and moved on to other things. Shortly thereafter, the picture book of the Lewis and Clark expedition was published. The dugout canoes in the book glided so smoothly on the surface of lakes and rivers that Antonio and his friends began rethinking their journey to the sea. But it was only a dream. The prospect of "felling a tree" and carving the inside into a viable canoe appeared so formidable that the project never got started.

THE DROWNING OF
TWO BROTHERS

Three miles upstream from where the raft washed away, a tragic event occurred that weekend. Felipe Molina and José Mojica walked their bicycles down the hill from the Jennings' dairy farm, until they reached the river at the bottom of the ravine. There, they mounted their bicycles and were halfway across the single-lane, wooden-plank bridge when they met a truck coming fast from the opposite direction. Cars and trucks always went down the hill fast. It was the kind of hill you had to break all the way down to keep from gaining excessive speed, the kind of steep hill that could be ascended only in low gear.

The boys were dressed in suits and were on their way to attend Sunday Mass. No one witnessed the accident, only their cries for help. Jorge Duran was fishing at the foot of the dam, thirty yards away, when he heard the truck start its descent, honking twice on its way down. He heard the deep rumble of the vehicle as it bottomed the ravine and started across the noisy, wooden-plank bridge. He said he heard one, maybe two voices scream at the same time. In his deposition to Sheriff Krause, he said he reeled in his line and ran to the bridge to see if anybody needed help. No one was in sight, but he found a bicycle hanging over the side of the bridge, caught by its rear-wheel spokes on an upright bolt that was part of the bridge support. The bridge had no railing.

Jorge lived on the Jennings' dairy farm and knew the owner of the bicycle. He climbed up the ravine and found the Molina family in their car, ready for the trip to church. They said Felipe and José had gone ahead on their bicycles. The family rode down to the bridge to view the suspended bicycle and concurred with Jorge that the boys had probably gone over the side and were swept away by the swift current of the swollen river. No other conclusion could be reached from the evidence left behind. Neither boy would have left the site without the other. The families of the two boys and their neighbors searched the river in hope of finding them alive, waiting to be rescued. Sheriff Krause came out with a group of nine men and scoured a large area downstream from the bridge.

That night the river began to recede, and by dawn the San Isidro River was overflowing its banks by fewer than five feet. At daybreak, Sheriff Krause and his volunteers resumed their search. The Sheriff said the boys' bodies were probably caught on submerged tree branches, but nobody wanted to believe that.

Juan Tomás put his motorboat into the water three miles downstream from the bridge and headed north. The current was swift and mirthless. Ponciano Cortez sat up front, scanning the river. It rained intermittently, while the search went on, and both men wore raincoats.

On the second day, one mile from the bridge, Ponciano signaled for Juan Tomás to move in closer toward the left bank. There appeared to be clothing caught on the branches of a downed tree. Juan Tomás positioned the skiff so Ponciano could view the object from up close.

"It's a body," Ponciano said, and moved back toward the center of the boat.

"Pull him in," Juan Tomás said.

"With what?"

"With your hands. Just grab on to anything and pull him in the boat."

"I can't do that," Ponciano said. "What if his eyes are open?"

"Throw your raincoat over him. I can't let the steering handle go, we'll get swept away by the current." He used his two hands and dragged the body into the boat by walking backwards. The body was fully clothed in a dark suit. Only the face and hands were visible. They were swollen and ashen blue. Neither man recognized the boy.

They then traveled north until Juan Tomás spotted Sheriff Krause on the river's edge close to the bridge. There were no banks. He revved up the engine and ran the boat out of the river into the tall grass.

A crowd of onlookers, mostly men and a few boys, gathered a short distance from the boat, where the body lay shrouded with the raincoat.

"We found one of them, Sheriff," Juan Tomás shouted to the tall man who was working his way through the grass toward the skiff.

"Which one is he," the Sheriff said.

"We don't know," Juan Tomás said. "He's kind of blue and puffed up."

"Yeah, they get bloated like that after they've been in the water a day or two," Sheriff Krause said.

He removed the raincoat from the body, and the crowd pushed forward, but did not immediately go to where the lifeless body lay. They looked cautiously in the direction of the boat, slowly shifting their focus from the boat to the boy's clothing, and finally to the boy's face. When they realized it was not a horrific sight that would shock their senses, they moved in still closer to study the teenager's face. Everyone except the Sheriff removed his hat.

"It's Felipe Molina," someone said.

"Are you sure?" Sheriff Krause asked.

"It's him," several voices said at once.

The Sheriff and Juan Tomás pulled the boat another ten feet away from the river's edge.

"Let's just leave him here until I can get an ambulance out here," the Sheriff said, and covered the body again.

The search for José Mojica continued. By that time, it was late in the afternoon, and the river had receded another foot. With every inch the river's level dropped, more fallen trees, branches and debris became visible, objects that had been hidden below the surface of the murky water. After the coroner came and the body of Felipe Molina was taken away, Juan Tomás and Ponciano put the boat back in the water and searched until nightfall. Around nine o'clock that night, they returned to the river with a large spotlight, powered by an automotive battery, and the two men searched from the boat most of the night.

Ponciano worked the spotlight, studying up close anything that resembled clothing. Five times during the night, they came upon pieces of clothing, but they were not what they were looking for. Each time they maneuvered in for a closer inspection, Ponciano prayed it wasn't the other boy. He still felt sick about touching the stiff body of Felipe Molina. When Juan Tomás first asked him to help with the search, he had readily agreed. It did not occur to him that he might encounter a dead person. Even the snakes they spotted in the water, now and then, did not produce in him the squeamish feelings of seeing a lifeless human body stuck on tree branches.

At six in the morning, after combing the river for nine hours, they pulled the boat out of the water. Both men were exhausted.

It was not until noon of the third day after the accident that José Mojica was found. The water level had receded considerably by then, and the Sheriff's group found the boy's body lodged on an uprooted tree. It was only a hundred yards downstream from the wooden bridge. José had been there all along, out of sight.

It was the first time anyone could recall of Anglos setting foot inside Santa Monica's Catholic Church. It was a Mexican church with all the services conducted in Latin and Spanish. Sheriff Krause, along with his wife and his Anglo deputy, attended the boys' funeral Mass, as did John and Janet Diviney, owners of the dairy farm where Felipe and José's families lived and worked. Reverend Bob Kellum was also in attendance, as were Jane Schneider, the principal, and her husband, and two teachers who accompanied them. Somehow the Anglos found each other and sat together close to the front, behind the Mojica family. Margaret Brandt arrived late and was escorted immediately by an usher to sit with her group, next to Reverend Kellum. Instead of wearing a hat, like the other Anglo women, she wore a black veil.

The two gray coffins lay silent and shrouded in mystery, one behind the other in front of the communion rail. No one had come forward to admit running the boys off the bridge.

Before delivering the homily, Father Erasti welcomed the "distinguished" guests in his torturous English, and the Anglo group acknowledged his greetings with a nod of the head.

During the Mass, the Anglos stood and sat with the congregation, but they did not kneel.

Lupe Rodriquez whispered, "They don't kneel at their church."

"I know," Antonio said. "Their church doesn't have any kneelers."

"They don't even have an altar or statues of saints," Lupe said.

"I can't believe Miss Brandt is here," Antonio said. "Everybody knows she hates Mexicans."

"Yeah. That's what I heard."

"Wonder why she's wearing a veil instead of a hat like the other Anglo ladies?"

"Maybe she heard that's what women wear in this church."

"Nah," Antonio said.

A week after the funerals, Sheriff Krause dropped by the J T Store and thanked Juan Tomás for his assistance in the search. "By the way, I've got something here that belongs to you." He reached into a large grocery bag and pulled out a raincoat.

"Oh, that. No, it belongs to Ponciano Cortez. He comes by here all the time," Juan Tomás said.

"Then see to it that he gets it back, awright?"

"Sure thing, Sheriff."

Juan Tomás hung the raincoat on a nail in the wall by the front door, and it remained there, on and off, for two months. Ponciano wanted nothing more to do with the raincoat after he used it to pull Felipe Molina's body out of the river, after which it was used as a shroud over the boy's body for hours before the ambulance took the body away.

"I don't think I want it anymore," Ponciano said.

"It's clean," Juan Tomás said.

"I know. It's just me."

"You're afraid of the raincoat, aren't you?" Juan Tomás laughed.

"Not exactly afraid. It's just that I know how it was used, and every time I wear it, I'm going to remember, and it makes me feel funny, like death might be contagious."

"In other words, you're afraid of it," Juan Tomás said.

"*Muy bien, compadre,*" Ponciano said. "I'm afraid of it. Tell you what, let's trade raincoats. They're the same size and almost the same color."

"No, I don't think so," Juan Tomás said.

"Makes you feel funny, too?"

Juan Tomás shrugged his shoulders. "I guess so."

The raincoat went back to the utility nail in the wall by the front door.

Whenever someone came by and admired the coat, Juan Tomás eagerly took it down and offered it to him. The raincoat made two trips out of the J T Store under the arm of different men. Each time, it took the new owners less than a week to learn of its lurid recent history, and the coat was hastily returned to the nail by the front door.

One night a straggly-bearded hobo came in asking for a handout. Juan Tomás had a soft spot for transients who were down on their luck, and always gave them something to eat or drink. Since the war began, the number of homeless drifters, always men, had increased. He offered the hobo a pint of ice cream.

"Now just move along," Juan Tomás said. "I've got work to do in the back." He went to the back room, leaving the hobo alone momentarily. When he returned, Ponciano's raincoat was gone and on its way by foot to Evet, Texas, the next town south.

The mystery of the drowning deaths of Felipe Molina and José Mojica was never solved. Sheriff Krause had a theory that perhaps the guilty person was not aware of his deed. There may have been no contact with the boys or their bicycles, he said. The sudden draft of air produced by the truck's momentum could have flung the boys into the raging waters as it sped past them, or maybe the boys panicked when the truck passed them and fell in. Since the road turned to the right immediately after the bridge ended, the driver may have been distracted, looking for oncoming vehicles as he maneuvered to make the sharp turn and did not see the boys fall.

"But with all the publicity," Ponciano said, "surely that individual knows he's the one who caused their deaths."

"He knows," Joaquin said, "but he also knows he is innocent of committing a crime. It was an accident."

"Would you turn yourself in and chance going to jail if you were sure you had not deliberately killed anybody?" Juan Tomás asked.

Good argument, everyone concurred. Under those circumstances, even Padre Erasti admitted he wouldn't fault that individual for not coming forward and turning himself into the authorities.

ON BECOMING AN AMERICAN

Antonio was in grade school, the first time he heard his father's lecture on successful living in America. Juan Tomás's lecture was based on a few observations he made during his army days, and Antonio would hear it many times over by the time he finished high school and went off to college. Juan Tomás reserved his words of wisdom for those occasions when he and Antonio were alone, and there was little to do.

"Remember, my son, that good living in the United States is Anglo. To succeed here, you must dress better than the Anglos, speak better than the Anglos, and be better educated than the Anglos. Only then will Anglos respect and accept you as a true American. Then you can go out and get a good-paying job which will allow you to enjoy the good things this country has to offer, like a house in a nice neighborhood where you can raise your family."

"Will I own a new car *papá*?" Antonio asked.

"You will be able to afford any car you want," his father said. "But remember, first you have to study hard. If you speak English poorly and can't communicate well with Anglos, they will always treat you like a *peon*, a laborer they hire to do their work for them, someone they don't care to associate with as a friend. I didn't have the opportunities you have because when I was your age, Mexican children weren't allowed in Anglo schools. But look at you, you're studying side by side with Anglo children. You're receiving the same education they are. You don't want to be an Anglo any more than you want to be Chinese or Russian. But since Anglos make the laws here and run the country, you must live their way to become a true American. If we lived in China, I would tell you to learn the Chinese language and adopt their way of living. The Chinese run China. Anglos run the United States. See what I mean?"

"*Sí, papá.*"

"At your age, your whole life is still ahead of you. You can study to become anything you want. I wish you had met my Mexican friends from

Chicago, the ones I met in the army when I was stationed in England. Then you would understand exactly what I'm talking about."

Antonio recalled the first time he heard that lecture. The conversation ended with his asking. "Have you ever seen a Chinaman, *papá*?"

"Yes, in the army...many times. Why do you ask?"

"Are they really yellow?"

"Not really. Well, maybe some of them are a little bit, but not yellow like mustard, more like the color of your aunt Maria Evencia."

Suddenly, Juan Tomás looked exasperated. "*Ay*, my son, you are not listening to me. This is not a discussion about the color of the Chinese people. We are talking about how to succeed in the United States of America. Listen to me, will you?"

"*Sí, papá.*"

NEW *PADRE* ARRIVES IN MEYERS

After his ordination in Spain, at age twenty-six, Padre Javier Galván's first assigned parish was *Nuestra Señora del Carmen* in East Los Angeles, where he served a seven-year stint. In the forties, East L.A. was a city of gangs, *pachucos*, and Zoot suiters. Even though Padre Galván stood only five feet five inches tall, weighed a hundred and thirty-five pounds, and possessed a squeaky mezzo-soprano voice, he had no problem in dealing with toughies. In his seminary days, he learned how to offset what he lacked in physical stature by talking tough, loud and fast. He knew he was most effective when letting go of his volley of words or punches before the opposition had a chance to think or react. After ordination, the Roman collar gave him yet another weapon in his arsenal with which to control people. The starched, white collar conjured an immediate aura of respect, which even a policeman in uniform did not possess, save for sticking his gun in someone's face. Impertinent, abrasive, and combative aptly describe this man of God.

Padre Galván soon discovered that the East Los Angeles parish was his calling. He enjoyed matching wits with the lowlifes, scoundrels, and cutthroats, who earned a living by taking advantage of the unfortunate souls who lived on the edge of society and at the bottom of everything from education to employment, to worldly possessions, to hygiene, and to good health. Padre Galván was nobody's fool and took no chances. He owned an illegal sawed-off shotgun, a German luger, brass knuckles, two Billy clubs, and an assortment of baseball bats, some with sharp nails and spikes protruding from all sides, He acquired his arsenal while breaking up fracases and in his own combats, trying to protect his or his parishioners' property or wellbeing. He made it clear to the entire area of Nuestra Señora del Carmen's parish hoods and vandals that he also had his turf.

The morning after a night skirmish, one could find the *padre* selling his latest acquisitions at Miss January's Jewelry and Pawnshop. The proceeds, he added to the church collection of which a percentage stayed in the parish and the remainder was forwarded to the provincial.

In his seven-years at Nuestra Señora de Carmen, he converted dozens of gang members through the shear admiration they acquired for him. Many became his cherished friends, and he did not hesitate to seek their help in time of need. He was stabbed twice, shot once, and beaten up badly enough for a three-day stay at the hospital. Twice the church mysteriously caught on fire, and his little house, on the same property as the church, was subjected to several drive-by shootings. In the end, though, the rowdy gangs learned where the official boundary lines were to the Padre's parish, and they opted to take their crime sprees elsewhere.

Nobody could ever be accused of falling asleep during one of his sermons. He adopted the language of the barrio and stripped himself of the smarter-than-thou Castilian dialect he brought with him from Spain. When he spoke, everyone felt he was one of their own speaking to them. This was not some Anglo *padre* who had little in common with anything in their real world. This was not some *padre* from Mexico or Spain, who talked down to them. Those were the spiritual directors they had known in the past. If people respected him, which they did, it was because he had earned their respect on the streets. Any *padre* is respected in his own church, but to be respected out in the streets, in the alleys, and in the bars took the qualities of a leader, because he operated without the backup muscle of a gang, most of the time.

He knew everyone in the parish, whether they attended his church or some other church, or, as more than likely was the case, no church at all. He carried a carton of cigarettes with him and stopped to befriend teen-agers at street corners and alleyways, wherever they happened to gather. Sometimes he sat on somebody's tumbledown back porch and listened to teenage gangs talk their talk. He would shoot the breeze with them and passed out packs of cigarettes until the youngsters felt he was part of the tapestry, not some intruder.

He knew every bar, every bartender, and every barmaid. He walked everywhere. He dropped in at all hours and picked up a cue stick, always finding a couple of curious fellows willing to challenge the little *padre*. He would buy a beer here and there, and seldom solicited anyone's presence to his church. They knew who he was and why he was there.

As time went on, new faces appeared at his church, and Padre Galvan could only surmise they were the fruit of his excursions around the parish.

Some men could not allow themselves to be seen worshipping on their knees, so they sent their families to attend Mass on Sundays and Holy Days of obligation.

This was the world Padre Javier Galvan stepped out of when the provincial decided it was time to reward him with a peaceful and tranquil parish, Santa Monica's Catholic Church in rural south Texas. In Meyers, nobody worried about the color and cut of one's clothes or if one was walking on the wrong side of the street or on the wrong side of town. No gangs or violence existed there. This was a lackadaisical community where the parish *padre* had almost always been a benign spiritual advisor nearing retirement or a freshly ordained *padre* in need of administrative experience.

Consequently, Padre Galvan's opening remarks to his St. Monica's parishioners were unlike anything they had ever heard.

"Today I saw people entering the church and blessing themselves with holy water. Then, they walked up the center aisle looking for a place to park. Up until this time, everything was okay. Next, they blessed themselves again and did a little Mickey Mouse bouncing motion facing the holy tabernacle, before dropping into an empty pew, and taking the first space next to the center aisle. Now, everybody coming after them will have to climb over them to sit down.

"First of all, my good people, this is not a Mickey Mouse church, this is the house of God. Watch closely. This is how you should genuflect. Take your right knee all the way down until it touches the floor. Like this. Next, stand up and move to the center of the pew. This way nobody must climb over you, whether they are coming from your right or left. Any questions?"

There were none.

Padre Galvan hurried from the sanctuary down the center aisle, pointing as he went. "I saw you…you… you… and you take the first space next to the center aisle when the entire bench was empty. Why? People had to climb over each one of you to sit down in your pews."

He pointed at Goyo Ferrer "Why?"

"I don't know. I guess I wasn't thinking," Goyo said.

"What about you?" he asked Cuca Arispe.

"I always sit here," the elderly woman replied. "I have for many years."

"You used to sit there, *señora*," Padre Galvan said. "From here on out, you will genuflect the way I showed you and move down the pew until you reach the center, like everyone else. Now, others coming after you can easily get in. See how nice and orderly this can be when you use your *cabeza*. The only exception is the mamas with babies. They must sit at the end of the pew, and they should leave the church when their babies start crying."

"How about you? Why are you sitting on the first space next to the aisle?" he asked José Juárez, an elderly man.

Before José could reply, Padre Galván said, "You don't have to answer, but the answer is plain enough. You're too lazy to take another three or four more steps toward the center of the bench."

He was scolding two of the most respected, elderly members of the parish.

"That woman over there says she always sits in the same place," he continued, "but the real reason she sits up front, next to the center aisle, is so everybody can watch her while she poses like a peacock. I know her type. She wants you to notice her clothes, her new rags. Well, this is God's house, my children. We come here to see Him—God, not that woman."

Evaristo Jimenez was the fourth person Padre Galván had pointed to. He looked straight ahead at the statue of the Immaculate Conception, whispering a prayer, and his prayer was answered. The *padre* turned around and headed back to the sanctuary.

Cuca Arispe wept silently. Pilar Núñez, who was seated next to her, reached over, and arranged the old woman's black veil so that it covered her grief from view. Then she sat back and patted Cuca's hands softy. The old woman looked at Pilar through the veil and whispered, "God bless you."

José Juárez' face was tight with embarrassment. He looked down until Mass began.

The congregation sat in a state of disbelief. The *padres* assigned to their parish had never spoken to them in such accusing terms. When Mass started, the congregation went through the motions of kneeling, standing, and sitting, but their minds lingered on what he had said, and how he said it.

After Mass, a large crowd gathered at the J T Store to fuel up and to discuss the new *padre*. While most members of the parish passed off Cuca Arispe as a busybody, they all agreed that the old woman did not deserve the tongue lashing given her. José Juárez was among those at the store, and a few men patted him on the back to let him know they sympathized with him. Everybody thought Padre Galván should have used more tact. A lot more tact.

"*Se salió el padrecito*," Esquique said. "He was way out of line."

Padre Galván's second Sunday at Santa Monica's was no less remarkable than his first. He stepped down from the sanctuary fully garbed in the green vestments used for the celebration of the Mass during the Ordinary Time of the Church. He looked over the congregation and pointed to the empty pews across the aisle from where the women and children were sitting. Only a few older men and some young boys occupied the pews on that side of the aisle.

"Where are all the men?" he said. "Does the town of Meyers, Texas, have mostly women?"

No one replied.

The *padre* pointed to a woman with her five stair-stepped children sitting next to her.

"What's your name?" he asked.

"Lydia Ramos."

"Lydia, who brought you to church today?"

"My husband," she replied.

"Is he here? Which one over there is he? Lydia's husband, please stand up."

No one answered his call.

"What is his name?" Padre Galván said.

Lydia Ramos brought her hand to the side of her face. "His name is Chano, but he's not here."

"Where is Chano?"

Almost in a whisper, she said, "Outside in the car."

"And what is Chano doing in the car?"

"I don't know. Maybe smoking and listening to music."

Padre Galván moved on to the next woman.

"What is your name, and where is your husband? You have three children with you. I assume you have a husband."

"I am Maria Chagoya. My husband's name is Ismael, and he is outside talking to his friends.

"I saw a lot of men outside after the bell rang. Do you suppose what they are doing is more important than hearing Mass?"

"*Pues, no,*" Maria Chagoya said.

"Of course, not. Everybody stay seated while I go ask them the same question." With that, Padre Galván rushed out through the side door.

In less than five minutes, he was back with all the men and boys he found outside. He directed them to the empty pews at the front of the church, where they remained for the duration of the services. The women looked at one another and smiled.

After Mass, the J T Store was abuzz with parishioners discussing the *padre*, again. In truth, as someone observed, he had simply repeated the same question outside he had asked inside: "Is what you're doing more important than attending Mass?" When they replied negatively, he invited them to follow him inside, and no one declined his invitation.

"Yes, but it was kind of *gacho* the way he led us in. Like we were a herd of cows," Esquique said. "It was embarrassing."

From April through October, weekends were a time to recuperate and relax for parents and a time to celebrate for their offspring. For single young men and young women, weekends meant going to a Saturday-night dance in San Marcos, where they had a chance to meet others their age from San Marcos and the surrounding communities, like Meyers, Wile, Martindale, Kyle, Buda, Lockhart, Maxwell, and Seguin. San Marcos was the hub of entertainment for young people, and the crowds of youngsters who congregated there on Saturday nights were the entertainment itself. The music was incidental.

San Marcos had three open-air dance pavilions, conveniently situated along Highway 81, almost midway between the San Antonio-Austin corridor.

Padre Galván made his rounds of these dance centers, keeping watch over his flock. On more than one occasion, he abruptly routed young lovers from the backseats of their cars when he came through peeking into cars with his long, four-battery flashlight. The security guards left him alone and kidded that soon he would start bringing police dogs. The security guards were not concerned with the romances in the parking lots. They were there to keep the peace and intervened with the crowds only when scraps broke out between rival factions who didn't appreciate for boys outside their group to talk with their girlfriends. But that was normal and expected, and seldom did anyone find himself arrested. Even drunks were placed in their own cars to sleep it off.

After his rounds of the dance centers, the *padre* headed for the beer saloons, where men from his parish were known to hang out. It struck him as absurd that the men were inside drinking and dancing, while their wives waited patiently outside in the family car, trying to keep their children from doing harm to each other.

The instant the *padre* entered a bar the atmosphere changed. The noise level dropped, and the mood turned somber. Men continued to drink, but the dancing stopped, and the dime-a-dance girls stood talking softly, bunched up at one end of the bar.

The first time Padre Galván eased up to the bar at the Cortez Bar & Grill and ordered a beer, everyone was appalled. There was something almost sacrilegious about a man of the cloth drinking in a public place like common sinners. What followed sent out additional shock waves. He asked Julio, the bartender, to serve the dancing girls whatever they wished to drink. At first, the women declined his offer, but when he insisted, they shyly accepted, and waved nervously at their benefactor.

The bartender, refused to take his money. "On the house," he assured the *padre*. "On the house. Absolutely!"

Padre Galván went over and introduced himself to the women. He asked their names and told each one something humorous as he shook their hands.

"I'm new in Meyers," he said, "and it strikes me that I haven't seen any of you ladies in church yet. I am personally inviting you to join me for Mass this Sunday at Santa Monica's Church. How about it, Emma? I really want you there."

Emma looked perplexed and rolled her eyes. "It's been such a long time, *Padre*. I don't know."

"That doesn't matter. I promise nobody will bite you or make ugly faces at you. The house of God belongs to everybody. Unless you have something more important to do on Sunday morning?"

"No, I don't. Yes, I'll be there," Emma said, and her girlfriends applauded and cheered her on.

"How about you, Isabel?"

Isabel was also reluctant at first. "I don't know," she said.

"Say yes, dummy. I'm going," Emma said.

"Okay, okay. I'll go," Isabel said.

Padre Galván knew he had won them all over. Emma and Isabel appeared to be their leaders.

"And the rest of you? How about it? Can I count on you to be there at 10 a.m. Sunday?" He reached in his coat pocket and brought out a handful of small, pewter crucifixes. He handed one to each woman.

"These were blessed in Rome by His Holiness Pope Pius XII. In the center, you can see a relic through the little glass window. That is a piece of cloth from clothing worn by Saint Catherine of Siena. She is one of the most important saints of the Catholic Church."

The women admired their unexpected gifts.

"*Gracias, Padre*," they said.

"I'll see to it they are all there for Sunday Mass," Emma said.

"Can we sit at the back of the church?" Isabel asked.

"Wherever you like, but I'll be expecting you."

Pedro Cortez, the proprietor, rushed to open the door. Padre Galván put a firm hand on Pedro's shoulder.

"Pedro. I'd like to see you there, too. Mass lasts only an hour. How about it?"

Pedro looked at Emma and the other dancing girls. They were all anxiously awaiting his reply.

He nodded. "I'll be there," he said.

Padre Galván pushed a crucifix into the Pedro's open palm. "I'll see you in church Sunday."

"Way to go, boss," Emma said.

Pedro Cortez was the oldest in a family of eight boys and two girls. He and his siblings started working in the cotton fields of South Texas as soon as they could drag a bag with a load of cotton behind them. That did not necessarily mean a bag for each child. If it took two children to pull a canvas bag between the rows, as was the case with his two sisters, Cristina, and Josefina, then that was the way it had to be until they had the strength to pull their own. Adelaida, their mother, died shortly after Benito was born. Their father Florencio died four years later. At age seventeen, Pedro found himself the head of the Cortez family.

Until their father's death, the Cortezes were migrant workers who followed the cycle of crops within the state of Texas. Soon after he took charge, Pedro concluded the family was going nowhere if they continued doing what they had always done. It was a mad man's method of existence with no relief in sight. Year after year, migrant families replicated the same routine until they became old and incapacitated before their time.

Pedro listened to some migrants talk about the fruit orchards in California, the factories in Ohio, and the beet and potato fields in Michigan. Those men talked about wages that far surpassed what Pedro and his siblings were earning. Wages that took a laborer beyond merely subsisting. And it wasn't just talk. Their families drove decent cars, some owned houses, and on weekends, they dressed better than the average farm hand. Talking things over with his brother, Julio, who was sixteen, they considered their options.

California sounded enticing, but from what Pedro heard, it was rigorous labor with field bosses constantly harassing workers to meet unrealistic quotas. Besides, the two brothers reasoned, California was next to Mexico, and chances were that a lot of Mexican laborers crossed over into California seeking work, just as they did in Texas during the harvest season. The factories in Ohio were out the question. Stories came back about fabulous wages paid there, but those jobs were for adults only. Pedro could qualify, maybe, but not his younger brothers and sisters.

"What do you think of Michigan?" Pedro asked Julio. And then without waiting for a reply, he added, "You know, the Medinas and the Delgados go up there every year. After the harvest, they come home and rest in Meyers. They bring back enough money, so they don't have to work for five months. Sometimes, they bring back new cars. Brand new cars, Julio. I mean cars that no one has ever owned or drove before."

"Wages must be really good," Julio said. "Do you think *papá* would have liked us to go to Michigan?"

"*Papá* is gone, Julio. It's me and you who must decide. We don't have uncles to tell us what we should do. We probably have relatives in Mexico, but I wouldn't even know where to start looking. *Papá* and *mamá* never talked about the old country. I say we go to Michigan this year and try our luck. I hear they even give the workers houses to live in. One for each family, during the planting and picking seasons."

Pedro used Julio as a sounding board, but ultimately, he made all decisions. Pedro chose Michigan, and that was the end of that. He approached the Medinas, then the Delgados, on how to go about getting to Michigan and whom to contact once there. It was also Pedro who met with the work bosses in Michigan to inform them he and his family were there and ready to work. Fortunately for the Cortezes, an amiable potato-field owner, E. Jones, was impressed with Pedro's initiative, felt compassionate toward Pedro and his young family, and hired them on the spot. He assigned them two little houses because they were a family of eight. He never regretted his decision. The young family worked out well in the potato fields. He was especially impressed with Pedro's ability to control his family. E. Jones tried him out as a foreman, when one of his field managers failed to report for work. Although the boy was years younger than most workers under his charge, everyone followed his orders without begrudging him.

At the end of the season, E. Jones came to Pedro's house.

"I'm glad I hired you and your family, Pedro. It worked out better than I thought it would."

"Thank you, Mr. Jones," Pedro said.

"I know you'll be leaving for Texas soon. If you come up this way next year, I promise you a job as field manager. That means more money in your pocket and a larger house," E. Jones said, shaking Pedro's hand.

And that was the beginning of a trek that took place every year, until the family grew up and went their separate ways. The breakup started with the girls. One year, the Cortezes went up to Michigan as usual, but the two girls did not return. They married locals they met at weekend dances. With Pedro's blessing, they broke away from the Cortez clan and remained in Michigan to start their own families.

José was the next one to pull away. He married a girl from Michigan. His father-in-law was a house-painting contractor—who rather than see his daughter go off to Texas—offered José a job with his company. José traded in his dirty field overalls for the white pants, shirt, and cap of a house painter, and never looked back. Not long afterward, Arturo saw the opportunity to learn a trade and landed a job alongside his brother José. But Texas was in Arturo's blood, and after spending two winters in Michigan, he returned to the big state, and went into business for himself in San Marcos. His first business cards read "Arturo's House Painting Co." Later that changed to "Art's House Painting & Remodeling Co."

When asked why he didn't stay in Michigan, Arturo promptly replied, "It's too darn cold up there. Even birds have enough sense to fly south for the winter. One year the snow that fell on Thanksgiving Day was still on the ground on Easter Sunday. That's just too much winter for a warm-blooded Texan like me."

As Pedro put it, love and money eventually broke up the family, until only he and Julio were left. Looking after their younger brothers and sisters until they left the nest must have soured the two oldest brothers on the idea of marriage. Neither Pedro nor Julio took interest in marrying and raising another family. After eleven years of working in the Michigan vegetable fields, Pedro and Julio opened a beer saloon in Aesop, Texas, and planted permanent roots in nearby Meyers. The treks to the North ended. Pedro now had the time to pursue his penchant for reading, a habit he developed while waiting up late for his family to return from their dates on weekends. He read books and magazines on everything from current events to novels. After he joined the *compadres'* nightly get-togethers at the J T Store, he turned his attention to the histories of Mexico and Texas.

Most of the members of the Cortez family were born in Texas. Only Pedro and Julio migrated to Texas with their parents, but they had hardly any recollections of Mexico. Pedro asked among immigrants if they had known his family in the old country. Some had known Cortezes, but those Cortezes were probably not his relatives.

Julio was glad when the trips to Michigan ended. He was a gregarious individual who enjoyed having people around him all the time. As bartender at the Cortez Bar & Grill, he had the perfect job.

PLUTARCO, PADRE GALVAN AND A SMALL-TOWN CULTURE

At the start of a new year, it was customary to post a list on the front door of Santa Monica's Catholic Church with the names of those families who had contributed money during the past year through their weekly envelopes. No amounts were given, only the names of the head of each household.

Padre Galván changed that. Not only did he post amounts donated, but he also read the figures from the pulpit, interjecting personal remarks as he went along.

"Benito Martínez," he called out. "Fifty-two dollars. That's a dollar a week. Not bad. Where are you, Benito? Stand up and show your face so everyone can see you and give you a hand."

Benito stood up briefly, and shyly accepted his ovation.

"Next on the list is Pancho Garcia with eight dollars and forty-five cents. That's for the entire year. That's about sixteen cents a week. Stand up Pancho, so people can see you."

An abashed Pancho stood up.

"Pancho blows a few dollars every Saturday and Sunday at local bars, and buys beer for his friends," Padre Galván said.

"He is a splendid and generous man with everybody except the Lord. Can you raise God's donation to one dollar a week like Benito Martìnez, my son?"

"*Sí, Padre*," Pancho said, and hastily sat down.

"Cuactemoc Castellon, thirty-five dollars. That comes out to sixty-seven cents a week. I know you have a large family to feed and clothe, Cuactemoc, but I also know you spend a little money here and there for your own pleasures. Can you manage a dollar a week?"

"*Sí, como no, Padre*. I will start with today's collection."

The *padre* could only surmise how grateful Cuactemoc was that he made no mention of his carousing with the girls at Cortez's Bar and Grill.

Next on the list was Tacho Longoria. Padre Galván was laying in ambush for the unfortunate young man.

"Tacho Longoria."

Tacho shot up immediately.

"As you know, Tacho's wife, Dionisia, died eight months ago. Very unfortunate that she was called away at such a tender age. But Tacho is getting over his grief now. I see him at dances, enjoying himself, and I'm glad for him because he's still a young man. You should see Tacho on the dance floor, spinning like a top. Tacho, you contributed seven dollars and fifty cents to the church the last year. That was about fifteen cents a week."

Tacho had heard enough and decided to head off the *padre* before he revealed some of his big indiscretions. Only the night before, the *padre* had startled him and a seventeen-year-old girl while they were romantically entangled in his truck. "I'm changing my donation to a dollar a week, starting today."

"Good. Very good, my son."

Padre Galván had done his homework, and the embarrassing and sometimes painful revelations continued. Every man whom he called quickly agreed to make a one dollar-a-week contribution rather than face disclosure of improper behavior.

After half an hour, Padre Galván stopped.

"That's enough for today. We will continue next Sunday, starting with those of you who don't contribute a dollar today."

Needless to say, no one dropped his envelope in the collection basket with less than the suggested amount in it.

These events were rehashed at the J T Store after Mass, followed by much conjecture and speculation. No resolution was reached as to what steps should be taken, but everyone agreed that Padre Galván had to go.

It was Juan Tomás who first expressed the problem aloud.

"*Ese padre está loco,*" he said.

When the men broke this news to their wives, the women made the sign of the cross and prayed to God that He forgive Juan Tomás for his vast stupidity. It was a sacrilege to speak in such a foul manner about a man who had been consecrated by the holy hands of a bishop. To give false testimony against another person was sin enough, but to bear false witness against Padre Galván was a very grievous sin, certainly worse than husbands drinking and dancing with the dime-a-dance hussies at the Cortez's Bar & Grill.

That night Juan Tomás and his *compadres* discussed the *padre's* behavior again.

"This *padre* is very different," Ponciano said.

"Yes. We all know that *compadre*," Juan Tomás said. "The question was had he crossed the line"?

Esquique looked at Juan Tomás. "What line?"

"The line of proper conduct. We've never had *padres* drinking in bars and snooping around dance centers to see how people behave."

"Or telling people where to sit at church or demanding a dollar weekly donation," Ponciano said.

Joaquin cleared his throat. "Don't forget he made some of us get out of our cars and go to Mass. I don't think he had the right to do that. He treated us like a bunch of dumb animals."

"I didn't appreciate that either," Esquique said. "But what happens when he crosses the line?"

"We report him," Ponciano said. "Padre Andrés in San Marcos is his superior. Padre Galván can't go around acting like he's, our boss."

"I knew a *padre* who did some odd things too," Pedro said. "Up in Michigan, there was a *padre* who charged five dollars a pew to hear Mass. Had a sign outside that said so. Of course, nobody sat alone. The church had long benches, and fifteen people could easily sit on one bench. That came out to thirty-five cents a person. If only two people sat in a pew, they had to split the cost. Two bucks and fifty cents each. But nobody did that. Everybody sat on crowded pews."

"That *padre* was crazy, too," Juan Tomás said. "His name wasn't Galván, was it?"

"No, he was a grouchy, old, Irish *padre*. His church was in the middle of the downtown area. Nobody belonged to his church because there weren't any houses around, only business buildings and hotels."

Esquique said, "Don't let Padre Galván hear that story. It might give him ideas."

The *compadres* laughed. They were in their element. They could take any issue that piqued their curiosity and view it through many different windows. They knew how to explore and squeeze all the nectar out of a topic, finding the levity and the seriousness in it. Whatever had little conversational value, they quickly spit out like the seeds of a watermelon.

"I have a gut feeling he'll cross the line soon, and remember when he does, it will be up to us to report him," Juan Tomás said.

The *compadres* nodded. They had no idea when it would come, but they were prepared, and, as things turned out, they did not have to wait long. Four months later, during the Sunday homily, Padre Galván met with their expectations and crossed the line big time.

When you drive through a small rural community, you would venture to think nothing of much consequence is happening there. At a distance, there may be a woman pinning up her laundry, or a man with his hands in his pockets, walking casually along the side of the road, or maybe there is someone's old hound lying in the shade with its eyes closed, pretending to be asleep. Small towns are like anthills, just dusty mounds on the surface. Below is where the action takes place. There you will find all the elements of a large city, the good and the bad. They are all present, except in smaller quantities, and sometimes one person plays multiple roles.

Plutarco Sánchez was such a jumping jellybean, as movers and shakers were known in those days. He was a gambler, a porno-magazine purveyor, an inventor, an entrepreneur, a con artist, and the conceiver of dozens of get-rich-quick schemes, none of which had yet succeeded

On a shelf in his bedroom were stacks of magazines about gangster mobs from New York, Chicago, Los Angeles, and Mexico City. Next to them lay stacks of sex comic books with all the popular comic-book characters of the day involved in orgies. The two most popular female mixers of the saturnalias were Blondie Bumstead and Betty Boop, with Superwoman trailing a close third place. These popular ladies took on every male hero character from Superman to Wimpy, the hamburger epicure. The comics were published in Mexico and the dialogue was captioned only in Spanish. But that didn't matter to Plutarco's clientele, since they enjoyed the artwork. Plutarco was ahead of his time, and you could either rent a comic book or buy it outright.

One day, Plutarco saw an advertisement placed by a science organization in a New Jersey publication offering one million dollars to the first person who could invent a perpetual-motion machine. The article said that such a feat had eluded the talents of many geniuses in the past, including Archimedes, Aristotle, Galileo, Leonardo da Vinci, Nikola Tesla, and Thomas Alva Edison. This did not discourage Plutarco one iota. He pondered on the elusive machine for several days before making his preliminary sketches.

The article said machine. A machine, Plutarco reasoned, has motion. Perpetual meant the machine had to continue operating indefinitely. The article said the invention had to be self-propelled and stand-alone. In other words, nothing could help it along—it simply worked, no wind, no fuel, no springs, no anything. It could operate in a vacuum.

His first model consisted of an upright wagon wheel set on an axle, which when larded with grease allowed the wheel to rotate easily for a long time. But eventually it came to a halt. This did not discourage Plutarco. Now all he had to do was come up with that little something that would keep the wheel turning.

After much cogitation, Plutarco concluded that if he attached three two-foot chains to the wheel, equidistant from each other, he could set the wheel in motion, and it should keep spinning on its own. The downward pull of the snapping action of the chains should suffice to keep the momentum of the wheel going. It was an excellent idea, except it didn't work, but it almost did.

"Plutarco," he said to himself, "now there's an inventor's name if ever there was one. Right in there with Archimedes and Aristotle, and it sounded a lot more like an inventor than Thomas or Leonardo."

When he took the sketches of his machine to the J T Store one evening, the *compadres* were impressed.

"I'm not one of those guys who gives up easily," Plutarco said. "I've made twenty-three improvements on it so far, but it's still not quite there."

"Well, don't give up. Edison tried over a thousand different elements in his light bulb before he got the results he was looking for," Juan Tomás said.

"I'm getting close, Juan Tomás. I doubt I'll have to make a hundred changes before I get it right."

Ponciano shook his head. "The perpetual-motion machine has been the challenge of the centuries. I think it's like trying to touch your chin with your elbow. You can almost do it, but it's impossible."

Plutarco was undaunted. He worked diligently for weeks on the machine that would catapult him into fame and fortune and spoke excitedly about the latest adjustments to his invention to anyone who would listen. But as time went on, his enthusiasm waned and so did the talk about the progress of the machine that would run forever. It took two months before he admitted to the same reality Archimedes and many others had faced decades and centuries earlier. It couldn't be done.

When Plutarco stopped by for gasoline one evening, the *compadres* asked about the progress of his invention.

"I put it aside for a while," he said. "I read somewhere that the great inventors of the past gave their projects a rest when they couldn't figure something out. Like Leonardo da Vinci. He worked on making man fly on and off throughout his life. He would work on the invention for months, and then put the project aside. Later he would return to it with fresh, new ideas."

"Did da Vinci make man fly?" Esquique asked.

"Well, no," Plutarco said. "But he succeeded with a lot of other inventions. Frankly, right now, I have other things on my mind—like making some money fast. Sitting at home working on inventions that don't work doesn't put bread on the table."

On another occasion, Plutarco read a magazine article that listed the mailing addresses of a hundred prominent people, including movie stars, singers, writers, business executives, politicians, and gangsters. If he could convince each one of those celebrities to send him a dollar, Plutarco reasoned, he would receive a hundred dollars. But they could easily afford a hundred dollars each, which would bring in the incredible sum of ten-thousand dollars.

That same day Plutarco sat down at his old Underwood and composed his first letter of solicitation. It read:

Dear Mr. Henry Ford II,
I am an investor and me and my company are inviting you to join us in an important business deal. Send me $100.00 and we will invest it in something they call the New York stock market with money other important people like yourself have sent to my company. In six months, we will more than double your money and mail you a check for $200.00. Like a good businessman I am sure you see what a great opportunity this is. My charge is that I keep all I make for you over $200.00. You pay me nothing! Send your check to myself at the address at the end.
Sincerely yours,
Plutarco
Mr. Plutarco Amogono Sánchez
General Delivery
Meyers, Texas
A second letter read:

Dear Mr. Clark Gable,

We haven't met yet and boy do I have an exciting business deal for you. Send me $100.00 and I will invest it in something called the New York stock market with money from other important people like yourself. In six months, I will more than double your money and send you a check for $200.00. I keep everything I make over $200.00. This is my fee. Like an intelligent man I am sure you see this is a tremendous deal. Mail your check to the address at the bottom.

Sincerely,

Plutarco

Mr. Plutarco Amogono Sánchez

General Delivery

Meyers, Texas

Plutarco composed twenty-five letters soliciting money from the illuminati. While they carried the same message, each letter was a separate creation, and no two were exactly alike. However, he soon realized that to men like Sticky-Fingers Gus and John Rockefeller, Jr., one or two-hundred dollars was an insignificant amount of money. Soon his letters read:

Dear Mr. Gene Autry,

We haven't met and I want to let you in a big business deal because you are my favorite actor and singer. I am a stock investor. Send me a $1,000.00 and I will invest it in the New York stock market along with money other famous people sent me. In six months, I'll more than double your money and send you a check for $2,000.00. I keep everything I make over $2,000.00. That is my fee. You pay me nothing. Like a wise person you are I am sure you see this is a great deal.

Sincerely yours,

Plutarco

Send to me here.

Plutarco Amogono Sánchez

General Delivery

Meyers, Texas

It took Plutarco two weeks to compose and mail letters to everyone on the list. His old Underwood had never seen so much activity. After mailing out the last letters, he went to the post office daily. A lot of people knew about Plutarco's latest venture, and they were curious to see what results the power of the written word might bring. After a while, some letters started to arrive, but they weren't what Plutarco expected. They were his own letters, being returned due to incorrect or incomplete address.

A few weeks later, he received the picture of a beautiful woman. The accompanying letter read:

Dear Mr. Sánchez,

On the advice of her financial advisors, Miss Young regrets that she cannot fulfill your request, but I can assure you that each one of them read your letter, as did Miss Young.

They said to mention that it is a very interesting offer.

I am enclosing a picture autographed by Miss Young for the interest you have shown in her.

Sincerely,

Ida Swasey

Promotions and Advertising

Plutarco proudly showed the picture and the letter around town.

"Those people have financial advisors who make their investments for them. I guess that's why nobody sent money," he said.

The picture was an excellent black-and-white glossy of Loretta wearing a cartwheel hat. He made sure everyone noticed it was autographed by her, although on close inspection, it was obvious that the signature was also a reproduction.

Months passed without any further correspondence until one day a cryptic letter arrived from New York state. The letter read:

Plutarco Sánchez,

Hey, pal, unfortunately the government confiscated all my assets before they sent me up. But I have a couple of good buddies in the Big Apple who can use a man like yourself. If you are a tough guy and know how to use weapons, especially a sub, you're the man they are looking for. Next time you're in Brooklyn, look them up. I would introduce them to you myself, but I will be indisposed for at least another seven years if things go as planned. Find a little lounge called Ciros in Lower Manhattan and ask the bartend for Flub and Walley. That's not their real names, but the bartend knows them.

When you talk to them, show them this letter so they know you're legit. They are always looking for muscle from out of town on the quiet. They'll put you to work right away. Good money, too. Not penny ante stuff like what you probably make in Texas. And by the way, tell them to come see their pal Gus every now and then.

I can't imagine how you got ahold of my address from way out there, but, hey, drop me a line now and then. Good to hear from someone in Texas. I am sorry I can't mail you the $5,000.00 you asked for.

Best of luck.

Gus

Old Sticky Fingers

No more correspondence came after Gus's letter, not even pictures. But that did not discourage Plutarco. As a good entrepreneur, he realized he had to have several projects going at the same time to find one that succeeded. Such is life.

Plutarco fancied himself the kingpin high roller of the county. He enjoyed his reputation as a clever scoundrel, who through wit and cunning managed to stay beyond the reach of the law. And although he did not deal in illegal booze, brothels, or extortion, he tried to portray himself as Mafioso in the ilk of Capone and Luciano. For this reason, he cherished his pen-pal relationship with Sticky Fingers Gus, who no doubt was tied in with organized crime. The fact that Gus was in prison added the right touch to Plutarco's persona as a dangerous man by association.

Anyone with a bent-on gambling knew Plutarco's mother's house was the place to go. Every Saturday night, a small group of men always gathered there to play blackjack. They played on his mother's dining room table and were limited to the dealer and five players. Men waited in line to play, and the demand was great enough for Plutarco to consider expanding his business. But there was a problem. The lot on which his mother's house sat was too small to add another room.

Again, Plutarco found the solution in an old magazine. He would dig a cellar under his mother's small four-room house. There he would set up a casino like the gambling houses from the Roaring Twenties era, complete with a secret entrance where access was gained by giving the password to the person behind a sliding panel on the door.

Most of the town stopped by to see the project under construction, as shovelfuls of dirt flew out from underneath the house. There had never been a house with a basement or a cellar in Meyers, and many wondered if the house itself would fall into the hole below. It took days to carve out Plutarco's casino. He placed supports under the foundation as the digging progressed, and when the basement reached the dimensions needed, he shored up the house with cinder blocks and heavy, timber beams.

The night of the inauguration, three local girls dealt at the tables, and the operation was a run-away success even though Sheriff Krause and his deputy swooped down and raided the blackjack tables, throwing Plutarco and his card dealers in jail. Plutarco paid everyone's fine and managed to stow away over half of the gambling proceeds in a secret vault. It was a winning proposition, and the gambling continued Saturday nights and so did Sheriff Krause's occasional official visits. After a while, the raids became less frequent, then, stopped all together. Sheriff Krause started dropping by to gamble a few dollars himself.

"Aw, heck," he said. "What's the harm. Ain't nobody complaining or getting hurt."

Plutarco finally had a winner.

PLUTARCO MARRIES

Once upon a time, there stood in the middle of Saint Lazarus Cemetery a one-room, wooden-frame house with a corrugated, sheet-metal roof and no paint on its walls, inside or out. It was called *el descanso*, the resting place. It had an entrance doorway, but no door, and no windows; a dirt floor, and a table in the center of the solitary room, which in years gone by had served as a bier. At one time, it had wooden benches inside, all around the room, but those had long since vanished, as had the door. Superstition being what it is, however, no one dared steal the seven-foot table where many corpses had lain.

The *descanso* was last used decades before. Back in those days, if a person passed on in the morning, his cadaver lay fully clothed on the table for viewing, while his grave was dug. That same day, before nightfall, interment took place. If the deceased had died after midday, the viewing went on all night, with burial taking place the following morning. Much to the shame of the male population, only women and children attended the all-night vigils. The men of the area were skittish about meeting up with ghosts wandering about in the cemetery after dark. They preferred not to encroach upon the territory of the dead. They had heard too many stories about eerie things happening at those nocturnal vigils for them to tempt the dead.

For many years after the advent of modernizations such as motorized hearses, funeral parlors, refrigerated holding rooms, embalming fluids, and fancily adorned metal coffins became part and parcel of the funereal convention, the *descanso* remained in disuse at the center of the cemetery with the same grey patina that all unattended lumber eventually acquires.

Plutarco had seen the *descanso* for over thirty years before he became aware of its potential. It was during Teodoro Ponce's funeral that it struck him. Here was another money-making opportunity. How could he not have seen it before with as many funerals as he had attended at Saint Lazarus Cemetery? The Catholic Church owned the cemetery, and that same afternoon he approached Padre Javier Galván.

After detailing the dilapidated condition of the *descanso* and its utter worthlessness to anybody, Plutarco brought his spiel to a close.

"How much do you want for the old shack? I don't know if I can salvage more than a couple of boards, but I thought I should help the church by tearing it down before it falls and kills somebody."

"Don't try to con me, Plutarco," Padre Galván said. "The old shack, as you call it, has some good lumber, but the church has no use for it. And you are correct. It could fall and injure someone. Take it, it's yours."

Plutarco was not sure he had heard what he heard. "Eh, how much, *Padre*?"

"Tear the awful thing down and get it out of there. It's yours. Do you understand that?" Padre Galván said.

Plutarco was flabbergasted. Free was even better than he had anticipated. "Yes. Oh, yes. Thank you, Your Excellency." And with that, he backed out of the sacristy, hat in hand, bowing gratefully every step of the way.

For once, Padre Galván allowed himself to smile. No one had ever referred to him by a title reserved for bishops and other hierarchy of the church.

Outside an elated Plutarco sped off for his first load of aged lumber and set about dismantling the descanso with a crowbar. The lumber moaned ominously as he pulled out the long, rusty nails. He worked carefully so the boards would not splinter. He had pried loose eight ten-foot boards from the front of the building when he realized it was almost dark. No sane person would remain alone in a cemetery after nightfall. He hurriedly slid the lumber onto the bed of the truck, glancing over his shoulder every few seconds, before jumping in the pickup.

The starter whirred when he turned the key, but the engine would not start. Suddenly, it was dark. A gust of wind shook the treetops, and the *Descanso* or grave put out a loud, sorrowful moan, louder than the sound of the lumber when he removed the nails. Plutarco leaped from the vehicle, leaving his keys in the ignition, and ran down the hill toward town. He didn't slow down until he reached the road leading to his mother's house. After he passed a pair of young lovers, who were out on an evening stroll, he felt safe and walked the rest of the way home. His mother's house was only two blocks farther.

Plutarco was thirty-five. He was one of those men who never left home. After his father died and his brothers and sisters came of age and left home, he remained with his mother. He was not a bad looking man, but because of his reputation as a gambler and con artist, women shied away from him. His quest, which had so far eluded him, was to amass a large fortune and find himself a good wife. He was reputed for negotiating a few very clever business deals, yet where women were concerned, he found it difficult to initiate small talk. The only woman in his life was his mother, and up until then, that suited him fine.

He sat down at the table, and he and his mother ate supper together. After a while, his mother looked outside and asked about the truck. Plutarco told her of his earlier visit with Padre Galván and about the truck stalling out at the cemetery.

"*¿Estás loco, hijo?*" she said. "Have you lost your mind?"

"Why? I'm going to sell the lumber. I stand to make a couple of hundred dollars out of it. Maybe more."

His mother became extremely disturbed about the *descanso*.

"That house belongs to the souls of the people buried in the cemetery. If you tear it down, they will come looking for you, Plutarco. That house is where the spirits of the dead gather after the sun goes down. They are children of the night. In the morning, get back out there and nail those boards back in place. Your truck didn't start because they were protecting their house from you. Just pray nothing happens to you tonight."

"That's hogwash. My truck didn't start because I flooded the carburetor," Plutarco said, but the seed was planted, and he could not help but wonder. The *descanso* had made sounds of a person in pain. The moans were real.

That night Plutarco awoke with a throbbing pain on his right shoulder. He turned every way possible, trying to make himself comfortable, all the while whining, until his mother got up and rubbed his shoulder with Vicks.

She said, "I told you." "And this is probably just a warning, if you don't put the *descanso* back the way it was."

The pain persisted, and Plutarco did not sleep the remainder of the night.

As soon as there was enough daylight, he began his trek to the cemetery. Somewhere along the way, he noticed his shoulder hurt less as he approached the city of the dead. By the time he reached his destination, the pain had completely left him. Plutarco took the boards from the truck and leaned them in place against the *descanso*. He loaded his carpenter's apron with box nails and climbed the stepladder. The *descanso* moaned as he hammered. Softly at first, then louder and deeper and more prolonged.

Plutarco was high on the stepladder when he hammered in the final nail on the last board, he had removed the day before. The house gave an enormous groan, leaned backwards, shuttered for a few seconds, and collapsed to the ground, leaving Plutarco untouched on the stepladder in the middle of the cemetery. The seven-foot table lay crushed under the rubble. It was a curious sight to see a man standing high on a ladder and the descanso flat as a pancake on the ground.

Plutarco scrambled off the ladder and got in his truck. This time the engine started the instant he turned the key, and he hurriedly drove away from the cemetery without knowing his destination. He decided not to rely on his personal judgment since this involved the spirit world of which he knew nothing. When he came to the road leading to Isaura's house, he turned her way. Surely the witch, or whatever the mystic woman was, could advise him. He did not have much faith in magic, black or white, but enough strange things had occurred in the past twelve hours to give credence to the existence of supernatural forces.

Isaura led Plutarco into her consultation room, where she measured the size of his head with a cloth tape ruler. Then she looked deeply into his eyes and murmured an undecipherable incantation. He did not understand the soft chant, but her voice was soothing, and she smelled so fragrantly, he was ready to believe whatever she suggested. He was glad he had gone to her instead of the *padre*, who was his other choice. Padre Galván would not have received him as warmly.

Isaura held Plutarco's right hand in both her hands. "The spirits dwelling at the cemetery are quite disturbed that you destroyed their *descanso*."

"It fell," he said.

"Yes, but it fell because you removed some boards and weakened the structure."

"That's probably true," he said. "Tell them to give me three weeks, and I'll rebuild it for them and even give it a coat of paint.

"You must have the gift of prescience," Isaura said. "That's exactly what it will take to pacify those poor wandering souls."

Plutarco gave a sigh of relief. "I'm glad to hear that."

"In return, you will receive a lifetime reward, Plutarco, and I will be there for the joyous occasion," she said.

"Reward? I don't need a reward." He drew in another lung-full of her enchanting aroma. "Just tell the spirits to lay off. No funny business. Tell them I'll have their house back up as soon as humanly possible."

"They'll be glad to hear that," Isaura said.

Word got around that the old *descanso* had finally fallen and that Plutarco, of all people, had volunteered to rebuild it. Men from the town showed up after work, hammers in hand, ready to assist Plutarco with his commendable project. New cedar posts, a few boards, nails, and cement were needed, and Plutarco went into town and bought the materials at his expense. With the rebuilding of the *descanso*, his life changed. Suddenly, Plutarco had new friends. Women now greeted him on the street and smiled. People were friendlier and nicer to him. He was no longer the low-life thug they had taken him for. Around noon, a couple of women showed up on the site with a warm meal and hot coffee for him. Monica Zapata, an attractive single woman, and devout church member started lingering around making conversation with Plutarco while he ate. By the time the descanso was finished, Plutarco was mesmerized by Monica's subtle charms, and he was no longer afraid of the spirits.

On the last day of the restoration of the resting place of the dead, with his face and clothes splattered with red barn stain, and before his fellow carpenters and newly found friends, Plutarco gallantly dropped on one knee and proposed to Monica Zapata, who although in her mid-thirties, blushed with all the bashfulness of a fourteen-year-old girl and accepted.

"Why don't we get married in the *descanso*. That way we will have the entire town in attendance, living and dead," Monica suggested.

"That's an excellent idea," Plutarco said, "except I was supposed to tear down the *descanso*, not rebuild it."

Monica was not disheartened. "I'll go talk to Padre Galván. He will understand."

And so, it came to pass a few weeks later, on a gloriously sunny day, that Plutarco Amogono Sánchez stood side-by-side with Monica Elena Zapata in front of the renovated *descanso* with the citizenry of Meyers, alive and dead as witnesses, while Padre Galván bound the couple in holy matrimony before heaven and earth. Plutarco glowed with happiness in his rented tuxedo. He could hardly believe all the good luck the *descanso* had brought him.

Never had the old cemetery played host to such jubilation. The *descanso* and the cemetery's fence were festooned with colorful ribbons and paper swags. It was the grandest wedding the town had seen. After the traditional chicken-and-mole dinner, the Mercado brothers showed up with their accordions and guitars and played and sang Mexican polkas until dusk. Couples danced outside the cemetery, until Padre Galván encouraged everyone to go inside and dance for their beloved departed.

The dance then moved inside the fenced cemetery, with couples weaving and shuffling around the graves. Norberto Perez, a photographer from San Marcos, took pictures of couples dancing and drinking beer. No doubt those pictures went into family albums to the bewilderment of future generations who would view them. Plutarco's mother stood smiling by her husband's grave and whispered: "He's our last one, Santiago. Now I can join you in peace."

Isaura tapped Antonio on the shoulder. "Shall we dance, handsome?"

"I don't know how," he said.

"No excuse. You look quite handsome in your grey suit," she said. "Let's get out there in the middle where everybody can see you."

She took Antonio's left hand, placed his right on her waist, and off they went, shuffling and sliding with the other couples, dancing on the grass between the graves. Antonio would recall in years to come how smoothly Isaura had led. He learned to dance that afternoon. He was thirteen, and the thirty-two-year-old *curandera* danced with such finesse that none of his friends kidded him about dancing with an older woman. On the contrary, they stood in awe on the sidelines as Antonio and Isaura whirled past them. Antonio thought his dancing partner, in her lavender dress and light azure eyes, was the prettiest girl at the wedding. Not only that she smelled heavenly.

Before leaving the reception, Isaura stopped to wish the newlywed couple happiness. It was the first time anyone had seen Isaura at a social gathering, and few people beside her patients recognized her. Most people thought she was one of Antonio's out-of-town aunts.

Suddenly Plutarco remembered her prediction. "Is Monica my lifetime reward?" he asked.

Isaura smiled and left the celebration.

Antonio had met Isaura earlier that summer, while he sat on the bank of the San Isidro River fishing quietly. In the hour he had spent there, he pulled up only three, small sun perch, much too small to eat, but beautiful to look at. They glistened with the colors of the rainbow as would be seen through a yellow filter. He studied the fish and wondered if the hooks hurt the little creatures, then he released them back into the river. He viewed with interest the eddies swirling upstream from where he sat. Now and then he caught a glimpse of a bigger fish, as it dealt with the little vortexes, and then swam away. There weren't many big fish downstream from the dam. Five miles upstream there was a state fish hatchery where larger fish, mostly bass and some catfish, were raised and released into the river waters four times a year. Only a few of those pan-size fish found their way through the flood-release gates or over the dam for him to catch. The riverbanks north of the dam were fenced in, with *Keep Out* and *Private Property* signs posted.

"Catch any fish today, Antonio?" she asked, the instant he heard a twig crack behind him.

Antonio spun around and leapt up from his sitting position. He was alone and face-to-face with a ghost in a white dress. His first impulse was to dive into the river and swim for the opposite bank. Only her straw hat kept him from going into the water. Ghosts don't normally wear straw hats.

He had never seen the woman before. The pupils of her eyes had very little color; they were almost crystal clear. Her hair was completely white, as were her face and her arms. She was the whitest person he had ever seen.

"Did I startle you?" she asked. "I'm sorry. I'm Isaura, *Doña* Zulema's niece."

"The *curandera*, the lady who lives in the little blue house?" he asked.

"Yes. She hasn't been well so I'm taking care of her. I'm a *curandera*, too."

"How did you know my name?" Antonio said.

"Well, that wasn't magic. I've seen you at the store a couple of times. My aunt said you are Antonio, the owner's son."

"What color are your eyes?" Antonio had to ask.

"They used to be azure blue. Now they're nearly colorless."

"Yeah. That's the first thing I noticed."

"It's a pigmentation problem. It also affects the color of my skin and my hair," she added. "I have to be careful when I go outside. If I'm exposed to too much sunlight, I get high fever and blisters."

"If you walk that way, along the riverbank, you can go almost all the way to *Doña* Zulema's house in the shade," he advised.

Antonio pulled his line out of the water and wrapped it around his bamboo pole.

"Why are you fishing alone?" she asked.

"I always fish by myself. When my friends are around, they make a bunch of racket and scare the fish away."

Antonio tied the pole to the frame of his bicycle. "If you're going home now, I can walk most of the way with you."

"That's nice. Thank you. I enjoy walking along the trail by the river."

Antonio estimated she was around thirty years old and certainly too pretty to be a ghost.

"When I was little, I used to think *Doña* Zulema was a witch. I heard she could cure sick people or cast evil spells on healthy people. Harold, this friend of mine, said that during thunderstorms, a *curandera* he knew stood out in the rain with her arms raised toward the sky and talked with the evil spirits in a strange language nobody understood."

Isaura laughed. "*Curanderas* aren't witches. We don't cast evil spells or turn men into frogs. We cure people with herbs and massages and prayers. Do you believe in *curanderas*, Antonio?"

"Yes. My father goes to see *Doña* Zulema when his muscles hurt a lot, especially his back and his shoulders. Mother doesn't believe in them. She goes to a regular doctor."

Isaura nodded. "A lot of people think there is something fake or evil about what we do."

"Can you tell somebody his fortune?" Antonio asked.

"I do it all the time. I can tell your fortune with Tarot cards or by reading the lines on the palms of your hands."

"Mother doesn't believe in all that, either. A friend of mine once brought a Ouija board to my house for us to play with, and mother sent him home. She told me the Catholic Church is against such things."

"Hmm. Interesting," Isaura commented.

"But my dad believes in fortune tellers," Antonio was quick to add.

"Good. Then I can still be your friend? We just won't tell your mother. Okay?"

"Sure."

When they came to the parting of their ways, they stopped and talked another few minutes before they went in different directions. Antonio mounted his bicycle and pedaled a short distance before he looked back to wave goodbye, but Isaura had disappeared. It did not seem possible that she could have walked out of his sight so quickly. Antonio hurried away, pumping his bicycle as fast as he could, until he reached town.

PADRE GALVAN
CROSSES THE LINE

When Padre Javier Galván crossed the line, he really crossed it. The congregation witnessed it at church, Juan Tomás and his *compadres* heard about it immediately after Mass, Reverend Reymundo Andrés, Padre Galván's superior, knew of it two hours later, Bishop Leland in Austin was briefed on it before retiring for the evening, and Padre Galván learned of his *faux pas* on the carpet at the bishopric the following morning.

"Padre Galván, just what have you done that has incited your parishioners to file serious complaints against you?" the bishop asked.

"I don't know, but people these days don't like to hear the truth about themselves or to be corrected, not even from the pulpit. And they have little respect for authority."

"According to this letter, you have engaged in strange behavior since your arrival at Santa Monica's, less than a year ago."

"I'm just looking out for the spiritual welfare of the souls entrusted to my care, in the way I always have," Padre Galván said.

"We've heard that your frequent bars and drink beer with women who are paid to dance. I hope you're not dancing with them," the bishop continued.

"Those accusations are taken out of context," Padre Galván said. "I go to bars to see how my parishioners are behaving. Occasionally, I'll join them and drink half a beer, if that much, but I never dance. Sometimes I buy beer for some individuals, and I also encourage them to attend church with their families."

"I see," Bishop Leland said. "This letter claims you are abusive, that you tell people where to sit in church and how much they should contribute to the collection."

"When I came to Santa Monica's, your Excellency, everything was in a state of chaos. Almost only women with their children attended Mass, while their husbands sat in their cars outside, talking or listening to the radio. The collection was nickels and pennies. Seldom could you find a dollar bill in the collection envelopes. These people didn't even know how to genuflect. Well, I've changed all that. There are dollar bills in the collection now, and more men attend mass."

"There is also the matter of improper language used in church. I'll ask Reverend Andrés to read aloud that part of the letter."

The bishop turned to Padre Andrés. "This last paragraph, please."

Reverend Andrés took the letter and read: "Padre Galván said he caught Chago Mendoza fornicating with an unknown girl in the back seat of a car at the Fiesta Baile parking lot. He said Chago had his pants down to his knees and that he was ramming the girl with great delight. He pulled Chago out of the car and ran the girl off after scolding them both in public. Later that evening, at the same dance, Padre Galván said he saw Tacho Longoria urinating in front of a car while three girls walked by. He said, 'Tacho stood with his dick in his hand trying to get their attention.' When the young ladies saw what he was doing, they turned their heads and ran away."

"Well?" said Bishop Leland.

"It's all true. I did witness both incidents and took corrective measures."

"The language, Padre Galván? Did you say from the pulpit that the young man was ramming the girl with great delight and referred to Juan's private part by the street name?" the bishop queried.

"I don't mince my words. I use the language of the people. I want to be understood. It serves no purpose to speak Castilian Spanish if no one understands it."

"This is not East Los Angeles. You don't find your language a little extreme, considering you are dealing here with peaceful, rural people"

"No, I don't. I know these people, and at times, I must kick their asses to get their attention...your Excellency."

Bishop Leland looked at Reverend Andrés with dismay. He could not believe the garbage that came from the mouth of the consecrated man.

Reverend Andrés shrugged his shoulders helplessly.

Two months later, Bishop Leland assigned Padre Galván to a rehabilitation center in New Mexico for alcoholic clergies. Padre Galván's case was unique. No facility was available for situations like his, so off he went to the rehab farm with other wayward clerics. Reverend Andrés took over the parish until Padre Fermin Urrutia, an old Spanish missionary, was brought in out of retirement.

In the nineteen-forties, the word sex was nonexistent in mixed-company conversations. The word fringed on denoting something evil, and men were careful not to say it or discuss the subject in the presence of women and children. Therefore, many boys and girls grew up knowing little about the origins of life. As far as most children were concerned, babies somehow mysteriously appeared from their mother's stomach. When children saw farm animals or dogs mating, their parents hurried them away in another direction, leaving the impression that the animals were doing something ugly, like defecating or urinating. Boys learned the basics of conception in the street from older boys, and mothers admonished their young sons not to touch themselves there or all kinds of bad consequences were likely to result, the least of which were a pimply face, shortness of stature, a deformed hand, and impotence. On the more grievous side, their mothers told them, they were buying a one-way ticket straight to Hell, from which there was no return.

Girls grew up even less informed, unless they had married sisters or a worldly-wise young aunt who explained what awaited them on their wedding night. The learning period after the wedding ceremony was short because while most young men expected to marry a virgin, they also expected their bride to perform like a loose woman on their wedding night. Consequently, many brides found the sex act unpleasant, but kept their bedroom experiences to themselves. Few brides complained to their friends that their adventuresome husbands demanded feats better suited for contortionists and which had nothing to do with procreation. In many instances, they were erotic acts that most brides found repulsive, but never did a girl return to her parents' home to divulge that she had married a sex maniac, although there was little doubt about it in her mind.

It was men like Ricky Móntez who introduced many young ladies to their first sexual experience. On the dance floor, he was a superb dancing partner, who knew all the latest moves and dance steps. All the girls talked wildly about Ricky and wanted to dance with him.

Ricky had a secret which he shared with dozens of girls on the dance floor. When a slow musical selection started up, Ricky would guide his partner to the center of the floor, where it was crowded, and movement was limited. It was there that Ricky embraced the girls firmly, until their bodies were fused from the knees up. Looking into the girls' eyes, he swiveled his lower body, slowly grinding it into theirs so they could feel his immense member pressing brazenly against their thighs. If the girls did not flinch, he grew bolder, and soon his hands were wandering all over their breasts and buttocks. The girls who enjoyed the fondling continued to dance with him. The ones who didn't like being manhandled simply turned him down after their first trip to the center of the dance floor. Only the most extroverted girls related their delightful experience to their friends.

One night, during the band's twenty-minute break, Ricky's extraordinary manhood was finally exposed. In an impromptu display of his dancing abilities, Ricky took to the floor alone with a wooden chair as his partner, accompanied only by the clap of his hands and the rhythmic click of the metal taps on his burnt-orange Bostonian wingtips. He maneuvered this way and that, making incredible leaps and splits, while twirling the chair on one leg and leapfrogging over it forward and backward, from one side to the other, bouncing like a rubber ball. It was an amazing display of showmanship that lasted ten minutes.

For his finale, he made a run from a corner of the dance floor toward the chair in the center, looping himself end-over-end, pirouetting in midair as he went. When he reached the chair, he attempted a forward somersault that wasn't quite high enough to clear the chair, and he went crashing down hard on his right knee, as dozens of spectators looked on. Ricky did not get up, he lay on the floor, moaning with his right leg bent at an abnormal angle that was painful to look at. The impact with the concrete floor had cracked his kneecap.

An ambulance was summoned, and within minutes, two medical aides were preparing him for the ride to the hospital. They placed a pillow under his head and tried to straighten his leg. One of the medics took a pair of scissors and slit Ricky's pant leg from the cuff to the edge of his boxer shorts. When he exposed the leg, the aides looked at each other and snickered aloud. It was obvious that something other than a leg injury had prompted their reaction, and the crowd moved in for a closer inspection. Taped to the upper side of Ricky's right thigh was a seven-inch cucumber. Despite Ricky's moaning, the girls tittered and placed a hand over their mouths to keep from blurting out into fits of laughter.

Finally, the medics arranged his leg in a position where he could be lifted, and they slipped Ricky into the back of the ambulance and drove him away with the cucumber still attached.

It took many months for him to recover, but even after he could walk again, he never returned to the San Marcos dance centers. Even so, Ricky Móntez remained in the minds of many girls for the rest of their lives. Every time they saw a cucumber at the grocery store, Ricky's name and a smile came to their lips.

DON SEVERINO
SCHOOLS ANTONIO

Antonio had just finished reading his history assignment on the evening the *compadres* told the stories of Severino Serrata and Irineo Solís. Through the cashiers window between the small office and the store, he could hear the *compadres'* voices clearly. Lately, they had discussed nothing of interest to him, but that night the stories were captivating. It wasn't long before he laid down his pencil and listened to the tales of two men who had lived in the area many years ago. Because of the lives they led and the way in which they died, they had become legends, and *corridos* were composed and sung about them.

Joaquin told his story first.

"One day," he began, "*Don* Severino was out in the field, mounted on his horse, supervising his field hands, when word came that his son appeared close to death. *Don* Severino's son Genaro had fallen victim to a serious illness, which Doctor Wrin diagnosed as the dreaded influenza that had killed millions of people around the world in the past three years.

"*Don* Severino was greatly distraught, especially since Genaro was his only son. He summoned all his workers to congregate before him and ordered them to kneel and pray the rosary in the middle of the field, where they were thinning out the young cotton plants for better growth. The field hands consisted of twenty-five men. Most of them seldom prayed, some, never, but they did not question their *patron's* orders.

"The men knelt on the raw ground facing their *patron*, and *Don* Severino led. They prayed for an hour and recited the complete rosary, which consisted of the Sorrowful, the Joyful, and the Glorious Mysteries. A complete rosary that had fifteen Our Fathers, one-hundred and fifty Hail Marys, and fifteen *Gloria Patris*.

"*Don* Severino went to church only once or twice a year, so it was surprising to hear him lead and recite prayers he probably had not intoned since his boyhood, when he accompanied his mother to church. As was the custom with most men, he attended church only on special holy days. Traditionally, only women and children attended Mass every Sunday.

"On this day, *Don* Severino not only prayed, but he also cried openly, begging the Lord God to spare his son Genaro.

"'Heal my son, Jesus, my God, my Savior,' *Don* Severino cried with arms outstretched toward the heavens, 'and I promise I will become the most devout Christian you have known. I will be like a saint, devoted to doing charitable deeds. I will give the church one half of everything I earn, starting with the crop that is now in the ground. Please, Lord, save my Genaro.'

"During the rosary, dark, ominous clouds moved in from the west and suddenly it was almost dark, as though night had arrived early. *Don* Severino was still on his knees when a boy came riding fast from the direction of the main house, and *Don* Severino stood up to hear the latest news. The message was brief and devastating.

'Doctor Wrin pronounced your son Genaro dead ten minutes ago,' the rider said.

"*Don* Severino hurled his rosary to the ground and mounted his horse. After his pleas and supplications, as well as those of his laborers, it was incredible that God should let Genaro die. He rode away swiftly to verify the bad news.

"After his son's death, *Don* Severino did not allow his wife or anyone else on the farm to attend church services, and even forbade them to pray. His wife, a religious woman, cried a lot on this matter and told him he was damming himself and everyone else along with him.

"'That's too bad,' *Don* Severino said. 'I made a pact with God, and He did not keep His end of our bargain. Your God doesn't have any powers. He is nothing, that…,' and he called the Lord a terrible name that nobody dared repeat."

"His wife cried and cried. 'God will punish us all. Don't talk that way about the Lord.'"

"'Not just about the Lord, I talk that way to God Himself.' And then he went outside and pointing to the heavens, he blasphemed, reviling the Lord God with profanities. 'If you have any power, come down and kill me now. Strike me dead. Show everybody how powerful and mighty you are. Prove me wrong, you fake.'

"Everyone present held their breath. The man was taunting the Lord God Himself, but nothing happened." *Don* Severino laughed and continued to ridicule God. Then he went inside the house and grieved the death of his son.

"It is said that from that day forward, he grew old and gray-haired very fast. He lost interest in farming, leaving the crops to his hired hands to cultivate without his supervision. He drank heavily in the town's *cantinas* and seldom spoke. Sometimes he went for days without speaking to anyone, except his horses."

"Early one morning," Joaquin said, "*Don* Severino unlocked the tool shed for the field hands. It looked as if the heavens were about to open with severe thunder showers at any moment. On mornings like those, the laborers did not enter the fields. The kind of clouds building up usually brought storms and sometimes, hail.

"One of the men, knowing *Don* Severino's absentmindedness of late said, '*Patrón*, it looks like a bad storm is moving in. Should we wait another few minutes…to see what happens?'"

"*Don* Severino was sitting tall on his horse with a quirt or short-handed whip in his left hand. He groused at the farmhand. 'What for? Don't you believe your God will protect you if it rains or hails? Well, you are right. Go home. Your God is useless. You can pray all you want, but He can't stop one drop of rain from falling on your head. He can't protect anybody from anything. *Nada!*'"

"Then raising his right hand, he pointed with his index finger toward the sky, and cursed God again. At that instant, a lightning bolt screamed out of the sky, striking *Don* Severino, and knocking him headlong off his horse to the ground. Four workers, close to their *patrón*, dropped next to him. They were not seriously injured and got up immediately. *Don* Severino's horse was also knocked to the ground, but it, too, was only momentarily dazed. *Don* Severino, on whose finger the bolt of lightning discharged, did not get up. He lay dead. His face and hands had turned gray. The forefinger of his right hand was black and burnt. Some of the flesh of the other fingers of his right hand was separated from the bone. His hair was scorched, and the odor of burnt flesh wafted around his body."

"*Doña* Jovita, *Don* Severino's wife, ran out of the house to where her husband lay."

"'Get him inside the house quickly before it starts raining. One of you men, take his horse and go look for Doctor Wrin. Tell him to come as soon as possible.'

"As the men carried the lifeless body into the house, one of the men spoke up. '*Patrona*,' and said softly. '*Don* Severino is no longer with us.'"

"'I know,' she said and began to sob. 'I saw it happen from the kitchen window. I saw him raise his hand just as the lightning struck him. Was anyone else injured?'" she asked.

"'No, *patrona*, only *Don* Severino,' the men replied.

"'Why was he pointing toward the sky?' she asked.

"The men looked at each other before one of them answered. 'He was telling us that it was about to rain.'

"'Yes, *Doña* Jovita,' another said, 'He did not want us out in the fields this morning.'"

"*Don* Severino's funeral was a fine undertaking, with all the pride, pomp, and circumstance befitting a rich man. Deviating from the custom that a person who dies in the morning should be buried by sundown of the same day, *Doña* Jovita ordered her husband's Mass and burial to be held two days later. Relatives, friends, and employees came to pay their last respects as he lay in a reddish mahogany coffin in the parlor of his house.

"'*Maravilloso*,' everyone said.

"In death, *Don* Severino appeared serenely asleep. He lay quietly at rest in luxury, dressed in his black, *vaquero*, gala suit with silver handiwork on the cuffs and lapels. He wore a shirt of fine silk with embroidery on the scalloped cuffs that matched the design on the shirt's collar and on the ribbon around the crown of his *sombrero*, which lay on the coffin alongside an enormous spray of yellow roses. The person who prepared him for viewing had used his powder puff generously on *Don* Severino's face and hands to hide the gray hue that covered them.

"*Doña* Jovita ordered her servants to keep the liquor flowing from the bottles of aged whiskey stored in the cellar. The wake went on continuously for two days and two nights with plenty of food and drink for all. *Don* Severino's sudden death kept the town captive, until his body was finally taken away and laid at his final resting place on Wednesday morning.

"Harrington Funeral Home came from San Marcos to transport the body of the deceased. The hearse was a sleek, black coach with windows on all sides, adorned with black, velvet curtains held open with tasseled, gold tiebacks. A team of six black horses was ready to pull the coach.

"Out front, the men studied the rig, as the horses stood at attention, waiting for *Don* Severino's body to be loaded. There was not a dash of white hair or blemish to be found on any of the six horses. They were completely black and indistinguishable one from the others. Their coats were well groomed and glistened in the sunlight.

"The twenty-five laborers who witnessed their *patrón's* death faced a dilemma. Maybe, they pondered, the *padre* should know the circumstances surrounding *Don* Severino's death. In the past, the *padres* had refused church funeral rites and a Christian burial to anyone who committed suicide. It was an unforgivable sin, the *padre* once said, to sin while dying. And although *Don* Severino had not literally taken his own life, they reasoned, he may as well have. He tempted the Lord God, and was it not a thing worse than suicide when God Himself chooses to kill you? He was in the act of cursing at God when God struck him dead. But who among them would speak up? Maybe it was too late anyway. Besides, would the *padrecito* believe their unlikely story?

"The hearse pulled up in front of the church, and the horses came to a halt. They remained ceremoniously erect while *Don* Severino's body was removed. *Padre* Eslava stood outside the church until all the parishioners had entered. Then, he signaled for the eight pall bearers to escort the body into the house of God.

"It is said that some heard mysterious low moans when the body entered the church. The walls creaked ominously, and the ceiling fans began to sway. *Don* Severino's field hands knew they should have told the *padre* about the circumstances of their *patrón's* untimely death. They knelt together, giving each other doubtful sidelong glances. It was too late to approach *Padre* Eslava. What could they do?

"They did not have to wait long for the answer. As the coffin eased down the center aisle, a thirty-pound ceiling fan broke loose from the ceiling and went crashing down at the feet of *Padre* Eslava.

"Without losing his place in the missal he was reading, he turned casually and asked two men to remove the fan from the aisle and place it inside the railing of the sanctuary. *Don* Severino's laborers did not witness the removal. As soon as the fan hit the wooden floor, they dashed down the side aisle and out through the big, double doors to safety. Nothing else irregular occurred during the Mass, as evidenced by those who stayed.

"Meanwhile *Don* Severino's twenty-five field hands were on their way to Saint Lazarus Cemetery to await the hearse after church services. Out in the open, what could possibly happen to them, they said among themselves, and to their great relief, nothing did."

"I've heard that story before," Esquique said. "Did it really happen?"

"*Claro qué sí.*" Joaquin said. "At least, that's the way I remember it."

When the story ended, Antonio pulled out his math book and started working the ten problems of his assignment while the *compadres* discussed and added tidbits to the story Joaquin had narrated.

After a while, Antonio heard Pedro say, "Something strange like that happened when I was a boy. We lived in Redden, a little town south of San Marcos. I must have been nine or ten at the time, so I know about it mostly from what people said. I remember that every time a young man came along who fancied himself a *Don Juan Tenorio*, a ladies' man, people brought up the story of Irineo Solís, and how his wife sent him straight to Hell."

"What do you mean his wife sent him straight to Hell? Only God can do that," Esquique said. "You don't know what you're talking about."

Juan Tomás nodded. "That's right he responded.

"Hold on a minute," Pedro said. "Let me tell my story. Then you decide. All right?"

"Let Pedro talk," Ponciano said.

Pedro leaned forward in his chair, his right elbow resting on his thigh, and gave his friends a furtive look, as though he were about to reveal a long-withheld secret.

"There was this gravely ill man, *¿me entienden?* His name was Irineo Solís. They say that Irineo was a very handsome man and had done lots of things he wasn't supposed to do."

"The usual fun stuff, like gambling, whiskey and women?" Esquique asked.

"*Como friegas,*" Ponciano said. "Let the man talk."

"Yes," Pedro said. "Exactly like that. He was a *parrandero*. He liked to have a good time with the prettiest girls and the best whiskey. And when I say he liked a good time I mean a very good time."

"We get the picture," Esquique said, and turned to see if that displeased Ponciano.

Ponciano sat stoically with his arms crossed.

"Irineo was still *un muchacho*, a young man, when his father died. He left Irineo a farm with eight-hundred acres of good, fertile land, a house, a tractor, dozens of cows, and pigs, and four horses. But Irineo was young and wild. He had just turned eighteen and did not know how to manage his business. Soon the farm started losing money.

"With his business sliding downward, Irineo decided to sell off a few acres, just enough to pay off some debts. But he did not stop there. The gambling, the drinking, and the womanizing continued, and so did the sale of land, a few acres at a time. By the time Irineo turned twenty-two, the entire farm: the land, the house, the tractor, the cattle, the pigs, and the horses were gone. In four years, Irineo squandered his entire inheritance.

"Now his female companions weren't barflies and prostitutes. Many were the wives and daughters of his wealthy friends and acquaintances, respectable women who did not play around with married men, until Irineo came along and seduced them—the man had charm and taste."

"In other words, his women weren't some old cowhides. They were classy, low-mileage babes," Esquique said.

"Well, yes. You could say that." Pedro said. "After all, he was a very handsome man, and women naturally chased after him. Even when he lay dying, and he was stone broke, women would not stay away. They took him food and whiskey. They didn't care that he was penniless. They loved him."

"What about the husbands and fathers of the women he seduced? Didn't they know Irineo was hiding the brisket with their women?" Esquique asked.

"Of course, they did. That's why he ended up at the cemetery long before his time. One day an irate farmer shot Irineo as he came out of the man's barn with the man's wife. Irineo had already seduced the farmer's daughter, and when he saw his wife with Irineo, that was too much. He shot Irineo twice in the gut with a 22-caliber rifle and dragged his wife by the hair back to the house."

"He didn't shoot his own wife?" Esquique said.

"No. He just gave her the proper beating she had coming, and that was it. They say the farmer didn't think Irineo would die from the wounds. He just wanted to teach Irineo a lesson. He figured his intestines would burn like hell for a few days, and then he would be all right. A 22-rifle shot is small, you know, and he used 22 caliber shots. Most of the time, those won't even kill a large dog."

"So Irineo didn't die on the spot?" Esquique asked.

"No. He went home to his wife Laura. She loved him and always forgave his indiscretions. She hoped the shooting had taught him a lesson, and maybe he would stay at home more often, like other husbands. The doctor removed two bullets from Irineo's stomach and assured Laura the wounds were not life-threatening. No organ had been seriously damaged. In a week or two, he said, the wounds should heal.

"But the pain did not go away, and the burning sensation grew more intense with each passing day. Irineo developed an infection that the doctor overlooked and later could not control."

"Laura remained at his bedside day and night, changing the herb compresses on his stomach every four hours. About a week after the shooting, Irineo started running a high fever, along with hallucinations, and he would not eat. Irineo himself came to the realization that he was nearing the end, and asked Laura to summon the *padre* so he could confess his mortal sins. He had many. A thousand or so, he told his wife, but Laura did not send for the *padre*. Neighbors said that toward the end, they could hear Irineo screaming for the *padre* to come, but all Laura did was pray for a miracle and kept changing his compresses every four hours. A neighbor, who visited the sick man, took it upon herself to go for the *padre*, but when he arrived, it was too late. Irineo was dead. He had died two hours earlier. Laura was by Irineo's side, praying and changing the herb compresses.

"Why didn't she send for the *padre*?" Esquique said.

Pedro shook his head. "As incredible as this may sound, Laura did not summon the *padre* because his visit would make it appear Irineo was dying, and that she could not accept. She wanted her husband to recover. The doctor said he would. He's just running a little fever, she said to anyone who asked about his condition. But as the doctor told her on his second visit, Irineo was a very sick man, leaning more in the other direction than this way. He advised her to notify his closest relatives immediately. Instead, she called on *Doña* Rosalia, a *curandera*, for her professional opinion.

"The *curandera* agreed with Laura. He was just running a fever. For two dollars, she sold Laura some new herbs she had just received from Mexico, which she claimed were more efficacious than those grown locally. The *curandera* assured Laura her husband was on his way to recovery.

"Irineo's body was cold and stiff with death, and still Laura would not accept that he was dead. That's when her aunt and cousins decided that all was not well with Laura. They took her away to her aunt's house and returned to make the necessary arrangements for the funeral.

"It is said that over five hundred people went by to pay their respects as Irineo lay on a large table in the parlor of his house. There was standing room only, as people filed slowly past the makeshift bier. Women knelt next to Irineo's body and cried unashamedly. Laura's brothers took her to see her husband, but when she kept talking to the corpse and tried to apply more herb compresses to his wounds, they took her away.

"Many men went to the viewing, and after carefully studying his remains, they went outside, where other men stood drinking quietly."

"'It's him, all right,' one man said. 'He really is dead…at last.'"

"'Yeah,' another said in a gruff voice. 'The son of a gun is gone.'

"The silent men nodded.

"Throughout the countryside, the story of how the handsome, young man died was told and retold, and everyone came to the same conclusion. His wife had condemned him to eternal damnation. If she had summoned the *padre*, they reasoned, Irineo would have confessed his thousand mortal sins, received absolution, and his soul would have drifted off to heaven, with the usual deviation of a temporary stop-off in Purgatory.

But his stay in Purgatory, as everyone knew, could be shortened with masses and rosaries said on his behalf, along with some twenty-five-cent, eight-day votive candles lit at the church's side altar.

"When you think about it, Irineo really didn't have many kinds of sins on his conscience. Mostly lust and heavy drinking, but he had a lot of each kind. Maybe about five hundred of each. Irineo didn't tell Laura, only that he had about a thousand mortal sins to confess.

"The story's ending, as told by those who were present, is that when the funeral coach approached the church, the four horses pulling the hearse became agitated and would not go near the church until the coachman jumped off the hearse and lead them by the bridle. The beasts remained still in front of the church for less than a minute. The instant the church bell tolled for the deceased; the horses bolted at full speed with the coach bearing Irineo's body bouncing behind them. The coachman watched helplessly as the horses hoofed it up the street, then cut off down a dirt road, galloping on until they were out of sight.

"Several men chased after the carriage by car and on horseback. It took the better part of five hours before the runaways were located, grazing along the riverbank, with Irineo's remains still in the hearse. They returned him to the church, and the second time, the horses remained calm throughout the ceremony. By the time the services were over, there was just enough daylight left to get Irineo to the cemetery and into his grave before the veil of night descended."

THE PERSISTENCE
OF ESTEBAN CRUZ

Because of his persistent, little cough, Esteban Cruz was exempt from the chores everyone else in the family was expected to carry out on the farm. The doctor who examined him said he had weak lungs and manual labor might exacerbate his illness and put him at risk of developing full-blown tuberculosis. Consequently, Esteban was free to while away his days sitting on the front porch of his father's house, listening to the radio, and watching the world go by. At times, he strummed his guitar or drove into town on errands, but anything that resembled manual labor, his father strictly forbade. That suited Esteban just fine, as he had no desire in joining his siblings in the fields, where they toiled long hours in hot weather like beasts of burden. But as only Esteban knew, his lungs were as clear as the sky on a hot summer day. He had feigned a cough from age thirteen, and so far, the ruse had freed him from his share of obligations going on five years.

The day he received his friendly invitation from Uncle Sam, Esteban knew his life of leisure was over. He drove to San Marcos and joined the Navy. Esteban preferred sailing to the wearisome life of a foot soldier. The idea of marching around with a ten-pound rifle and a backpack strapped to his body did not appeal to his delicate nature. On the other hand, a ship sounded like a restful place. How much walking could one do on a boat?

The truth of the matter was that Esteban had never been closer than a hundred miles to the nearest ocean, and the largest boat he had seen was an eighteen-foot pleasure craft he once spotted on a lake.

Much to his family's astonishment, Esteban received an A-1 classification on his physical examination. The cursory chest x-ray the Navy gave him did not detect even a speck of damage to his lungs, as Esteban knew it wouldn't, and within days, he left the farm and went off to war.

Life in the Navy was a series of shocks to Esteban. The first time he saw the ocean, it terrified him. The horizon, the line where the sky meets the ocean, appeared higher than the shoreline, and it seemed to him that at any moment the ocean would come crashing inland and swallow up everything in sight. Esteban stood petrified on the beach until a recruiting officer assured him that in thousands and thousands of years, this had never happened. Not since Noah, anyway. Next came the shock of seeing the ship he was assigned to. It was a steel, seven-hundred-foot behemoth, which he was curtly corrected that the USS Warlord was not a boat, but a United States naval vessel, a warship.

Esteban couldn't comprehend how a steel craft weighing over 30,000 tons could remain afloat even after taking on board 1,200 men. It clearly defied the laws of nature. Petty officer second class Bill Wilkes spent the better part of an hour lecturing the astonished Esteban on the laws of buoyancy and assured him that all was copasetic. Nevertheless, when they sailed away, a wary Esteban Cruz made sure he had easy access to the lifeboats.

Esteban never saw combat. When the USS Warlord reached the Philippines, he was one of the first sailors stung by the Anopheles mosquito, and in nine days, he developed a virulent case of malaria. Drugs had little effect on the infection, and he fell into a coma. Soon thereafter, the ship's doctor had him transferred to a hospital in Honolulu, Hawaii, where he spent the remainder of his military career. The malaria led to a crippling anemia, which left him bedridden for months at a time. Rest and a little exercise were the only way his body could fight the disease, but his recovery was slow, and he remained hospitalized throughout the war. Two years after the war ended in 1945, Esteban was finally discharged and sent home, even though he was still a sick man. He was among the last soldiers to go home.

Esteban picked up his civilian life where he had left it before he joined the Navy. He went back to the wooden bench on the front porch of his father's house.

After welcoming him home with a dinner party, his family decided to allow him to rest for a period—a little vacation. But when a month elapsed, and then two more, and Esteban was still sitting on the front porch, his father approached him one evening at the dinner table.

Everyone was eager to hear Esteban's plans.

"Esteban," his father said, "you can't imagine how happy I am to have my three sons' home, safe and sound. Joel and Lupe came home when the war ended. You stayed gone a while longer. But I guess the five years in Hawaii were beneficial to your lungs and your health. You don't cough anymore, and you've never looked better.

"Now, I don't mean to hurry you none, son, but as soon as you are rested up, I expect you to take your place alongside your brothers. There is so much to do. While you boys were gone, the farm went to the dogs. It was too much work for me and your sister to handle."

Esteban had a forlorn look on his face. "It was terrible out there, *papá*—horrible. I can't start to tell you of the atrocities I saw. There was this young man with his nose blown off by a shell that exploded on the deck. And there was the twenty-five-year-old captain without legs. And a professional musician, a guitar player, who lost his right hand. And then..."

"I thought you didn't see any action?" Mariana, his sister, said.

"He didn't," Joel, his oldest brother, said. "He heard those stories in the hospital, where he was laid up resting and flirting with the cute nurses. The only action he saw was sending his buddies post cards with pictures of hula girls."

"Joel and me are the ones who saw atrocities," Lupe said. "We're the ones who got shot at."

"Now, now, boys. I'm sure the war was bad enough everywhere, but let's move on for now. I'm sure Esteban will join you in the fields soon."

"In time, *Papá*, maybe, but not too soon. Right now, what I need is two thousand dollars," Esteban said.

"Two thousand dollars. Whatever for?" Mariana said.

"Well, I've been talking to this lawyer in San Marcos, and he needs two thousand to take my case. I'll pay you back when the case is settled—with interest."

"Are you in some kind of trouble?" his father asked.

"No, *Papá*. I'm suing the Department of the Navy and the United States government. Malaria is a terrible disease. Once you get it, it stays in your body for life. Some people lose their eyesight, or get seizures, or just die from it."

"And what's your big *problema*?" Joel commented, "Or should we ask?"

"Well, ever since I contracted malaria, years ago, I don't have the energy to do anything," Esteban said.

"Yeah, tell us something new," Joel said. "You must have had a bad case of malaria before you joined the Navy."

"Joel, you know better than that. Your brother might have a point," their father said.

"When I wake up every morning, I must force myself to get out of bed. It's that difficult," Esteban said.

"Tsk. Tsk," Lupe said. "Sounds more like a serious case of lard-assitis or lazy heaviness."

"My lawyer thinks I stand a pretty good chance of recovering some money. I'm suing for one million dollars."

Joel howled. "You're out of your ever-loving."

"Think about it," Esteban said. "Two thousand dollars is all my attorney needs to file the preliminary paperwork. His take is forty percent of the million, plus the up-front two thousand."

Esteban did not get his loan, and regardless of the pleas from his father and Mariana Esteban made the bench on the front porch his habitat. Joel and Lupe did not plea. They harassed, taunted, and ridiculed him. A month later, his two older brothers decided to move the front porch to the back of the house, leaving two steps by the front door with no shade. At the rear of the house, there was no view of the road with cars and pickups going by and people waving. The panorama at the back of the house was the shed where the tractor and tools were stored, the old, two-hole outhouse, and tall grasses bending with the wind.

The change in scenery didn't faze Esteban. Soon he started receiving visitors: men in naval uniforms and expensive-looking business suits. Sometimes they stayed for hours. At times, Esteban called to Mariana that he was going into town, and he rode off with the strangers. Nobody asked Esteban about his business, nor did he come forward with information, until his father decided it was time to stop playing games.

"I understand some men in suits and uniforms came today," his father said at dinner.

"Yeah. They were naval lawyers and my lawyer, Mr. Blevins, looking into my case."

"But you didn't have the money for the lawyer," Mariana said.

"Mr. Blevins says my case is good enough to take a chance on me."

Joel looked at Esteban. "That joker can't be serious," he said.

"Serious enough to take my case."

"So, if you get a million or six-hundred thousand dollars, or whatever, what are you going to do with all that money?" Lupe asked.

"We're going for two million, but we'll settle for one. When the money comes in, I'm going to get us a new John Deere tractor for the farm, indoor plumbing for the house, and a rocking chair for the porch.

"Dream on," Joel said.

Their father didn't know what to say. All the talk about millions of dollars was so far flung. He suspected he knew what he had, a lazy son.

As the months went by, attorney Blevins' visits became more frequent. He brought manila envelopes with mysterious documents, which he discussed with Esteban, and which Esteban sometimes signed. At other times, the attorney picked up Esteban in his pre-war Buick, and they went off for several hours.

One day, Mariana served Esteban a large glass of fresh lemonade and sat down with him to share the moment. It was then she realized she had not noticed Esteban lately. He looked older. More than old, he looked haggard and worn out. He had become as old as his brothers.

"Are you ill Esteban?" she asked. "Do you feel all right?"

"Finally, somebody bothers to ask," Esteban said. " No, I don't feel all right. I tried to tell y'all that shortly after I got home, but nobody listened."

"What's the problem? I'm listening."

"Can you keep a secret for a short time?" Esteban asked.

"Of course," Mariana said.

"I'm not well at all. I'm dying," he said.

"Dying? Dying from what?" she asked.

"Anemia. Cancer of the blood. I won't last long."

"That's impossible. The doctors approved your release from the hospital when the Navy discharged you."

"They did what they could and sent me home to die." Esteban said.

"Die when?" she asked.

"Who knows? Today, tomorrow…a year from now."

One week later, a new, oak, rocking chair appeared on the porch. It was the high-back rocker Esteban had described to Mariana. That evening, Esteban felt compelled to speak after supper.

"To whom it may concern," he said, "Thank you for the rocking chair. I can't thank you enough, but don't you dare move the porch to the front of the house. I like it where it is now."

Joel and Lupe looked at each other, and a moment later, the room exploded with laughter.

"You just say the word, son, and I'll see to it that certain parties put it wherever you want it," his father said.

To the end, nobody mentioned his illness. They were kinder to him and took every opportunity to see after his comfort.

Esteban's case was litigated when he had grown too weak to appear in court and his case was settled in his favor within weeks after his death. In accordance with Esteban's wishes, a new green-and-yellow farm tractor soon appeared in the shed, followed by indoor plumbing.

ESTEBAN CRUZ WRECKS

O ne Friday evening, when the *compadres* were deep into their nightly discussions, a car drove up to the gasoline pumps. Antonio put down his history book and hurried out of the office to wait on the customer.

"It's Esteban Cruz," Juan Tomás said. "I'll take care of him."

Esteban Cruz was in his early twenties. He was a tall, slender man with white skin as transparent as an albino's, who, as far as anyone could recall, had never worked. People said Esteban contracted tuberculosis in his infancy, and the illness had left him with a weak set of lungs, precluding him from prolonged physical labor. Esteban lived at home with his father, two brothers and a sister. Everybody in the household worked in the fields, except Esteban, and his siblings were content with the meager pay their father gave them at the end of the week. Esteban whiled away his time running small errands for the family, reading magazines, and strumming his guitar. He was the family chauffer, and once a week went into town for groceries and gasoline. He always wore clean khakis with sharp pleats and a pressed white shirt.

People avoided Esteban's breath whenever he spoke to them, turning their heads away or shielding their mouths and noses with a cupped hand. Some did both, as one would in avoiding someone's offensive breath. Nobody wanted to contract the deadly tuberculosis. The old-timers still remembered how the disease had wiped out entire families during a severe outbreak many years before. Back then, it was called consumption, but it was the same pernicious disease.

Esteban went about his errands oblivious of people's fears or ignoring them altogether. On that evening, he went to the J T Store for gasoline and soda waters. He always bought Coca Colas and Pepsi Colas by the case, four of each.

As soon as Esteban entered the store, Juan Tomás's *compadres* cascaded out through the sliding side door, leaving Juan Tomás to tend to his customer.

The accident occurred only sixty feet in front of their eyes, as they waited for Esteban to leave. The *compadres* had been watching the

Mercado brothers push their Ford station wagon up the road in their direction. The car had once been an elegant vehicle with blond, wooden, exterior panels decorating its sides, but that was long ago, long before Macario Mercado purchased it from its second owner. On this night, the old station wagon was out of fuel, and the four Mercado brothers were drunk. Instead of sending someone ahead to buy a gallon of gasoline, they concluded their best option was to push the vehicle from where the tank ran dry to the nearest service station. As Macario, the eldest, pointed out, it was only four or five miles to the J T Store.

With a half-moon in the sky and not a cloud in sight, the night was clear. Macario was at the wheel, steering the vehicle down the center of the road, where the pavement was smooth. They cruised slowly under manpower and without lights.

Approaching them from the opposite direction were four men, just as inebriated, in a rattletrap pickup truck that had just passed a slow-moving car. Nobody knows why these things happen or what the chances are that this could occur on a farm-to-market road where a car or a truck might pass by every ten minutes at that time of the night, but it happened. Right there before the *compadres'* eyes the crash took place with such impact that for an instant the sky lit up as the two vehicles collided head on. The "inebriated ones," as we shall refer to the men occupying the rattletrap pickup truck, to keep them mentally apart from the drunk Mercado brothers, crashed into the Mercados' station wagon in the middle of the road at the pickup's maximum speed of fifty-two miles an hour.

Who was right, who was wrong? No one can say. The only thing for sure is that one of the inebriated ones, who was riding on the flat bed of the pickup truck, was decapitated during the collision and that his head went rolling down the road, veered off to the side, hit a telephone pole with an ugly thud, then bounced back onto the pavement again. Even at that late hour, thirty people from nearby houses rushed out to view the mangled mess. It is not every day one has an opportunity to witness such a catastrophic event, especially one that includes decapitation. It took exactly twenty minutes more for the entire population of the town of Meyers to converge at the site—all 301, to wit.

Juan Tomás's four *compadres*, the only true witnesses to the horrific crash, re-created the accident as they saw it for those arriving to see the wreckage. The new arrivals listened intently and passed the news along to those who came later, and those, in turn, did likewise to the ones who arrived after them, until everybody was giving everybody else their own spin on the sequence of events, as though they had all been present when the wreck occurred. Even the four *compadres*, who witnessed the accident, were informed about how it all happened by someone who had just arrived.

The honking-goose squabble came to a sudden halt when a hearse came wailing down the road. In small towns, hearses often doubled for ambulances, but as anyone present would have attested, the hearse was the correct vehicle in this instance, because the headless body lying by the side of the road was dead.

Gerónimo Pastrano was the unfortunate man's name. He was one of the inebriated ones who had passed-out drunk on the bed of the truck. Upon impact, the driver's door flew open, striking Geronimo on the neck like a guillotine. No one knew him except the other three inebriated ones riding in the pickup. They said he was a farmhand, who showed up at a farm near Luling three weeks earlier. He was a Mexican *bracero* from somewhere in the state Oaxaca, spoke no English, and had no relatives in the United States that they knew about.

While everyone was busy watching the flashing, red lights of the hearse as it approached the scene, Esteban Cruz decided he would take a closer look at the deceased.

The man's shirt was torn off his torso, and where his head should be, there was nothing left but bloody tendons protruding from the neck area. The sight overwhelmed Esteban. He reached for his throat, retching, and gasping for air, but was overcome. Esteban fell so neatly beside the headless Geronimo that when the hearse arrived, the two attendants picked up both bodies and laid them side by side on the floor of the hearse.

When the crowd saw this, the gaggling started all over again. Where did the second body come from? Had there not been only one fatality, not two? Well, yes, that was what everybody else thought, too. Neither the drunkards nor the inebriated ones could answer the question. Soon two ambulances arrived from Lockhart. The drunk Mercado brothers were hustled into the first ambulance and the inebriated ones into the other. Despite the tremendous impact, except for minor cuts and lots of bruises, nobody else was seriously injured.

After the vehicles left, the crowd moved over to the J T Store's parking lot, where there was sufficient light to discuss the sudden appearance of the second corpse.

Two bodies?

The mystery continued.

On the hearse's return trip to Luling, Esteban Cruz woke up. He lay staring at the overhead dome light and listening to the drone of the driveshaft under the floor. He was strapped down. Up front, two men were talking and smoking. He turned his head to view his surroundings and met with the bloodshot eyes of a severed head wedged between his shoulder and a body lying next to him. The eyes were partially open, as though he were falling asleep. Esteban's eyes rolled up, and he was out cold for the duration of the eleven-mile trip.

The attendants on the hearse were not in the habit of calling out the medical examiner late at night just to have him pronounce someone dead, who was obviously dead. They drove directly to the morgue. The dead were not predisposed to go anywhere. The required details would be handled in the morning.

The final segment in this cavalcade of events came when Esteban found himself with several defunct bodies at the morgue. The room was refrigerated and dimly lit. He awoke freezing, viewed his surroundings for an instant, and flew off the examination table. In one leap, he reached the double doors eight feet away and went running down the hall.

Fortune Walker, the lone night watchman, was in the habit of resting by the front door with one eye fixed down the hall at the double doors, where the bodies were stored. The front door was always unlocked in the event he had to make a hasty exit. He had worked there for three months, and it had not happened yet, nor had it happened to anyone who held the position before him. But on that night, Fortune was not to be disappointed nor denied. He was sitting facing the long, dark hall with his legs crossed on top of a desk when he heard the noise. It sounded like the squeaking of casters. Fortune had just enough time to lower one leg. The sharp squeak was immediately followed by a loud bang, as the double doors down the hall flew open. Before Fortune could stand up, Esteban was in the middle of the hallway, running in his direction.

"Y'all get back in that room, y'all hear," Fortune cried out, trying hard to outrun his own voice, while he made his escape out the front door.

"Mr. Jones, the manager, is gonna be mighty mad at y'all in the morning. Help me, somebody! Help! Help! Y-e-o-o-o-w!"

In his lifetime, Fortune Walker would hold many kinds of jobs, as we shall see, ranging from part-time Baptist minister to miracle worker, but he always remembered working as night door-rattler at the morgue as the worst of the lot.

FORTUNE WALKER–USED CARS AND OTHER GOODS SALESMAN

Fortune Walker is the most renown citizen Meyers, Texas, ever produced. At the height of his career, he received nationwide acclaim. Fortune was a talker, and it is said he could convince anyone of almost anything. When he became a salesman at the Four Aces Used Cars in San Marcos, he knew he had found his calling. The owner of the car lot brought Fortune, a black man, on board with the hope that sales to minorities would improve, and he was not disappointed. The lot had three other salesmen, all Anglo, and immediately Fortune took the lead in selling more cars than the others. Soon the Anglo salesmen were spying on and plotting against him. But no matter how they tried to derail his sales, Fortune managed to outsell them month after month, often to the tune of twice as many sales as the next best salesman.

When asked how he did it, Fortune would always give the same reply. "Easy. I give the customer what he wants."

"Like what—exactly?" a White salesman asked.

"Well, it's like when I was younger. I used to hang around the Greater Hay Loft in San Antonio. Farmers would pull in with their twenty-foot flat-bed trailers loaded down with bales of hay, and there they sat for days. They didn't know how to sell. Their idea of selling was to sit in the cab of their rig until somebody walked by and bought their load. Well, I tell you what. I would approach those farmers and tell them I could sell their hay in a matter of hours for a small commission."

"So, did you have any takers?"

"You bet," Fortune said, "and by sundown, most times, I had me at least one, sometimes two commissions in my pocket. Like I say, you just must give the customer what he wants.

"For instance," Fortune said, "one day a Negro, like myself, came along, sniffing at my hay. Well, right off, I knew it was probably for his boss. Ain't too many Negros buying a trailer load of hay for themselves. So, this brother looks around and finally asks, 'How much?'

"My asking price is the going asking price, same as the other guys on the lot, but here's where the difference came in. I reached in the cab and pulled out three dark-green velvet boxes, each one a different size.

"'Lookie, here,' I said, 'let me show you something.' I opened the largest box slowly right in his face, and said, 'If you buy from me today, I'll throw this in for free. Makes a nice gift for your wife or lady friend.'

"There before his eyes was a necklace with ten emerald-green stones staring up at him.

"'Man,' he said, 'that's nice, but I don't know.'

"I scratch my head and act like I'm in deep concentration. 'Well, I tell you what. You want to go home, and I want to go home. Let's do this. You buy my hay here and now, and I'll lower my price ten dollars. You can go right down the line of trailers here and find nobody cheaper."

"You really had the lowest prices?" one of the salesmen asked.

"I don't know, man, but no matter, they hardly ever checked."

"'On top of that,' I said, 'I'm, gonna give you something else to go with the necklace.'

"Then I opened the smallest velvet box and show him a set of earrings that matches the necklace, two large emerald-green studs. The man's eyes lit up like Christmas-tree lights. He can see himself making big-time points with his lady.

"But I'm not through with him just yet. Here's the clincher. At this point, I put the necklace and the earrings in his hands, like I don't expect them back.

"'Lemmie show you one more thing.' I said,' I have a bracelet here that matches the necklace and the stud earrings. They're a set, and I really don't want to split them up.'

"'Give me ten dollars for the bracelet,' I said, 'and the complete set will be yours.'

"I then opened the third velvet box, and there lays a bracelet with a double strand—mind you—a double strand of green stones that's nothing but class.

"'But it's up to you, brother,' I said. 'Just thought I'd show it to you 'cause they belong together.'

"The brother is hooked. We're not talking hay anymore, we're talking jewelry. We're talking about pleasing his ladylove. So, he bought the jewelry for a couple of hundred dollars, and I threw in the hay.

"Then I carefully put his jewelry in a bag, made him out a receipt for the hay, and assured him we would deliver by noon the next day. The costume jewelry cost me seven dollars and ninety-nine cents. My job was done, and I still had six hours of daylight left to sell more hay.

"So that's one way I have used in selling. You just give the customer what he wants, and you've got yourself a sale."

"'But what about selling to Mexicans and Whites, they're our bread and butter.'

"Actually, they are easier to sell to than Negroes," Fortune said. "Take Mexicans, for instance. When I was selling hay, a Mexican fella came along one afternoon giving my hay the once-over. He talked like an arrogant type of fella, probably a foreman at the farm where he worked. Anyway, I pretended like I wasn't really interested in his business.

"It was a Tuesday. Well, I know the sooner he buys his hay, the sooner he'll be heading back to the farm. Won't have much time left for drinking and socializing with the *señoritas*.

"'How much you want for the trailer load?' the Mexican prospect asked.

"Now the man said trailer load, not just a few bales. Still, I kinda ignored him,

'How much for the load of hay, padnah?' Pancho repeated, this time in a higher pitched voice that told me he was getting a bit aggravated with me.

"And I answered like I didn't care if he stayed or left, 'That's all right. I think I might have it sold.' And here goes the clincher: 'Besides, I don't think you can afford it.'

"Now, he was offended. I had stepped on his pride. If you want to sell something to a proud person, tell him he cain't afford it. It's like waving a red bandana in front of a mad bull. Here this proud Mexican has a Negro telling him he cain't afford a load of hay. Man! You guys ain't that fella, so you cain't begin to imagine the amount of insult I was heaping on him. It's kinda like burning the American flag and then stomping on it. See what I mean? Why he'll probably pay twice the asking price, if he's mad enough, just to prove me wrong.

"'The trailer load is going for two-hundred dollars, delivered within sixty-five miles,' I finally said.

"The Mexican snorted at me in disgust,

"'I can afford two loads like that one, padnah,' he said, and showed me a wad of twenty-dollar bills to prove it."

"Then I said, 'Lookie here, man. When is your boss expecting you back at the ranch?'

"Thursday or Friday. Why?"

"So, I said, 'Tell you what. I'll knock off ten dollars off the price, and I'll hold the load here and deliver it whatever day you say. That will give you time to shop, do a little drinking, look around town a bit, maybe visit with the *señoritas*. I know a couple of *cantinas* on Zarzamora Street where they have young girls you can dance with for a dime. Now that's a better deal than anyone around here will give you. Check 'em out.'

"You can bet your bottom dollar that *hombre* was hooked. He now had a load of hay at a good price for his boss and a couple of days to paint the town red. Always keep in mind there ain't nobody in this world more romantic than a young man on the prowl. Old ones, too, when they can get more than two-car lengths away from the house."

"Now, White folks, you ask. I guarantee nobody sells faster to a White man than a poor Negro like myself, if I play my cards right. When a White man buys something, he doesn't want anyone giving him a bunch of sass. Most White men think they know all about what they're buying and what they're willing to pay for it. They love to haggle.

"A White man looked at my trailer and said with a disdainful huff, 'This has got to be the sorriest load of hay I've seen all day. Look at the dark spots on it. That's rot. Look at how loose the bales are wired to-gether. These bales are practically falling apart. Boy, you're cheating the public out of ten pounds on every bale.

"All this time, I just stood there looking dumb, saying, 'Yes, suh. I sees what y'all means. Yes, suh. Shore do.'

"When he heard my price, he made a face and stomped off in conster-nation, mad and cussing at me and my hay, but I can tell he's interested. My hay looks every bit as good as everybody else's, the bales are tight as the next guy's and just as clean. I knew I had him hooked because he thought he'd found himself a sucker. Acts like he ain't nothing but smart, and I ain't nothing but dumb. Don't ever let a White man suspect you're smarter than he is, or you just lost the sale.

"Sure enough, after a while Whitey wandered back my way, figur-ing he could drive home the bargain he was looking for. He quoted me the ridiculously low price he was willing to pay and said that under the circumstances, he was probably bidding too high. Acted like he was doing me a favor. Well, I knew the going price of hay, so I knew he was low-balling me. I quoted him somewhere around seventy-five dollars more than the lowest price I was authorized to accept and let him dicker his way down from there.

"When I said my boss would fire me if I went any lower, he thought that was my rock-bottom price, whether it was or not. I had me a sale, and I just kept yes, pushing him until his final dollar bill was in my pocket.

"But these are just examples of sales I've made, and they can apply to any race or nationality. Study your customer. In every race and nationality, you'll find the guy who wouldn't mind getting a little extra something for his money, or the proud man who wants you to believe he can afford to buy anything, or the man so full of himself, he thinks he knows everything. Like I said, study your customer."

Armed with these revelations from Fortune Walker, the three White salesmen headed for the front door of the Four Aces Used Cars, ready to psychoanalyze the next man or woman who dared to set foot on their lot.

THE FORTUNE WALKER'S STORY

Fortune Walker's feats of persuasion were legendary, and people liked to tell of one incident because it involved the richest landowner in Thimble County, namely Mr. W.W. Wentworth, III, the kingpin, to whom people referred to as W.W. the Turd, although never to his face, of course.

W.W. owned some land in the center of Meyers, Texas, which comprised a small building with a sizeable parking lot and eight acres of unimproved land next to it. The old building was last used as a grocery store many years before, but it was the parking lot upon which Fortune Walker descended one morning with a pair of divining rods, which were nothing more than a couple of warped branches from a chinaberry tree that he had lopped off the day before and soaked overnight in linseed oil.

"Uh-huh," Fortune said, as he walked around the lot. "Uh-huh, there's something here all right."

It was Saturday morning, and with nothing more interesting to do, some twenty men gathered across the street to watch Fortune, as he walked about repeating his "mantra."

"What y'all looking for, Mr. Walker?" a small boy finally asked. "Y'all think there's water down there?"

"Water? You say water?" Fortune said. "There's a lot more than water here, boy. There's buried treasure. Maybe, gold. Not sure what, just yet."

"Gold, you don't say?"

Fortune ignored the boy and continued following his sticks wherever they led him. He remained there most of the day, approaching the property from different angles to be certain his readings were accurate. By that afternoon, the crowd across the street had doubled. Fortune took measurements with his magical sticks, and occasionally he picked up four or five rocks and piled them together here and there. The observers did not bother Fortune. He was deeply engrossed in his work. Surely the small clusters of rocks were markers, they surmised.

At about three-thirty that afternoon, Fortune finally stopped and walked over to the crowd, who awaited his findings almost as anxiously as a farmer awaiting the deliverance of an unborn calf.

"It's gold," Fortune said. "Yes, sir. Lots of gold. Probably a trunk or two of Spanish doubloons. That's a kind of gold coin the Spaniards used for money."

"Well, you better talk to W.W. the Turd before you go to digging any holes on his property," someone in the crowd shouted.

"Thank you, brother," Fortune said. "Thank you for reminding me who the property belongs to. Yes, yes. I'm going to go talk to Mr. Wentworth first thing Monday morning and draw up our legal contract."

And with that Fortune clambered into his pickup and drove away.

The crowd milled about for a while, giving their opinions on what to make of Fortune and his claim.

"*Está loco,*" Ponciano said. "The trunks of gold coins, he was talking about, the Spaniards transported in *buques,* ships. There never were any *buques* here. We're over a hundred miles from the ocean."

"Maybe not in *buques,*" Joaquin said. "There is an old legend that before Presidente Porfirio Diaz was run out of Mexico, he had several, large, wooden chests full of gold coins buried in Texas, because he thought he would escape here. Instead, the revolutionaries chased him off to Spain, but they say his gold is still buried in Texas. Somewhere."

"All I know is them divining rods has got magic in them, when used by someone who knows what he's doing," Jimmy Ray said. "And my cousin, Fortune, knows how to use them. I've seen him find water where people said there warn't none."

A tall cowboy spoke out. He had just picked up his mail at the post office across the street and lingered a while to see what the commotion was all about. "Well, Fortune had better take his sticks with him when he's goes to see old W.W., 'cause he's gonna need them to find the fastest exit to the building when the Turd chases him out," the cowboy said.

The crowd laughed loudly and started breaking up.

"Can you imagine," someone said, "Fortune Walker wasted the whole blessed day messing 'round with them silly sticks, pretending he found gold. Stupid, man. Stupid."

"Yeah," someone behind him said. "And we wasted the whole day watching him."

The building across the street from the large parking lot housed the business offices of W.W. Wentworth, III. From there he micromanaged his lands, his leases, and all his other dealings, business and personal, large, and small. It was there that Fortune Walker presented himself at ten in the morning on Monday. Fortune chose the hour of his appearance, estimating that W.W. was probably busy the first couple of hours with unfinished business from the previous working day, and he guessed correctly.

"Mr. Fortune Walker," he introduced himself, "looking to speak to Mr. W.W. Wentworth, III, on urgent business matters."

"What kind of business matters, Mr. Walker?" Clara Ann, the receptionist, asked.

"It's a business venture," Fortune replied, with all the enthusiasm he could imbue into the words.

"And what is the nature of the venture, Mr. Walker?" she said.

A tall, elderly man came through the doorway of the adjoining office. "Oh, hell, Clara Ann, we don't need all those questions. Everybody knows Fortune Walker. The only question I have is what's so almighty interesting about the parking lot out front that warranted such a crowd of onlookers Saturday? Come on in here, son," he said, and Fortune followed him triumphantly into his office.

"Okay, Mr. Walker, have a seat. What's on your mind? I don't suppose this is a social call."

Fortune found himself at ease, not tense as he had imagined he would be. He had slept little, worrying about a confrontation, and here was this kindly gentleman talking to him in a most respectful manner. W.W. was not at all what he had expected. Fortune disregarded the speech he had planned to spit out in rapid-fire sequence. Instead, he found himself saying, "I'm very good at reading divining rods. I have found water for people many times. I have also found lost articles, rings, and things someone lost."

"And what do you think you found on my vacant lot?" W.W. asked.

Fortune glanced towards the open doorway that led to the receptionist's office and leaned forward, whispering what everybody on the street already knew. "Gold," he said. "Lots of gold."

"Oh, ho, ho! Gold, you say, and lots of it," W.W. repeated. "How can you be sure?"

"These things are never a sure thing. It's not just the sticks, it's the one working them, too. If you are good at it, you can feel it as the rods lead you around. You almost know for sure when you locate something, but you're never a hundred-percent positive as to what you have found," Fortune said.

"And?" W.W. Wentworth, III, said. "What do you propose? What's the catch?"

"No catch. I don't know how far down the gold is. I don't even know if it's in coins or bullion, but I believe it's down there. If you allow me and my men to bring it up, I'll split it fifty-fifty with you. You get half, and I get half and with Fortune Walker you have nothing to lose, Mr. Wentworth. In fact, I have already marked six places where the gold is more than likely buried."

"Hmm," W.W. said, "Maybe your idea of gold isn't as cockeyed as it sounds. Before the Mexican American War, there were a lot of rich Mexican landowners hereabouts. *Hacendados*, they were called. When the Mexican American War ended, they had to make a hasty escape to Mexico when the onslaught of White settlers came through with deeds to their lands, issued by the United States government. The *hacenda-dos* were run off lands that had been in their families for generations. Some were killed and buried on their own property. That was bad. The lucky ones loaded up their wagons and fled, sometimes leaving valuable heirlooms and gold behind, buried in the ground. At least, that's what history tells us."

"Yeah, I've heard," Fortune said.

"What about the diggers?" W.W. Wentworth asked, catching Fortune off guard.

"The diggers? Oh, the diggers. Well, they work for me. I pay them. I'll take care of them out of my half."

"And what about the holes?"

"No problem, Mr. Wentworth," Fortune said. "Me and my men will fill them all up when we're done. All I need is your permission to start digging, and we're in business. I don't even need a written contract. That is unless you want one."

W.W. Wentworth, III, chuckled. "No, a handshake will do just fine, Mr. Walker. But I do have this concern. I don't want anybody falling headlong into one of those holes at night and breaking his neck. Cover them up every night, with boards or something. You hear?"

"Oh, yes, sir, Mr. Wentworth. Yes, sir."

Fortune floated out of W.W.'s office and wafted down the street toward his pickup truck. He was bursting with energy to get started. There was only a matter of convincing five or six speculating souls to work for free until the gold was found and sold.

Meanwhile W.W. Wentworth, III, sat at his desk going over the events of the morning. "Interesting, indeed," he said to himself. He pondered briefly about a written agreement and decided the handshake would suffice. After he was gone, he didn't want his heirs ridiculing him for entering such a far-flung covenant. They would think him a doting fool. And yet, what if gold were found in large quantities? Would they fault him for giving away half of it? He dwelled on that question until he decided they would think him even a greater fool if he went after the gold himself and came up empty-handed.

It took Fortune two days to assemble his crew of three black men, one Mexican, and one Anglo. Among them, they gathered the necessary tools: picks, shovels, buckets, ropes, hammers, ladders, boards, and kerosene lamps. The crew first met two nights later. They had already put in a full day in the fields and agreed to dig for three hours every night, until they struck some *hacendado's* cache. Since there were five diggers, their share would be one fifth of half of Fortune's portion. The mathematical hocus pocus of halving a whole and then subdividing half of one half into fifths was beyond their comprehension, but Fortune assured his men there would be plenty for everybody. After all, the gold had been collected and hoarded for generations by some family until it came to rest in the hands of the *hacendado* who fled to Mexico without his treasure. In the unlikely event the cache was not as lucrative as they hoped, Fortune promised to find his crew a bonus by skimming from W.W.'s half, which he would never miss—the Turd was already made of gold.

The project got underway at the southwest corner of the lot, which was farthermost from the vacant store. The store, an old, red-brick building, and the land once belonged to Sam Diviney, where he ran a grocery store for many years. After Sam died, his wife put the property up for sale. W.W. saw the For-Sale sign going up and walked across the street and bought it on the spot. He had no specific plans for the property, but as was his custom, he bought real estate cheap and sold none of it. He knew sooner or later some profitable use would come along.

Fortune's crew started with a round six-foot-wide hole. They dug for three hours every night with someone always in the hole, digging or shoveling out dirt. At the end of the night, Fortune entered the hole with his divining rods and took a reading. Then they covered the hole with boards and stored their tools in the vacant store. Fortune proudly flaunted the new brass key to the store. On his enormous key ring, he carried the keys to every car, truck, house, toolbox, gate lock, suitcase, and pad lock he had ever owned. The display of keys jangling on his belt clip made him feel important, but it was also the source of much ridicule. People laughed when they saw over two pounds of keys hanging at his side. They said he carried more keys than the warden at the federal prison.

One night, Sheriff Krause drove by the site while the men were engrossed in the excavation. He was making his rounds of the small communities under his jurisdiction, when he saw the men digging under the cover of night. The sheriff turned the cruiser around and quietly drove toward them with the car lights off. When he was almost on top of the diggers, he flipped on the spotlight and jumped out of the car with his holster unsnapped. He caught the men by surprise.

"Just what in blazes do you think you're doing?" Sheriff Krause called out.

Fortune was away at the time, so his cousin Jimmy Ray answered for the group.

"We're digging, sir" he said.

"Yeah, I can see that. What for?" the sheriff asked.

"We're digging for gold."

"Gold? Now that's a good one. Where's your digging permit? This is private property, you know," the sheriff said.

"I don't know nothing about that, but Fortune Walker has permission from Mr. Wentworth hisself," Jimmy Ray said.

"To dig at night? Unlikely," Sheriff Krause said. "Where's Fortune?"

Jimmy Ray looked at the others for help, but none came. "Well, we don't rightly know. Sometimes he goes off to the J T Store for sody waters."

"Just passed by there. It's closed," the sheriff added. "Tell you what. You boys shake off all that dirt from your clothes and shoes and get in the cruiser. I'm taking y'all in for questioning. Looks to me like y'all are trespassing and damaging private property."

Mel Strong, the only Anglo in the group, moved in front of the spotlight beam where the sheriff could see him. "What about me, sheriff. I just happened to be here, kinda helping a little bit. Do you mean me, too?"

Sheriff Krause lumbered over to where Mel stood and took a hard look at him. "I ain't exactly sending out written invitations. When I said you boys, I meant everybody who was digging. Understand? Look at the dirt all over you. Shake that stuff off before you get in my car."

When Juan Tomás opened the store the following morning, the telephone was pleading to be answered. It was Tacho Longoria, one of the men apprehended the night before.

"*Soy yo*, Juan Tomás. *Sí, sí*, Tacho Longoria. I'm in the can. We need your help." He explained the situation.

"What do you want me to do?" Juan Tomás said.

"We need for you to find Fortune Walker and tell him to bring Mr. Wentworth's permission to dig in writing, so the sheriff will let us out of jail. *¿Entiendes?*"

"*Sí*. I'll see what I can do."

"*Pero* hurry up—*por favor.*"

Juan Tomás knew all about the gold dig. He had bet Ponciano five dollars no gold would be found. Juan Tomás thought it over and decided to call W.W. instead.

The old man roared with laughter when Juan Tomás related what Tacho Longoria had told him. "I'll take care of it," W.W. said. "I'll put a call through to Sheriff Krause right now and get those boys released. Thank you for calling, Juan Tomás." Before hanging up, he said, "In fact, here comes Fortune Walker now. Ho, ho. This is going to be an interesting day."

By the time the five diggers showed up that evening, wanting some explanations, Fortune had a letter from W.W. posted on the wall of the brick building, authorizing each one in the crew by name to dig on the property. As usual, Fortune glazed things over, and within the hour the crew was back in the hole digging and shoveling out dirt.

The project went on without incident for another two weeks. Then one night it happened. When Fortune's crew was putting away their tools, Fortune went into a frenzy.

"It's here," he cried out. "It's in here."

"What's in here, 'cuz?" Jimmy Ray asked, looking around for something out of place.

"The gold, man. The gold. It's in here, somewhere in these walls or under the floor. I'm double sure," he said.

"The walls is made of brick, and the floor is solid concrete. You think old man Turd is going to let us bust up his building? You's crazy," Jimmy Ray said.

"Look, man," Tacho Longoria said. "We already dug several thirteen-foot holes, hit water, and filled them back up. We got one going at eight feet, now. Maybe, it's time to give up, and just say it was a nice try. Know what I mean?"

"It's in here, I'm a telling you people," Fortune said.

Fortune's crew looked at each other for guidance. Then Mel Strong suggested. "Fortune, how about this? If old man Wentworth gives his okay to tear into the floor and the walls of the store, we'll do it. But we ain't gonna dig outside no more."

The other diggers nodded.

Fortune Walker approved of the plan. "That's do-able, boys. That's do-able. First thing tomorrow, I'll have a talk with W.W."

True to his word, Fortune posted W.W.'s authorization on the front door of the empty store the next day. The agreement was not only permission to the dig holes in the parking lot, but also to break up the old building as they saw fit.

W.W. also re-arranged the terms for the distribution of the gold. Fortune explained it to his men. "Well, boys, it's this way. We now have written authorization to bust up this building anyway we see fit to get at the gold, but a couple of things have changed. Now we are destroying property. We're not just digging holes we can fill back up. Consequently, W.W. figures he should have a little more of the take."

"How much more is a little more?" Mel Strong asked.

"Well, you still get a fifth of half of whatever I get, same as before, but W.W. wants seventy-five percent of the gold. Says he's taking a costly risk."

"In other words, we're probably getting less than half of what we were getting before," Mel said.

"Don't worry, boys. When we find the stash, we'll skim some off the top and W.W. will never know the difference. I told y'all that before."

The crew wasn't pleased on settling for less than was originally promised. Their fifth had suddenly plummeted, and they wondered aloud how much a fifth of half of twenty-five percent of a million dollars might be.

In the end, it didn't matter if each one was entitled to a fifth or a hundred percent, because after breaking up the concrete floor and knocking massive holes in the walls of the old store, at the end of the month, the venture came up empty handed, and all parties agreed it was time to give up the search.

W.W. Wentworth, III, looked at the eyesore across the street from his office. He was the laughingstock of the town. His empty building looked like the target for field artillery exercises. His friends ridiculed him for allowing Fortune to con him. They said the Alamo survived in better condition after it was battered by 1,500 Mexican troops for thirteen days. No doubt about it, the building was in shambles, and what remained standing served as a daily reminder to W.W. of his dealings with Fortune Walker.

But money goes to money. Not a year had elapsed before the district manager of the United States Postal Service and his advisors approached W.W. Wentworth, III. They were looking for some acreage where they could set up a hub for the postal service, and Meyers, Texas, was as centrally located as they could find. W.W. escorted the gentlemen to the property across the street from his business offices.

"This is as good as it gets," W.W. said. "I'll finish knocking down this old building, and you will have over eight acres to build on. And it's next door to your present post office. I'll even offer to put up the building and lease it back to you if you prefer. I'll give you as long a lease as you need."

W.W. was angling with his best bait, and the fish did not get away. It wasn't long before the postal service started construction of a spacious building, and W.W. could not be happier. His business principle remained intact. He did not sell the land, and he now had a beautiful structure on his property, which would automatically become his in sixty years. Not that he intended to live to age a hundred and thirty-five, but he had good feelings about the transaction. Surely someone in the family would live to claim it.

THE ORTIZ MURDER

By far, the most shocking event to take place in Meyers, Texas, was the murder of Padre Luis Ortiz. When Ismael Sustaita shot and killed the new *padre* in a fit of jealous rage, the town knew he was a self-condemned man. He had ended the life and works of one of God's handpicked representatives. Ismael also murdered his own wife about three seconds later, but no one faulted him on that account. After all, he was only protecting his honor.

Padre Luis Ortiz spent thirteen years studying for the priesthood. From the tender age of fourteen until he turned twenty-seven, he lived a life surrounded by priests, male professors, and fellow seminarians. There were no women in his life. The finished product upon ordination, when he took his perpetual sacerdotal vows, was a scholastic well versed in the teachings of the patriarchs of the Church, who spoke Latin, Greek, English, and Spanish. He could quote from the bible as well as any biblical scholar, and now that he possessed the powers of celebrating Mass and of forgiving sins, he was also thought capable of assuming the responsibilities of a parish.

Eight months after his ordination, Provincial Emilio Cardona assigned Padre Ortiz to his first parish, Santa Monica's Catholic Church, in Meyers, Texas. There the young *padre* was surrounded by women, young and old, all-in competition with each other, vying for his attention. The affection lavished upon him overwhelmed Padre Ortiz. The ladies treated him like a celebrity. Some were very pretty, and they all smelled divine. Almost immediately, the young *padre* found himself wrestling with his conscience. He was attracted to women. He had not known this before because he had never been around them. Now, he understood why some fellow seminarians took leave from their studies as their ordination day drew near. Only a scarce few returned to receive their holy orders. None had ever returned with explanations as to why they chose the secular life. The reason was women, most seminarians surmised. What else could it be?

Padre Luis Ortiz's handsome looks did not go unnoticed. The younger wives tried to outdo each other preparing their best meals for him. They washed and ironed his clothes, they made his bed and cleaned his house. In return, he gave them small gifts, like inexpensive rosaries, crucifixes, small prayer books, and holy cards, which his family and friends had given him during his long years of preparation for the ministry of Christ.

A certain attractive wife came into his ken and he into hers, so that soon he was spending a lot of time with Mona Sustaita, Ismael Sustaita's wife. Alone in his house, they talked and laughed. She was prettier and smelled even better than the others. She was taken in by the fact that an educated man like him enjoyed her company. She had only a sixth-grade education. In one hour, the *padre* talked to her more than Ismael did in a week. They began to see each other daily, and quickly fell deeply in love.

Mona, who was baptized Ramona, shortened her name to Mona, which in Tex-Mex meant a smartly dressed or chic woman. When she was single, Mona often viewed herself in her full-length mirror and knew those models in fashion magazines had nothing on her. She longed to go off to a big city and become one of them, but her parents stifled her aspirations. She was not allowed to date or attend the Saturday-night dances, like her friends, and yet, young men swarmed around her wherever she went. She wanted out, where she could breathe on her own. In an attempt at freedom, she married Ismael Sustaita.

He was a hardworking, decent man four years her senior, as good as could be expected by a girl of her social status. But from the beginning, she knew she had under-married, and that her marriage was a mistake.

As those things usually go, Ismael was the last person to notice that his marriage was about to derail. When his friends pointed out his wife's sudden zealous involvement with the church, he thought nothing of it. That was the sign of a good woman. It would help in raising their family in the Catholic tradition he was raised in. Besides, since they did not yet have children, she had ample time to devote to God and the parish.

The week of Mona's birthday, Ismael stopped at Strickland's Gold and Diamond Shop in San Marcos, where he asked to see a pair of gold earrings in the shape of maple leaves with a green stone mounted on each leaf. Their price was more than he had intended to spend, but when the jeweler offered to let him pay for them in installments, the way he had paid for Mona's wedding ring, he decided to buy them.

In the same glass, display case was a beautiful string of pearls that changed colors when viewed from different angles. The salesman said they were rainbow-iridescent, cultured pearls. Ismael knew they were beyond his financial reach. Even Mona's wedding ring had not been that expensive.

It was still four days until Mona's birthday, and Ismael put the earrings in the glove compartment of his truck. The gift was not wrapped, and he left it in the small velour box the jeweler put them in. Several times a day, he reached for the box and opened it, pretending it was Mona who was seeing the earrings for the first time. Her look of surprise, her laughter, the big hug he would receive, they all played in his mind. Her birthday would fall on Saturday. They would go dancing, and she would wear the earrings so all her friends could admire them. Surely none of them owned anything quite as beautiful. Ismael wondered if this was the kind of gift a wealthy man would give his wife.

Twice, when Mona was riding with him, he fought off the urge of taking out the velour box and putting it in her hand. He wanted to see the excitement the earrings would create, but both times he overcame the temptation. A birthday gift was supposed to be given and opened on a person's birthday, not before.

Saturday morning Ismael could withhold his secret. Without saying a word, he left the little black box on the kitchen table and went in the parlor to browse through some magazines. When Mona entered the kitchen, she picked up the box, just as Ismael knew she would. He watched her open it.

"How nice," she said. "Are these for me?"

"Who else would I buy something like that for, my love? Happy birthday."

"I'm surprised you remembered," Mona said, but the ebullience Ismael had expected wasn't there. She didn't thank him or embrace him.

"How nice" was the extent of her gratitude.

"I'm taking you dancing tonight," Ismael said.

"Okay," she said. "Your breakfast will be ready in fifteen minutes."

Saturday-night dances started at sundown and broke up around midnight. They usually featured a Mexican polka *conjunto* with three or four musicians, an accordion, a bass, a guitar, and sometimes a tuba. The musicians took turns singing.

Ismael and Mona arrived in time to find seats on the permanent benches that encircled the concrete dance floor. On the way to the dance, Mona's neck and shoulders were covered with a black shawl. Now that the shawl was off, she lustrated her green dress under the bright lights for all its worth. Ismael took her hand and backed away to admire her. She was the most beautiful woman at the dance, and he told her so. When they danced, his gaze was fixed on her birthday present. The emerald-green stones of the earrings complemented her green dress. He led her past her girlfriends, where they could admire her, and after four fast polkas, they returned to their seats.

One of Mona's friends followed them. "Oh, my gosh, look at this," she said. Two other girlfriends arrived at her side with their dance partners.

"Let me see. Let me see," one of them said. "Wow! That's beautiful."

"*Qué mona*, Mona," the third woman said, and her partner nodded.

It was then that Ismael took his eyes off the earrings and noticed what everybody was so fascinated by. It was a pearl necklace, one he had never seen her wear before.

Two more couples stopped and commented on the necklace, but not a word about the new earrings.

"Is the pearl necklace your birthday present?" one of Mona's friends asked.

Under the incandescent lights, the pearls exploded with color, and Ismael faced the reality that the pearls eclipsed the earrings. He had never seen anything so beautiful. They appeared like the string of pearls he saw at the jewelry store.

As the night progressed, more people commented on the necklace, but nothing was said about the earrings, except by Mona, and then only after he asked how she liked his gift.

Whatever possessions Mona brought with her at the time of their marriage, he assumed were rightfully hers, and no inquiry about their origin was proper. But all night the question burned in Ismael's mind. Where did the pearls come from? To the woman who asked if the necklace was her birthday present, Mona said, "It was a gift. I've had it a long time."

How long? Ismael wondered. How long before they were married, and what had she done in exchange for such a luxurious gift? And why did she stop seeing the man who gave her the pearls? Perhaps he was already married.

"I've never seen you wear that necklace before," he said on the way home.

"Oh, it was at the bottom of my little jewelry box. I thought it went well with this dress, so I wore it."

He dared not pry further. Obviously, she did not want to talk about it, and he did not want to cause a rift between them. They had been married seven months and had not had their first serious argument. Some things were better left unspoken, but still, he wondered and lost sleep over the pearls.

After Mona's birthday, their lives grew quieter and apart. Mona spoke mostly when necessary or in response to his questions. Her tone was not strained, just terse and polite, but Ismael sensed that more than just the honeymoon was over.

Three weeks after Mona's birthday, Ismael dropped by Strickland's Gold and Diamond Shop and discovered a clue to the tear in his marriage. Ismael handed the clerk ten dollars and his payment card. She rang it up, punched the date paid on the card, and returned it to him. It was the first installment payment on the earrings.

Ismael drifted to the case where he first saw the earrings. Another less attractive pair occupied the space now. The string of rainbow-iridescent, cultured pearls was also gone. In its place was a gold necklace with blue stones.

The clerk moved silently across the showcase from Ismael. "Is there something I can show you, Mr. Sustaita."

"No, ma'am. There was a pearl necklace here last month, but I see it's gone now."

"Yes," she said, almost lamenting the fact. "It sold."

She pulled out a small catalog and turned a few pages. "Is this the one?"

Ismael studied the picture intently, it was like Mona's, but he couldn't be certain. "I think so."

"Sorry, but it's gone," the saleslady said.

"Thank you anyway," Ismael said and left the store.

Ismael got into the pickup but did not immediately start up the motor. He sat drumming his fingers lightly on the steering-wheel hub. He was confronted with a problem, and the jewelry store clerk probably knew the answer. Minutes passed before he threw the truck in reverse and began to back up slowly, but it was no use. He couldn't leave without finding out the truth. It cost nothing to ask, and the saleslady appeared nice enough. Ismael put the truck in first gear and re-parked in the same spot. A car that was waiting for his parking space honked twice and drove past him in a hurry.

Inside the store, the salesclerk came out to meet him as soon as she heard the doorbell chime. "Mr. Sustaita. Back already? How can I help you?"

Ismael pointed to the spot where the pearls had been. "Do you know who bought the pearl necklace?" he asked, and the question reverberated loudly inside his head.

"No, I don't know," she said. "George—I mean Mr. Strickland, the owner, must have sold it when I wasn't here. I work four days a week."

Ismael nodded. "A man helped me the last time I was here."

"That would be Mr. Strickland. I'm sorry we no longer have the item you are inquiring about. It went fast. We can order you one, but we can't guarantee it will be exactly like the one you saw. They never are. The one we had was beautiful, wasn't it."

"And very expensive," Ismael added.

"Pearls of that quality do tend to be a bit pricey," she said.

As Ismael headed home, a miasma of questions filtered into his brain, and everything he did from that time forward occurred in slow motion, like the movements of a man walking in water up to his chin. He stopped in Meyers and filled up with gasoline, although the gauge indicated the tank was over half full. Juan Tomás would later recall how Ismael stood staring blankly toward his farm, which was four miles away. He paid for the gasoline and bought a box of twelve-gauge shotgun cartridges. To the small talk Juan Tomás tried to initiate, Ismael said, "Yeah, you could say I'm going hunting."

The last four miles were an eternity. Something strange was going on at his house, and he intended to get to the bottom of things. Mona had changed. They hadn't made love in weeks, even before the silent treatment began. Not since shortly after the new *padre* arrived at Santa Monica's Catholic Church. Maybe Padre Ortiz was to blame, stuffing his wife's mind with strict moral ideals.

At first, it did not cross his mind there could be a romantic link between the *padre* and his wife. *Padres* don't have romantic affairs, he thought. They take a vow of celibacy, and Mona wasn't like some other women who fall in love with men who shower them with attention. A protestant minister had run off with a farmer's wife some time back in a town nearby, but protestant ministers can marry, not *padres*

In the past month, Mona had invited Padre Ortiz to supper every evening on weekdays. She cooked extraordinary meals, usually reserved for special occasions. She baked pies, and she acted giddy whenever he was around.

Educated people made Ismael uneasy. He never knew what to say and felt that Padre Ortiz talked down to him. He joined them the first two times the *padre* was their guest. Mona dressed in her finest. Each time he had to shower and put on clean clothes just to eat in the presence of a man one year his junior. The *padre's* conversations bored him. After the second evening of dining with the *padre*, Ismael stayed away until supper was over before he headed for home and ate alone. By that time, Ismael was not sure of what his wife was capable.

As he drove home, he eyed the orange-and-green box filled with cartridges. What could he expect to find? He was arriving home an hour early. How would he react if he found Mona in a compromising situation he did not even want to think about?

No. Not Mona. Not my Mona, he thought. She was raised a good girl, a respectable lady. And Padre Ortiz? Granted, he had only been around a short time, but one didn't question his integrity. He was a man of God. He was a spiritual person, and it should be an honor having him home for supper.

But the *padre* was also young and handsome. Mona had never mentioned his looks, only his hands. At supper, one evening, she commented on how smooth and white they were. Like they were made of white candle wax, she had said.

"Imagine," Mona said, filled with wonderment, "a twenty-seven-year-old man who has studied all his life, a man who has never stood in the middle of a cotton field. And do you know, Ismael, he plays the piano and speaks four or five languages. How marvelous."

And how handsome, she said to herself.

Disturbing images flashed through his mind as he drove. They were hugging, they were kissing. Ismael tried desperately to put the foolishness out of his head to no avail. As he reached the long driveway that led to the farmhouse, the images became more intimate. Mona was in their bed with a man. It was Padre Ortiz, and he was naked. She was naked.

He turned off the headlights, threw the pickup into neutral, and let the truck roll quietly to a stop beside the house. The *padre's* green Plymouth was in front of the car garage. Ferdie, their watchdog, stood up lethargically from where it lay and did not bark. Ismael took the 12-gauge shotgun from the gun-rack behind him and slid out of the truck. On the wooden porch at the back of the house, he put one boot in front of the other on the boards he knew from experience would not squeak. He opened the unlocked screen door and let himself in. His right index finger was on the trigger, and his hands trembled as he made his way into the house. The radio in the kitchen was blaring Mexican music from an Austin radio station.

Mona was alone in the kitchen, slowly stirring a pot over the stove. She glanced toward the door and saw her husband.

"Padre Ortiz is washing his hands. Why don't you join us, we're about ready to eat." she said.

"I think I will," he said, and waited to observe her reaction.

"Good," she said.

That was only the third evening meal Ismael, and his wife would have together with the *padre*. Mona turned down the volume on the radio, but Ismael could still hear the constant strum of the guitars and the arpeggios of the button accordion as the musicians belted out a popular *norteña* polka.

Mona was in a bubbly mood. "Do you care for Mexican polkas," she asked the *padre*. "All the days you have eaten here, and I never thought to ask. I can put something else on if you like."

"No, no. The music is fine," Padre Ortiz said.

"That's our music, you know. I enjoy listening to it when I'm eating or working. Some people prefer popular or country music, but it's mostly the *gringos*. It's their music."

"Personally, I enjoy all kinds of music," Padre Ortiz said, "especially if it's happy music."

"I like *ranchera* music," Ismael said.

"What about romantic songs, *Padre*? They can be so sad, but I love them," Mona said.

The *padre* nodded. "That's true. Some waltzes are like that, even without words, they play with the strings of your heart."

"I like *ranchera* music," Ismael repeated.

Mona squealed. "That's beautiful. 'They play with the strings of your heart.' I'll have to remember that."

Ismael resigned himself to eating. There was a conversation going on at the table, but obviously he wasn't included. It was the same treatment he received the previous times he sat down to eat with the *padre* and Mona. They talked only to each other, had eyes only for each other, and laughed only with each other. Once in a long while, they threw bits of conversation his way, like throwing scraps at a hungry dog to keep him at bay.

"What do you play on the piano?" Mona asked.

"Oh, the music of the great composers like Beethoven, Mozart, Schumann, Liszt, Chopin. The old masters. On the organ, I prefer to play the works of Bach, Palestrina, and some of Schubert's," he said between bites.

"Isn't he wonderful?" she said. "He plays the organ, too."

Wonderful, Ismael thought. Here was a woman even more ignorant than himself trying to impress the good-looking *padre*. She wouldn't know the difference between classical music and a cat pouncing on a piano keyboard in the dark.

After enjoying a sumptuous dinner of pork roast with mole and all the side-dishes that usually accompany that entrée, Mona cleared the table to make room for dessert. She went into the bedroom and returned quickly to serve everyone a cup of coffee with a slice of pie. When she sat down, she was wearing the rainbow-iridescent, cultured pearls.

Both men noticed them at the same time. The *padre* smiled and nodded at Mona. She smiled back. Ismael looked hard at the necklace, taking in every detail, and when he looked away his face was ashen. He knew. Mona had no idea how he had stumbled into the truth, but he knew. She sensed he was on the verge of exploding and turned with a distraught expression toward Padre Ortiz, who understood. Next to him sat a very somber Ismael.

"You know, Ismael," Padre Ortiz said, "I receive money which I never spend. My family and my friends constantly send me money and gifts. But I don't need any money or gifts. Everything I need is provided and paid for by the diocese: my house, my car, my gasoline, my food, my clothes. Everything.

"Since I can't use them, I like to give the money and the gifts to those deserving parishioners who give so generously of their time to the church."

Padre Ortiz placed his pale hand on Ismael's shoulder. "Ismael, you should be very proud of your wife. She keeps fresh flowers on the Blessed Mother's altar, she helps with the sweeping and cleaning of the church interior, she washes and irons the linens for the altars. She even finds time for the upkeep of my little house. She is active in two of the church's religious associations and is more dedicated toward the welfare of our parish than anyone else. That is why I found it fitting to give her something special on her birthday, as a reward for all she does for our mother the Church. I'm glad to see she's wearing the necklace tonight."

His remarks let the wind out of Ismael's sails. Ismael looked questioningly at his wife, and she at the *padre*. Now she had been caught in a lie.

The necklace had not lain at the bottom of her little jewelry box as she had told her husband.

"I'm wearing the necklace for a reason, *Padre*," Mona said. "I intend to return it to you, but first I wanted you to see how it looks on me."

"Why?" Padre Ortiz asked. "It's your reward. I don't know how else to thank you for everything you do, including these wonderful meals. No, no. Please, keep it."

"I can't. I wore it to a dance on my birthday, and it attracted so much attention I knew it wasn't right for me. People like us," she said, nodding toward Ismael, "don't buy jewelry like this. It's too fancy, too expensive."

Mona removed the string of cultured pearls and arranged it carefully in the velour box and laid it beside the padre's plate. "Thank you, though. It's very beautiful."

Ismael wasn't sure what had occurred in the past few moments. He didn't know if what he heard was true, or whether the truth had slithered past him. He looked at his wife, then turned toward the padre.

"She's right," Ismael said. "That's the kind of gift a doctor or a lawyer would buy for his wife—not a man like me, who earns his living raising crops on a small farm. We buy shiny things for our wives that we hope look expensive, but we seldom buy the real thing. When we do, it's something small and not very expensive, like the gold earrings with green stones Mona's wearing. The stones are colored glass, they only look like emeralds."

Everyone finished dessert quietly. For the first time that evening, tranquility set in.

After the Padre left, Mona lingered for a while in the kitchen. She knew the question in her husband's mind, and she had the answer ready before he asked.

Mona entered the bedroom and jumped playfully on her side of the bed. Ismael was already in bed, paging through an old magazine. Before he could utter a word, Mona turned to him.

"I'm so glad you made him take the pearls back. Poor man. I didn't know how to tell him, but you solved the problem for me. Didn't you, my love? You explained it better than I could have. You're so smart, you know that?"

"Then why did you tell me you've had them a long time?" Ismael said.

"Because I didn't know what else to tell you. If it had been a crucifix or a rosary, that would be okay. But when he showed up with a pearl necklace on my birthday, I didn't know how to refuse it without hurting his feelings. I wanted to tell you, but I was afraid…afraid you might mind."

"Why should I mind?" he asked.

"Well, you know. I didn't know *padres* gave personal gifts like that."

"Then why did you wear it to the dance?"

"Oh, that was just me. You know. I wanted to wear it just one time in public. Women are peacocks. We love to show off," Mona said.

"And the earrings I gave you aren't beautiful?"

"Of course, they are, silly. Next to my wedding ring, they are the most precious possession I have. I'm glad the pearls are gone," she said, and planted a kiss on his cheek.

She snuggled closer to her husband and put her arms around him for the first time in weeks. He asked no further question, and she knew he was convinced nothing was going on behind his back.

Ismael stared at the dark ceiling and wondered. Could a man of God find his wife attractive, attractive in the way most men find women attractive, and could his wife find the *padre* attractive in the natural way women are drawn to men? Long after Mona started breathing heavily, Ismael pondered the two questions until a third one entered his mind. If so, would they do anything about it?

From that day on, Ismael had supper with his wife and the *padre* every evening, so he could analyze their every word and gesture. Why did she look at the *padre* in that way? What did he mean when he cleared his throat twice?

The corn fields were too far from the house to see if she had visitors when he was working, but he went past the house several times during the day to keep an eye on things. Mona had an older model car, which she kept in the garage behind the house. Unless the garage doors were open, it was impossible to tell if she was home. At first, Ismael was proud of the fact that his wife was the only woman among friends who owned her own car. His friends let him know they could do the same, but they didn't want their wives traipsing about without their knowledge. Now he understood, and he was becoming a crazy man driving back and forth past his own house to see what was going on.

WHO DONE IT?!

There was an open shed behind Isidoro Chávez's house, where he and a handful of his cronies played dominoes every afternoon. It was next to Santa Monica's Catholic Church. When more than three of Isidoro's friends showed up, they switched to cards and played poker. These were all elderly men: *dons*. They played their games while they smoked hand-rolled cigarettes, told jokes, and complained about their illnesses. They reminisced about the past, of happy and sad events, and they observed everything. Now, Mona's navy-blue Ford was parked behind the church, in front of Padre Ortiz's house.

"What do you make of that woman's visits?" Donato said.

Isidoro tapped the domino in his hand on the table. "Are you suggesting something inappropriate is going on?"

"I didn't say that. All I'm saying is that I find it strange that she arrives and leaves at the same time, Monday through Friday. She stays exactly one hour. We know that Padre Ortiz and the woman are alone in the house during that time. She carries nothing in and takes nothing out, and she's too well-dressed for house cleaning. What are they doing?"

"She sure acts suspicious, the way she rushes out to get in her car," Cipriano said.

"She always covers her face with her hand or looks the other way," Fermin added.

Isidro was troubled by the conversation. "That's Mona, my godson's wife."

"Well, maybe you should find a way to tell her husband about this," Donato said. "Don't say anything's wrong. Just tell him it doesn't look right."

Cipriano chuckled. "Can you imagine the vicious *chismes* that would start flying if certain women found out about this?"

Fermin shook his head. *¡Ay, chihuahua!* Women think the worst. They have such evil minds."

"And they have big mouths to match their evil minds," Cipriano said.

Suddenly there came the sound of heels moving rapidly across the *padre's* wooden porch, as Mona rushed out of the house to get in her car.

Exactly one hour had elapsed since she arrived. None of the four men looked in her direction, even when she started the engine and drove away. Mona was sure of it. She observed them in her rearview mirror.

"I will talk to my godson tomorrow, when he is out in the field alone," Isidoro said.

In the early afternoon the following day, Isidoro parked his truck at the end of the field and waited for Ismael. It wasn't long before his godson headed in his direction.

"*Padrino*, what a pleasant surprise," Ismael said, and extended his hand to greet his godfather. "To what do I owe this unexpected visit?"

"It concerns something that I believe should be brought to your attention," Isidoro said, and he related what he and his friends had observed.

"What time does she get there, *padrino*?" Ismael asked.

"At three, every afternoon, Monday through Friday, and she leaves an hour later," Isidoro said. "See, my godson, there's probably nothing wrong with what she's doing, but it just doesn't look right. A woman alone with a man who is not her husband—every day. *¿Quién sabe, m'hijo?* If word about this gets around, it could ruin Mona's reputation. Vicious gossip travels like a grass fire on a windy day and is impossible to stamp out."

"Thank you, godfather. I'll take care of this matter."

"It is painful to come and report such things, but I thought it was my duty as your godfather."

"You did the right thing, *padrino*. Only your best friends and your worst enemies will tell a man such things. You are my best friend, *Don* Isidoro."

Ismael waited until Isidoro's pickup was out of sight before he turned the tractor around and headed home. He pulled up next to the house and walked over to the garage. Mona's car was gone. It was two-forty-five. He hurried into the house for his shotgun and a box of cartridges.

There may have been a shred of suspicion in his godfather's mind, but there was no doubt in Ismael's. Lately, he had become a stranger in his own home. Mona's laughs were forced. She did not smile with him anymore, and she ignored him when Padre Ortiz was present. Her only attempt at levity came on the night she explained her lie about where the pearls originated. She had smiled and laughed, even kissed him, to convince him she was telling the truth, but every evening, Ismael caught them with eyes locked on each other's over the dinner table.

Ismael opened the orange and green box, removed two cartridges, and slid them into the twin barrels of the twelve-gauge shotgun. He snapped the gun shut and placed it on the rack in the cab of the pickup. He turned the truck around and revved the engine as he hurried out of his driveway.

"Here we go," he said.

Those had been the last words he and his army buddies cried out before dashing forward during an attack. They were in Italy, precariously positioned behind the stone walls of bombed-out buildings. To overtake the enemy, they had to leave their safety zone and advance forward. Some said a quick prayer, others counted to three, and then with a sudden rush of adrenaline, they shouted in unison, "Here we go," and scrambled ahead to find another temporary haven before doing it again and again. There was no turning back. This was the only way to rout the enemy, a building at a time, a few yards at a time.

Isidoro and his friends were at their domino game when Ismael pulled up alongside his wife's Ford. He got out quickly and headed for the *padre's* house without closing the door of the truck. Isidoro and his friends stood up as soon as they saw Ismael was armed.

Ismael climbed the stairs and crossed the porch quickly. He turned the knob on the door, and, finding it unlocked, went in. It was a small house. The bedroom was to his left. He caught them in the middle of the sex act.

No mistake about it.

How could he be mistaken when his wife was lying naked under the man of God, and they were both sweating with pleasure.

Padre Ortiz turned toward the doorway with an astonished look on his face. He opened his mouth to speak just as Ismael raised the shotgun and fired into his face at close range.

"Oh, my God, Ismael, don't," was all Mona managed to say before Ismael fired the second cartridge into her chest.

Ismael walked slowly out of the house, dropped the weapon on the porch, and drove away.

Isidoro and his friends heard the two blasts and understood something horrific had occurred. They saw Ismael come out of the house and leave. They waited a short time, and when no one else emerged, Isidoro hurried down the street to call the sheriff from *el telefón* at the J T Store.

He returned minutes later. "The sheriff said for us to go in and see if there is anyone we can help, but not to touch anything."

The bedroom was a slaughterhouse. Padre Ortiz's face was gone as was part of Mona's chest. She was still lying under the *padre* with her legs open. He was slumped over her right shoulder. It was a ghastly sight, even for the four elderly men who had witnessed atrocities in Mexico during the Revolution. They made the sign of the cross and filed quietly out of the house, not wanting to disturb anything.

Within a half hour, an ambulance with its siren at full tilt turned into the church's horseshoe driveway, and the four domino players guided the driver to the house behind the church. Two men, dressed in white, jumped out as soon as the ambulance came to a halt, and the wailing siren faded to nothing. Sheriff Krause pulled up seconds later, accompanied by a deputy. He stationed his cruiser behind Mona's car.

Soon the first body appeared, shrouded with a white sheet. By that time dozens of the town's people were on hand, staying their distance, but watching intently.

"*¿Qué pasó?*" the crowd whispered from the rear to the front. The alternating, flashing lights on the sheriff's cruiser were on, and they drew the children to the front of the crowd. A second covered gurney came out of the house, and the crowd gasped in unison. When the news circulated that Padre Ortiz and Mona had been murdered, some of the women knelt on the gravel driveway and began to pray.

"Mona. *¿Cuál* Mona? Mona Lopez?" a woman asked.

"*No, no.* Mona Sustaita. Ismael's wife."

"Mona Sustaita? *Dios mío.*"

The ambulance sped away with its siren wailing, as the crowd huddled around the four old men who were telling Sheriff Krause what they had seen and heard. They pointed to the table under the shed, where they were sitting when it all happened. They had seen Mona arrive first and later Ismael when he got there armed with a shotgun. The sheriff jotted everything down on a note pad, including Isidoro's address. No, he did not have a telephone, Isidoro said. He had called the sheriff's office from the J T Store. Juan Tomás, the owner, was in the crowd, and Isidoro pointed him out.

"Where does Ismael Sustaita live?" Sheriff Krause asked, his note pad still open.

"Well, you take this road, like you are going to San Marcos, but before you cross the iron bridge, you take a right. You go about a mile and take a left and follow that road a good quarter mile." Isidro continued with his directions, pointing with his index finger at every turn of the way. Finally, he said, "Maybe it's better if I go and show you. It's hard to explain how to get to Ismael's house."

The sheriff agreed, and they left together in a hurry, spraying loose gravel behind them.

Isidoro rode in the backseat of the cruiser, giving directions until they approached Ismael's driveway. "That's his truck over there," he pointed out.

"The one he was driving when you saw him at Padre Ortiz's house?"

"Yes, that's the one."

They turned and drove up the driveway slowly. A hundred feet from the house, Sheriff Krause stopped the car, and he and his deputy emerged with rifles drawn. He signaled for Isidoro to stay in the car.

"Ismael, this is Sheriff Krause," he called out. "Come on out, I want to talk to you."

Both lawmen ran toward the house stooping down as they neared it. The sheriff called out to Ismael a second time, but no response came. Sheriff Krause approached the house from the front while his deputy scurried around the right side and entered the house through the back door. Seconds later, Isidoro saw the deputy come out of the front door. He threw his arms open, signaling that Ismael was not in the house.

Both men went to the back yard. The pickup's door was open on the driver's side. The deputy looked in the bed and under the truck while the sheriff opened the door of the one-car garage. They found nothing. They moved on beyond Isidoro's line of vision, behind a cluster of low trees where the windmill's tower for the water pump stood. The windmill sat atop a tall derrick, forty feet from the ground.

Isidoro waited in the car, concerned that his grandson would consider him a traitor for bringing the law to his door. He felt like a Judas ram. If he hadn't told Ismael about Mona's visits, none of this would have taken place. Ismael had done what any honorable man would do, but he wondered about the appropriateness of his own actions.

The deputy appeared from the back of the house, signaling in Isidoro's direction.

"Come on. The Sheriff wants to show you something."

Isidoro got out and hurriedly followed the deputy. Sheriff Krause was standing close to the derrick, looking at something in the Johnson grass.

"I didn't know Ismael. Is that him?" the sheriff asked.

Isidoro moved forward in the tall weeds until he saw the man lying on the ground. The man's head was twisted in an unlikely position. His eyes were half open. Only then did Isidoro realize what had happened. He cleared his throat, not sure if words would come out.

"Yes, that's him," he said. "He was my godson."

"Looks like he took a dive from the tower—headfirst," the deputy declared.

Now Isidoro knew he was Judas himself. He had driven his godson to his death, just as Judas had delivered the Divine Master to the Roman soldiers to be crucified.

After their deaths, Padre Ortiz and Mona went their separate ways. Padre Ortiz was sent by rail to Los Angeles for burial, where his relatives lived. Mona's parents had recently moved back to Lubbock, and they laid her to rest there among relatives in a family plot. Only Ismael remained in Meyers.

Many wondered if Ismael would receive Christian funeral rites. After all, he had died in sin. He murdered two people and then committed suicide. Three heinous sins.

It came as a complete surprise when Padre Andrés announced Ismael's funeral Mass would be celebrated at Santa Monica's Catholic Church with burial to follow at Saint Lazarus Cemetery. In the past, people who committed suicide were forbidden church funeral rites or burial in consecrated ground.

Unbeknown to the parishioners were Padre Andrés's supplications before Bishop Leland.

"I knew Ismael Sustaita all his life. I baptized him, you confirmed him, Your Excellency. This year, I presided over his and Mona's wedding ceremony," Padre Andrés verified. "We know he was a good Catholic."

"But what you want me to do is forbidden by our church's teachings. I cannot allow Ismael Christian funeral rites.

"That's just the point, you can. You have the power to override that belief."

"What if you are wrong, Andrés?" Bishop Leland asked.

"If anyone thinks Ismael was a bad person, I'll be by Ismael's side at the Resurrection to prove him wrong."

Padre Andrés had been in and about the Meyers community since his arrival forty-five years earlier, recently ordained in Spain. He was an old man, now, in his seventies. When he arrived in Texas, many years before, he spoke his native Castilian with the rapidity of someone trying to say everything at once, as many Spaniards do, but over the years he tempered the delivery of his speech to meet the graceful lilt of the Mexicans in that area. He was a kindly *padre*, some said saintly.

At the beginning of the homily, Padre Andrés looked out over the congregation Padre Ortiz left behind. The church was filled.

"It is no secret why I am here today and why we are holding funeral services for Ismael Sustaita," Padre Andrés told the faithful. "But I ask you not to pass judgment on his soul. Only God is entitled to do that.

"One winter morning, two men were standing on a bridge when a desperate man approached them. He had committed a terrible crime and could no longer live with the sin on his conscience. Before their very eyes, the desperate man threw himself over the bridge rail into the icy waters of the river far below and drowned. Then a marvelous thing happened. The man's soul arose from the waters of the river, shining pure and clean as snow. He went straight up through the clouds to heaven. The two men were in awe at what they had witnessed and hurried away to relate it to a holy man they knew.

"The holy man listened, and when they finished telling their story, he said, 'The desperate man may have leaped to kill himself, but there was an eternity between the bridge and the river below.'"

The congregation nodded and thought they understood. They wondered if there had been an eternity between the top of the derrick and the ground below.

FORTUNE, MIRACLE WORKER

Early one spring, news about a miracle worker in Austin, Texas, began trickling out of the local radio stations. They were remarkable stories of a man with the power to heal the sick, the sort of thing hardly anyone believed, but everyone wished were true. Antonio was by then out of college and working as an accountant for a beer distributor in Austin. Like everybody else, he discussed the sensational news with his co-workers, and dismissed them as improbable. Miracles like those the Reverend Willie Brown was allegedly performing were a thing of the past. They had not occurred since biblical times.

Congregations approached their religious leaders about the news, who were prompt to reply, "Fraud. Don't waste your money or your time on that charlatan."

"That's what we think too," their flocks said, and the whole thing would have been ignored and soon forgotten were it not for the fact that the miracles continued. Within days, the magnitude of the healer's powers reached the mainstream of the nation. Radio stations and newspapers throughout the country carried daily reports of the black minister in Texas, who could cure the sick, regardless of their afflictions. Surely it was a scam, the cynics argued. But when the media reported that Reverend Brown worked without compensation and refused all donations, except food and water, many non-believers reconsidered, and the hoopla grew so loud that pastors like Padre Erasti in Meyers, Texas, felt obligated to make a statement from the pulpit.

"The scriptures tell us we shall see many strange things toward the end of the world," he said. "Antichrists will roam the earth, who will claim to be the true Christ, and they will perform miracles. I urge you to beware of false prophets. This so-called healer in Austin isn't even Catholic. Stay away from him. He is an evil man."

But as the weeks passed, and the black minister continued healing the sick, more families began taking their ailing loved ones to him from near and far. An invalid was reportedly flown in from Tampa, Florida, and went home a cured man. A woman suffering from an acute hearing loss flew in from Phoenix, Arizona, and her hearing was restored. People suffering from arthritis claimed they felt a warm sensation and instant relief the moment the minister touched them. Patients with other maladies likewise said they felt better right away, and it was reported that few patients went home disappointed.

Reverend Brown ministered to the sick in front of his house in full view of the public. He did it quickly and in an orderly manner. He tended only to patients arriving by ambulance, which were readily available for a hundred dollars five blocks away.

As soon as an ambulance arrived, his aides brought out the patient on a gurney and placed him before the healer. Reverend Willie Brown closed his eyes and laid his hands on the afflicted person while he prayed. He told the patient to have faith, and he would feel better soon, although he might not be completely cured for a few days. After the brief encounter, the two attendants slid the patient back into the ambulance and was quickly driven away. It took Reverend Brown fewer than five minutes to dispatch a patient.

People gratefully stuffed his shirt pockets with ten and twenty-dollar bills, but he handed the money back to the crowds.

Manuel de Jesus Vásquez, Juan Tomás's father, had suffered a severe stroke six months earlier and was beginning to walk again with the aid of crutches. His wife urged him to go see the miracle worker, but he refused. He had seen miracle charlatans in Mexico, and was, therefore, not eager to meet another one. If in the end he consented to the sixty-mile trip, it was to keep peace at home. Almost everyone in the Vásquez family believed the stories the media put out and insisted that Manuel de Jesus allow Reverend Brown to heal him.

After waiting an hour in the long queue of ambulances, Manuel de Jesus reached the healer's house, where two aides brought him out immediately and placed him in front of the healer. Manuel de Jesus's wife, Pola, stood by the gurney holding his crutches.

Reverend Brown sized up the patient's situation and whispered, "*¿Anda?* Can he walk?"

"*Poquito,*" his wife said.

"Stand him up," Reverend Brown ordered his attendants. He laid his hands on the sick man's head and stepped back several paces. "Look into my eyes and walk toward me. *Anda para acá, hombre.*"

Manuel de Jesus took five small steps forward before the healer took his arm and walked him back to the gurney. The aides immediately laid the man down and slid him back in the ambulance, while the healer raised Manuel de Jesus's crutches in the air.

"This man was lame, and now he walks. Praised be the Lord. Hallelujah!" Reverend Brown proclaimed, and the crowds applauded and cheered, while Manuel de Jesus was driven away.

That evening Antonio called his father. He found Juan Tomás in a foul mood.

"The healer is a fake," Juan Tomás said. "He led everybody to believe that *papá* can't walk and that he had cured him. He did nothing for him."

"I told you he was a fake. Even grandfather knew that" Antonio reminded them. "There's a couple of guys at work who know sick people who went to see Reverend Brown, and they tell me those people are still as sick as ever, some sicker."

"There went a hundred dollars up in smoke that Ramón and I gave mother for the ambulance," Juan Tomás declared.

"You just watch. One of these days they'll expose him as a fraud," Antonio told his father.

Not long after that, Antonio picked up the newspaper and read the latest chapter on the man who had captivated the public's attention, and who had supposedly cured his grandfather. The newspaper article said that the Reverend Willie Brown, the renown black healer, had suddenly shut down his healing practice, leaving a disappointed public crying in the street in front of his rented house. The article stated that the minister had sold his fleet of used ambulances to a company in Austin and disappeared. The miracle worker's rollercoaster ride lasted three months and netted him an estimated income of $200,000 in ambulance fees, according to the publication. Another source, it said, had it at almost double that amount.

Antonio laughed when he read that the wonder worker's real name was Fortune Walker, a former used-car salesman from San Marcos, Texas, and part-time Baptist minister. Antonio knew him well. He was the man who had conned W.W. the Turd into believing there was a buried treasure on his property. He was Clear Walker's father, a boy Antonio grew up with and had once planned to navigate down the San Isidro River aboard a raft all the way to the Gulf of Mexico.

BELEN DIES, JUAN TOMÁS
HAS A HEART ATTACK

The year after Antonio graduated from Meyers Elementary School, Margaret Brandt became Mrs. Margaret Kellum, but the happy union was short-lived. Reverend Kellum developed pancreatic cancer and died exactly ninety days after he was diagnosed with the deadly disease. The marriage lasted only four years. Rumors flew that Margaret inherited a sizeable estate from her husband, which included a hefty acreage in Missouri the reverend's first wife had brought into their marriage. But Margaret Brandt Kellum loved her profession and she continued to teach well past retirement age. She hung up her pointing stick at age seventy-one, when the arthritis in her swollen legs became so acute, she could no longer stand for more than a few minutes at a time.

After high school, Antonio moved to Austin, where he rented an apartment and clawed his way through college with part-time jobs. Those were happy times for Antonio. For the first time in his life, he was living beyond the reach of his father's control. He felt liberated and able to do as he pleased, despite the fact he had never been busier, studying and working.

By the time Antonio was out of college, he was an educated young man who spoke English without an accent. He was the man his father had hoped he would be, a city slicker like Juan Tomás's three Mexican American army buddies from Chicago, the ones who conversed and joked in English with anyone, including their commanding officers. After college, Antonio settled into his first fulltime job.

Soon Antonio's thoughts turned toward his sweetheart Elena and marriage. Unlike his father, however, Antonio and his father did not go to his girlfriend's house to ask for her hand in marriage. Elena's parents were third-generation Americans, born and raised in the United States with few ties to Mexico or its customs. Antonio proposed to Elena after a dinner date at an Italian restaurant, where he presented her with the engagement ring from a set of rings she had admired at Gil's Jewelry.

Antonio and Elena set the wedding date for January, six months away, to give themselves enough time to plan and finance their wedding.

Two weeks before Christmas, tragedy struck. Antonio's mother died suddenly and without warning of a heart attack. Belén's death was the greatest shock ever in the lives of Juan Tomás and Antonio. It was incredible. She had always been there for them, the devoted wife and mother, the heart and soul of the Vásquez family. She was the healthiest member of the family, the one who arose quietly before everyone else and saw to it that her family got off to a good start. Now she was gone. She exhaled her last breath in her sleep and died peacefully.

"The day she died was the low point in my life, *m'hijo*," Juan Tomás said.

"Mine too, *papá*. The lowest."

Maria Evencia, Juan Tomás's divorced sister, moved in to care for him, but home wasn't like home anymore. The essence that transformed their house into a home was missing.

"Do you mind if we postpone our wedding for a while?" Antonio asked.

"Of course not," Elena said.

"How does June sound?"

"Sounds good to me. I've always wanted to be a June bride," she told him.

"And I, a June groom."

Elena laughed. "Seriously, I understand, and I don't mind it at all. Nobody should get married soon after a parent passes away."

"When Dad proposed to Mom, her father set a *plazo* of one year. Then her uncle died, shortly before the wedding date, and her father postponed it another year," Antonio said.

"So, they waited two years to get married?" Elena said.

"No way. My mother didn't put up with her father's old customs. She threatened to elope."

"Good for her. Enough is enough."

Antonio offered, "They gave her dead uncle the benefit of a two-month grieving period, and then got married."

"An uncle is close family, but not like one's parents," Elena opined.

Juan Tomás was at a loss to accept his wife's sudden death. He was the one with the lifelong heart problems, the one who should have died first. For years he had worried about what would become of Belén and Antonio if he had an early death, but once Antonio finished college, he knew his son would be there for her.

Four years after Belén's death, Juan Tomás suffered his first heart attack. The J T Store remained open, but the mechanic bays were closed. The doctor forbade Juan Tomás to engage in strenuous, physical labor and to refrain from lifting anything heavier than twenty-five pounds. Juan Tomás tired easily after the attack and was restricted to selling gasoline and store merchandise. Even simple oil changes and lube jobs proved too much for him to handle.

The evening discussions and storytelling continued with Ponciano and Esquique, his only two *compadres* still living in Meyers,

Antonio had always looked on his father as a strong, domineering parent, someone to fear and obey. After the heart attack, that changed. Overnight, Juan Tomás became feeble and slow. The resolute man Antonio had known all his life suddenly became a parent in need of care and supervision.

Everything was changing. After the war, fewer customers patronized the J T Store. By official count, Meyers's population remained at a constant three hundred and one, while that of the surrounding rural areas dwindled drastically. With the advent of technological inventions for raising and gathering crops, fewer hands were needed to operate farms, and people moved to the cities, where jobs were available. The same phenomenon was occurring across the United States. America was fast becoming an urban nation, and small rural communities began to die.

When a second heart attack struck, and Juan Tomás was further debilitated, Antonio urged his father to go live with him and his family. Juan Tomás, his mind in a stupor from illness and medication, compliantly moved to Austin. But it did not work out. Juan Tomás longed for his friends and his home. Antonio could see his father was withering away, sitting in the same chair, staring out of the same window, day after day. He was an unhappy man.

After nine months, Antonio moved his father back to Meyers and reopened the J T Store with sufficient stock to restore Juan Tomas's dignity as a bona fide businessman, but not enough to tire or stress him out. Maria Evencia again took charge of the household.

Although his wife had died four years earlier, Juan Tomás still missed her greatly. Antonio hoped that taking him back to his beloved, little town, where he and Belén grew up, was a consolation to his father. Juan Tomás was back in his familiar surroundings: his friends, his business, and the comfort of his own bed. He was home to live out the remainder of his days.

When the end came, a year and nine months later, he died of a massive stroke while tending to a customer who had purchased four dollars of regular gasoline. Juan Tomás opened the cash register with the four one-dollar bills clutched in his right hand and collapsed.

IN LIFE ALL THINGS MUST END

Antonio knew his father would not last long, and he wanted him to die happy on the acre of land where he had lived most of his life. Antonio called the Cross Gulf Oil Co and placed a fuel order for ethyl and regular gasoline, the same order his father had called in for over two decades. The station was not equipped with extra pumps or tanks for diesel, super octane, or any of the new blends.

The following morning, a young man, no more than twenty-five years old, appeared with the delivery truck. He looked familiar, although Antonio was certain they had never met.

"My father will run the station," Antonio said, while the young man pumped gasoline into the underground tanks. "We shut the store down last year due to illness, but Dad says he's ready to try it again. He has been a Cross Gulf client since I was five years old."

"Did you know John Cross?" the young man asked.

"I knew John Cross senior and John junior very well," Antonio said.

The delivery boy's face lit up. "They were my grandpa and my pa'. I'm John, too," he said, and turned so Antonio could see the embroidered name with a *III* following his name on the pocket of his khaki shirt.

"I suppose it's time for me to just be John Cross. Pa' was killed in a motorcycle accident when I was nine, and we buried Grandpa in December. My grandpa and grandma helped Ma' raise me."

"They were good people," Antonio said. "I knew them well."

"I've always added *III* to my name for Grandpa's sake. He liked that. It reminded him of his son, that one time there was a number one and a two."

ANTONIO, THE EXECUTOR

As executor of his father's will, Antonio returned to Meyers to dispose of Juan Tomás's business and the family home. He had planned on staying a couple of weeks, but within a week, almost every item on his list was checked off.

The house went first. The Guerras, Juan Tomás's long-time neighbors, bought it for their expanding family. Cresenciano Guerra had five sons, all married, four of whom had built their houses on acreage adjacent to his. Only his youngest son, Frank, and his wife had not settled down yet, and for the present were living with him and his wife. Lately, Cresenciano sensed his daughter-in-law's dissatisfaction in not having a home of her own. She married Frank three years earlier and had lived with her in-laws since their wedding day.

Cresenciano did not hesitate when Juan Tomás's house went up for sale. He readily co-signed on the mortgage with Frank for the property. It was his dream that all his sons should live close to him and his wife, where they could enjoy their grandchildren. He did not quibble over the asking price, although he felt it was on the high side. Cresenciano was afraid Frank, and his wife might move away, maybe to another town, if he ignored the opportunity to buy the Vásquez house.

"I'm glad my parents' house is going to Frank, a good friend, instead of to strangers," Antonio said. "Frank and I grew up together. Our birthdays are two days apart."

Cresenciano's face lit up with pride. Nothing pleased him more than to hear others talk about his sons.

"Frank is a hard worker," he said. "He drives a Ford pickup truck he bought from his *patrón*. Looks like new."

"Who did Frank marry?" Antonio asked.

"He married Socorro Martínez, the daughter of Genaro Martínez, the Martínez family that lived on the Wilson farm. My daughter-in-law is an amazing woman. She can pick 135 pounds of cotton a day. That's just five pounds less than what a healthy strong man can pick."

"Amazing," Antonio said.

"Yes. We're very proud of her," Cresenciano said.

Antonio couldn't help but wonder what Socorro looked like.

Whenever Antonio returned to Meyers, oppressive feelings always awaited him. Even at home in Austin, he could never dwell long on his first year at school without dark emotions creeping in. When he drove past his old elementary school, feelings of injustice committed against him swelled up within him, clutching at his throat with such force that at times he found it difficult to talk. It was as though a crime had once been committed against him at that site, and the adrenaline of the moment still dwelled within him. The perpetrator of his anxiety was Margaret Brandt. He could not think of his first-grade teacher without arousing his anger. Even after all those years, she remained tucked away, hidden in his mind, only to surface from time to time and torture him. He hated that he loathed her in such an unwholesome way, because he was torturing himself and nobody else. Chances were that Margaret Brandt, if she were still living, hadn't thought of him since the day he last sat in her classroom. And that was over twenty years in the past.

Antonio was grateful that his father raised him with a thirst for knowledge, at a time when few parents appreciated a formal education for the quality of life it could impart to their children. Juan Tomás had drummed his mantra into Antonio's mind until it became a way of life to him.

"In America, good living is Anglo. If you want to be accepted as a true American and to succeed in the United States, you must be better educated than Anglos," and so on. Antonio learned that lesson well, and when the time came, he passed it on to the following generation.

After the Second World War ended, Mexican Americans became better educated than in the past, thanks in large part to the G.I. Bill, and they began making their voices heard. Dozens of racial barriers that had existed for over a century fell in the next two decades. Antonio and his father had played a role in that liberation. Now Mexican Americans ate at any restaurant they chose, sat anywhere they pleased on public transportation and in theatres, lodged at any hotel they could afford, and used the same drinking fountains and restroom facilities as Anglos. It had been a long struggle, but Mexican Americans were finally beginning to be accepted as Americans.

Through a front window at the J T Store, Antonio looked out as the day ended. Despite the negative recollections about his hometown, he felt sadness, knowing it would be his last day in Meyers.

Unlike the city, where people associate a sunset with the faltering of sunlight, in the country, a sunset is a glorious exhibit of the sun sinking slowly into the western horizon, where it expires in a blaze of glory. Antonio watched the last eight minutes of the setting sun in wide-eyed wonderment, as though he were witnessing it for the first time. The sun's final panoply of colors was so magnificent that he wondered whether there might be some mystic message hidden in the event. Fourteen days had passed since Juan Tomás was laid to rest, and Antonio could not help but see the analogy of his father's death in the ebbing solar rays. An era had ended with his father's passing.

Juan Tomás was not a religious man, though he firmly believed in God and in His divine mercy. Whenever the *compadres* discussed the life hereafter, he said he hoped that God would grant him a place in heaven, even if it were the humblest location in Paradise. *Un rinconcito*, some out-of-the-way dark corner where he could kneel and worship God.

Antonio recalled the evening the *compadres* broached the topic of being someone else. It was the kind of supposition Ponciano enjoyed putting before his friends.

"If you could be anybody else of all the people from the past and present, who would you like to be?" Ponciano asked.

Esquique answered immediately. "Jorge Negrete, the most famous Mexican singer and actor of all times."

"I wouldn't mind being General Douglas McArthur," Pedro said.

Ponciano nodded at Pedro's reply. "That's not a bad choice, but if I was going to be a general, I would choose Alexander the Great. He conquered all the civilized world by the time he was thirty-three years old."

"If I could be someone else," Joaquin said, "I would choose Mexico's greatest president, Benito Juárez. He did more to bring justice to his country than Abraham Lincoln or Simón Bolívar brought to theirs."

The *compadres* thought Joaquin had made an excellent selection.

"Juan Tomás, what about you?" Esquique said.

"I wish I could have been the man the Roman soldiers crucified to the right of Christ," Juan Tomás said.

"He was a thief. Why would you want to be a thief?" Esquique asked.

"Because when that thief asked Jesus to remember him when He reached His kingdom, Jesus turned to him and said, 'On this day, you will be with me in Paradise.'"

"In other words, the man had an iron-clad guarantee he was going to heaven," Pedro said.

"*Híjole*," Esquique said. "That sure beats the pants off of Jorge Negrete, and General McArthur."

"Great choice," Ponciano said. "I wasn't even thinking along those lines."

"As I get older," Juan Tomás said, "sometimes I lie in bed staring at the ceiling and wonder what will become of me after I die. I know I haven't done enough to deserve heaven. At times like those, I know I should be living a better life—one closer to the church and God's commandments."

"Saints and other do-gooders will receive the choice places in Heaven, *compadre*," Joaquin said. "Sinners like us will be lucky to get their foot in the doorway to heaven and maybe find that *rinconcito* you were talking about."

J T STORE—
THE MEXICAN *TIENDA*

Just before sundown, Antonio switched on the store's lights, and continued cleaning out his father's desk. He found only old magazines and invoices, yellowed with age. He dumped the contents from the six drawers in the trash barrel and paced the store for things he might have overlooked. The building looked bare and strange.

Around 7:30 pm, a dark-green Buick pulled up to the gasoline pumps. This would be the store's last customer. There were only thirty gallons of gasoline left in the regular tank. The ethyl tank was empty. Antonio went outside to take care of the customer.

"Good evening. Fill up?" Antonio said.

He had greeted customers and asked that question how many times in his younger days? Hundreds, maybe thousands of times. It was a gimmick the Gulf Oil Company taught its agents to induce customers to purchase more gasoline than they intended to buy. Otherwise, the company claimed, the undecided customer would buy only a few gallons or a couple of dollars' worth.

"Yes. Fill up with regular, and the hood's okay," came the reply from the woman in the car, Antonio pumped the fuel and promptly returned to the customer. As evening fell, the temperature dropped, and he could feel the cold air bite the back of his bare hands. The smell of gasoline was everywhere. For some reason, the odor of gasoline was always pungent on cold nights.

"That comes to three dollars and fifty cents," he said.

The woman extended her hand to pay with a ten-dollar bill.

"Antonio, I'm so sorry about your father. I attended the Mass and went to his graveside services, but it was so cold, you know. I left immediately after the services. All my bones were aching badly."

Antonio studied the woman's face. Before him was a woman wizened by age with sadness in her eyes. Her hair was completely white and long. He tried, but he did not recognize her.

"Thank you," he said, through the white vapor that spouted from his mouth. He produced her change from his pocket.

"I hear about you now and then," she said. "I understand you're married and doing very well in Austin. You did the smart thing, Antonio. You went off to a large city where there are better career opportunities. I always knew you would succeed. You were a good student."

"I'm an accountant," Antonio said. "It's a good field. I'm taking my CPA exam next month."

"That's wonderful," she said. "Do you remember when you first started school? I was your first-grade teacher," adding, "Oh, my, that was so many years ago."

Antonio felt a dagger pierce his soul and the suppressed anger of a lifetime began to rise like magma from deep within a volcano, racing to the surface.

"Do you remem...," he said, and his voice cut itself off. His heart was pounding wildly. The words wanted to gush out, but he couldn't find a place to start. There was so much he had suppressed, so much he wanted to say. The humiliations he suffered at her hands, the whippings she gave him, the head lice he didn't have, the slap that knocked him to the floor, the oversize desk, the suspension from school, the detentions during recess, the false accusations, the rigged white shoebox, the Christmas he received the gift he took to school, the pony ride...the darned pony ride! Where to start? His brain scanned swiftly through his past and picked one painful incident. His words poured out involuntarily.

"Do you remember when you made me sit in that huge, broken-down desk for an entire year, while the other children changed desks every month?"

Margaret Brandt Kellum's eyes became glassy. She could not look at him.

"Antonio, hear me out," she cried out, before he could say more. "Teachers don't behave like that anymore. That was a long time ago. I'm so ashamed I was mean to you. My husband urged me to write you and ask for your forgiveness, but I never did. I wanted to, but I was too ashamed. You have no idea how much pain treating you badly has caused me. I think about it often. The J T Store is always here to remind me of you. I'm sorry, Antonio. What else can I say?"

She began to cry.

"Discrimination is so ugly, but thanks to God it's becoming a thing of the past," she said.

Antonio looked at her small, wrinkled face. The hardness in her look, which he remembered well, was gone. Before him was a frail, old woman in the winter of her life. He didn't have the heart to upbraid her.

"Do you want to hear something funny?" Antonio said. "Years ago, my grandfather disowned his daughter Monica because she married an Anglo. He said mixed marriages between different races were against the laws of nature. My grandfather believed God created different races for a purpose. And yet, ten years later, when my uncle Mario came home from the war with a blonde, blue-eyed bride from Germany, Grandfather thought that was wonderful. He said she fit into our family just right."

Margaret pulled a handkerchief from her purse and dried her tears. "Times are changing, Antonio," she said, "...for the better."

Antonio managed a thin smile. "Maybe I live too much in the past. I wouldn't want to be like that old Confederate soldier who was fighting the war in the Tennessee mountains twenty years after the Civil War was over. He didn't know the war had ended."

"That's a story I used to tell my students," Margaret said

"I know," he said.

Margaret smiled and extended her hand toward Antonio. "I better leave before it gets colder. My legs are giving me a lot of trouble."

Antonio took her hand in his hands.

"The war is over," he said.

"God bless you, Antonio. Goodbye."

Antonio returned to the store, as Margaret Brandt Kellum drove away. He watched the Buick from the doorway until the red and blue taillights disappeared into the night. The brief encounter with his first-grade teacher had brought his life full circle. The pang in his heart was gone, and he was breathing normally again. The hatred he had harbored all those years, which he thought could only end in an explosion, had vanished. The volcano had dissipated. The Margaret Brandt he knew as a child no longer existed.

It seemed like only yesterday that he sat in the store listening to his father and his *compadres* wax on for hours on many topics, no matter how insignificant. He heard heated declamations about the meaning of life on one night, followed the next with an explanation of why leaves turn yellow and fall off trees in autumn. He heard several variations of the legend of the dead woman who went looking for her lost infant sons. He remembered vividly the night Ponciano reenacted the murder of Julius Caesar. He learned about the Mexican Revolution through the eyes of his father and his friends, most of whom had witnessed it firsthand. And the music, the songs of the Revolution had come alive in that very room. All these things, he heard there in his youth, many years ago.

Only Ponciano and Esquique remained of the five colorful individuals who gathered nightly at the J T Store, weaving their amazing stories, and singing their nostalgic songs. Pedro died shortly before Juan Tomás. He rested in Saint Lazarus Cemetery, four miles up the road, where Juan Tomás was recently interred. No one seemed to know the exact whereabouts of Joaquin, only that he had returned to Mexico.

The night was cold and clear. A full moon adorned the sky. Antonio took a last look inside the building where his father had worked most of his life. Then he pushed the sliding door with his shoulder until he heard the large, steel pin drop in place, securing the building from the outside.

One by one the lights inside the houses in Meyers, Texas, went off for the night.

Without any fanfare, the J T Store closed its doors forever.

JESSE NATAL SÁNCHEZ went to meet his maker August 11, 2020. His entire life he demonstrated love for reading and collected books, as a passionate believer in life-long learning. Because of his love for language, he was an active member of readers' and writers' clubs and had a strong predilection for the Latino Club. He attended San Antonio College and went to St. Mary's University where he majored in philosophy. Jesse and Norberta traveled throughout Mexico two-weeks a year, to expand their cultural knowledge. Also, he was an accomplished piano player and composed many songs for his wife. For forty-one years, Jesse worked for transportation lines, and, in 2001, he retired as Director of Pricing and Traffic Manager for the Southwestern Motor Transport. All who knew Jesse remember him for his keen sense of humor and his love of family.